'This is a richly woven story about family, but it's also a unique take on *Little Women*. There are no heroes or villains here, only people – flawed and loving and striving like the rest of us. "Generosity" is the word that comes to mind when I reflect on this gorgeous novel' Allegra Goodman, *New York Times* bestselling author of *The Cookbook Collector* and *Sam*

'This is an emotional, heart-wrenching family drama featuring complex and richly drawn characters – have tissues to hand' *Women's Weekly*

'Napolitano's novel will make you think deeply about sisterhood and what we choose to share with those we love' *Town & Country*

'In *Hello Beautiful*, Ann Napolitano treats readers to that rare pairing in fiction: intelligence and tenderness. And what a treat that is! This is a story about family, and sisters, and storytelling, but it's also an examination of identity, and the consequences of doing love badly, and how love can be redeemed. I was moved by the Padavano family's journey through all of that. Read this book! You'll be glad you did' Therese Anne Fowler, *New York Times* bestselling author of *It All Comes Down to This*

'A sprawling, hugely affecting novel [filled with] empathetic characters and rich writing . . . [*Hello Beautiful*] has rightfully earned comparisons to Louisa May Alcott's *Little Women*, with its four close, vibrant sisters and the lonely outsider who infiltrates their circle' Shondaland

'A family drama with echoes of classics and characters who are distinctly written. As a reader, you'll laugh and grieve with William and the Padavanos as they go through life – soaring as much as they stumble' Book Riot

'*Hello Beautiful* is the work of a great author at the height of her powers. Equally immersive, emotional and brilliantly crafted, this is an early contender for best novel of the year' J. Ryan Stradal, *New York Times* bestselling author of *Kitchens of the Great Midwest*

Hello Beautiful

A NOVEL

Ann Napolitano

PENGUIN BOOKS

PENGUIN BOOKS

UK | USA | Canada | Ireland | Australia
India | New Zealand | South Africa

Penguin Books is part of the Penguin Random House group of companies
whose addresses can be found at global.penguinrandomhouse.com.

First published in the United States of America by The Dial Press, an imprint of
Penugin Random House, a division of Penguin Random House LLC 2023
First published in Great Britain by Viking 2023
Published in Penguin Books 2024
001

Printed and bound in Great Britain by Clays Ltd, Elcograf S.p.A.

The authorized representative in the EEA is Penguin Random House Ireland,
Morrison Chambers, 32 Nassau Street, Dublin D02 YH68

A CIP catalogue record for this book is available from the British Library

ISBN: 978-0-241-99849-6

www.greenpenguin.co.uk

Penguin Random House is committed to a
sustainable future for our business, our readers
and our planet. This book is made from Forest
Stewardship Council® certified paper.

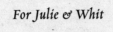

For Julie & Whit

Has any one supposed it lucky to be born?

I hasten to inform him or her it is just as lucky to die, and I know it.

I pass death with the dying and birth with the new-wash'd babe,
 and am not contain'd between my hat and boots,

And peruse manifold objects, no two alike and every one good,

The earth good and the stars good, and their adjuncts all good.

—WALT WHITMAN, "SONG OF MYSELF," VERSE 7

HELLO BEAUTIFUL

William

FOR THE FIRST SIX DAYS OF WILLIAM WATERS'S LIFE, HE WAS NOT an only child. He had a three-year-old sister, a redhead named Caroline. There were silent home movies of Caroline in which William's father looked like he was laughing, a sight William never saw again. His father's face looked open, and the tiny redhead, who pulled her dress over her face and ran in giggling circles in one of the movies, was apparently the reason. Caroline developed a fever and a cough while William and his mother were in the hospital after his birth. When they came home, the little girl seemed to be on the mend, but the cough was still bad, and when her parents went into her room to get her one morning, they found her dead in her crib.

William's parents never mentioned Caroline while William was growing up. There was one photograph of her on the end table in the living room, which William traveled to occasionally in order to convince himself that he'd actually had a sister. The family moved to a navy-shingled house on the other side of Newton—a suburb of Boston—and in that house, William was an only child. His father was an accountant who worked long hours downtown. With his daughter gone, the man's face never opened again. William's mother smoked cigarettes and drank bourbon in the living room, sometimes alone and sometimes with a female neighbor. She had a collection of ruffled aprons that she wore while preparing meals, and she became agitated whenever one became stained or messy.

"Maybe you shouldn't wear the aprons while you cook," William said once, when his mother was red-faced and on the verge of tears over a dark blotch of gravy on the fabric. "You could tuck a dish towel in your belt instead, like Mrs. Kornet does."

His mother looked at him as if he'd spoken in Greek. William said, "Mrs. Kornet, who lives next door? Her dish towel?"

From the age of five, William would walk to the nearby park most afternoons with a basketball, because basketball, unlike baseball or football, was a game he could play alone. There was a neglected outdoor court that usually had a hoop free, and he would shoot for hours, pretending he was a Celtics player. Bill Russell was his favorite, but to be Russell you needed someone else to block or defend against. Sam Jones was the best shooter, so William was usually Jones. He tried to imitate the guard's perfect shooting form while pretending the trees that surrounded the court were cheering fans.

One afternoon when he was ten years old, he showed up at the court and found it occupied. Boys—maybe six of them, about William's age—were chasing one another and a ball between the hoops. William started to back away, but one of the boys called, "Hey, wanna play?" And then, without waiting for William to answer: "You're on the blue team." Within seconds, William was swept into the game, his heart pounding in his chest. A kid passed him the ball, and he passed it right back, afraid to shoot and miss and be told he was terrible. A few minutes later, the game broke up abruptly because someone needed to get home, and the boys spilled off the court in different directions. William walked home, his heart still rattling in his chest. After that, the boys were occasionally on the court when William showed up with his ball. There was no discernible schedule to their appearances, but they always waved him into the game as if he were one of them. This never stopped being shocking to William. Kids and adults had always looked past him, as if he were invisible. His parents hardly looked at him at all. William had accepted all of this and thought it was understandable; he was, after all, boring and forgettable. His primary characteristic was pallor: He had sand-colored hair, light-blue eyes, and the very white skin shared by people of English and Irish descent. On the inside, William knew, he was as uninteresting and muted as his looks. He never spoke at school, and no one played with him. But the boys on the basketball court offered William a chance to be part of something for the first time, without having to talk.

In fifth grade, the gym teacher at his elementary school said, "I see you out there shooting baskets in the afternoons. How tall is your father?"

William stared at the man blankly. "I'm not sure. Normal height?"

"Okay, so you'll probably be a point guard. You need to work on your handle. You know Bill Bradley? That gawky guy on the Knicks? When he was a kid, he taped cardboard to his glasses so he couldn't look down, couldn't see his feet. And then he dribbled up and down the sidewalk wearing those glasses. He looked crazy, no doubt, but his handle got real tight. He has a perfect feel for how the ball will bounce and how to find it without looking."

William sprinted home that afternoon, his entire body buzzing. This was the first time a grown-up had looked directly at him—noticed him, and noticed what he was doing—and the attention threw him into distress. William had a sneezing fit while he was digging for a pair of toy glasses in the back of his desk drawer. He visited the bathroom twice before he carefully taped rectangular pieces of cardboard to the bottom of the glasses.

Whenever William felt sick or odd, he worried he was going to die. At least once a month he would crawl under his covers after school, convinced he was terminally ill. He wouldn't tell his parents, because illness wasn't permitted in his house. Coughing, in particular, was treated as a horrific betrayal. When William had a cold, he allowed himself to cough only in his closet with the door closed, his face muffled by the row of hanging button-down shirts he had to wear for school. He was aware of that familiar worry tickling his shoulders and the back of his head while he ran outside with the ball and glasses. But William had no time for illness now, no time for fear. This felt like the final click of his identity falling into place. The boys on the court had recognized him, and the gym teacher had too. William might have had no idea who he was, but the world had told him: He was a basketball player.

The gym teacher gave him additional tips that allowed William to develop more skills. "For defense: Push kids away with your shoulder and your butt. The refs won't call those as fouls. Do sprints: Get a quick first step and beat your man off the dribble." William worked on his passing too, so he could feed the ball to the best players in the park. He wanted to keep his place on the court, and he knew that if he made the other boys better, he had value. He learned where to run to provide space for the shooters to cut in to. He set screens so they could take their favorite shots. The boys slapped William on the back after a successful play, and they always wanted him on their side. This acceptance calmed some of the fear William carried inside him; on the basketball court, he knew what to do.

By the time William entered high school, he was a good-enough player to start for the varsity team. He was five foot eight and played point guard. His hours of practice with the glasses had paid off; he was by far the best dribbler on the team, and he had a nice midrange jumper. He'd worked on his rebounding, which helped offset his team's turnovers. Passing was still William's best skill, and his teammates appreciated that they had better games when he was in the lineup. He was the only freshman on the varsity team, and so when his older teammates drank beer in the basement of whoever's parents were willing to look the other way, William was never invited. His teammates were shocked—everyone was shocked—when, in the summer after his sophomore year, William grew five inches. Once he started growing, his body seemed unable to stop, and by the end of high school he was six foot seven. He couldn't eat enough to keep up with his growth and became shockingly thin. His mother looked frightened when he lurched into the kitchen every morning, and she'd hand him a snack whenever he passed nearby. She seemed to think his skinniness reflected badly on her, because feeding him was her job. His parents sometimes came to his basketball games, but at odd intervals, and they sat politely in the stands, appearing not to know anyone on the court.

His parents weren't there for the game when William went for a rebound and was shoved in the air. His body twisted while he fell, and he landed awkwardly on his right knee. The joint absorbed all of the impact, and all of his weight. William heard his knee make a noise, and then a fog descended. His coach, who seemed to have only two registers—shouting and mumbling—was yelling in his ear: "You okay, Waters?" William generally responded to both the shouts and the mumbles by phrasing everything he said as a question; he never felt sure enough to lay claim to a statement. He cleared his throat. The fog around him, and inside him, was dense and laced with pain that was radiating from his knee. He said, "No."

He'd fractured his kneecap, which meant he would miss the last seven weeks of his junior-year season. William's leg was immobilized with a cast, and he was on crutches for two months. What this meant was that for the first time since he was five years old, he was unable to play basketball. William sat on the desk chair in his room and threw crumpled-up paper into the bin by the far wall. The clouds that had descended with the injury remained; his skin felt damp and cold. The doctor had told him that he would make a full recovery and be able to play in his senior-year season, but still, William felt slightly panicked every minute of the day. Time became strange too. He felt like he would be locked in this cast, in this chair, in this house, forever. He began to think that he couldn't do this, couldn't sit inside this broken body any longer. He thought of his sister, how Caroline was gone. He thought about her gone-ness, which he didn't understand, but as the clock hand labored from one minute to the next, he wished that he were gone too. Off the basketball court, he had no usefulness. No one would miss him. If he disappeared, it would be like he'd never existed. No one spoke of Caroline, and no one would speak of him. Only when William's leg was finally freed from the cast, and he could run and shoot again, did the fog and the thoughts of disappearing recede.

Thanks to his decent grades and promise as a basketball player, William was offered a handful of scholarships from colleges with Division I basketball programs. He was grateful for the scholarships, because his parents had never indicated that they would pay for college, and because he took it as a promise of guaranteed basketball. William wanted to leave Boston—he'd never been more than ninety miles from the city center—but the swampy heat of the South made him nervous, so he accepted a scholarship from Northwestern University, in Chicago. In late August 1978, William kissed his mother goodbye at the train station and shook his father's hand. With his palm pressed against his father's, William had the strange thought that he might never see his parents again—that they'd only ever had one child, and it wasn't him.

IN COLLEGE, WILLIAM GRAVITATED toward history classes when filling his schedule. He had what felt like gaping holes to fill in his knowledge of how the world worked, and it appeared to him that history had the answers. He appreciated that the academic subject looked at disparate events and found a pattern. *If* this happened, *then* this happened. Nothing was completely random, and therefore a line could be drawn from the assassination of an Austrian archduke to a world war. College life was too new to be predictable, and William struggled to find any sense of equilibrium in the face of excited students who offered him high fives while he made his way down the noisy hallway in his dorm. He divided his days between studying in the library, practicing on the basketball court, and attending classes. In each of these locations, he knew what to do. He sank into every classroom chair, opened his notebook, and felt his body sag with relief when the professor began to talk.

William rarely noticed other students during classes, but Julia Padavano stood out in his European history seminar because her face appeared to be lit up with indignation and because she drove the professor—an elderly Englishman who held an oversized handkerchief balled in one fist—crazy with her questions. Her long, curly hair shifted around her bright face like curtains while she said things like: *Professor, I'm interested in the role of Clementine in all of this. Isn't it true that she was Churchill's main adviser?* Or: *Can you explain the wartime coding system? I mean the specifics of how it worked? I'd like to see an example.*

William never spoke in class or utilized the professor's office hours. He believed that the role of a student was to keep his or her mouth shut and soak up as much knowledge as possible. He shared the professor's opinion of the curly-haired girl, which was that her frequent interjections and inquiries, though often interesting to William, were impolite. The fabric of a serious classroom was created by students listening and the professor providing wisdom in a carefully unrolled carpet of words; this girl poked holes in that fabric, as if she didn't even know it existed.

William was startled one afternoon after class when she appeared at his elbow and said, "Hello. My name is Julia."

"William. Hi." He had to clear his throat; this might have been the first time he'd spoken that day. The girl was regarding him with wide, serious eyes. He noticed that in the sunlight her brown hair had honey-colored highlights. She looked lit up, from without and within.

"Why are you so tall?"

It wasn't unusual for people to remark on William's height; he understood that his size was a surprise whenever he entered a room and that most people felt compelled to say something. Several times a week he heard, *How's the air up there?*

Julia looked suspicious when she asked the question, though, and her expression made him laugh. He stopped on the path that crisscrossed the quad, and so she stopped too. William rarely laughed, and his hands tingled, as if they'd just woken up from an oxygen-deprived sleep. The overall sensation was one of being pleasantly tickled. Later, William would look back at this moment and know that this was when he fell for her. Or, more accurately, when his body fell for her. In the middle of the quad, attention from a specific girl reeled in laughter from the nooks and crannies within him. William's body—tired and bored by his hesitant mind—had to set off fireworks in his nerves and muscles to alert him that something of import was taking place.

"Why are you laughing?" Julia said.

He managed to mostly tamp it down. "Please, don't be offended," he said.

She gave an impatient nod. "I'm not."

"I don't know why I'm so tall." Secretly, though, he believed that he'd willed himself to this height. A serious basketball player needed to be at least six foot three, and William had cared about that so badly that he'd somehow defied his genetics. "I'm on the basketball team here."

"At least you're making a virtue of it, then," she said. "Perhaps I'll come to see one of your games. I generally don't take an interest in sports, and I only come to campus for classes." She paused, and then said quickly, as if embarrassed, "I live at home to save money."

Julia told him to write her phone number on his history notebook, and before she walked away he'd agreed to call her the next night. It was to some extent irrelevant whether he'd fallen for her or not. In the middle of the quad, this young woman seemed to have decided they would be boyfriend and girlfriend. Later, she would tell him that she'd been watching him in class for weeks and liked how attentive and serious he was. "Not silly, like the other boys," she said.

Even after he met Julia, basketball still took up most of William's time and thoughts. He'd been the best player on his high school team; at Northwestern, he was dismayed to discover he was among the weakest. On this team, his height wasn't enough to set him apart, and the other young men were stronger than he was. Most of them had been weight lifting for a few years, and William was panicked not to have known to do the same. He was easily shoved aside, knocked over, during practices. He started going to the weight room before practice and stayed on the court late to drill shots from different angles. He was hungry all the time and kept extra sandwiches in his jacket pockets. He realized that his role on this team would probably be as a "glue guy." He was good enough at passing, shooting, and defense to make himself useful, even though he wasn't a gifted athlete. His most valuable skill was that he rarely made mistakes on the court. "High basketball IQ, but no hops," William heard one of the coaches say about him, when they didn't know he was within earshot.

His scholarship required that he work a job on campus, and from the list of possibilities, he chose the one that took place in the gym building, because it would be convenient for basketball. He reported to the laundry facility in the sub-basement of the enormous building at the assigned time, where he was confronted by a skinny woman with a tall Afro and glasses. She shook her head and said, "You're in the wrong place. They told you to come here? White boys don't get assigned to laundry. You need to get yourself to the library or the student rec center. Go on."

William looked down the stretch of the long narrow room. There was a row of thirty washing machines on one wall and thirty dryers on the other. It was true that as far as he could see, no one else was white.

"Why does it matter?" he said. "I want to do this job. Please."

She shook her head again, and her glasses waggled on her nose, but before she could speak, a hand clapped William on the back and a deep voice said his name. He turned to see one of the other freshmen on the basketball team, a strong power forward named Kent. Kent had nearly the opposite set of basketball skills from William: He was a supreme athlete who dunked theatrically, crashed the boards, and sprinted every minute he was in the game, but he made bad reads on plays, caused multiple turnovers, and never knew where to be on defense. The coach gripped his head while he watched Kent run the court, presumably reeling at the disparity between the young man's physical potential and his high-speed, erratic play.

"Hey, man," Kent said. "You working down here too? I can show him the ropes, if you like, ma'am." Kent gave the stern woman a wide, charming smile.

She softened and said, "Okay, fine, then. Take him off my hands and I'll pretend he's not here."

From that point on, William and Kent timed their shifts in the laundry so they could work side by side. They washed hundreds of towels and the uniforms for every team. Football uniforms were the worst, because of the smell and deep grass stains that required a special bleach to be scrubbed into the fabric. William and Kent developed a rhythm to each step of the laundry process; with their focus on timing and efficiency, the work felt like an extension of basketball practice. They used the time to break down plays and figure out how their team could improve.

One afternoon, while they were folding an enormous pile of towels, William explained, "It goes: Guard-to-guard pass to initiate, forward comes off the baseline screen, and a guard screens down for the big." William paused to make sure Kent was following. "If the pass goes to the big, the small steps out to the corner and the other forward comes off that screen, and the other guard screens down on the weak side."

"Picking the picker."

"That's right, and if the big passes to the forward, then the flex continuity repeats."

"Too predictable! Coach wants us running the same thing over and over. . . ."

"But if we do it right, there's not a lot a defense can do to stop it, even if they know it's coming, especially if we—"

"Boys," the man at the next dryer said, "do you know that you're making no sense? I mean, I watch basketball, and I have no idea what you're talking about."

Kent and William grinned at him. At the end of their shift, they went upstairs to the gym, where it was twenty degrees cooler, and shot baskets.

Kent was from Detroit, had loud opinions on all the NBA players and teams, and often broke his sentences in half to laugh at one of the dumb jokes that flew like paper airplanes around the locker room. During practices, he was repeatedly yelled at by the coach for show-boating, which Kent apologized for but was unable to stop himself from doing again five minutes later. "Fundamentals!" the coach thundered, over and over.

Kent claimed to be related to Magic Johnson, who was a senior at Michigan State and was widely considered a lock as the first pick in the upcoming NBA draft. It was so easy for Kent to make friends— everyone liked him—that William wondered why Kent chose to spend his time with him. All he could see was that Kent seemed to delight in William's quietness as an opportunity to manage their friendship. Kent did most of the talking, and only slowly did William realize that Kent told personal stories in order to get William to share his own. After hearing about Kent's grandmother's leukemia, which had stunned everyone in the family—apparently, she'd claimed she would live forever and was such a powerful force that they'd all believed her—William told Kent that he'd exchanged only one letter with his parents so far and that he was going to stay at school for Christmas break.

After a long night practice, while they were walking slowly across the quiet quad, their muscles cramping with exhaustion, Kent said, "Sometimes I have to remind myself that it doesn't matter if the coach benches me or bawls me out because he doesn't appreciate my beautiful game. I'm going to med school. He can't stop my future from happening."

William was surprised. "You're going to be a doctor?"

"Hundred percent. I don't have the tuition worked out yet, but I will. What're you going do after college?"

William was aware of his cold fingers. It was early November, and when he breathed in, the air felt icy in his lungs. William never considered life after college; he was aware that he kept his eyes averted from the future on purpose. He wanted to say *basketball,* but he wasn't good enough for that to be his career. Kent asking the question confirmed that he didn't think William was good enough either.

"I don't know," William said.

"We'll start thinking about it, then," Kent said. "You got talents. We got time."

Do I have talents? William thought. He wasn't aware of any, off the basketball court.

Julia attended a Friday-night basketball game in early December, and when William noticed her in the stands, his eyesight blurred and he passed the ball to the other team. "Hey," Kent yelled as he powered by William on the court. "What kind of bullshit was that?" On the defensive end, William made two steals that turned the momentum of the game in favor of the Wildcats. On offense, at the top of the key, he made a bounce pass to an open shooter in the corner. Kent crowed just before halftime: "I get it! You got a girl here! Where is she?"

After the game—the Wildcats won, and William had played his best minutes of the early season—he climbed into the bleachers to see Julia. Only when he got closer did he see that she was seated with three girls who resembled her. They all had the same boisterous shoulder-length curls. "These are my sisters," Julia said. "I brought them to scout you. That's basketball language, right?"

William nodded, and—under the scrutiny of the four girls—he was suddenly very aware of how short his basketball shorts were and of the flimsiness of his sleeveless jersey.

"We enjoyed it," one of the younger-looking girls said. "It looked exhausting, though. I don't think I've ever sweated in my entire life as much as you did. I'm Cecelia, and this is my twin, Emeline. We're fourteen."

Emeline and Cecelia pointed friendly smiles at him, and he smiled back. Julia and the sister on her other side were studying him like jewelry appraisers sizing up a stone. If one of them had pulled a watchmaker's loupe out of her purse and held it to her eye, he wouldn't have been surprised. Julia said, "You looked so powerful . . . out there on the court."

William blushed, and the tops of Julia's cheeks pinkened too. He could see this beautiful girl's desire for him, and he couldn't believe his luck. No one had ever wanted him before. He wished he could take her in his arms, in front of her sisters, in front of the entire arena, but that kind of bold action wasn't in William's nature. He was drenched with sweat, and Julia was speaking again.

"This is my sister Sylvie," she said. "I'm the oldest, but only by ten months."

"Nice to meet you," Sylvie said. Her hair was a shade darker than Julia's, and she was more petite, less curvy. She continued to study William, while Julia beamed like a peacock with all her feathers on display. While he stood there, he watched one of the buttons on Julia's shirt come undone, pulled too tight across her generous chest. He had a glimpse of her pink bra before she realized and pulled everything back into place.

"How many siblings do you have?" Either Emeline or Cecelia asked this. They weren't identical, but they looked very alike to William. Same olive complexion, same light brown hair.

"Siblings? None," he said, though of course he thought of the framed photo of the redheaded toddler in his parents' living room.

Julia already knew he was an only child—it had been one of her first questions during their first phone call—but the other three girls looked comically shocked.

"That's terrible," Emeline or Cecelia said.

"We should invite him to our house for dinner," Sylvie said, and the other girls nodded. "He looks lonely."

And so, four months into college, William found himself with his first girlfriend, and a new family.

Julia

JULIA WAS IN THE BACK GARDEN, AN EIGHTEEN-BY-SIXTEEN-FOOT rectangle hemmed by wooden fences, watching her mother dig up the last of the season's potatoes at the exact time William was due at the house. She knew he'd be punctual and that one of her sisters would let him in. William would probably be flustered by her father, who would ask him if he knew any poetry by heart, and by Emeline and Cecelia, who wouldn't cease moving or talking. Sylvie was working at the library, so he'd be spared her inquisitive stare. A few minutes alone with her sisters and father would help William to get to know them—Julia wanted him to see how lovable they were—and, as a bonus, he'd be extra-thrilled to see *her* when she walked inside. Julia was famous within her family for making an entrance, which really just meant that she thought about timing, whereas no one else in her family did. As a young child, Julia would twirl into the kitchen or living room, calling out, *Ta-da!*

What would William think of their small house, squeezed in next to identical squat brick houses on 18th Place? The Padavanos lived in Pilsen, a working-class neighborhood filled with immigrants. Colorful murals adorned the sides of buildings, and in the local supermarket, you were as likely to hear Spanish or Polish as English. Julia worried that William would find both the neighborhood and the inside of her family's home shabby. The floral couch covered in plastic. The wooden crucifix on the wall. The framed array of female saints next to the dinner table. When Julia's mother was frustrated, she named them aloud, her eyes fixed on the women's faces as if imploring them to save her from this family. *Adelaide, Agnes of Rome, Catherine of Siena, Clare of Assisi, Brigid of Ireland, Mary Magdalene, Philomena, Teresa of Avila, Maria Goretti.* All four Padavano girls could recite these names better than the rosary. It was unusual for a family dinner to conclude without either their father reciting poetry or their mother reciting her saints.

Julia shivered. She wasn't wearing a coat; it was forty degrees out, and most Chicagoans refused to consider it cold until the temperature dropped below freezing. "I like him," she said to her mother's back.

"Is he a drunk?"

"No. He's a basketball player. And an honors student. He's going to major in history."

"Is he as smart as you?"

Julia considered this. William was clearly smart. His brain worked. He asked questions that let her know he was interested in understanding her. His intelligence didn't register in the form of strong opinions, though. He was interested in questions and uncertain in his answers; he was moldable. William had studied with Julia a few times at the Lozano Library, which was only a few blocks away from the Padavanos' home. Sylvie worked at the library, and everyone in their neighborhood used it as a meeting place, but studying there meant that William had to commute an hour back to his dorm late at night. When making weekend plans, he always said, "Let's do whatever you want to do. You have the best ideas."

Julia had never considered the idea of physical intelligence until she'd attended William's recent basketball game. She was surprised by how exciting she found watching William compete with his team. She'd seen a more forceful side of him than he exhibited off the court: yelling commands to his teammates, using his strong, tall body to block an opponent from the basket. Julia had no interest in sports and didn't understand the rules, but her handsome boyfriend had sprinted and leapt and spun with such pure physicality, and such intensity of focus, that she had found herself thinking: *yes.*

"He's a serious person," Julia said. "He takes life seriously, like I do."

Rose climbed to her feet. A stranger might have laughed at the sight of her, but Julia was accustomed to her mother's getup. When she gardened, Rose wore a modified baseball catcher's uniform, topped off with a navy-blue sombrero. She'd found all of it on the street. Their end of the block was 100 percent Italian, but many of the streets in the neighborhood were filled with Mexican families, and Rose had plucked the hat out of someone's garbage can after a Cinco de Mayo celebration. The catcher's equipment she'd picked up when Frank Ceccione, two doors down, got into drugs and quit his high school baseball team. Rose wore his huge leg guards and had sewed large pockets for her gardening tools onto the chest protector. She looked ready for some kind of game—it was just unclear which one.

"So, he's not smarter than you." Rose lifted the sombrero up and pushed her hand through her hair—wavy like her daughters' but laced with gray. She wasn't nearly as old as she looked, but starting years earlier Rose had forbidden any celebration of her birthday, a personal declaration of war against the passage of time. Julia's mother trained her eyes on the dirt rows of her garden. Potatoes and onions were all that remained to be harvested; most of Rose's work now was devoted to preparing the garden for winter. The only sections of non-growing soil were reserved for a narrow path between the plants and a white sculpture of the Virgin Mary, which leaned against the back-left corner of the fence. Rose sighed. "It's just as well, I suppose. I'm smarter than your father by a million miles."

Julia could see how "smart" was a tricky term—how did you quantify it, especially when neither of her parents had gone to college?—but her mother was correct. Julia had seen photos of Rose, pretty and tidy and smiling in this same garden, with Charlie at the beginning of their marriage, but her mother had eventually accepted and donned marital disappointment the same way she strapped on her ridiculous gardening outfit. All of her considerable efforts to propel her husband toward some kind of financial stability and success had died in their tracks. Now the house was Charlie's space, and Rose's refuge was the garden.

The sky was dimming, and the air growing colder. When freezing temperatures arrived to stay, this neighborhood would quiet, but tonight it chattered as if trying to get in its final words: Distant kids shouted laughter; the older Mrs. Ceccione warbled in her garden; a motorcycle coughed three times before starting up. "I suppose it's time to go inside," Rose said. "Are you embarrassed by your old lady looking like this?"

"No," Julia said. She knew William's attention would be on her. She loved the hopeful look William directed at her, as if he were a ship eyeing the ideal harbor. William had grown up in a nice home, with a professional father, a big lawn, and his own bedroom. He clearly knew what success and security looked like, and the fact that he saw those possibilities in Julia pleased her immensely.

Rose had tried to build a solid life, but Charlie had wandered away with, or kicked over, every stone she laid down. Julia had decided, halfway through her first conversation with William, that he was the man for her. He had everything she was looking for, and as she'd told her mother, she just really liked him. The sight of him made her smile, and she loved fitting her small hand inside his large one. They made an excellent team: William had experienced the kind of life Julia wanted, so he could direct her endless energy while they built their future together. Once she and William were married and established in their own home, she would help her family. Her solid foundation would extend to become theirs.

She almost laughed out loud at the relief on her boyfriend's face when she entered the living room. William was seated next to her father on the squeaky couch, and Charlie had his hand on the young man's shoulder. Cecelia was lying across the old red armchair, and Emeline was staring in the mirror hung beside the front door, adjusting her hair.

Cecelia was saying, in a serious voice, "You have an excellent nose, William."

"Oh," William said, clearly surprised. "Thank you?"

Julia grinned. "Don't mind Cecelia. She talks that way because she's an artist." Cecelia had special access to the art room at the high school, and she considered everything in her sightline to be source material for future paintings. The last time Julia—intrigued by the focused expression on Cecelia's face—asked her sister what she was thinking about, Cecelia had said, "Purple."

"You *do* have a nice nose," Emeline said politely, because she'd noticed William blush and wanted to make him feel better. Emeline read the emotional tenor of every room and wanted everyone to feel comfortable and content at all times.

"He doesn't know a word of Whitman," Charlie said to Julia. "Can you imagine? William didn't get here a moment too soon. I gave him a few lines to tide him over."

"No one knows Whitman except for you, Daddy," Cecelia said.

The fact that William didn't know any of Walt Whitman's poems was additional validation for Julia that her boyfriend was different from her father. She could tell from Charlie's voice that he'd been drinking but wasn't yet drunk. He had a glass in his hand, half filled with melting ice cubes.

"I can reserve *Leaves of Grass* for you at the library, if you'd like," Sylvie said to William. "It's worth reading."

Julia hadn't noticed Sylvie, who stood in the doorway of the kitchen. She must have just gotten home from her shift at the library, and her lips were the kind of deep red that meant she'd been kissing one of her boys in the stacks. Sylvie was a senior in high school and spent her free hours working as many shifts as possible to save money for community college. She wouldn't earn an academic scholarship like Julia had, because she hadn't matched her older sister's determination to get one. Sylvie aced the classes she was interested in but got C's or D's in everything else. Julia had operated her determination like a lawn mower and mowed through high school with the next step in her sights.

"Thank you," William said. "I'm afraid I haven't read much poetry at all."

Julia was sure William hadn't noticed her sister's lips, and even if he had, he wouldn't know what they meant. Sylvie was the sister Julia was closest to, and she was also the only person who stymied Julia, who left her at a loss for words. Her sister had read hundreds of novels—it had been Sylvie's only interest, and hobby, for their entire lives—and out of those books she'd plucked a life goal: to have a great, once-in-a-century love affair. It was a child's dream, but Sylvie was still holding on to it with both hands. She was looking for *him*—her soulmate—every day of her life. And she made out with boys during her shifts in the library to practice for when she met him.

"It's not right to practice like that," Julia would tell Sylvie, when they were lying side by side in their dark bedroom at night. "And the kind of love you're looking for is made up, anyway. The idea of love in those books—*Wuthering Heights, Jane Eyre, Anna Karenina*—is that it's a force that obliterates you. They're all tragedies, Sylvie. Think about it; those novels all end with despair, or death."

Sylvie had sighed. "The tragedy isn't the point," she said. "We read those books today because the romance is so enormous and true that we can't look away. It's not obliteration; it's a kind of expanding, I think. If I'm lucky enough to know love like that . . ." She went quiet, unable to put into words how meaningful this would be.

Julia shook her head at the sight of her sister's red lips, because this dream was bound to backfire. Sylvie cared too much and lived too much in her head. She would be branded a slut and eventually marry a good-looking loser because he stared at Sylvie in a way that reminded her of Heathcliff.

Emeline was talking about her homeroom teacher, who was on probation for smoking marijuana. "He's so honest," she said. "He told us how he got caught and everything. I'm worried he's going to get in more trouble for telling us about it. He doesn't seem to understand the grown-up rules for what to say and what to keep to himself. I kept wanting to tell him to shush."

"You should also tell him not to smoke pot," Cecelia said.

"I suppose we should eat?" Rose had come out of her bedroom, clean and wearing one of her nicer housedresses. "It's lovely to meet you, William. Do you like red wine?"

He stood, unfolding his long body from the low couch. He nodded. "Hello, ma'am."

"Sweet mother of Mary." Rose tipped her head back to look up at him. She was barely five feet tall. "You didn't think to mention that he's a giant, Julia?"

"He's a marvel, though, isn't he?" Charlie said. "He's got our Julia soft around the edges, which I wouldn't have thought possible. Look at her smile."

"Daddy," Julia said.

"What position do you play?" Charlie asked William.

"Small forward."

"Ha! If you're the small forward, I'd hate to meet the big one."

"I wonder what the evolutionary explanation is for that kind of height," Sylvie said. "Did we need people who could peer over walls to see if the enemy was coming?"

Everyone in the room, including William, laughed, and Julia thought he looked a little teary in the middle of the action. She made her way to him and whispered, "Are we too much for you?"

He squeezed her hand, a gesture she understood meant both yes and no.

Dinner wasn't delicious. Despite the fact that she grew beautiful vegetables, Rose hated to cook, so they took turns battling dinner onto the table. The vegetables weren't intended for them, anyway—they were sold by the twins each weekend at a farmers' market in a nearby wealthy neighborhood. It was Emeline's turn to cook, which meant they had frozen TV dinners. The guest got to choose his TV dinner first; William selected turkey, which came on a tray with small compartments for mashed potatoes, peas, and cranberry sauce. The family members chose carelessly after him and started eating. Emeline had also made Pillsbury crescent rolls, popped out of the tube and baked in the oven. Those elicited more enthusiasm and were gone in ten minutes.

"My mother made this same brand of dinner when I was growing up," William said. "It's nice to have it again. Thank you."

"I'm glad you're not appalled by our entertaining," Rose said. "I'd like to know if you were raised Catholic."

"I went to Catholic school in Boston all the way through."

"Will you go into your pop's line of work?" Charlie asked.

This question surprised Julia, and she could see that it startled her sisters too. Charlie never mentioned work, never asked anyone about their job. He hated his job at the paper plant. The only reason he wasn't fired—according to Rose—was that the man who owned the company was his childhood friend. Charlie regularly told his daughters that a job did not make a person.

"What makes you, Daddy?" Emeline had asked a few years earlier in response to this comment. She'd spoken with all of her little-girl sweetness; it was commonly agreed that she was the gentlest and most earnest of the four girls. "Your smile," Charlie had said. "The night sky. The flowering dogwood in front of Mrs. Ceccione's house."

Julia had listened and thought: *That's all nonsense. And useless to Mom, who's doing strangers' laundry every week to pay the bills.*

Perhaps Charlie was trying to ask the kind of question he believed other fathers asked their daughters' boyfriends. After the words left his mouth, he finished his drink and reached for the wine bottle.

"Daddy looked frightened," Sylvie would note to Julia later that night, in the dark. "And did you hear Mom use the word *appalled*? She never talks like that. They were both showing off for William."

"No, sir," William said. "My father is in accounting. I—" He hesitated, and Julia thought, *This is difficult for him because he doesn't have the answer. He lacks answers.* A shiver of pleasure climbed her spine. Julia specialized in answers. From the time she was old enough to speak, she'd bossed her sisters around, pointing out their problems and providing solutions. Sometimes her sisters found this irritating, but they would also admit that having a "master troubleshooter" in their own home was an asset. One by one, they would seek her out and say sheepishly, *Julia, I have a problem.* It would be about a mean boy, or a strict teacher, or a lost borrowed necklace. And Julia would thrill at their request, rub her hands together, and figure out what to do.

William said, "If basketball doesn't work out, I might ..." His voice stopped, and he looked as lost as Charlie had a moment earlier, suspended in time, as if his only hope was that the end of the sentence might magically appear.

Julia said, "He might become a professor."

"Ooh," Emeline said approvingly. "There's a nice-looking professor two blocks over, and the ladies follow him around. He wears excellent jackets."

"Professor of what?" Sylvie said.

"No idea," Emeline said. "Doesn't matter, does it?"

"Of course it matters."

"A *professor*," Charlie said, as if Julia had said *astronaut* or *president of the United States.* Rose talked about college all the time, but her education had ended after high school, and Charlie had dropped out of college after Julia was born. "That would be something."

William shot Julia a look, part thanks, part something else, and the patter at the table continued around them.

Later that night, when they went for a walk around the neighborhood, William said, "What was that about me being a professor?"

Julia felt her cheeks flush. She said, "I wanted to help, and Kent told me you were writing a book about the history of basketball."

William let go of her hand, without seeming to notice. "He did? It's not a book—it's more notes at this point. I don't know if it will ever be a book. I don't know what it will be."

"It's impressive," she said. "I don't know any other college kids who are writing a book in their free time. It's very ambitious. Sounds like a future professor to me."

He shrugged, but she could see him considering the idea.

William was tall and shadowy above her. A man, but young. Pilsen was muted tonight under a navy-blue sky. They were on a smaller side street. She could see the spire of St. Procopius, where her family attended Sunday mass, a few blocks to the right. Julia thought of Sylvie being kissed against a row of science-fiction novels under the bright lights of the library. She reached over and tugged on the front of William's coat. *Come down here.*

He knew this signal and lowered his head. His lips met hers— gentle, warm—and they pressed together in the middle of the street, in the middle of their romance, in the middle of her neighborhood. Julia loved kissing William. She'd kissed a couple of boys before him, but those boys had approached kissing like it was the starting pistol in a sprint. Presumably, the finish line was sex, but neither of the boys had expected to get that far; they were simply trying to cover as much ground as possible before Julia called off the race. A cheek kiss veered into kissing on the lips, which escalated rapidly to French kissing, and then the boy was patting her breast as if trying to get a feel for its measurements. Julia had never let anyone go further than that point, but the whole endeavor was so stressful that she'd only been able to experience kisses as wet and reckless. William, though, was different. His kisses were slow and not part of a race, which allowed Julia to relax. Because she felt safe, different parts of her body lit up, and she pressed her soft body against his. With William, she wanted more for the first time. She wanted him.

When they finally pulled apart, she whispered into his chest, "I'm going to leave this place."

"Where? Your parents' house?"

"Yes, and this whole neighborhood. After college. When"—it was Julia's turn to hesitate—"when my real life starts. Nothing starts here; you saw my family. People get stuck here." She pictured the soil in Rose's garden: rich, pebbly, sticky to the touch. She rubbed her hand against William's jacket, as if to wipe off the dirt. "There are much nicer neighborhoods in Chicago. They're a different world from here. I wonder if you'll want to go back to Boston?"

"I like it here," he said. "I like your family."

Julia realized she'd been holding her breath, waiting for his response. She'd decided William was her future, but she wasn't sure he felt the same way, though she suspected he did. "I like them too," she said. "I just don't want to *be* them."

When Julia crept back into the house later that night and into the tiny bedroom she shared with Sylvie, she found all her sisters waiting there in their nightgowns. They offered her triumphant smiles.

"What?" she whispered, unable not to smile in return.

"You're in love!" Emeline whispered, and the girls pulled Julia onto her bed, a celebration of the first of them to take this step, the first of them to hand her heart to a boy. The twins and Sylvie collapsed onto the single bed with her. They'd done this countless times; it had gotten trickier as their bodies grew, but they knew how to tuck their limbs and arrange themselves to make it work.

Julia laughed with her hand over her mouth, careful not to make noise and wake up their parents. She was surprised to find tears in her eyes, wrapped up in her sisters' arms. "I might be," she said.

"We approve," Sylvie said. "He looks at you like you're the bee's knees, which you are."

"I like the color of his eyes," Cecelia said. "They're an unusual shade of blue. I'm going to paint them."

"It's not your kind of love, Sylvie," Julia said, wanting to make that clear. "It's a sensible kind."

"Of course," Sylvie said, and kissed her on the cheek. "You're a sensible person. And we're so happy for you."

WILLIAM PROPOSED WHEN THEY were juniors. This had been the plan, Julia's plan. They would marry right after graduation. She'd shifted her major from humanities to economics, after taking a fascinating organizational-psychology course. She learned about systems, how every business was made up of a collection of intricate parts, motivations, and movements. How if one part was broken or out of step, it could doom the entire company. Her professor was a business consultant who advised companies on how to make their workflow more "efficient" and "effective." Julia worked for Professor Cooper during the summer between her junior and senior years, taking notes and drawing business-operations charts on architectural paper. Her family made fun of her navy pumps and skirt suit, but she loved walking into the air-conditioned chill of office buildings, loved how everyone dressed like they took themselves and their work seriously, even loved walking through clouds of cigarette smoke on her way to the ladies' room. The men looked how she thought men should look, and she bought William a crisp white button-down shirt for his birthday that year. She planned to add a corduroy blazer at Christmas. William had decided to make Julia's suggestion that he become a history professor a reality. Julia appreciated the elegance of her plans: engaged this summer, graduation and wedding next summer, and then William would enter a PhD program. Julia loved living in this moment, with her life directly in front of her instead of off in the distance. She'd spent her entire childhood waiting to grow up so she could be *here,* ringing all the bells of adulthood.

William was spending his last full summer at Northwestern in basketball training camp, and Julia would often meet him at the athletic center at the end of the day so they could have dinner together. She ran into Kent on the quad occasionally, when he left practice early for his summer job at the college infirmary. Julia liked Kent, but she always felt slightly uncomfortable around him. It seemed like their timing was off, to the extent that they often spoke at the same moment. When they were with William and he said something, they both responded and ran over each other's words. Julia respected Kent—after all, he was planning to put himself through medical school—and thought he was a good influence on William. Part of her discomfort was a desire for Kent to like her. She wasn't sure that he did. In his presence, she flipped through possible conversations in her head, looking for one that would put them on solid ground.

"Good evening, General," Kent said, when he saw her that evening. "I hear you're burning it up in the corporate world."

"Don't call me that," she said, but she smiled. It was unthinkable to take anything Kent said as an insult; his tone and ready smile didn't allow for that possibility. "How's basketball?"

"Joyful," he said, and the way he said the word reminded Julia of when Cecelia had answered a question with an excited *purple.*

"Our boy was feeling himself at practice today," Kent said. "He's having fun this summer. It's good to see."

This had a note of chiding to Julia's ear, but she couldn't see what Kent would be chiding her about. Did he think she didn't want William to have fun?

When Kent said goodbye, she sat down on a bench to wait. She shook her head, annoyed at how she allowed William's friend to fluster her. She pulled a compact out of her purse and reapplied her lipstick, then stood up when she spotted her handsome fiancé leaving the gym in the middle of a flock of tall, gangly young men. She'd run into an acquaintance from her freshman biology class on the street recently, and the girl had said, *I heard you were engaged to that tall boy with the beautiful eyes. He's very cute.* Julia held tight to William's hand while they walked to a café for dinner.

William was slow-moving and unable to hold a conversation until he'd eaten a thousand calories and the color returned to his face. Julia, on the other hand, was rattling with excitement, unable to stop talking about every moment of her day.

"Professor Cooper says I'm a natural problem-solver," she said.

"He's right." William cut his baked potato into a grid and then ate a square.

"I was wondering, have you been working on your writing?" She'd learned not to call it a book. "You could use it as your senior thesis."

"It's a mess," he said. "I haven't had much time for it lately, and I can't figure out how to focus the material."

"I'd love to read it."

He shook his head.

She wanted to ask, *Has Kent read it?* But she didn't want to hear William say yes. She wanted to read the book because she was interested and so she could have a sense of how good it was. Whether it had the potential to build a career around.

"I'm going to start this year," he said. "Coach said my playing has taken a leap."

"Start?"

"Start every game. I'll be part of the best five. When NBA scouts come, they'll see me play."

"That's fun," she said. "I'll cheer for you."

He smiled. "Thank you."

"Have you told your parents about our engagement yet?"

He shook his head. "I haven't. I should, I know. But"—he hesitated— "I don't think they'll be interested."

Julia gave a smile she knew was too tight. He'd been avoiding telling his parents for weeks. She believed it was because he was embarrassed to tell them that he'd asked an Italian American girl from a poor family to marry him. He'd told her enough about his upbringing that she knew his father had an impressive job and his mother didn't need to work. They probably had airs and expectations for their only child, but William wouldn't admit this, and she wouldn't state her fear outright. Now she said, in a tight voice to match her tight smile, "Don't be ridiculous. They're your parents."

"Listen," he said, "I know it would be strange *not* to invite them to the wedding, but I don't think we need to invite them." He saw her face and said, "I'm just being honest. I know it's unusual."

"You'll call them tonight," she said. "And I'll be on the phone with you. I'm charming. They'll adore me."

William was quiet for a moment, and his eyelids drooped in a way that indicated he had gone far away from her. When he looked up, he regarded her as if she were a problem he needed to solve.

"You love me," she said.

"Yes," he said, and the word seemed to settle something inside him. "Okay, let's do it."

An hour later, sharing the hard wooden stool in the old-fashioned phone booth in his dorm hallway, they called Boston. William's mother answered the call, and William said hello. The woman sounded surprised to hear from him, though she was polite. Then Julia spoke—her voice sounding overamplified to her own ears, as if she were speaking through a megaphone—and William's mother sounded far away. She said she had something in the oven and it was nice they were getting married, but she had to go now.

The entire call was finished in less than ten minutes.

Julia gulped for air when she hung up the receiver, winded from trying to reach, to touch, the distant woman on the end of the line.

When she could speak, she said, "You were right. She doesn't want to come."

"I'm sorry," he said. "I know that's disappointing to you. Your vision of the wedding had everyone there."

Julia was pressed against William on the tiny seat. The hallway booth was warm. The temperature and the disappointment and Julia's sympathy for this boy rose inside her—this boy who deserved parents who kissed his cheek the way her parents kissed hers. They had planned not to have sex until they were married, though they had come close to breaking that resolution once or twice. The remote woman on the phone had handed William off to Julia in a way that felt as significant as a wedding vow. She needed to take care of him; she needed to love him, with every part of her. In fact, she had to, right now. She was flushed, her skirt was twisted around her waist because of the seating arrangement, and she needed to be closer to him in order for anything to be all right.

She said, "Can we have privacy in your room?"

His roommate was gone for the summer. William nodded, a question on his face.

She took his hand and led him down the hall, into his room, and locked the door behind them.

Sylvie

THE LOZANO LIBRARY OVERLOOKED A THREE-WAY INTERSEC-
tion in the center of Pilsen. Sylvie loved every inch of the spacious library and the wall of floor-to-ceiling windows that showed whatever
light and weather the city had to offer. She loved how the library welcomed everyone and how the librarians dutifully answered every
question presented to them, no matter how arcane or ridiculous. Sylvie had been working in the library since she was thirteen; she'd started
by shelving books and now, at the age of twenty, she bore the title of
librarian's assistant.

Sylvie was shelving copies of *What Color Is Your Parachute?* when
Ernie, a boy her age with a dimple in his chin, smiled his way into her
row. They had gone to high school together, and he sometimes stopped
by after his morning session of electrician school. After checking that
no one else was in sight, Sylvie stepped into his arms. They kissed for
about ninety seconds, making two slow turns down the aisle with his
hand on her lower back, and then she tapped him on the shoulder, and
he was gone.

Sylvie told Julia she kissed boys to practice for her great love, and
that was true. But she also did it because it was fun. She'd waited
through her entire childhood, scanning classrooms for her person, her
version of Gilbert Blythe from *Anne of Green Gables.* Sylvie hadn't found

him yet, but she enjoyed the thrill that accompanied a boy taking her in his arms. Sylvie was naturally shy and bookish; she'd blushed when Ernie looked into her eyes. "I'm getting better at kissing," she told Julia when they returned to the subject at night in their beds. "It's clearly a learned skill."

Julia had shaken her head. "People are talking about what you're doing with those boys. If Mama hears about it . . ." There was no need to finish this sentence, because they both knew Rose would be furious. And if Sylvie tried to explain that she was practicing for the love of her life, Rose would be bewildered and probably lock Sylvie in her room. Rose had never uttered the word *love* in front of the girls; they simply knew she loved them because of the furious attention she pinned on them. They also knew, in the same unspoken way, that Rose loved Charlie. It was *because* she loved him that Rose had been so disappointed by her marriage and why it was essential that her girls grow up strong and educated, able to stand on their own two feet, unbowed by something as tricky and undependable as love.

Julia used to dismiss the idea of love too, but now she was in love with William Waters. Sylvie found it fascinating to watch the person she knew better than anyone succumb to romance. Julia walked through her days smiling, unbothered by things that normally ruffled her: the sight of Charlie pouring a second or third drink; Cecelia sliding into her chair, late for dinner; Emeline playing outside with younger neighborhood kids, when Julia considered her too old to do so. Love had made Julia happier and lighter, but she saw it as part of a well-constructed life, not a reason for living, like Sylvie did.

Julia believed in several direct steps: Education led to a good marriage, which led to a reasonable number of children, to financial security and then real estate. Julia found Sylvie's behavior in the library distressing because there was a murky abandon implied in allowing boys, plural, to cover Sylvie's face with kisses, to slide a hand over her sweater and cup her breast, even though Head Librarian Elaine—she insisted everyone address her this way—was only two rows away. "Just date one of them at a time, like a normal person," Julia pleaded with Sylvie. She wanted her sister to behave in a way that made sense.

"I have no interest in dating," Sylvie said. "Dating is about getting dressed up and pretending you're a pretty girl who thinks about nothing but marriage and babies. I *don't* think about those things, and it makes me sad to pretend to be something I'm not. Oh—" She propped herself up on her elbow so she could see her sister in the dim light. "I thought of a metaphor today while I was shelving. Imagine that I'm a house, and when I find my great love, I'll become the entire world. Our love will show me so much more than I'm able to see on my own."

"You're ridiculous," Julia said, but she smiled while she said it, because she was tender inside her own love story and because she wanted Sylvie to be happy, even if Julia thought her dream was nonsensical.

Sylvie wasn't entirely impractical. She would earn a degree in English literature, which would allow her to understand some of the mystery and beauty and symmetry in the novels she loved and qualify her for a job in teaching or publishing. She would give her mother whatever money she could spare, to make Rose's life easier. She and her mother didn't get along well; they picked small fights with each other all day long. Sylvie didn't like how Rose left used drinking glasses and dishes all over the house; the twins did this too, but Sylvie excused them because they were the babies of the family. Rose would complain that Sylvie didn't care about her garden, which was true. Sylvie was the only daughter who insisted that all her chores take place inside the house; she went out back only to hang laundry on the multi-tiered clothesline. When Rose came upon Sylvie reading a book, she made a face and then gave a noisy sigh. This mystified Sylvie—how could her mother disapprove of her reading, when she had been the one to demand that all four girls go to college? Sylvie had observed that her mother and Julia often shared a peaceful silence at the kitchen table. But when Sylvie and her mother were together, the air crackled as if filled with static electricity.

Rose smoothed Emeline's and Cecelia's hair and bossed them around like they were still young children, and the girls accepted it. They did most of the weeding in the garden and helped Rose fold laundry. The twins had always seemed to need only each other, and they often seemed pleasantly surprised by the affection their parents and older sisters showered on them. Emeline, in particular, looked startled when another member of the family joined a conversation she was having with Cecelia, as if she'd forgotten that other people lived in the house. The twins had their own made-up language, which they'd spoken until the end of elementary school, and they still used some of the vocabulary when they were alone.

Sylvie closed her eyes, a book in her hands, so she could relive Ernie's kiss. The people who called her easy, or a slut, were lazy thinkers. She had never done more than make out with Ernie, or Miles, or the man in the suit with the thick eyebrows. These young men seemed happy to kiss her, and the ninety-second limit meant nothing serious could develop, which suited Sylvie perfectly. If a steady boyfriend or sluttiness were the two available doors, she had found and opened a third. What made her most excited about her future was the idea of finding more third doors. Her soulmate would qualify; he would be more than a boyfriend or a husband. He would *see* Sylvie, as if through a pane of clear glass, and not want to change any aspect of her. Sylvie watched her mother try to change her father every day, and now she could see Julia lovingly nudging William into the shape of her ideal future husband. Sylvie would love differently. She would celebrate whoever her beloved happened to be; she would be curious about his distinctiveness and sink into a love that was unblinkingly honest.

My heart is open, she thought, and then wondered at the phrase. Was it a line from a poem? Had she heard her father recite those words in the house? She shared her father's affection for Whitman. When Charlie recited his poems, she pictured the bearded poet standing on the back balcony of a steam train—the words, the beauty he saw in the world, bringing tears to his eyes.

When Sylvie emerged from the row with her cart, she saw Julia and William sitting at the table they favored. It was partially hidden from the front of the library by a structural beam, so they had a little privacy, though Sylvie had never seen them do more than hold hands. They were leaning toward each other now, eyes locked. Sylvie understood her sister's laser focus. She knew that Julia had gone all in on William Waters; he would be her husband, the structural beam of her future. Julia was willful, and her formidable engine was powering her and William forward. "I know why you like him so much," Cecelia had teased her older sister. "Because he does whatever you tell him to."

Sylvie didn't know William as well as she knew her sister, of course, but she did sense some kind of fear in him, though he presented as steady and calm. He was holding on to Julia like a life raft, and Sylvie wondered why. She wasn't prone to gossip, but she liked to understand the whole arc of a story, especially when it came in the shape of a six-foot-seven man her beloved sister had brought into their family.

She pushed her cart up to their table, and they both smiled hello at her.

"You're so good about studying." Sylvie stared hungrily at the spread of books that covered their tabletop. She'd had to drop out of community college when Charlie took another pay cut. She now worked as many shifts at the library as were available, saving money so she could re-enroll.

"I'm not as smart as your sister," William said. "I have to study a lot, or my grades will drop and I won't be able to play basketball."

"You'll be back in college soon," Julia said to Sylvie.

Sylvie shrugged and felt her cheeks grow warm. She didn't want to discuss her financial issues in front of her future brother-in-law. "How's wedding planning going?" she asked. "It will be nice to meet your family, William."

A strange look crossed his face, and Sylvie wondered if she'd said something wrong.

"Actually," Julia said quickly, "his parents aren't coming to the wedding. They don't want to."

Sylvie tilted her head to the side and tried to make sense of this. People *don't want to* exercise, or eat salads, or wake up early. Saying your own parents don't want to attend your wedding sounded like a mistake. "I don't understand," she said.

William looked tired; something in him faded, to match his faded blue eyes. "I don't think you or your sister *can* understand," he said. "Your family loves one another. I don't think my parents love me."

He looked surprised by what he'd just revealed, and Sylvie was surprised too. She sat down in the empty seat at their table. Julia put her hand over William's. She said, in her most determined voice, "Our wedding will be wonderful without them."

"Of course it will!" Sylvie said. "I'm sorry I asked. . . . I didn't know."

"They're not bad people," William said. "You're just lucky to have Rose and Charlie as your parents."

"Yes," Sylvie said. Sunlight was boring into the library through the spread of windows. They were all caught up in its shine for a moment—they blinked, put hands up to shield their eyes—until a cloud moved or the sun sank a degree and normal color returned to the room around them.

Head Librarian Elaine made a loud tutting noise from somewhere, and Sylvie stood.

"Are you hiding a boy in one of these stacks?" Julia said.

"Not right now," Sylvie said. "It's just me and a thousand books."

A MONTH LATER, SYLVIE was back in college, thanks to her sister. Julia sat in the Lozano Library one afternoon and paid close attention to the regular patrons. One older man, who came in at lunchtime and read Sylvie her horoscope from the newspaper, happened to work in the neighborhood bank. Julia beelined for him, and when she explained the situation Sylvie was in, he said he'd be delighted to help. That same afternoon, he arranged for Sylvie to get a small student loan. "Can't have a light like you buried under a bushel," he said, when he handed Sylvie the papers.

This generosity—from the man and her sister—made Sylvie teary, even though she rarely cried. Head Librarian Elaine tutted at the sight of her pink face and streaming eyes and said, "Well, I suppose you'll want to rework your schedule around your classes again."

"Yes, please, ma'am."

Her sisters baked her a cake, and Cecelia drew a banner that said, *Congratulations, Sylvie!* She hung the banner in Sylvie and Julia's tiny bedroom, though, so the sight of it wouldn't hurt Charlie's feelings. He had been ignoring the fact that Sylvie was out of college—because it was his fault—and so would prefer to ignore that she'd had to re-enroll. The four girls ate the cake on the floor of the bedroom, cross-legged and talking over one another.

"This cake is for you too." Sylvie nodded at her older sister. "I wouldn't be going back if it weren't for you."

Julia swallowed a bite and said, "You should have thought of this solution yourself, you know. Everyone in that library adores you. If they'd known you needed help, you would have had it earlier."

Voices erupted outside the door, from the direction of the living room, and the four girls went silent to listen. Rose's voice climbed to a pitch that meant she was unhappy, then Charlie responded, and Rose's voice leveled. What at first sounded like a marital fight subsided into a conversation, and the girls relaxed.

"Here's what you're going to do," Julia said.

"Oh, goodie," Cecelia said, and Emeline put down her fork in anticipation. The twins had just turned seventeen and started their senior year of high school. Sylvie was twenty, and Julia twenty-one. They were getting too old to play this game, which had started in early childhood, but they hadn't been able to give it up. Julia ran the game and told each of them their future. She picked up an invisible fortune-teller's ball and shook it like a snow globe to find different answers for the four girls each time. When they were in elementary school, she'd gone through an animal-loving phase in which she would be a veterinarian and Sylvie her assistant. Julia couldn't bear to give the animals their shots, so she needed an assistant to take on that responsibility. In this future vision, Emeline and Cecelia would be zookeepers. There had been myriad professions and husbands since then, a kaleidoscope view of the years ahead.

"Sylvie will meet a tall, dark-eyed stranger named Balthazar on a train and commence the great love affair of her life. She'll also write the great American novel and be awarded the Pulitzer Prize before she's thirty."

Sylvie pushed her bare foot against her sister's thigh in appreciation, her mouth filled with sugary icing.

"I'll marry William next summer and we'll have two perfect children. We'll live in a genteel single-family house with a proper yard— probably in Forest Glen—and you three will come over every Sunday, at least, for dinner. And I'll run the school board at my children's school and be the perfect faculty wife."

"What if he makes it into the basketball league?" Emeline said. "Isn't that what he really wants to do?"

Julia pushed her curls away from her face. "Being an athlete isn't a career—it's something you do during school."

"So you'll run everything," Cecelia said, wanting Julia to move on.

"Yes. And you, Emmie, will marry a Scottish doctor and have three sets of twins. You'll live on a farm next to a moor."

One of the futures always featured a moor—the girls were collectively fascinated by the idea of that mysterious landscape, which featured in nearly all the English novels they loved.

"Ooooh," Emeline said, and fell back on the bed in delight. Her greatest wish was to be a mother, a role she'd been practicing for her entire life. Ever since she was a toddler, she'd carried snacks and Band-Aids in a little purse, to minister to her sisters whenever they were hungry or hurt. The younger children on their block waddled after Emeline like baby ducks, basking in the attention she gave them. She was the most sought-after babysitter on their side of Pilsen and, as a result, had an impressive bankroll stored under her mattress.

"Three boys and three girls," Julia said, before Emeline could ask. The girl nodded, satisfied.

"My turn!" Cecelia said.

"You'll go to art school and become a famous painter. You can't be too far from Emeline for too long—"

"Or we'll die," Emeline said.

"—so you'll keep an apartment in Paris and one in Scotland near her farm, which makes sense because you love the rain."

"Yes," Cecelia said. "I'd like to paint the rain in the same way Van Gogh painted the night sky."

Emeline nodded. "I'll hang your paintings all over my farmhouse."

Sylvie had to force herself to swallow her next bite of cake, because the taste was suddenly laced with bitterness. She almost said something unkind, like *None of this will ever happen.* But she stopped herself. The game was no longer fun for her, and she could tell that Julia had to feign enthusiasm for it as well. Sylvie had never admitted, even to herself, that writing a novel was a dream. But her sister had snaked the truth out of her and said it in front of everyone, and—even though Sylvie knew Julia had meant well—that felt painfully, strangely, like a loss. The dream was now in the air, at risk of the elements, beyond her grasp.

ON JULIA'S WEDDING DAY, Rose woke the four girls at dawn.

"What's wrong, Mama?" Emeline said, in response to Rose's frantic expression.

The girls rubbed their eyes and yawned their way into a panicked silence, awaiting the worst. William had died, or run away, or the church had burned down, or Charlie was too drunk to make it to the wedding. Or perhaps something terrible had happened to the garden: a flash flood or an army of killer ants.

"There's. So much. To do," Rose said, winded by having to speak the words. "Get up!"

Julia was already standing, smoothing her hair. She followed her mother into the kitchen, narrating her own to-do list aloud. "We need to make sure there's a chair for William—separate from the ones for the old people. He can't stand for long because of his knee. Sylvie will get the flowers from Mr. Luis. The cookies?"

"Are ready to go into the ovens."

The four houses up and down from theirs had offered their kitchens to Rose and were poised to bake their portions of the five hundred cookies needed for the reception. At ten o'clock, Emeline was due to run from house to house and shout, *Now!* The cookies would be slid into the ovens simultaneously.

The wedding would be at St. Procopius at noon, and then a wine-and-cookies reception would be held in the church's side yard. Julia's dress had been made by an Italian seamstress two streets over. Rose had been laundering the seamstress's dresses and fabrics for free for months in exchange for the wedding gown. Rose was a world-class barterer. In the back left corner of her garden, she grew a specific varietal of squash only because the local butcher missed it terribly from his childhood in Greece; she gave him the entire crop each year in exchange for cuts of chicken and beef for her family. She'd orchestrated everything they needed for the wedding except the wine. Charlie was drinking buddies with the owners of the four liquor stores within walking distance, and Rose insisted that after all the business he'd given them, the least they could do was donate a case each for the wedding of his eldest daughter.

"Sylvie, you're not going to marry and leave me, are you?" Charlie was in his armchair in the living room, wearing an old white T-shirt. He held a mug of coffee with both hands.

"Oh, Daddy." Sylvie crossed the room and kissed the top of his head. "No matter what," she said, "I wouldn't leave you."

"Emmie? Cece?"

"Don't be silly, Daddy," one of the girls called from their bedroom. "Of course we're going to get married. Someday."

Charlie leaned back in his chair. He looked older than Sylvie had ever seen him. He turned toward the window, which was just beginning to show the first light of day, and nodded. "You'll all set sail, as you should, and leave your mother and me here. It's a tale as old as time."

After breakfast, Sylvie walked to the florist, which was six blocks away. Mr. Luis, a tiny Ecuadorian, sniffed at her from behind the counter and told her that the flowers would be delivered to the church on time. He was insulted that she had checked on him. "Surely you have something better to do with yourself on a day like this. Do your hair, put on lipstick. Do something to make yourself look special, child."

Sylvie frowned. Did she look that bad? She was the maid of honor, which meant she would stand at the front of the church next to her sister during the ceremony. She wanted to look pleasing for Julia, but that required one of those magical good-hair days; Sylvie was never able to convince her own hair to look presentable. She hadn't checked in the mirror this morning, but Mr. Luis seemed to suggest that she wasn't in luck. Sylvie thanked him and left the shop. She counted how many steps she had to travel away from the door before she could no longer smell roses: thirteen.

She passed the library, which was just about to open, and waved through the window at the girls behind the desk. She felt an urge to duck inside and work a shift. To spend this day within the library's cool stacks. The wedding, the sunlight, the mandatory smiling—it all seemed exhausting to her. She knew it was a strange contradiction, but despite her interest in love, weddings made her uncomfortable. They were too showy, too public. Deep love between two people was a private, wordless endeavor, and to place the lovers in fancy clothes in front of a crowd seemed antithetical to the nature of the thing. No one could *see* love—this was what Sylvie believed, anyway. It was an internal state. Watching that moment between two lovers felt wrong to her, almost blasphemous.

Sylvie was happy for Julia and William, but still, she would have to pretend the kind of girlish joy that she knew weddings were supposed to elicit in her. She would be kissed by all the old women in the neighborhood. *You're next* would be said to her again and again, and this would make her feel melancholy too, because her true love hadn't yet appeared, and what were the odds of him showing up at the Lozano Library, where she spent most of her time? What if she never found him?

Sylvie almost tripped over Cecelia, who was sitting on the curb just beyond the library. "What are you doing here?" she asked, surprised. Had Rose built time into the schedule for sitting on curbs, staring into space?

"Oh," Cecelia said. "I'm waiting for Emeline. She went into the pharmacy."

Sylvie sat down on the concrete, next to her sister. If there was time built into the schedule for this, she wanted part of it. She could use a quiet moment before reentering the manic energy of their house.

"I'm Beth today," Cecelia said.

Sylvie nodded. This was from a long-running conversation between the four Padavano sisters. When Julia had first read *Little Women,* she told her sisters about the four fictional sisters in the book, and they began to argue over which of them was which March girl. Julia and Sylvie both saw themselves as the feisty Jo, and they were both right, Sylvie thought. They had Jo divided between them. Julia had Jo March's exuberance and passion, and Sylvie had her independence and literary leaning. Emeline and Cecelia passed the identities of Meg and Amy back and forth between them, but whenever any of the sisters was sick or forlorn, she'd declare herself Beth. *One of us will be the first to die,* they would take turns telling one another, and all four girls shuddered at the thought.

"What's wrong? Do you not feel well?"

"I have a secret," Cecelia said. "You can't tell Julia. I'll tell her after her honeymoon. Maybe."

Sylvie waited. The neighborhood streamed around them. Loud teenagers jostled each other as they walked; a kid bounced a basketball, waiting to cross the street; a row of Hasidic men turned the corner. People with ancestors from every part of the world headed in every direction. It was a Saturday, and a beautiful June morning, so everyone looked a touch happier than normal, a touch more free.

"I'm pregnant."

A breath caught in Sylvie's throat, and she coughed. She thought, *But I haven't even had sex yet.* She said, "No, you can't be. You're seventeen. You're wrong."

Cecelia shrugged. She and Emeline had just graduated from high school, an event that was overshadowed by Julia's college graduation and wedding. Charlie had looked older this morning; Cecelia did now too. "It was a boy in my class who I've always liked. I drank too much at Laurie Genovese's party. He doesn't know. I'm not sure what I'm going to do."

Sylvie's second reaction was anger. She had been *so careful,* only kissing boys, only allowing herself moments of risk-free pleasure. Julia had been planning and executing her life with military precision since grade school. Neither of them had left room for any surprises. Sylvie could see now that they'd believed their sheer example would keep Emeline and Cecelia safe, following directly behind them on the path to adulthood. Keep them careful. But that had been lazy on Sylvie's part. She knew about third doors. If she and Julia had been marching in and out the same door, of course there was a chance that Emeline and Cecelia would find another exit. Cecelia was adorable: small and curvy. She had a generous laugh and drew portraits of her many friends for their birthdays. Boys had swarmed to her, and her older sisters hadn't told her how and why to fend those boys off. As Charlie had said this morning, it was a tale as old as time.

Sylvie felt welded to the curb. Even when she stood up, when she walked home with her two little sisters, when she let Rose bustle her into her pink maid of honor dress and tried to improve her unruly hair, she felt like she was on that curb, watching life rush past. The library to her back, Cecelia a walking time bomb, Julia so happy she appeared to be shooting off sparks, William on the cusp of joining a new family, Rose and Charlie unaware that a new generation was already on its way. When the sun was high overhead, and Sylvie was standing at the altar—a smile affixed to her face—she was still sitting on that curb, trying to figure out if she was too late to pull everyone back.

William

THE ACTION—FROM THE BODY ANGLES OF THE PLAYERS TO HIS own leap in the air—felt so familiar that when William rose for the block, he thought, *Be careful.* Those words were still in his head when a colossal center with dreadlocks and goggles slammed into his chest. William was stronger than he used to be, so he shoved back, still in the air, and was propelled backward. He collided with another player and tipped sideways. When he hit the floor, he landed hard on his right knee.

Kent leaned over William and offered his hand to help him stand up. "You all right?" Kent said.

William could barely hear his friend. His knee was buzzing. He was unusually aware of the *inside* of his knee, which felt like a sand-castle being knocked down by a sneaky wave. He stared at the joint while the referee blew his whistle and men carried a stretcher onto the court. William had recognized the play, and now he recognized the accompanying fog, and the pain too.

He needed two surgeries, because the knee had to be reconstructed. Every time the surgeon or attending came into the hospital room, William listened carefully, wanting to understand. The knee was the only subject he could pay attention to; all other information seemed to travel from an impossible distance. He caught words, fragments, but not meaning.

He was lucky to have a hospital room to himself. Normally, a patient would have been sent home for the two weeks that separated his surgeries, but since William needed to keep his injured leg immobile and elevated, and his dorm room was up three flights of stairs, they kept him in the hospital. The nurses said a roommate might arrive at any time, but one never appeared. Kent visited when he could, but between schoolwork, basketball, and his job in the laundry room, he didn't have much time to spare. Julia visited at least once a day, sometimes twice. She tried to make William laugh by performing an entrance: She twirled, like a ballerina entering the stage, or strode in with her chin up, playing a stern nurse. Once she came in with several books balanced on top of her head; she made it halfway across the room before they toppled. William enjoyed the entrances but didn't need them. He was just happy she was there.

Julia brought his textbooks so he could try to keep up with his coursework. Finals were less than two months away, and then came graduation. "We'll remember June 1982 as the best month of our lives," Julia said. "Graduation and a wedding." She named the two events with pleasure, savoring the solidity of the milestones. William liked it when his fiancée spoke like that; he admired how Julia saw her life as a system of highways to be expertly navigated, and he was grateful to be in her car.

When she left the room, though, William was often alone for hours. He ignored the textbooks and flipped between channels on the television in the corner. He watched Bulls games on mute. Kent had brought William's mail on his last visit, and William had recognized his father's spidery script on one of the envelopes. When he'd touched the letter for the first time, an icy sweat covered his skin. William had thought that he'd deadened himself to hope in regard to his parents, but with the appearance of the letter the emotion had shot, unwanted, through him. He'd stuck the envelope under his pillow while he worked to shoo the hope out of him, like a bird out a window. William had always accepted the fact that his parents didn't want him in their lives. He'd felt mostly calm while he and Julia phoned his mother about the wedding, because he'd known what the result would be; his only concern that evening had been for Julia and her disappointment.

But his parents would have had time to consider everything, in the wake of that phone call, and now they'd gone to the effort of writing him a letter. They couldn't know he was in the hospital—how would they have heard? The university was covering his medical bills, and when the surgeon had offered to speak to William's parents, he'd said that wasn't necessary. William thought it was *possible* that his mother and father had written to him because they felt some remorse. Now that William was a man and getting married, perhaps they'd realized how much of his life they'd missed. Perhaps they wanted to be part of his adulthood. He hoped—again, the hope showed itself in an icy sweat—they might have written a long letter, one that included an apology for having been so uninterested in him for so long. The letter might ask for William's forgiveness and for the chance to attend his wedding.

William switched off the television and pried open the envelope. He could tell right away that there was no letter inside. There was only a check. On the memo line, it said: *Congratulations on wedding/graduation.* The check was for ten thousand dollars. William looked at the zeros and thought, *It's really over now.* He wouldn't deposit the check—he knew that immediately. He wouldn't touch their money. William's heartbeat slowed to a murmur in his chest, and he had to breathe in a funny way to keep from crying. He was surprised by how upset he was; it felt like something had broken inside him.

WILLIAM'S BASKETBALL TEAM AND coach visited between the two surgeries. His teammates, several of whom had to duck as they walked through the doorframe, were wearing team sweats. Everything inside William sank while the group gathered around his hospital bed. It felt like his insides—his self—had narrowed to the point of a pencil. All color and lines vanished.

Every visitor wore a careful smile intended to cheer him up.

"You're okay," Kent said. He was nearest to William, and he tapped his shoulder twice, as if to hammer in some kind of certainty with the words. *You're okay.*

I don't think so, William thought.

The coach cleared his throat and said, "Son, you were lucky to have it happen when it did. You made it to the tournament and got that experience. You served us well during the meat of the season. And I hear you're getting married soon?"

"Yes, sir."

"Wonderful news. That's the real stuff. See, everything is looking up."

You don't mean that, William thought. *You know I won't be able to play anymore. You know I'm finished.*

Their point guard, Gus, handed him a get-well-soon card they'd all signed, a couple of guys made jokes about hospital food, and then, thankfully, they filed out.

The physio—a bearded man named Arash—hung back, though, and approached the hospital bed. He frowned and said, "What was the history with that knee?"

William nodded in appreciation of the question; the knee did have a history. The pencil point inside him softened, and he was able to gather enough air to breathe. "I broke the kneecap my junior year in high school. During a very similar play, actually."

"I thought so. So the kneecap shattered the way it did because of an earlier weakness."

Arash had the X-ray in his hand; he looked down at the image. William's kneecap looked dustier, messier, than the bones above and below in the X-ray. The white knob was traced with multiple lines. "Looks like a mosaic."

"A career-ender," William said.

"That too. Look, I know you love the game," Arash said. "I saw that, and I saw your weak knee. You can stay in basketball, you know. You can coach or be a trainer or play another role. Look around at all the support staff and see what appeals to you. Basketball is a big machine with a lot of parts."

William leaned forward. "What do you mean, you saw my weak knee?"

Arash was a stocky man with powerful-looking forearms. "You protected it once or twice. I could also see how you used your other side to pivot and jump. That's what happens when an injury occurs at a young age. The knee doesn't operate in isolation. The hip and ankle start to get used differently, and your overall balance is thrown off. There's interplay between the various joints, and no one told you to build the weak leg back to full strength. I bet you came out of the cast last time and immediately returned to the court without changing anything, right?"

William nodded.

"That's what I thought."

Julia arrived a few minutes after Arash had gone. She scanned William's face; she could see he was riled up somehow. "Did something happen?"

"My knee is killing me."

"You poor thing. Try to think about something else. Think about the wedding. You have something wonderful to look forward to, right?"

"That's what Coach said too."

She brightened. "How nice!"

She handed him her clipboard, which had pages of plans: the guest list, floral arrangements with taped photos of different flowers, a minute-by-minute schedule. A timeline of things to do and dates to have each item done by. A spreadsheet to show who was responsible for what. Almost every box had either Julia's or Rose's name beside it.

William flipped through the pages. The wedding was nine weeks away. It was a concrete event he could comprehend, like the reality of his knee. He needed to show up for one and be careful with the other.

Julia smoothed William's hair; her touch felt good.

She was talking, so he tried to focus. "When I went into the history department to get your work, I asked around about teaching-assistant jobs. Turns out there's a position for next fall that hasn't been listed yet. Should I hand in your résumé for you?"

William would start the graduate program in history at Northwestern in September. He'd been surprised and relieved when the program accepted him. He thought of himself as a mediocre student, but the truth was that studying alongside Kent and Julia for the prior four years had changed that. His friend and girlfriend had modeled hard work and taught him how to study effectively. These skills, combined with William's constant fear that a low grade-point average would knock him off the basketball team, had vaulted him onto the dean's list.

The PhD application had required him to declare a historical period to focus on, and he'd struggled with the choice. His favorite part of history was its *breadth,* the sweeping connections between events and figures. How Leo Tolstoy had inspired Mahatma Gandhi, who had in turn inspired Martin Luther King, Jr. William didn't see how he could confidently plant his feet in any particular century, continent, or war. When he'd discussed this quandary with Kent, his friend shook his head and said, "You already have an area of focus, dummy. You're writing a book about the history of basketball." This surprised William—it hadn't occurred to him—and he said, "I can't study *basketball*. That wouldn't be seen as a serious academic subject." But he'd applied to study American history from 1890 to 1969, a time frame that would allow his private interest and his legitimate work to at least exist side by side.

William would need teaching-assistant jobs to provide him and Julia with some income during the long PhD program. He arranged his face to show that he was paying attention to his fiancée and her plans, but somewhere inside was a repeated whisper of *wedding, knee.*

"Sure?" he said. "But I'm not sure my résumé is ready to go out."

"I'll clean it up; I'm good at that. I read so many résumés for Professor Cooper last summer, remember? You need a haircut when you get out of here." Julia touched his arm. She paused and then said in a low voice, "I wish I could climb into bed with you."

William imagined her curves fitting against his side. He imagined what would happen when he pulled the sheet over their heads.

"Kiss my hand?" he said.

She leaned forward and took his hand in hers. She kissed the outside, in the soft spot between his thumb and index finger. Then she turned his hand over and kissed the palm. Softly, over and over. *Wedding. Knee.*

ROSE AND JULIA CHAIRED a run-through meeting at the Padavanos' dining room table a few days before the wedding. Charlie wasn't there, but his absence wasn't mentioned, and William wondered if the meeting had been timed for when he would be out. Sylvie sat in the corner farthest from her mother and read a book that she was holding on her lap. She paid attention only when she was addressed directly. Emeline had been told to take notes on decisions that were made, so she sat at the ready with a pad and pencil. Cecelia leaned against her twin's arm, looking bored or sleepy.

It had taken William a while to get a handle on the differences between the twins, but he now had no trouble telling them apart. Cecelia always had flecks of paint on her hands and clothes, and she went from good-spirited to annoyed with startling speed. She liked to try out stern looks on people, in a way that reminded William of Julia. Emeline was more placid and slower to react than her twin. She was the quietest of the four sisters, but when the phone rang in the small house, it was usually a request for Emeline to babysit. William once had the thought that his fiancée seemed to stride about the world with a conductor's wand, while Sylvie brandished a book and Cecelia a paintbrush. Emeline, though, kept her hands free in order to be helpful or to pick up and soothe a neighborhood child. Every time Emeline had seen William since his injury, she'd asked if she could carry something for him or open the door in his path.

William listened while Julia and her mother took turns reciting the schedule and the assigned tasks. When Rose stated that on the morning of the wedding Charlie would pick William up at Northwestern, he said, "That's not necessary. I can get myself to the church."

"You're injured," Rose said, in a tone that suggested the shattered kneecap was his fault. "And how exactly are you intending to get to the church in your wedding suit, on crutches—the city bus? Charlie will borrow our neighbor's car, and he'll drive you. That's that."

Emeline grinned. "Mama just wants to make absolutely sure that you're at the church on time."

"If that's true, then she shouldn't have appointed Daddy to be the driver," Cecelia said.

Rose shook her head, her gray hair flying. "You girls be quiet. William and Charlie will look after each other, and they'll both be there on time."

"Oh!" Emeline said, and patted the table with her open palm. "That makes sense. You're giving Daddy a responsibility and making Daddy William's responsibility. You're an evil genius, Mama." She held her hand up in front of her mother's face for a high five, which Rose ignored.

Rose said, "Have you given instructions to the best man?"

"Kent knows where he needs to be, at what time."

"Will he be drunk?"

William looked at her, surprised. "No?"

"Don't mind her," Julia said. "She always assumes every man drinks too much."

"Only until proven otherwise," Rose said. "Cecelia, why are you lying on the table during a meeting? Sit up, please."

"I feel like we're all set," Sylvie said. "This wedding is going to run like a finely tuned watch. I have to go to work soon, remember?"

Rose turned toward William and said, "After the wedding, you'll call me Mom, or Mama. No more Mrs. Padavano."

She glared at him while she said this, but he could feel another message being delivered with her eyes. She regretted that his parents weren't coming to the wedding, and she regretted that his parents didn't love him. She would love him, to fill their absence.

Julia squeezed his good knee under the table.

It took him a moment to find his voice. "Thank you," he said.

"Nonsense." Rose had already turned back to her list.

But he thanked her again and covered Julia's hand with his own.

Later, it occurred to William that Rose had called the meeting to tell him this. She didn't need to run through the plans. She was the commander-in-chief, and she would direct her soldiers on the day. She didn't delegate—she ordered. She'd simply wanted to make this declaration to him, in front of witnesses.

GRADUATION FELL ONE WEEK before the wedding, and since that event included its own celebrations of various sizes, the days began to feel punctuated by William climbing into or out of nice clothes. The night before the wedding, he and Kent went out for burritos and toasted their way through too many beers. On Monday, Kent was moving to Milwaukee for medical school. "It's less than two hours away," he said. "I know you're going to miss me, but we can both visit. We'll do laundry together, for old times' sake."

Sareka, the laundry room boss who had tried to send William away the first time he showed up in the basement, had attended their graduation and cheered wildly when William's and Kent's names were announced. She never officially changed her tune; she always professed to distrust William and like Kent, but by his junior year it was clear she was pretending, and William took her affection as the highest compliment. He'd invited her to the wedding, but she'd said no without hesitation. "I prefer not to be around that many white people."

"You're going to be a great doctor," William said.

Kent eyed him. "Are you looking forward to being a professor?"

"Did I tell you that Arash noticed that my right knee had a weakness before the injury? He told me in the hospital."

"No shit. That's interesting. I'm not surprised, though. That guy has a talent. He told Butler that his ankles were moving stiffly, and a few days later he broke one of them in a scrimmage. Remember that?"

"If I'd known, I could have strengthened the knee and avoided this break."

"Nuh-uh."

"Nuh-uh what?"

Kent shook his head. "Stop talking like that. We're graduated. Rehab that knee and we can get serious about pickup ball, but it's time for us to be full-grown men now." He lifted his beer bottle. "A toast to you and the General, and to me and a million hours of studying."

CHARLIE WAS RIGHT ON time, and William was waiting on the curb. It had taken him a long time to get dressed that morning. He'd taken two freezing showers, because he felt overheated and worried about sweating in his nice suit. Once he had the suit on, he attached and detached his knee brace countless times, trying to make sure his pants were pulled smooth around the metal brace and not bunched up.

William slid his crutches into the back seat of the blue sedan Charlie had borrowed and lowered himself into the front seat, after sliding it back for maximal legroom.

"Big day." Charlie was wearing a suit; he looked small and uncomfortable behind the wheel. "I only wear this thing for funerals, usually," he said, as he pulled out into traffic.

William looked at the buildings and houses outside the window. He felt like he was playing a scene in a movie: young man with his almost father-in-law on brink of wedding. He wanted to act his part as well as possible.

"You're going to be good to Julia." Charlie stated this like it was a fact.

"Yes, sir. I will be."

Charlie took a corner smoothly, then switched lanes after checking his mirrors. A fat truck appeared in front of their car, and he slowed to allow enough distance between the vehicles. He was a good driver, which surprised William. Julia's father always presented as the distracted, mildly incompetent man his daughters and wife believed him to be. It was interesting to see him be competent, and William wondered, for the first time, how much of Charlie's usual behavior was an act.

"Did you know that Rose and I eloped? We didn't have a wedding. I think that accounts for her feverishness about this one. It's for her *and* for Julia."

William shook his head. "I didn't know that."

"She was pregnant with Julia, and our mothers didn't like each other. Some beef from the old country. We drove to Las Vegas."

William smiled at the idea of Rose and Charlie on the Las Vegas Strip. Did Julia know that she'd been conceived before her parents' marriage?

As if he'd heard his thought, Charlie said, "Julia knows. It's family lore; we never hid the truth. Rose hated Las Vegas, though—she said she was disappointed in all the people that go there every year. She's never gotten out of the funk Las Vegas put her in."

This was supposed to be a joke, but Charlie's overall mood was too somber for it to land. William felt bad for him. Charlie was about to give away his eldest daughter, and he was completely sober, which was a rare occurrence. Alcohol made Charlie lighter.

"I've never been good at providing Rose with what she wanted, other than the girls," he said. "Try to give Julia what she wants, whenever you can. Julia's strong, willful, like her mother—she'll give your life a backbone. Rose holds me up, in a lot of ways, and I'm a lucky man. You're a lucky man too."

William felt the truth of this: He was lucky. Julia had already given him so much. All she seemed to want from him was his love and his enthusiasm for her plans. He could keep providing both of those things, easily, and he hoped that would be enough. From the outside, Charlie and Rose's marriage seemed complicated, like a clock with inner workings that spun but didn't quite connect.

Charlie leaned forward and peered through the wide windshield. "There's the church. Look for a parking spot I can swing into."

For the next six hours, with the exception of the time at the altar, William felt like he was always in the wrong spot. Julia, Rose, or Charlie kept calling his name. Asking him to speak to a distant cousin, hug the girls' first-grade teacher, talk basketball with a Bulls fan or talk Boston with an uncle who had been there once. His knee ached no matter what position he was in. Julia would get upset that he wasn't sitting and then pull him across the lawn to shake hands with the man who had done the flowers. Kent, who had the magical ability to make himself comfortable in any situation, hand-shook his way across the grass as if he were running for mayor. William noticed that he was always trailed by a flock of pretty young women. Sylvie, Emeline, and Cecelia revolved around William and Julia like pink constellations. "So much smiling," Sylvie said to him once, in passing. Toward dusk, Cecelia handed William her high-heeled shoes and then walked away across the lawn. Charlie, hair standing up straight, a drink in his hand, clapped William on the back whenever they came near each other.

All of that was blurred, though, by Julia's luminescence. Her white dress was covered with tiny white beads that swished when she walked. Her hourglass figure was hugged by the fabric; her hair was pinned up on top of her head; her eyes were bright. She looked like she had been plugged in to a power source the rest of them didn't have access to. William was grateful all over again every time she took his arm or kissed his cheek. "My wife," he whispered.

Rose came to find them when the limousine arrived. "It's time for you to leave. You two have a wonderful time, and I'm going to sleep for three days."

Julia hugged her mother, and the two women gripped hard and hung on for a long moment. When Rose pulled away, she said, "William?"

William took in the entire scene: the stone church; the crowd of tipsy, smiling people; his basketball teammates, taller than everyone else, their long legs wavering with drink. The white streamers connecting the tree branches overhead. His new sisters-in-law working the edges of the party, kissing the older guests goodbye.

"Thank you for everything, Mom," he said. *Mom* hurt his throat on the way out; he'd rarely used the term—his own mother had seemed to prefer he call her nothing at all, so he'd done that. The word had long been dormant, covered with rust, inside him.

Rose nodded, satisfied, and turned to clear a path for them to the waiting car, to whatever happened after *wedding, knee,* and the rest of their lives.

Julia

JULIA FOUND HERSELF STRANGELY UNPREPARED FOR THEIR honeymoon, which took place at a resort on the shore of Lake Michigan. She'd spent so much time and energy planning the wedding that she hadn't given much thought to her and William's trip. In moments of daydream, she'd pictured them lying side by side on sun loungers, holding hands. In reality, there were heavy winds for the five days they were at the lakeside hotel, which choked the beach with whipping sand, and it was difficult for William to walk on uneven terrain with his crutches. In fact, it was difficult for him to walk anywhere. After he traveled about a hundred feet, his forehead creased and he grew pale. The steps he did take were so slow, Julia had a hard time restraining herself to his pace. She developed a habit of walking ahead and then circling back. They were both exhausted from the end of the school year and the wedding, so once Julia stopped feeling like they had to *do* something—explore the town, go out to lunch, look at antiques because the area was known for antiques—they were able to enjoy the last day and a half, when they barely left their bedroom.

Back in Chicago, they went straight to their new apartment in the married-housing building on Northwestern's campus. They qualified for the housing because William would start graduate school there in the fall, and he'd gotten a summer job on campus in the admissions office, helping to reorganize their filing system. Julia immediately loved the place. It was a one-bedroom with a living room window that looked out over a quad. Sunlight poured in. She'd never lived anywhere other than the small house on 18th Place, with her parents and sisters. This apartment was almost impossibly peaceful, with just her and William. They had their own kitchen, bathroom, and small round yellow table to eat meals together.

She went with William for his checkup with the surgeon. The man examined the lacework of scars around and across his kneecap and declared his healing excellent. "Time to ditch the crutches, young man. You need to increase your walking too," the doctor said. "These muscles need to move or they won't strengthen. You're a ball player, so I recommend you go for a long walk every day while dribbling a ball."

"I *was* a ball player," William said.

"Dribbling the ball is for the distraction and to get your balance back," the doctor said. "Your wife is paying attention, in any case."

"I'm paying attention." William sounded offended.

The doctor looked at Julia. "Make sure your husband walks. If he's sedentary, the knee will always be a problem. Don't let him disrespect my work."

The following Monday, William reported to Northwestern's admissions office, and Julia went grocery shopping. This was delightful too. She could buy bananas, even though Rose hated the smell of bananas and refused to have them in the house. Emeline was allergic to peanuts, so they never bought peanut butter, but Julia could put a jar in her basket now. She bought cold cuts, bread, and a fancy mustard for William's packed lunches. She took more time than was necessary, trailing up and down the aisles of the market. When she got back to the apartment, she found her three sisters standing in front of her door. Her heart leapt at the sight of them.

"I missed you!" she said. "But what are you doing here? We're coming over to the house for dinner tonight."

"We wanted to see your place," Sylvie said.

Julia tried to frown, but her face wouldn't stop smiling. She was happy to be the subject of her sisters' collective attention. She knew she was beaming, and she could see the girls' pleasure in causing it. "Next week, I said. I wanted to add some touches first, hang pictures. So it looked really nice when you saw it for the first time."

"Was the honeymoon terribly romantic?" Emeline leaned against the wall, as if in a mild swoon.

"We're not here to see your house," Cecelia said. "Let's go inside, though."

Julia handed off her shopping bags and opened the door with the key.

Her sisters gave similar sighs of pleasure.

"How lovely!" Sylvie said.

It did look lovely, with the morning sun streaming in. The three visitors understood the preciousness of having your own space. When you grew up in a crowded, small house like they had, much of the dream of adulthood became living somewhere less crowded. Somewhere that was your own and didn't need to be shared.

Julia gave them a brief tour, and then they sank down onto the sofa and armchair in the living room. Julia noticed that Cecelia was carrying something under her arm, and said, "What is that?"

"Oh." Cecelia pulled it free. "It's my scarlet letter, from Mama. She wants me to carry it everywhere for a week, at least. I told her I would." It was one of the framed saints from the dining room wall. Julia stared at it, trying to match the woman with her name. She knew the saints only in context, listed in a row, on the wall of their house.

"St. Clare of Assisi," Cecelia said.

Sylvie and Emeline looked down, as if to study their own legs and feet. Their mother had taught them lessons related to each saint, but she'd never removed a saint from the wall, much less assigned one as a traveling penance to a daughter.

Julia remembered this saint now. St. Clare had refused to marry at the age of fifteen and had run away from home. She'd cut off all her hair and devoted her life to God. She created the Order of Poor Ladies, and her own sister and mother went to live with her in her abbey. She was the first woman in history to write a monastic rule, which the Order of Poor Ladies lived by. Julia studied her youngest sister. Cecelia had been born three minutes after Emeline, so they sometimes called her Baby. Charlie liked to croon Frank Sinatra at her: *Yes sir, that's my baby. No sir, I don't mean maybe.*

"What happened?" Julia was aware that her hands were freezing and she was scared.

"I'm pregnant. Almost five months along." Cecelia spoke the words calmly. "Mom has decided that I'm headed for a life of destitution. But I'm going to keep the baby. I'm not telling the father, because—" She stopped for a second. "Because there's no good to come from his knowing."

Julia shook her head in refusal. This couldn't be correct. "You're pregnant?"

"Yes."

"You're having a baby, at the age of seventeen."

"I'll be eighteen when the baby's born."

Julia felt something inside her harden. She studied her other sisters; clearly she was the last to know. They had already swallowed this news and found a way to accept it. Emeline was unconditionally loyal to her twin, and besides, she adored babies. Sylvie *was* disappointed in Cecelia—Julia had seen this in her sister's eyes—but Sylvie looked at life like a story, and she would be impressed at how their younger sister had made herself a main character in their shared narrative.

Julia said, "I'm supposed to have the first baby."

Sylvie and Emeline looked up from their feet, surprised.

"I'm sorry," Julia said. "But this is ridiculous. You should obviously give the baby up for adoption. Why should you ruin your life because of a mistake?"

Cecelia stood, and when she did, she straightened her posture and the pregnancy was visible for the first time. How long had she been walking slumped over, with carefully arranged clothes? She was wearing a lavender button-down shirt, and the hard mound of her belly pushed the fabric outward. "You and Sylvie see us as children," she said. "Mama thinks everyone is on the verge of catastrophe at all times. I'm neither of those things. I never wanted to go to college. I'll study and make art on my own, with my baby. This is my life, and my choice. I'll never be a burden on anyone." Five foot two, shoulders back, she growled the last sentence.

Emeline said, "Mrs. Ceccione said Cecelia could move into Frank's room and that she would help with the baby, if we cooked dinner and did chores. I'll start college in the fall, of course, but I'll work too. And I have a fair amount of money from babysitting that will help us buy what we need."

Julia stared. "You're going to move two doors down?"

"I can't stay home," Cecelia said. "Mama made that clear. And I'm sorry you feel like I unseated you, Julia. I know how much you like to be first."

Cecelia said this kindly, and even though Julia's hands were ice and she was mad at this truth in front of her—this mess—she nodded acceptance. She willed herself to stand up and hug her sister, but her cold body refused to move.

Sylvie cleared her throat and looked at Julia. "Mama asked us to tell you not to come to dinner tonight. She said she'll receive you when her mourning period is over."

"I'd like to leave now," Cecelia said, "but I need to pee. Can I use your bathroom?"

When she'd left the room, Julia, Sylvie, and Emeline looked at one another. Sylvie's face was worried, and Emeline had a mournful line between her eyebrows.

"Daddy?" Julia said.

"He's not talking. Mama says she's not talking, but she never shuts up. Daddy's coming home later than usual." This meant drunker than usual.

"They look old," Emeline said. "They don't want Cecelia to move out, but Mama told her that if she made this decision and didn't go to college, she had to."

Why? Julia thought, when her baby sister came back into the room and when her sisters filed out of the apartment. *Why ruin everything? Why would you do this to us?* Julia had tried so hard to do everything right, and she had. She felt overheated now and pushed open the window. She stared at the memory of Cecelia standing in the middle of her beautiful, perfect apartment in her purple shirt. She wished that they had told her the news somewhere else. Anywhere else. Julia went outside at one point and walked around the path that framed the quad.

There was a bench on the far side, which she sat on until she needed to return to motion.

When William came home that evening, she said, "I think we should have a baby."

He stopped where he was, his crutches pushed ahead of him for the step he'd been about to take. He looked like a tree propped up with wooden stakes. William was using the crutches only at home, when his leg was exhausted and sore. "Now?" He audibly swallowed. "I thought . . . we need to get on our feet first. Julia, I haven't even *started* graduate school."

"You got the teaching-assistant job for the fall. You're wonderful."

She was building something in her head. An answer to the mess, a way to fix everything, to put her family back to rights. Julia would save as much as she could from William's small salary and give that money to Cecelia, or Mrs. Ceccione, to make sure her sister had what she needed and was okay. The independence Cecelia had shown that afternoon felt like a flag planted into sandy ground. It was an announcement, a wish, from the pregnant girl; it wasn't who she was. She didn't have the strength she was pretending to have, and living down the block from Rose's tsunami of grief and judgment was going to throw Cecelia against the rocks. So more money would help. And Julia would get pregnant as soon as possible, because as a newly married woman, her pregnancy would be celebrated. It would be undeniably accepted. Julia would put her pregnant belly beside Cecelia's. Rose and Charlie would embrace both their grandchildren, because they would come as a set. Everyone would be back together again, and there would be enough love to go around. Julia had a sun-soaked image of two babies sitting on a blanket; one of them was hers, but she wasn't sure which one.

"You haven't even asked about my first day," William said. "Did something happen?" He paused and pulled his crutches back to his sides. He was now an upright tree. "You seem . . . agitated?"

Julia smiled at the questioning uplift to his voice. He was full of questions, and she loved him. She was full of answers. She walked closer and pressed herself against him. She reached up and undid the top button on the white shirt she'd given him for his birthday. Then the button below that. She ran her finger across the soft white T-shirt underneath. "Are you hungry?" she said, in a voice no louder than a whisper.

He shook his head.

She tugged on his shirt, and he lowered to her. *This will work,* she thought, distracted, as his lips covered hers and she led him in a slow, swaying, backward walk to the couch.

THE NEXT DAY, JULIA took the bus from Northwestern to Pilsen. She didn't want to go, but it was impossible to hear that news and not appear before her mother. Julia wouldn't have been able to put into words why, exactly, but she needed to show her mother the respect of her presence.

She found Rose sweating in the garden, bent over the herbs. Heat was rising from the soil in waves; summer in Chicago was punishing. Julia knew from experience that tending to the herbs demanded the most rigor and attention to detail. Rose insisted that whoever was working in that part of the garden use a magnifying glass and tweezers. Tiny bugs needed to be spotted and removed, and a special spindly weed that had a proclivity for climbing up the herbs and strangling them needed to be caught early.

"She's not here," Rose said. "If you're here to see *her.*"

"I came to see you."

This seemed to surprise Rose, and she stopped in the middle of yanking out a clump of young crabgrass. She put her hands on her thighs, and Julia was able to see her mother's face for the first time. Rose looked wrecked, as if she'd been in a car crash. All the familiar pieces were there, but wrong and somehow broken.

"I had to draw a line," Rose said.

Julia found it difficult to bear her mother's distressed face, so she looked up at the hot, low sky. She searched her mind for the right thing to say, words that would make her mother feel better. Before she'd found them, Rose said, "I only asked one thing of you girls."

"That we go to college."

Rose glared. "No. I asked you not to mess up like I did. Was that too much to ask?"

Julia shook her head, even though she couldn't recall her mother ever making that specific request. Rose had repeated, over and over: *You have to go to college.* She'd never actually told them not to get pregnant before marriage. That expectation was unspoken, but it turned out to have the highest stakes.

"You girls were supposed to do more than I did," Rose said. "I wanted you to be better. That," she said, her voice as gravelly as the soil at her feet, "was the whole point of my life."

"Oh, Mama," Julia said, taken aback. In the heat of the news the day before, she hadn't considered that Cecelia was repeating their mother's history. Rose had gotten pregnant with Julia when she was nineteen and unmarried, and Rose's mother had stopped speaking to her. The mother and daughter never spoke again. The girls had never met their grandmother. Charlie always said that it wasn't a loss, because their grandmother was an unfriendly, bitter woman. But when the subject of her mother came up, Rose always turned away. She never said a word. Now Rose was the mother turning away from the daughter, and the grandchild. Rose was axing a branch off her own family tree, which meant she was both inflicting and experiencing pain.

"I failed," Rose said.

"No, you didn't. You were a great mother."

"I failed." This time she said it in a soft voice that sounded like Emeline's. Julia had never heard her mother speak in that tone before and wouldn't have believed she was capable of it. Julia wondered if all four girls' voices lived inside their mother. Emeline's earnestness, Julia's clear directives, Cecelia's excitement about the palette of colors that made up the world, Sylvie's romantic yearning. Perhaps Rose simply masked her daughters' voices with her own gruff tone, her own twist of anger and disappointment, but they were all there, buried within her.

"Look at me," Julia said. "I'm married, with a college degree. It didn't mean anything that you got pregnant with me before you were married. It doesn't have to *mean* anything." Julia had never been both-ered by the fact that she was conceived before her parents' marriage. It wasn't uncommon in their neighborhood, and she'd always felt a thrum of pride that she had started their family. Without her, Charlie and Rose might not have married. Sylvie, the twins, this house, would not have existed. Julia was the catalyst.

"At least Charlie married me," Rose said. "Your sister is pretending the father doesn't exist, doesn't matter. She refused to tell me his name, so I couldn't call his parents and set this right. Do you know who he is?" Her eyes flashed with sudden hope.

"No, I don't."

"Fiddlesticks," Rose said to the dirt.

Julia couldn't see how pulling another person into a mistake did anything other than make it a bigger mistake, but she kept this opin-ion to herself. "Cecelia has all of us," she said. "She has our family. We can give the baby everything he or she needs."

Rose's face darkened. "The baby might be fine," she said. "But Ce-celia's life is over."

She might as well have said, *My life was over when I became pregnant with you.* Julia wasn't offended, though, because her mother was seeing everything wrong. Rose was in a black mood, and so she only saw darkness. Rose scanned her garden, and Julia could tell that her mother was seeing only what was wrong with it: the chewing bugs, the leaves with holes, the possible rot, the weak stems.

Rose said in a dull voice, "How's William?"

"He's good. He's barely using his crutches anymore."

Rose nodded, but Julia knew that she hadn't heard her, couldn't hear her. Rose had failed, and so she was a ruin: a cracked statue like the Virgin Mary leaning against the fence in the corner of the yard. Julia wanted to say, *Don't worry, Mama. I'm going to get pregnant. I'll make sure our tree branches remain intact.* But she couldn't say that. Her plan was just that, a plan. Not yet an answer to her mother's heartbreak. Julia thought about Cecelia's baby and how, unless she fixed this, that child would arrive the same way she had, on the heels of scorn and outrage. With a mother and daughter's separation. She felt a warmth toward Cecelia's baby, a kinship, for the first time.

When Julia left, she was worn out, as if she had grabbed a shovel and assisted her mother in the garden. On the bus ride home, she wondered what the point of her own life was. She'd never considered it in those terms before. Her father had called Julia his rocket ever since she was a little girl—*I can't wait to watch you fly,* he'd say—and she was the one who fixed problems. A large challenge lay before her now, though: her largest yet. It was a ball of yarn with her entire family woven into it, which meant everyone she cared about was at stake. Her sisters, her parents, William, the babies who weren't yet here. Julia felt a wave of fear that she wouldn't succeed, and then quashed it. She had never failed at anything she'd put her mind to, and this would be no different. It couldn't be any different.

CECELIA WENT INTO LABOR in late October, when Julia was almost four months pregnant. Mrs. Ceccione drove Cecelia to the hospital, and her sisters met her there. Only one person was allowed into the delivery room during the birth, and the nurse, gowned and masked, announced to the waiting room that the young mother had asked for a woman named Julia.

Thrilled, Julia tugged on a hospital gown and did her best to contain her hair beneath the shower cap she was handed. When she entered the room, she found Cecelia crying. "I want Mama," she said. "I want her so much, and you remind me of her."

"Baby girl," Julia said, and smoothed Cecelia's hair off her flushed face. This was what Rose called her daughters in times of sickness or sadness.

"I miss her so much." Cecelia looked wild-eyed at her sister. "You wouldn't believe it. Every day, I've had to fight not to go home. It's like the baby wanted to see her. My body hates being away from her."

"Do you want me to call her now?" Julia said. "She would come." She wasn't sure this was true, but she knew it was what her sister wanted to be true, and in the face of Cecelia's anguish, Julia would try her best to alter reality.

Cecelia twisted her body under the sheets and cried out. She grabbed Julia's hand and squeezed so hard that Julia gasped. How was her sister this strong? Julia experienced the waves of contractions with Cecelia for the next twenty minutes, feeling the magnitude of creating and meeting a new human wash over her. She wiped sweat off Cecelia's forehead with a cloth and allowed her hand to be throttled. She was certain their mother was wrong to turn her back on this: on her own baby, on the arrival of her first grandchild. Julia promised herself that she would never be that stubborn.

"I feel like I need to poop," Cecelia said, in a loud whisper.

"That means it's time to push the baby out." This came from the bored-looking nurse in the corner, whom Julia hadn't even noticed was there. "I'll get the doctor."

The infant arrived—yelling, pink, wrinkled—so furious that Julia and Cecelia both cried in relief.

"She's here," Cecelia said, when the baby was lying on her chest.

The infant patted her fist against her mother's skin. Julia watched her take in quick breaths and then let them go. This brand-new being seemed to be concentrating all of her tiny form on the act of living.

Julia said, "Look at her." She wished everyone they knew was in the room with them to look. In fact, she wished thousands of people were crowded in here with them—all of humanity—because the sight was so amazing.

"Isabella Rose Padavano," Cecelia said. "We'll call you Izzy. Welcome to the world."

"Mama's not going to be able to resist her." Julia stared in wonder at the infant. Her perfect eyes, perfect tiny nose, perfect pink mouth. "She's irresistible."

LATER THAT NIGHT, AFTER Julia and her sisters left the hospital, Charlie visited. Mrs. Ceccione must have told him the news.

When he appeared in the doorway of Cecelia's room, he didn't mention the prior five months, or Rose's anger, or the fact that he had never walked the twenty-four steps from his house to Mrs. Ceccione's to visit his shunned daughter. Charlie just looked at Cecelia and the baby for a long moment. Then he smiled with so much warmth it was as if a sun had risen inside him. "Hello beautiful," he said. And with those words, Cecelia knew that she was forgiven, and she forgave him too.

He kissed Cecelia's cheek and sat in the chair next to her bed with the baby in his arms. Izzy stared up at her grandfather, her dark eyes serious and bright. Charlie gazed down at her and said, "She's hardly heard any language yet. Shall we start her off with an incantation, with some magic?"

"Yes, please," Cecelia said.

He cradled the baby to him and whispered into her tiny ear: *"For every atom belonging to me as good belongs to you."* He pressed kisses into her soft cheek. He appeared to be sober, and he gave his granddaughter all of his love, Cecelia said to her sisters later. Then he stood up and carefully handed Izzy back to Cecelia. He kissed his daughter again. "Thank you, sweetheart," he said.

Charlie made it halfway down the hospital hallway before collapsing to the floor. A nurse around the corner heard and recognized the sound of a human body in surrender. She reached him in less than a minute, but his heart had already stopped. None of the machines or experts in the hospital were able to bring him back.

Sylvie

THERE WAS A LINE OUTSIDE THE FUNERAL HOME DURING THE three sessions of the wake. Inside, Sylvie stood in a row beside Rose, Julia, and Emeline and said *thank you so much* every time a stranger told her how wonderful her father had been. One woman said she'd stood next to Charlie at the bus stop on Loomis every day for years, because their commutes lined up, and he'd been kinder to her than anyone else in her life. Mr. Luis, who had provided the flowers for Julia's wedding and now for the wake and funeral, said that when he'd first moved to Pilsen, Charlie had helped him negotiate a low rent for the flower shop. "My business never would have existed without him," Mr. Luis told the Padavano women. "I didn't believe in myself, but Charlie, who had just met me, somehow did."

Charlie seemed to have had a habit of helping young mothers: Several women said he had bought them baby formula when they couldn't afford it. Head Librarian Elaine appeared before Sylvie at the second wake and told her, in a stern voice, that her father had been a lovely gentleman and that he'd once done her a meaningful favor. Sylvie wasn't aware that her father and Head Librarian Elaine—who was fifteen years older than her parents—had ever met or even been in the same room together. A few men, who must have been drinking buddies, entered the funeral home worse for wear and were eyed nervously by Rose's friends. Co-workers from the paper factory arrived wearing white shirts and dark ties, as if it was their uniform. "It's impossible he's gone," one of the youngest workers said.

Sylvie agreed. It was impossible.

Many guests wept, on and off, as if their tears were for Charlie but also for their own personal heartbreaks. An early lost love, a miscarriage, the pounding headache of never having enough money. In a setting where weeping was acceptable, they would take their opportunity. They followed a clear path: First they waited on the line that hugged the far wall, then stopped in front of the open casket, then turned left to give their condolences to the Padavano women. At that point, they either exited the room or moved into the center, where there were seats. The Padavano women never spoke publicly at the wake, but during each session a different man, from a different part of Charlie's life, would rise and speak about him in a choked voice.

Sylvie never approached the casket. She'd glimpsed her father when they'd first arrived in the room. Dead Charlie looked still, waxy, gone, and she had no desire to see his empty body up close. She stayed rooted to her spot as if it were a locked cell. She listened to her voice express thanks or whatever other words seemed appropriate. She watched her hands be enveloped by strangers' hands. When old women insisted on kissing her, she allowed them her cheek. William carried over a chair at one point for his pregnant wife, but Rose sat down on it instead, despite the fact that she had been turning down offers of chairs the entire night.

Mrs. Ceccione ducked in and out without coming near the Padavano women. She had been avoiding Rose since Cecelia moved in with her, but she was no doubt worried she would go to hell if she didn't show her respect for the dead. Relatives and cousins Sylvie had met only a handful of times because so-and-so hated so-and-so arrived and departed in tears or huffs. "That woman," Rose whispered angrily to her daughters at least once per wake session, but usually Sylvie didn't even know to whom she was referring. There was an infrastructure of grudges that had shaped Charlie's and Rose's extended families and kept them away from one another. When the Padavano sisters thought of family, they'd always pictured only the six people who lived under their roof. Aunts, uncles, grandparents, and cousins had always been framed as enemies or potential enemies. Sylvie watched people wash in and out of the room on a tidal schedule of theatrical grief, but she was mostly aware of who was missing: Cecelia and the baby.

Cecelia and Izzy had been released from the hospital that afternoon. The original plan, constructed largely by Julia, had been for Cecelia to go straight from the hospital to Rose, where the baby would serve as a peace offering between the mother and her youngest daughter. But that plan had evaporated when Charlie died. Sylvie had been the one to answer the kitchen phone when Cecelia called from the hospital, crying so hard Sylvie didn't know who it was at first. Rose had taken the news as if it were a bolt of lightning. Her body tightened, then released, and she fell to the living room floor. Sylvie knelt next to her. Emeline—the terrible sentence, *Dad is dead,* still in her ears—ran back to the hospital to be with Cecelia. Julia didn't know yet; she was sitting peacefully on a bus to Northwestern.

The first thing Rose had said, in a strange new voice, was, "*She* was the last one to see him? He was with *her?*"

Sylvie had been confused at first. "Cecelia?"

"Her," Rose said, in the strange voice.

"He died in the hallway," Sylvie said. But she knew then that the opening to Cecelia and the beautiful new baby had been shut. This death, and the betrayal Rose saw in it, had ruined any chance of reunion. Sylvie stayed on the floor, but she drew back from her mother. Charlie had always tempered Rose and insisted she be softer. He had no doubt been thinking the baby would be the fix as well. Sylvie wished she had spoken to him about it; she and her sisters should have brought him in on the plan. If they had, maybe he wouldn't have gone to visit Cecelia in the hospital. Maybe this wouldn't have happened.

Still, she told her mother, "It has nothing to do with Cecelia. His heart gave out."

"Not with me," Rose said. "It wouldn't have happened on my watch."

Charlie's favorite armchair was behind them. The armchair where he spoke in meter, and drank his drinks, and told his daughters how much he loved them. Sylvie had never cared if his paycheck got smaller or if he drank too much. He had been her person, and they'd passed books back and forth between them her entire life. She had noticed as a little girl that Charlie never went into the back garden, and so Sylvie never did either. That early impulse to follow her father, to imitate him, had built a fence between her and Rose.

The funeral took place five days after the death. So many people showed up at St. Procopius that they couldn't all fit inside the large church. Rose wore a black dress with a piece of black lace pinned to her hair. She sat in the front row with Sylvie and Julia at her sides. William flanked Julia in his dark wedding suit. On Sylvie's other side, Emeline twisted in her seat to see if her twin had entered the church, because surely Cecelia wouldn't miss this. Sylvie caught her sister's eye to ask, *Do you see her?* Emeline shook her head.

Sweating under her thick dress and tights, Sylvie remembered the last time she'd been alone with her father, about a month earlier. After dinner one night, Rose had sent the two of them to pick up a big order from the market. She'd done the shopping earlier; their job was to carry it home. The order wasn't ready, so Mrs. DiPietro gave Charlie a small glass of beer and they waited on the back steps of the shop. There was a small, spiky garden at their feet, and Charlie studied it. "Doesn't hold a candle to your mother's," he'd said.

"How would you know?" Sylvie held her hair up over her head, trying to get some air on her neck. The sun was setting, but it had been an unusually warm September day. "You never go in the backyard."

He gave a small smile. "I presume her greatness."

Her father looked tired, and Sylvie remembered wondering if he'd been sleeping poorly. Probably his heart was beginning to fail; it was failing that day on the stoop, with the beer in his hand. Maybe Charlie had sensed it, because he'd said, "Sweetheart, I knew that you skipped a heap of classes in high school."

Sylvie looked at him in surprise. "You did?"

"Butch was an old friend, so I told him to turn a blind eye for as long as he could and then give you a harmless punishment."

Butch McGuire had been Sylvie's high school principal, and after more than a year of missing more math and chemistry classes than she attended, he told her that the penalty was repainting the wall behind the school. Cecelia had helped her, always happy to have a brush in her hand. Emeline tended to them with snacks. Sylvie had believed that both her parents were unaware of her truancy and her punishment. "Why?" she asked, meaning, *Why did you do that, and why are you telling me now?*

"What were you doing during those missed classes?"

"Reading." Sylvie waved her hand. "The classes were a waste of my time. If I'm not interested in something, I have no hope of learning it." She'd read in a park near the school, storing novels in the hollow of an ancient oak she thought of as her friend. Sylvie didn't tell her sisters what she was doing, because she knew Julia would be furious and insist she return to the classroom, and she didn't want the twins to think that what she was doing was acceptable. That had been, perhaps, when Sylvie first became aware that she was choosing a different path than Julia. Sylvie was reading novels she hid in a tree—a tree she talked to about her thoughts and worries—while Julia was leaping every academic hurdle placed in front of her.

Charlie nodded. "You're too young to really understand that life is short, but it is. I didn't want to stop you when you were walking away from something that didn't matter to do something that did. You and I are cut from the same cloth, baby girl. Neither of us would expect school or work to fill us up. We look out the window, or into ourselves, for something more." He studied her. "You know that you're more than a librarian's aide and a college student, right? You're Sylvie Padavano." He said her name with delight, as if she were a famous explorer or warrior. "It's *because* you know that more is possible that you'll always see the pointlessness in following a stupid rule or clocking in and out of a boring class. Most people can't see that distinction, so they just do as they're told. Of course, this makes them bored and irritated, but they think that's the human condition. You and I are lucky enough to see that it doesn't have to be that way."

The truth in Charlie's words shivered up Sylvie's spine.

He grinned at her. "I'm giving a bit of a speech, aren't I? Well, so be it. We're not separated from the world by our own edges." Charlie set down his beer glass, empty now, and rubbed his hand up and down his arm, as an example of one of his edges. "We're part of the sky, and the rocks in your mother's garden, and that old man who sleeps by the train station. We're all interconnected, and when you see that, you see how beautiful life is. Your mother and sisters don't have that awareness. Not yet, anyway. They believe they're contained in their bodies, in the biographical facts of their lives."

Sylvie felt like her father had shown her a part of herself she hadn't known existed. When Sylvie looked back on that moment—now, from the funeral pew, and later, over the course of her life—it would always be one of her great joys that her father had said this to her and that she was able to delight *him* by paraphrasing one of his favorite poems: "We are not contained between our hats and boots." And then Mrs. DiPietro had come outside with their bags, and the father and daughter had walked home, their arms touching, molecules dancing between them, and the stars turning on like tiny lightbulbs in the evening sky.

The priest was talking about Charlie, trying to make his job sound important, trying to make it seem like Charlie had run his household, even though the priest knew it was Rose who made every decision, and Sylvie ached at how this priest and all the people at the wake defined Charlie with his biographical facts, when he had been so much more. He was vast, and beautiful, and more present in the gift of baby formula to a young mother than in any day he'd spent at the paper factory. He *was* his acts of kindness, and his love for his daughters, and the twenty minutes he'd spent with Sylvie behind the grocer's that evening.

That conversation had helped Sylvie understand herself in a new way. She looked for third doors because she was like her father. Julia sought to collect labels like *honors student, girlfriend,* and *wife,* but Sylvie steered away from labels. She wanted to be true to herself with every word she uttered, every action she took, and every belief she held. There was no label for kissing boys for ninety seconds in the library, which was part of why it made Sylvie happy and Julia uncomfortable. Sylvie would keep boycotting boring classes to read in parks. She wouldn't settle for less than true love, even though her sisters had issued a collective sigh when she told them that Ernie had asked her out on a proper date and she'd turned him down. She would wait, forever if necessary, for a man who saw the expanse of her, the way her father had. Sylvie shifted in the pew, her thoughts bunched up in her head. Rushed and hot and mucky with the tears she hadn't yet shed. She knew now—inside her body, her bones, her cells—that her father was gone. He was gone and no one else really knew her. Julia, Emeline, and Cecelia each saw a slightly different Sylvie: She was soft with Emeline, in response to her sister's softness, and playful with Julia because they enjoyed challenging each other. Sylvie was curious in Cecelia's presence, because her artist sister spoke and thought differently from anyone else she knew.

Sylvie looked around at the bent heads, her sweating, weeping sisters and her rock-faced mother, and knew they were all in trouble. Charlie had seen and loved each of them for who they were. When any of his girls—including Rose—had come into view, he'd always given them the same welcome, calling out, *Hello beautiful!* The greeting was nice enough to make them want to leave the room and come in all over again. He'd delighted in Julia's ambition and nicknamed her his rocket. He'd taken Cecelia to the art museum on Saturday mornings. He'd kept a shared inventory of the neighborhood kids with Emeline, because Charlie loved to watch his daughter light up while explaining a child's interests and the specific reasons he or she was remarkable. Sylvie and her sisters had known themselves under their father's gaze. And with that gaze gone, the threads that had tied their family so tightly together had loosened. What had been effortless would now take effort. What had been home for all of them was now merely Rose's house. Emeline was already sleeping on Cecelia's floor at Mrs. Ceccione's to help with the baby. Julia was married. Sylvie knew in that moment that she would have to move out too.

She walked back to the house with Rose after the funeral; she intended to talk to her mother about moving out but didn't want to do it that day. Perhaps they could agree on a timeline that wouldn't seem too abrupt for either of them—maybe a month? But Rose didn't look at her, or speak, while they made their way home. Rose walked straight into her bedroom and changed into her gardening clothes. On her way outside, she passed Sylvie with her face turned away.

"Can I do something for you, Mama?" Sylvie said. "What would you like for dinner?"

Rose stopped. "Your sisters all left me," she said, her voice thin. "Everyone has left."

Sylvie said, "I'm right here," but her mother gave no indication of having heard her, and Sylvie wondered if maybe she wasn't right here. Her certainty wavered, and with it her sense of self. Sylvie had the sensation of fading away in her black dress and tights. Under Charlie's gaze, Sylvie had been whole; now, in front of her mother, she was porous, disappearing.

"You should go stay with one of your sisters," Rose said. "I'd like to be alone." She opened the back door and walked outside. Sylvie stood still for a moment in the empty house, fighting for air, because it felt like her lungs had seized up. Rose's second daughter wasn't enough, and would never be enough. When she was able to breathe normally, Sylvie went to her room to pack her belongings.

That night she slept on William and Julia's couch. She brought her clothes in paper grocery bags. Sylvie was surprised at how little she owned. The room she and Julia had shared all their lives was so tiny, there had never been room for more than their single beds and a dresser. Sylvie had never bought books, because of her relationship with the library. Lying on the couch in her nightgown, under a rough blanket, with the grocery bags lined up neatly in sight, she felt tangled in a net of grief. Her father was dead, and her mother had turned her away. *My soulmate would save me,* she thought. *He would see me, and I would feel more solid.* But this brought a fresh sadness, because if she ever did meet this man, he would never have known her father. Sylvie studied the ceiling for most of the night. She felt tears deep inside her, but they couldn't seem to find a way out. She still hadn't cried.

The next morning at the library, she pinned a notice to the huge public bulletin board: *In need of a house sitter or pet sitter? Need someone to water your plants while you're on vacation? I will do chores in exchange for a bed. Please find Assistant Librarian Sylvie at the front desk.*

No one came near her, though. Not even her boys, though she would have loved to have been kissed or held, even for a moment. Two of them, Ernie and Miles, had attended the wake but avoided making eye contact with her. She hadn't told them about her father, but someone had hung the funeral mass and death announcement on the library bulletin board. Everyone Sylvie encountered seemed to sense that she was wearing death, so they gave her a wide berth. Once or twice she sniffed her clothes, to make sure she wasn't emitting a terrible odor. She pushed her cart up and down the stacks. She did her college reading in the library when she wasn't on a shift, and then slept on Julia and William's couch at night.

"Did you tell Mom you'd be staying here for a while?" Julia asked.

Sylvie shook her head. "She's relieved I'm not there."

"But she's so alone," Julia said. "She's never lived alone before."

"You visited her this afternoon."

Julia reached up to make sure her hair was behaving itself. "I think she's in the garden all day, every day. She hardly spoke while I was there. I know she's mourning, but . . ."

Sylvie spoke with certainty. "Mama doesn't want me there."

The next afternoon at the library, Sylvie saw her mother walk past the wide windows. Rose was still in black, though she no longer had the piece of lace on her head. She walked slowly, with an erect carriage. She didn't look into the library, even though the chance of her daughter being there was always high. Sylvie didn't run outside to speak with her either. She stayed frozen at the desk and watched as Rose walked the full length of the windows before she disappeared.

JULIA DEVELOPED A HABIT of climbing onto the couch with Sylvie in the middle of the night. Because Julia had a new curviness—she wasn't visibly pregnant to strangers, but she'd had to buy larger bras—this involved Sylvie lying on her side on the very edge of the cushions. She had to wrap her arms around Julia to keep from falling off. The night pulsed around them, and Sylvie was grateful to be crushed against her sister. It was late November; several blurry weeks had passed since their father had died.

"What are we going to do?" Julia whispered.

With her eyes closed, Sylvie could pretend they were in their single beds, in their childhood room. They had, after all, talked back and forth in the darkness for as long as either of them could remember. She said, "You're going to have a baby. I'm going to qualify for a higher paycheck soon, and I'll find my own place."

Sylvie had switched her college focus from English literature to library sciences, because she knew Head Librarian Elaine needed a new librarian and would hire her if she had the necessary qualifications. Every day, Sylvie looked at studio apartments in the classifieds, reassured that with the new job she would be able to afford a tiny studio.

Julia said, "I feel like Beth."

Sylvie hugged her sister closer. While they were growing up, only Sylvie, Emeline, and Cecelia ever made that pronouncement. Julia had never said she was Beth before. When Julia was sick with the flu or a cold, she drank orange juice and sucked zinc tablets and ate salads, in order to fuel herself to get to the other side. Sickness or disappointment was simply something to be conquered. She wouldn't even joke about surrendering.

But Julia's eyes had looked panicked ever since Charlie's death. Because Sylvie understood her older sister so well, she knew Julia was not only mourning him but reeling from the fact that he had died at all. Julia hadn't planned for him to die, and that shock threatened her entire worldview. Their father's absence was, after all, unfixable.

"We'll figure it out," Sylvie said. "You'll come up with a new plan. You always do. It's probably just hard to do that when you're pregnant. Give yourself some time."

"Was I wrong to try to fix everything?" Julia laid Sylvie's hand on her abdomen. The baby's movements had become discernible in just the last few days.

Sylvie went quiet, because when the baby did move, the sensation was delicate and impossible to catch unless you were still. She had the thought that Julia's small bump felt like a drum, but the percussion was inside the instrument. Sylvie felt something and was thrilled: bubbles, perhaps the waving of a tiny hand. "No," she said. "You weren't wrong."

There were moments of quiet, when one sister or the other would almost fall asleep. Only once had they both slept deeply, and William found them curled around each other in the morning. Usually they slid in and out of rest. Sylvie clung to her sister in part because she felt unmoored at night. She was swallowed up by the sky and her blanket and the paper bags holding her clothes. In the darkness, Charlie was missing, and Rose glared in Sylvie's direction with an anger she didn't understand but that made Sylvie's body tighten with guilt nonetheless. Sylvie knew that Cecelia cried at each milestone Izzy reached because she'd lost both her parents and the world her little girl was supposed to grow up in. Rose, brutally silent, two houses away from Cecelia and her granddaughter, was descending deeper and deeper into stubborn grief. The last time Julia had been to see her, Rose sent her away.

Sylvie was almost asleep when her sister said, "After the funeral, William asked to be excused from his teaching-assistant job for the rest of the semester—he told the department that he needed time with me because my father died."

"That was nice of him."

"But we need the money. I was counting on it, and he didn't ask me before talking to his adviser. I'd rather William taught, anyway—this makes a terrible first impression. The professors there are going to think he's lazy, or soft." Julia said the word *soft* as if it was the most damning criticism she could think of.

Sylvie considered this. Her brother-in-law limped around the apartment and smiled at Sylvie to let her know that he didn't mind her being there, although of course he must. She didn't feel in a position to criticize him. "Did you tell him any of this?" she said.

"It's too late to change anything. Will you do me a favor?"

This didn't need a response, so Sylvie simply waited.

"Will you read his book? He calls it a work in progress. I nagged him until he finally let me read it, and I don't know what to make of it. At all." Julia looked at Sylvie with wide eyes. "I've been avoiding having conversations with him, because I don't know what to say. You're the reader—you'll see what he's trying to do. And if it has potential to help him? Get a job after graduate school?"

This many question marks from Julia were unusual. *We're all unstitched,* Sylvie thought. *How much longer can this continue?*

"Of course. I'll read it tomorrow at the library. Or today, depending on what time it is."

Julia kissed her cheek. "Thank you so much. You can't tell him you read it, obviously."

Sylvie tried to read her watch in the dark, a bubble of panic threading up her middle. What time was it? Was it close to dawn? With no sleep, the days took on the emotional cast—and the loud losses—of the night.

SHE STARTED READING AT a library table before her shift, and continued while eating a sandwich at lunch, and picked it up again on the bus on the way to class. Julia had handed her a physical mess: about two hundred typewritten pages held together with a rubber band, inside a paper bag. Sylvie's first impression was that it was indeed a work in progress. Some chapters started and then stopped in the middle of a paragraph. There were question marks inside sentences, intended for William to answer at some point. There were footnotes filled with suggestions, ideas, and queries from William about what direction the material might go in.

It was ostensibly a book about the history of basketball, and it started in 1891 in Massachusetts, when Dr. James Naismith invented the game—using peach baskets as hoops—in order to keep off-season track athletes in shape during the frigid winter. The book jumped around according to what seemed like William's whims, but still, it was roughly chronological. It covered the sport's first league in 1898, Dr. Naismith's thirteen rules, and the fact that until 1950 all the players and coaches in the official games were white. When the narrative broke off, William was in the middle of explaining the battle between the American Basketball Association and the National Basketball Association in the 1970s, when the two leagues fought for stars like Dr. J and Spencer Haywood. Interspersed with the history were the stories of specific games: A game in Philadelphia when Bill Russell battled the giant Wilt Chamberlain. A 1959 college game in which Oscar Robertson had 45 points, 23 rebounds, and 10 assists. The manuscript ended in the middle of game five of the 1976 finals between the Boston Celtics and the Phoenix Suns. The game went to triple overtime and was the longest finals game ever. William's writing was solid—clean and unobjectionable—but Sylvie found herself little interested in the main narrative of the story; it was the footnotes and embedded questions that fascinated her. The footnotes seemed to be a conversation William was having with himself. He wrote things like:

Why am I so interested in Bill Walton's injuries?

Am I just writing to catch up with the present day? Is that enough?

How could my father and so many other men in Boston hate Russell so much? I can't even bear to write about what happened to his home there.

Where is the science on why these men grow so tall, when their parents are often short?

There's no thread to this project.

This is terrible, I'm terrible.

Several times, William wrote: *What am I doing? Why am I doing this? Who am I?*

Once, toward the end of the unfinished narrative, a footnote read: *It should have been me, not her.*

Sylvie reread the footnotes. They felt like an answer key for a different story, not the history of basketball they were attached to. What did *It should have been me, not her* mean? That statement couldn't be connected to basketball, could it? Was the *her* Julia?

The anxiety embedded in the questions made Sylvie shiver, and the bus rattled beneath her as if in agreement. Charlie had said to Sylvie: "We look out the window, or into ourselves, for something more." In these footnotes, William was looking inside himself, but what reflected back was apprehension and uncertainty. *Who am I?* William didn't seem to recognize the person in the mirror, or perhaps he didn't see anyone there. Sylvie remembered the last time she'd stood in front of Rose and the feeling that she was disappearing. Sylvie had felt that way, to some degree, every minute since her father died. She'd become worried that it was her father's attention that kept her intact, kept her *Sylvie,* and she felt great sympathy now for her brother-in-law. Sylvie had been feeling this way for only a month, and it was terrible. The size of this manuscript, and the effort in its pages, showed that William had been in this place for a long time.

When Sylvie finished reading, she was on the bus back to Julia's apartment after her night class. She fit the manuscript into the paper bag and stared at the window, which showed her glassy reflection. She saw the outline of William's face overlaying her own. Sylvie had always liked her brother-in-law; she felt comfortable around him, and they shared a smile occasionally when Julia talked with a lot of exclamation marks. Emeline, the barometer of everyone's moods, had always described William as sensitive. But William had belonged to Julia from the moment Sylvie met him, so she'd never truly considered him as anything other than the man her sister had chosen. She wondered now, for the first time, if Julia had made a mistake. The writer of these pages was filled with her sister's least favorite qualities: indecision, self-doubt, sadness. Julia was like a star baseball player who lived at the plate, smacking away any uncertainties with her bat. The only explanation that made sense was that Julia didn't know this lived inside her husband—or hadn't, until she'd read these pages too.

Sylvie felt a heightened physical awareness on the bus seat, her cells tingling as if they had just woken up. She felt the weight of the manuscript on her lap, the cloudy windowpane, Julia's possible mistake, the tiredness of having spent weeks barely sleeping on someone else's couch, her father's gone-ness. Sylvie felt something move inside her too, but before she could figure out what it was, she'd started to cry. She fought to stay silent, so as not to draw any attention to herself on the half-filled bus, but the salty tears slicked her cheeks and soaked the front of her coat.

When she got back to the apartment it was late, and her sister and William had already gone to bed. Sylvie brushed her teeth, tugged her nightgown over her head, and fell onto the couch. She felt William's questions like pinpricks to her skin. They reappeared in the darkness and seeped into her, demanding answers.

What am I doing? I'm lying on a couch in my sister's apartment.

Why am I doing this? Because my father died, and he was my home.

Who am I? Sylvie Padavano. She heard her name in Charlie's voice, said with relish, and smiled.

This last question, and the answer, made Sylvie realize for the first time why her mother had always frowned at her and not at her sisters.

Rose recognized in Sylvie what had always bothered her about her husband. "Ugh, Whitman," Rose would say in disgust when Charlie recited his lyrical lines. Not because Rose cared about Walt Whitman, but because she blamed the poetry inside Charlie for his lack of success in life. The reason his salary stayed small, the reason he refused to get upset when the furnace broke and yet would drag her outside to admire a full moon, the reason he didn't care what people thought of him and yet hundreds of people turned out for his funeral. Sylvie was spiked with the same stuff Charlie was, and so when Rose looked at her daughter, she didn't see *Sylvie;* she saw the failure of her own marriage and her personal failure in convincing Charlie to be who she'd wanted him to be. Sylvie thought of Julia, who had so much of Rose inside her. She knew that any glimpses Julia caught of the faltering sentences inside William would also be despised.

With her eyes closed, Sylvie placed herself on the wide expanse of her brother-in-law's uncertainty. It resembled one of the foggy, rambling moors she and her sisters had loved in Victorian novels. Sylvie felt at home on the rough terrain, filling her lungs with murky air. Since Charlie's death, she'd felt like she was spilling out of her edges and messily trying to scoop herself up at the same time. Her sisters and mother were safe, with their aspirations and routines; Sylvie *was* her heartbreak and loss. William wasn't safe either, and his questions kept Sylvie company. She and her brother-in-law were both struggling to inhabit their own skin, a goal that would sound absurd to almost anyone else.

When Julia appeared, Sylvie scooched over and hugged her older sister harder than usual.

"Are you okay?" Julia whispered.

Sylvie shook her head and buried her face in her sister's neck. She could feel the baby flutter inside her sister and then into her own flat belly. She needed this hug, and she was also buying time before Julia asked her questions and Sylvie tried her best to answer.

"Is the manuscript good?"

"Yes and no."

"Will it help him get a professorship?"

"No."

"What does it mean . . . what is it?"

"I don't know. I've never read anything like it."

ROSE CALLED A FAMILY meeting on a Saturday when Julia was eight months pregnant and Izzy was four months old.

"A family meeting, including Cecelia?" Julia had asked, when she visited their mother in her garden. ("Her getup has gotten even worse," Julia told Sylvie that night. "She wears Daddy's pajamas under the baseball equipment.")

"Of course not," Rose had said. "You, William, Sylvie, and Emeline."

The listed people turned up at the house at four o'clock on the designated day. All three sisters paused on the front step and glanced down the street toward Mrs. Ceccione's house. None of the sisters had told Cecelia about this meeting—they couldn't bear to tell her she'd been excluded—but of course she knew. Sylvie had gotten Cecelia a part-time job at the library, and their shifts often overlapped. Emeline slept on a cot in Cecelia's room, and Julia called Cecelia once a day to see how she and the baby were. Cecelia, like all of them, listened to everything her sisters said and everything they didn't. This meeting had been so clearly omitted, this hour wiped off the shared calendar, that it might have been the only thing Cecelia knew for sure.

Rose was already in her spot at the dining room table when they came in. She looked thinner in the cheeks and was wearing a faded housedress.

"I have to sell this place," she said, when they were seated around her. "I can't afford to live here anymore." She waved her hand casually, to indicate the walls, bedrooms, and history that surrounded them. "I don't need its size either."

Sylvie leaned back in her chair. It had never occurred to her that this house could be sold. When Rose and Charlie were first married, Charlie had gotten a great deal on the purchase, probably through a drinking bet—though that was never clearly stated—during a period of racial tension in Chicago, when a lot of white people were fleeing the city. Closing this deal had been perhaps the greatest achievement of Charlie's life, in Rose's eyes.

Sylvie's sisters looked as shocked as she felt: Julia's face had gone white, and Emeline was blinking more than normal, which is what she did when she was scared or surprised.

"I thought you owned the house outright," Julia said. "Daddy always boasted about not having a mortgage."

Rose frowned. "I had to take one out about ten years ago, so we could feed and clothe you girls."

This sank in. The saints on the walls stared down at them. There was a blank spot where St. Clare of Assisi had been. They all knew that the framed image now lived under Cecelia's bed down the street.

"You can't leave your garden," Emeline said. Julia, William, and Sylvie nodded with relief. That statement was true. What was Rose without her garden? Rose's existence had always taken place in the garden, as if her roots sat beside those of the herbs, lettuce, and eggplants.

"Too much work," Rose said. "I'm finished. This house is finished. You've all moved out."

She didn't look at Sylvie when she said this, but Sylvie felt the dart her mother had thrown twist into her chest. *You said you wanted to be alone,* she thought. *I did what you asked.*

"I'm moving to Florida," Rose said. "To a condo on the beach. I know a few ladies from the neighborhood there, and they're setting me up. With the sale of this house, I'll be fine."

"Florida?" This was the first word William had spoken since they'd sat down. "You can't do that."

Rose fixed her eyes on him.

"Your daughters need you." He took a breath. "Mom. We need you."

"I'm about to have the baby," Julia said. "You need to wait, please."

The air in the room felt strange: heavy yet about to move, as if on the threshold of a storm. The Padavano girls shifted in their chairs. They could all feel Cecelia down the street, holding her daughter as if she was a life preserver, trying to listen to words she couldn't hear.

"I wanted to let you all know in person," Rose said.

Where are you? Sylvie thought. *Are you already in Florida?* She remembered her glimpse of Charlie in the coffin—waxy and gone. This was almost worse. Her mother was in front of them, blood pumping through her body, but she was absent. She'd taken leave: Perhaps since the day of the funeral? While Sylvie sat on the floor beside her, right after the news? Or had she been wanting to be somewhere else for years, and now she saw the chance to break free?

Emeline said, "We all miss Daddy. We should be together. I brought pictures of Izzy, Mama. She's so beautiful."

She pulled the photos out from under the table, but the mention threw Rose onto her feet. She was walking away while she said, "Feel free to take some food from the garden on your way out."

Three of the four Padavano girls were left gripping the dining room table, as if everything were being pulled away from them at once.

William

WILLIAM ADHERED TO A DAILY ROUTINE. BREAKFAST, THEN he food-shopped for Julia or did any other necessary household errands. He was trying to please his wife, to make up for ground he'd lost through a miscalculation. He'd assumed Julia would appreciate the fact that, after Charlie died, he asked to be released from his teaching-assistant position for the rest of the semester. The department was understanding; after all, they had plenty of graduate students to fill his spot in the classroom. But Julia had looked panicked when William told her—she didn't like surprises—and he realized he'd made a mistake. Julia depended on more than just his love and attention; she needed him to make money, even though they had enough in savings from wedding gifts to last the rest of the semester. His wife also didn't know about the uncashed check that was hidden in his dresser drawer; he had no intention of using it, ever, but it existed in case of an emergency. Julia didn't need William at home to have company either; Sylvie had moved in, and it was usually to her that Julia turned when she was feeling mournful. This made sense to William, of course, but he was dismayed by how he'd gotten the math wrong on every count.

After William had washed the breakfast dishes and asked if there was anything else he could do, Julia shook her head and held the door open for him to leave. Thankfully, she kissed his cheek on the way out, to let him know her disappointment was temporary. He walked to the Northwestern library, where he studied for his evening classes. On his way to his favorite study carrel, William usually passed the elderly history professor in whose class he'd met Julia. The old man appeared not to recognize William, but William didn't take that personally. He suspected that this would be the professor's final year of teaching. The old man's eyes leaked tears when he spoke, and his nose wept too. William wondered if the professor still cared about the subjects he lectured on. Did he have new thoughts on the Molotov–Ribbentrop Pact of 1939 or the capture of Berlin? Or were these just words the old man recited, like lines from a play?

William took a break from studying at lunchtime and walked to the athletic building. He sat in the bleacher seats, with the basketball court before him, and ate his packed lunch. Sometimes there was a gym class going on, with an array of students of all shapes and fitness levels being coaxed through calisthenics by a teacher. Sometimes a few of the team's shooters were there for extra practice. William knew all the players except the freshmen, and once or twice after finishing his sandwich he let the guys convince him to take a few shots from the corner. He knew his knee couldn't take pivoting or even jogging from one spot to the other, so he stood still and drilled one long shot after another while his former teammates hooted with pleasure. When the ball swished through the net, William's breathing slowed to normal, and he could pretend that he still inhabited a recognizable life.

With the basketball in his hands, he could forget that his father-in-law had dropped dead, his sister-in-law slept on his couch, and every time he saw his wife he was startled. Julia wasn't obviously pregnant, but she no longer looked like the woman he'd married. Her hips flared dramatically, and her cheeks were often flushed. She was beautiful, gorgeous, heaving with life, but on a fixed journey from conception to birth that William found hard to locate on any map. *Where are you?* he wanted to ask her. *Do you know where you're going? Are you sure it's the right way?*

He was embarrassed to admit the truth even to himself, that he'd never given thought to having a child. William had fallen in love with

Julia—he still swam in an ocean of gratitude that he went to sleep beside her every night and woke up with her every morning—so marriage had made perfect sense. But creating a new person, and raising him or her, was an entirely different proposition. He'd told Julia that he was happy and excited about her pregnancy, because he knew that was what he was supposed to feel, but William was unable to imagine himself as a father. When he tried to picture himself with a baby, the image was blurred. Perhaps he should have voiced some hesitation over Julia's plan, but his wife had suggested they get pregnant, and for the next month, every time he walked into the apartment she seemed to be waiting for him, naked. William was unable, and unwilling, to talk through the pros and cons of parenthood when Julia wasn't wearing clothes.

Now he lived with a pregnant wife and a sister-in-law who swept guiltily in and out of the apartment. He no longer sat on the couch, because it was Sylvie's bed. He read textbooks over his meals and reviewed his notes, trying to memorize all the moving parts of a particular year in American history. When William woke up in the middle of the night, Julia's side of their bed would be empty, and he'd find her asleep in her sister's arms. Watching them, William felt a strange loneliness. They looked like they belonged together, and when he walked back into his bedroom, he had the thought that perhaps it was he, and not Sylvie, who was the intruder.

After lunch at the gym, William returned to the library to read about the Panic of 1893. William's graduate adviser was a bright-eyed professor who always wore a bow tie and had a hard time sitting still, presumably because everything excited him so much. During their initial meeting, in the first month of the program, the professor had asked William what he *really, really loved* about the period of American history he'd chosen as his focus. With this question, William had felt everything at motion inside him—his blood, his lungs, his heart—slow almost to a stop. He was mortified; it had never occurred to him that he was supposed to bring *love* to this endeavor. Finally, he managed to say something about the great changes the country had gone through between 1890 and 1969—the Gilded Age, two world wars, the civil-rights movement—but it was too late. There was confusion in the professor's eyes, and he seemed to be thinking: *How strange, I don't feel any historical passion coming from this young man at all.*

Most days, William stayed at the gym later than he intended to after finishing his lunch. He needed to review chapters for his evening classes, but he delayed returning to the library. It was on one of those afternoons that Arash saw him while crossing the court and came to sit beside him.

"How's the knee?" he asked.

"Fine." This was William's standard response when asked about his knee. He thought it was the correct answer, since the knee functioned and allowed him to walk from place to place. It always ached—the pain was worst at night—but it seemed unmanly to admit that. And who cared? He no longer needed a pain-free knee. Professors could sit, after all. His body was now more or less irrelevant.

Arash studied him. "I heard you're in grad school here. Congratulations."

William was surprised. "How did you hear that?"

Arash smiled. "We track you boys. I track my injuries, so you're on my list. But we like to keep tabs on all our players. We're not heartless, you know. We can't send a nice note in celebration of some achievement if we're not keeping tabs."

William considered this. He hadn't been prepared for kindness, and it made him think of Charlie. His father-in-law's funeral was the first William had ever attended. He'd listened at the wake to the stories of how generous Charlie had been to people in Pilsen and at work. After a trio of drunk men tried to explain how Charlie had helped them appease an angry landlord, William had the urge to stand up and tell the room that his father-in-law had been an excellent driver and that he had hidden his competence, or perhaps it had been ignored by Rose and their daughters. *How much else did Charlie feel like he had to hide from us?* he wanted to ask. Instead, he watched Rose harden, hour by hour, and watched panic and grief etch his wife's beautiful face.

After the casket was lowered into the ground, Julia had brought William to visit Cecelia and her baby girl. The infant was placed in William's arms with no warning. He'd never held a baby before, but his wife and Izzy's mother turned away from William casually, as if they trusted him to somehow know what to do. The baby stared up at him and her face quivered; she was considering tears. She was unbelievably tiny and wrapped up in blankets so he couldn't see her limbs. She seemed very warm. Did she have a fever? Were the blankets necessary? William sat down in a chair, so that the baby would have less far to fall if he dropped her, and then slid down to sit on the floor. Julia and Cecelia laughed at him, but with affection in their eyes, and then the two women sat on the floor with him, as if to say that what he'd done was perfectly fine.

"Nice finish!" Arash said, his eyes on the court. "That freshman there, the power forward? He's been an excellent replacement for Kent. Good first step."

"Who's replaced me?"

Arash scanned the floor. "There's a new guy who rebounds well. He's all elbows, though; he's not an IQ guy like you." Arash nodded, as if agreeing with his own assessment. "Have you read *The Breaks of the Game*?"

"The what?"

"It's a book about smart players like you, how they play and *think* the game. Run through film in their mind, understand how to use space. The greats are always playing chess out there. You should read it."

William tried to absorb Arash's words; he knew immediately that he would replay this conversation later, when he was alone. These felt like the words, and sentences, he had been waiting for. William committed what felt like tiny failures and disappointments during every hour of his current life; he wished that he was still a basketball player with positional intelligence, who was part of a team. A memory flashed into his mind: He was standing on the park court as a ten-year-old, watching the boys who had just welcomed him into their game run away to get home in time for dinner. *Come back,* the young William thought.

Arash clapped him on the shoulder. "Got to get to an appointment. Maybe I'll see you here again?"

"I'm here most days," William said, and was confused by the feeling in his chest—was it longing?—as the man walked away.

———

WILLIAM AND JULIA SPENT several weeks that December repeating the same argument every time Sylvie was out.

"We should move into the other apartment before I get huge," Julia said. She and William now qualified for a two-bedroom apartment in married housing, because they were expecting a child. "I want to get organized," she said. "We're going to have to put together a crib and a changing table, at least. You'll go back to teaching next month, so we should use this window to move, while you have a little free time." She paused. "Why do you keep looking at me like that?"

William tried to make his face neutral. "Like what?"

"Like what I'm saying is shocking. You realize we're having a baby in April, right?"

"Of course. I'm just saying that we're comfortable in this apartment. You've always said that you loved this place. Let's stay here until the end of the school year. We can move in the summer."

Julia looked at him with wide eyes, annoyed. "It's too small, with Sylvie staying with us. If we move now, she could sleep in the baby's room. I don't understand why you're arguing with me."

William didn't know what to say, how to explain that he simply wanted to push off moving for as long as possible. Nothing inside him would make sense to his wife. He thought dumbly: *If we don't move, then the baby won't be born, because he or she won't have a bedroom.* The larger apartment was in a nearby campus building, so it wouldn't be a big change, but now, with Charlie's death and Julia growing and Sylvie on his couch, everything felt uncertain to William. He needed to wake up in his bed in his current bedroom, and eat two pieces of toast with strawberry jam, and then walk to the library. He needed to sit in his favorite study carrel and spread his books out in the precise way he liked. He needed to take a break from studying to eat lunch in the gym— sometimes with Arash—and remember what it used to feel like to run the court in front of him with a basketball in his hands. At the end of each day, after he attended classes, William returned home to the woman he'd fallen in love with only a few years earlier. The beats of this exact routine gave William an infrastructure, and the idea of any alteration made him stare blankly at his wife, even though he knew she was being reasonable and he was not.

SEVERAL DAYS A WEEK, Arash brought his soup and small brown roll—his lunch never varied—and sat beside William in the bleachers. Arash talked to William like he was a colleague, which was a kindness William appreciated.

"I have concerns about Paterson," Arash said, nodding toward the sophomore shooting guard who was bouncing up and down on the court, waiting for his turn to shoot.

"He has a nice stroke," William said. "Don't you think?"

"Good technique in his shot, yes. But pay attention to how he lands."

William watched the lanky kid dribble around three cones and then shoot. "I don't see a problem."

"Try to slow your vision down while you watch. Watch him in slow motion for his next three turns."

William had no idea what Arash meant by this, but he watched carefully for the next twenty minutes. He tried to pull apart the different parts of Paterson's movements: the angle of his body when he ran, the rotation of his knees when he pivoted, the abandon with which he leapt toward the basket. On the fourth viewing he noticed Paterson's torso twist while he shot, which caused him to be off-balance when he landed. He tried to explain this to Arash, who nodded.

"That's right. I think he might need to work on strengthening his ankles—there's possible ligament weakness there. Your experience made me rethink my work, you know. I want to find out about the players' prior injuries. If I have that information, I can help build them out. I'm concerned they'll lie to me if I just ask them about the injuries straight up, though." He made a face.

"They won't want you to think there's anything wrong with them. They don't want to be viewed as damaged and get less playing time."

"Exactly," Arash said. "Goddamn knuckleheads."

William nodded and put a hand on his weak knee. "This semester—for the next month, anyway—I'm not teaching," he said. "I have some free time. Would you mind if I watched you work sometimes? Shadowed you?"

Arash turned in his seat to look at William. It occurred to William that he knew very little about this man. He'd been a physio at Northwestern for more than a decade, but did he have a wife? Kids? Did he live on campus? Where was he from? Studying history was about scope, about understanding the terrain that surrounded the critical event. Nothing and no one existed in a vacuum. Charlie in his armchair in his house had been only one slice of his terrain. The wake had revealed the woman at the bus stop, the friends he shared drinks with, fellow poetry-lovers, nice men at his miserable job. Bitter relatives, stunned daughters.

"Aren't you in graduate school full-time?"

"I can get everything done," William said.

Arash looked back at the court.

"I won't get in your way." William cringed because his voice sounded desperate, but also because he realized he *was* desperate. Something opened inside him in this gym, as he watched the players. He wanted to be here more. He needed to be here, to have any chance of feeling okay.

"That would be fine," Arash said. "I could use your help."

WILLIAM REGRETTED GIVING JULIA his book the moment he handed it to her. If Charlie hadn't died, he never would have caved to her repeated requests, but he couldn't bear to make her more unhappy than she already was. Also, William felt like he owed her something in return for her reluctant agreement to stay in their current apartment through the end of the school year. He said, "It's not in a readable state yet. You're not going to know what to make of it. This is a draft, a messy draft."

"I understand that. I'm so glad you're letting me look at it. Thank you."

The next morning William saw her reading the pages at their yellow kitchen table, but then he never saw her reading again. A few days later he saw the manuscript on the couch, wrapped in the paper bag, and he flinched to see it out in the open. He felt like he'd handed his wife the muddled insides of his head, or perhaps his soul. He'd been writing the book for almost five years, but he'd done so in fits and starts. He didn't actually think of it as a book—that's just what Julia called it. For William, it was something he worked on because there was a silence inside him that sometimes frightened him. Basketball was noisy—the game took place at tempo, with ten men jumping, shooting, guarding, cutting at every moment—and writing about it masked William's internal quiet. He could listen to the thumping of the basketball, in the gym or on the page, and imagine that it was his own heartbeat.

He used to return to his dorm room after a hard practice and re-create a famous game on the page. When he wrote about the signature moves of great players—Oscar Robertson's head fake, or Kareem Abdul-Jabbar's glorious skyhook—he felt the ripples of those moves in his own body. Those ripples were the only times the stillness deep inside him broke, and he'd experience some relief. But because of the way William wrote, the narrative in the book was convoluted and followed only the fitful path of his enthusiasms. He knew it would make no sense to his wife, and having the pages out of his hands made him feel like he'd lost part of himself. Days went by without Julia mentioning the book, and she seemed to go to great effort not to meet his eyes. The fog that had arrived with William's injury returned to his peripheral vision, like cloud cover circling a mountain. The book was terrible; he was terrible.

Finally, one night at bedtime, Julia handed him the stack of pages and said, "It's good!"

He closed his eyes so he couldn't see her bright, forced smile. "You don't have to say that. It's not true. It's just for me. I'm sorry it won't get me a job after graduate school."

"You won't need a book for that," she said. "We'll get you a job."

Fog nipped at the edges of him, and he felt bad for his wife. She had to pretend she thought he was better than he was. She had to pretend she wasn't worried she'd hitched herself to a bad horse. This wasn't the first time William had seen this kind of strained smile on Julia's face, and he hated that he'd put her in this position. A dark mist saturated him.

She said, "The footnotes were very interesting. Very unusual."

"I need a glass of water," he said, and climbed out of bed. He walked fast into the living room and then reared back, his heart racing, at the sight of Sylvie on the couch. He'd forgotten she was here; he'd forgotten everything.

"I'm sorry," she said. He'd frightened her too.

"It was my fault," he said. "Rushing into the room."

"Are you all right?" she asked.

There was something in Sylvie's voice, some knowing, that made William pause. He pictured his wife and Sylvie sleeping side by side on the couch. The two sisters were careful and kind with each other; he'd always admired that about them. One of the things he loved most about Julia was how she treated her family. The sisters were so close that, in reality, his wife never operated alone; the four Padavano girls shared their lives, celebrating and utilizing one another's strengths, covering for one another's weaknesses. Julia was the organizer and leader, Sylvie the reader and measured voice, Emeline the nurturer, and Cecelia the artist.

William's wife wasn't much of a reader anymore. Of course—he realized—Julia would have asked Sylvie to read his book. Not as an act of betrayal but as a way to bring her best self to the task. Julia's love and ambition plus Sylvie's critical-reading skills.

William stood still at the edge of the living room in the dim light while this knowledge unfolded inside him. He could feel Julia, anxious, behind him. William had always known that he'd married not just his wife but her family too. At the start of their relationship, Julia had brought her three sisters to his college basketball game to make it clear that she came as part of a unit, and he'd accepted that. Julia had legally changed her last name to his, but for all intents and purposes, he'd joined the Padavanos. The deepest union in this apartment was between the two sisters who fell asleep in each other's arms.

Sylvie was sitting upright on the couch now, as if she were a visitor and not a woman wearing a nightgown with her hair down. She gave William the same worried look his wife was directing at his back.

William walked away from both women, into the kitchen. He needed to be alone. He needed to wrestle his breath under control.

He leaned against the refrigerator and rested his hands against his thighs. He panted as if he were running the court, an hour into a game that his team was losing by a landslide. No matter how many minutes remained on the clock, there was no chance of victory.

IN JANUARY, WHEN THE new semester began, William resumed teaching, on top of attending classes. Julia was clearly relieved that he was earning a salary and made a small fuss when he brought his first paycheck home. William was pleased she was happy, but he now found his days so long and demanding that he had to manage his energy to get from one end to the other. The history program believed it was beneficial for the graduate students to teach outside their area of focus, so William was now the teaching assistant for an undergraduate class called The History of Ancient Egypt. Each class meeting required an immense amount of preparation on his part, and William was always tired, even when he slept well at night. He developed a habit of shaking his head sharply, once, before walking into a graduate lecture, and this turned on an internal motor that allowed him to nod and smile and take notes while the professor spoke. A more powerful motor was required when William was the TA in front of his own class. His heartbeat revved up, and the minutes seemed to fly out the open window, winged with anxiety. He had to constantly check his watch to make sure he wasn't covering the material too quickly. He felt like he was doing time wrong; a better professor would pace himself to finish just as the class ended, lining up the minutes with some internal clock that William lacked.

When he arrived home late at night, William tried his best with Julia, and he could tell she was trying her best with him. William knew, though, that reading his manuscript had permanently damaged Julia's opinion of him. For her, his "book" had loomed large through their entire relationship: In the beginning she'd been thrilled by it, because she saw the project as a sign of William's maturity and ambition. Over the years, she'd used the idea of it to paper over any worries she had about his lack of personal plans and goals. Julia had been counting on his book to prove that he was the man she'd chosen. And now that she'd read it, she knew he wasn't. William had dreaded this happening; it felt like stepping off a cliff, and he didn't know in what state he would reach the ground. He wondered, every day, if he should tell her that he'd understand if she wanted to leave him. But Julia was pregnant—visibly now—and so she was trapped. They were trapped: He was becoming less of the man she'd married by the day, while their family was only growing.

Julia told him about a doctor's appointment she'd had that afternoon and asked if he wanted to rest his hand on her taut belly. William placed his hand where she pointed, but he knew he didn't have the right expression on his face—some of his fear must have showed through. Julia sighed and turned away, saying she needed to go to bed. William was relieved on the nights that he arrived home and Julia didn't try. She just waved to him from her seat on the couch next to her sister but didn't stand up to get him dinner or ask about his day.

"You're not excited about the baby," Julia said to him once, as a statement of fact.

It took William a moment to recall what excitement was, and then he said, "I am." But he knew he'd failed to sound convincing. "I'm sorry."

"Please stop apologizing. Sometimes, William, I feel like I'm having the baby with Sylvie, and you're just some guy who lives here."

Julia challenged him with her eyes. She wanted a response, she wanted him to push back, to be insulted, but all he could come up with was another expression of regret.

LATE ONE EVENING, WILLIAM was walking home from class when he noticed, through the darkness, a woman sitting on a bench. He blinked in her direction for a moment, not understanding why she held his attention, and then realized it was Sylvie. William's heart gave a quick rattle in his chest. He might have crossed the street or turned a corner before his sister-in-law could see him, but it was too late. She'd noticed him too.

For weeks he'd been avoiding Sylvie. Every time he was in the same room with her, he thought, *You read my ridiculous footnotes.* This made him want to drop through a hole in the floor; he knew Sylvie must have been horrified at what she'd read. He hadn't removed the manuscript from the paper bag since Julia gave it back to him; this was the longest he'd ever gone without adding to its pages.

"I left my apartment keys at the library," Sylvie said, from her seat on the bench.

William noticed that she looked tired and remembered that she also took night classes. He looked at his watch; it was almost ten o'clock. "What were you going to do?"

She shrugged. "I was trying to figure it out. It's too late to phone, because Julia needs her sleep, and I wasn't sure you'd be home. My guess is that I was going to sit here for a little while longer—it's not too cold—and then get a bus to go sleep at Mrs. Ceccione's place."

William sat down on the edge of the bench, next to her. "Well, problem solved, because I have keys."

She smiled. "I was also admiring the stars."

"The stars?" At first he didn't know what she was talking about, but then he tipped his head back. There they were.

"Are stars not your thing?"

This is a strange conversation, William thought. But he'd stepped outside his daily routine, and he felt less nervous with Sylvie in the shadowy darkness than he did inside the apartment. "I guess not?" he said. "I mean, I have nothing against them."

They were quiet for a few moments, with their heads leaned back to take in the sky.

"I miss my father all the time," Sylvie said. "I keep thinking it's going to get easier."

William looked over at her, and there were tears on her cheeks. He could see tears trapped in her eyelashes, and he lost his breath. He could see her sadness traced across the lines of her body, overlaying her arms and legs and the oval of her face. This struck him; he'd never been able to see so clearly what another person was feeling.

Sylvie had been hurt by Charlie's death; Julia had been shipwrecked too. Charlie Padavano had felt essential to his daughters, as if he was part of their own construction. William missed his father-in-law as well; he remembered Charlie asking him to explain basketball. William had found himself drawing the court on a piece of paper and explaining the actions of the five players on a team, the older man nodding in concentration beside him.

William said, "That kind of loss . . . must be hard."

"I didn't expect"—she paused—"for it to be part of everything, every minute. I didn't know that you could lose someone, and that meant you lost so much else."

William considered this. "Like it's all connected."

She made a small noise next to him, neither a yes nor a no.

He shifted his weight against the wooden slats of the bench. His body felt odd, like blood was rushing though it at a faster pace than normal. He watched a policeman stroll down the sidewalk on the far side of the street.

Sylvie said, "You look tired."

William turned toward her and found himself looking directly into Sylvie's eyes. He had the strange sense that she was looking inside him, to the truth of him. He hadn't known this was possible. When Julia gazed at William, she was trying to see the man she wanted him to be. She couldn't see, or didn't want to see, who he actually was.

William thought of Charlie again; his father-in-law had seemed interested in knowing *him*. And then, briefly, he thought of his parents. Had his mother or father ever looked straight at him? He didn't think so. He imagined that his mother must have held him as a baby with her face turned away. Maybe this was why he had a hard time picturing himself as a parent, because his own parents had wanted to leave every room he was in.

William took a jagged breath. Why was he having these thoughts? It felt like Sylvie's attention had revealed him to himself. And the stars were so bright overhead. Aggressively bright.

"I've been very tired lately," he heard himself say.

"Me too."

"You lost your father and your home." He hadn't considered this before, but he knew, as if the air between them were stacked with answers, that this was the truth.

"Yes," she said, and her voice wavered.

Something wavered inside William in response, and he was

afraid—for a split second—that *he* might cry. But he couldn't do that in front of his wife's sister; too much had already passed between them. He stood up and said in a brusque voice, "Let's get inside."

A few days later, Julia told him, upset, that Sylvie had found a place of her own; she was moving out. William felt a stab of something sharp in his chest and thought, *That's my fault too.* Something had happened to him on the bench, and since then he'd found his daily routine even more difficult to power through. He'd almost wept in front of his sister-in-law, and he never cried. Not since he was a child, anyway, and William had few memories of tears even then. His unstitching must have looked distasteful to Sylvie. Understandably, the combination of reading his embarrassing footnotes and that moment on the bench had been too much—too much what, he wasn't sure—for Sylvie to take.

A MONTH LATER, ROSE announced she was moving to Florida, and the sisters gathered the following evening at William and Julia's apartment. William wanted to be helpful but didn't know how. He sat in the armchair and watched the four sisters roam the living room. The women shared the same crease between their eyebrows and the same need for movement. They passed Izzy back and forth among them, even though the baby kicked and wriggled in their arms.

"She's working on crawling," Cecelia said in apology.

"Of course she is." Julia spoke as if she were running out of air. She was so pregnant she had a hard time filling her lungs. "Izzy's brilliant."

None of the women smiled, because Julia wasn't joking and they all agreed with her.

"What can we do?" Emeline said. "If Mama wants to leave, we can't stop her."

"She might not like Florida. She might come back," Sylvie said.

William had made eye contact with Sylvie very briefly when she arrived. They exchanged a nod that felt like shorthand for: *I saw you that night, and you saw me, but we're fine.* Since Sylvie had moved out, William was careful to never be alone with her. He'd finally regained some sense of momentum that allowed him to get through his days, and he didn't want to lose it. Also, he'd seen Sylvie's emotions as if they were drawn all over her body, and that seemed alarmingly intimate, as if he'd seen her without clothes. William didn't understand what had happened between him and his sister-in-law on the bench that night, but it felt dangerous, like a shining dagger that could cut through his life as if it were made of paper.

He scanned the other women in the room. No one here had ever been to Florida or even on an airplane. Rose already had her ticket. William had looked in the local real estate section of the newspaper that morning and seen that her house was on the market, for far more than he would have thought it was worth.

"I can't believe she's leaving *now*," Julia said. "She'll probably miss the baby being born."

Izzy was passed from Sylvie to Julia. Julia kissed the baby girl's cheek and then nuzzled her face into her neck.

The three other sisters looked distressed, their eyes on their oldest sister; Julia was their leader, and she didn't have a plan. William felt a surge of annoyance at them for expecting Julia to fix this. His wife was having a hard time sleeping, and her back hurt all the time. "I feel like the baby is crowding me out," she'd told William that morning at breakfast. She looked uncomfortable and swollen every minute of the day.

"Older people often move south when they retire," he said, and noticed that his deeper, male voice sounded odd in the room. "It's very common. This isn't bad news necessarily . . . you just weren't expecting it."

There was a beat of silence. No one met his eyes. He wondered if he had no credibility on the subject because his own family tree had shriveled so prematurely. Or did he lack credibility simply because he was a man in his armchair, like Charlie had been?

William looked down at his weak knee.

"Would anyone like something to eat?" Julia said. "We have pasta. Or eggs?"

"This has been a hard year." Emeline sounded like she was delivering a speech she hadn't written and didn't fully believe in. "But we'll be fine by ourselves. We'll take care of one another. I arranged my college classes to be at night, so I can work full-time, and I got a raise at the daycare. Cecelia and I will be able to move into our own place soon."

"I'm painting murals on the walls at the daycare," Cecelia said. "And if that works out, I'll do the same at other daycares and maybe schools."

"You two"—Emeline gestured at Julia and William—"are doing wonderfully. Sylvie is about to be an official librarian, the best one in the city."

"We're still lucky," Sylvie said tentatively, as if testing out the twins' hypothesis.

"We'll make it through this," Julia said.

William walked into the kitchen to boil water for pasta and to hide the fact that he was moved by how the sisters had just knit themselves back together in front of him. He felt alone, in front of the sink, with a rickety knee and a palpitating heart. He cooked the pasta, added the refrigerated marinara sauce Julia had made earlier in the week, and brought the bowl to the table. Emeline jumped up to get plates and utensils.

"Thank you," Julia said, and he saw the gratitude in her eyes.

"I'm just going for a walk," he said. "I'll be back in a little while."

The four sisters regarded him, and the baby gave a sudden happy shout, which made the women smile in his direction before turning to Izzy. William left the brightly lit apartment and closed his eyes with relief to find himself alone in the purple twilight. He thought for a moment of his book, but it was behind him, indoors, and he didn't want to return until everyone but Julia was gone.

He looked at his watch; there would be a pickup game going on at the gym or perhaps a late team practice. He crossed the campus in long strides, gulping the night air. He would take his regular seat in the bleachers and scan the gaits, leaps, and landings of young men, looking for future injuries. Every weakness he was able to spot on the basketball court could be fixed.

Julia

J ULIA AND ROSE DIDN'T SPEAK ON THE WAY TO THE AIRPORT. William hadn't wanted Julia to drive the borrowed car; she was so pregnant her belly touched the wheel even with the seat pushed back. He'd offered to chauffeur them to O'Hare, but Julia knew it had to be just her and her mother. If Rose was going to communicate something to Julia—some missing information to explain her leaving, or regret for the decision—it wouldn't happen with William present. But Rose kept her face stony as they parked the car, checked her luggage, and walked to the gate.

Julia said, "I'll send you a photo of the baby when he's born."

Rose nodded. "Don't be so sure it's a boy."

"Everyone says it is, because of how I'm carrying."

Julia and Rose stopped suddenly. Cecelia was standing by the gate, holding Izzy on her hip. She was wearing her painting clothes: jeans and a splattered long-sleeved shirt. Her hair was held back with a yellow bandanna that used to belong to Charlie. She mirrored her mother's stony expression.

Cecelia said, "I won't let you leave without meeting your first grandchild."

Rose's eyes darkened. She looked pale and hard. Julia could tell she was thinking about her husband lying on the hospital floor.

"My first grandchild is right here." Rose pointed at Julia's belly.

"No," Cecelia and Julia said, at the same time.

Rose took a step back.

Izzy, who was missing her morning nap, rubbed at her eyes with the backs of her hands and frowned at everyone.

"It's going to be so hot in Florida," Julia said, trying to steer the conversation to a place that made sense, that had potential for peace. As the words left her mouth, though, she knew they were meaningless. "You've never liked the heat, Mama."

"You don't have to be this stubborn," Cecelia said.

Julia felt a tremor run through her body. She'd known there would be an important conversation with her mother at the airport—she'd felt this in her bones—but she hadn't known it would include Cecelia. She felt a pinch of jealousy, because her younger sister had stepped in front of her again. Cecelia was almost nineteen and seemed more powerful, more certain, in motherhood than she had been before. She was pretty and wearing clothes that fit her. Julia felt as big as the ocean, and her thoughts swam like fish in her head.

"Are you trying to kill me too?" Rose said to Cecelia. "Right before I get on an airplane to have some relaxation for the first time in my life?"

Oh no, Julia thought.

"You can't really, truly believe that I had anything to do with Daddy's death." Cecelia pointed a look at Rose that said, *If it's anyone's fault, it's yours.*

There were people all around them—eating snacks, drinking coffee, making sure they had what they needed in their carry-on bags—but Julia couldn't have said whether there were ten strangers in the terminal or one hundred. Were they watching and listening to her mother and sister stab each other in the heart?

"Daddy said that you never spoke to your mother again after she turned you out." Cecelia shook her head, and so Izzy shook hers too. "I wanted to say goodbye and tell you that I always loved you and that I'll tell Izzy only good stories about you. And you know why? Not for you, Mom. I'm going to do that for me. I don't want to get bitter and angry like you. I *want* to miss you, because I love you."

"You shouldn't talk like this," Rose said. "I'd like to sit down." And she went to sit in one of the waiting-area chairs. The tremors coursing through Julia's body seemed to pass over her mother's face, but Rose said nothing until the boarding announcement was made.

"Do you have everything you need for the flight?" Julia said, and then thought, *Why can I only say stupid things?* She wanted to be *in* this moment with her mother and sister, but she wasn't. She was a cheap bouncy ball in the middle of a gunfight.

Rose directed her attention at Cecelia. "I choose what conversations I have, young lady. Not you. There's no virtue in being mouthy." Rose nodded, as if in agreement with herself, and then walked slowly toward the boarding tunnel, where she showed the flight attendant her ticket and disappeared from sight.

Izzy made a soft noise and bounced in her mother's arms.

The two sisters looked at each other. "I didn't know I was going to come here when I woke up this morning," Cecelia said. "I just found myself walking to the train."

The airport thrummed around them: overhead announcements, the clack of bags being set down, the murmur of conversation. Julia said, "Could you drive the car back to the city? I think the baby is coming."

"Now?" Cecelia's eyes widened, and she kissed her sister on the cheek. Izzy leaned forward from her mother's arms to do the same. One firm kiss, and one butterfly-light.

"Of course he's coming," Cecelia said. "Let's go."

"You were so brave," Julia said, as she let herself be led down the hallway. Her voice was dim in her own ears, and these would be the last words she would say out loud for a while. She could feel some kind of vast power pulling her within herself.

They didn't have a car seat, so Julia half-sat and half-lay in the back seat, holding Izzy with both hands.

"Hang on," Cecelia said. "Just hang on until we get to the hospital. I thought it was so silly when Daddy taught us to drive, since we live in a city and never owned a car. He told me that it was a valuable life skill and that I could be the driver when the four of us robbed a bank one day."

Julia knew her sister was talking to keep her attention away from the pain, but it wasn't *pain* exactly—more a smothering intensity. Every few minutes, she felt like she was being sat on by an invisible elephant—the weight crushed her—and then the elephant stood up, and she was herself again. Julia focused on keeping her hands on Izzy, who had fallen asleep beside her. She looked so perfect and beautiful in her sleep that Julia started to cry. *No baby could ever be this cute again,* she thought. *Which means my baby won't be this cute.*

"There's the river," Cecelia said from the front seat. "Five more minutes. I'm going to paint a picture of Izzy and your baby together. I'll paint one for each of us."

When the elephant stood up, Julia thought, *Mama is in the sky right now. She's not even on this earth. She's literally unreachable.*

Cecelia seemed to hear her thoughts. "It's Mom's loss, not yours," she said. "She's going to miss everything, but you won't. I won't. I'll call William and the others when we get to the hospital. All of us will be there."

They reached the hospital, Cecelia peeled Julia's fingers off Izzy's onesie, and people—faceless strangers whose voices she couldn't understand—helped her into a wheelchair. Julia wondered if they were the same people from the airport. She could hear the timbre of Cecelia's voice, but the words wouldn't separate into distinct shapes. Julia kept shifting her weight, twisting in the seat, trying to evade the elephant, who now refused to stand up.

Later she would be told that her labor was surprisingly fast for a first birth and that she arrived too late to have an epidural. Cecelia called the history department at Northwestern, but no one could track William down right away. It took thirty minutes before he was found in the university gym and then he ran, despite his bad knee, to the corner of the Northwestern campus where it was possible to find a cab. Sylvie abandoned her desk at the library. Emeline had been sitting alone in the house they grew up in, intent on spending every minute of the last day their family owned it inside its walls. She ran out the front door, though, when she got the call from her twin.

Because everything moved so quickly and William hadn't yet arrived, Cecelia was in the delivery room, just as Julia had been with her.

The ability to hear and understand words was the first of Julia's capacities to go. Soon she was thinking in sentences without prepositions or adjectives. *No, no more, stop, baby coming.* It felt like a wall had fallen inside her and revealed that she was no more than an animal. This was a surprise to Julia, even from that place. She growled and mooed and caterwauled as her body somehow squeezed itself. The noises seemed to come from inside her and outside her, and she felt no shame. She felt power. She felt like a lioness, covered in sweat, rising up on the hard bed they'd laid her on, announcing, "Push," as everything she was made of, in lockstep, guided the baby out of her body.

"It's a girl!" Cecelia cried.

The elephant evaporated, the squeezing stopped, and Julia was herself again. Mostly herself, anyway. She realized that she was most certainly a mammal and had the ability to shake the world apart and create a human when she unleashed her power. She was a mother. This identity shuddered through her, welcome like water to a dry riverbed. It felt so elemental and true that Julia must have unknowingly been a mother all along, simply waiting to be joined by her child. Julia had never felt like this before. Her brain was a gleaming engine, and her resources felt immense. She *was* clarity.

Julia held the baby for what felt like only a few seconds before the nurse whisked the infant to the nursery to be washed and wrapped in a blanket. Cecelia left the room to tell the others the news. Julia shook her head, in disbelief and joy. She couldn't believe how fast her mind was moving, but perhaps these truths had been inside her all along and were accessible now because she'd given birth. She saw everything so clearly. She had spent her whole life trying to fix other people—her parents, her sisters, William—but that had been a fruitless endeavor; she could see that now. She couldn't keep her father alive or her mother in Chicago or Cecelia celibate or William ambitious. She'd just been fine-tuning her skills for now, for what mattered, for motherhood. She would protect and celebrate her baby girl and let everyone else do whatever they wanted. With her daughter, Julia was complete. She realized, amazed: *I love myself.* That had somehow never been true before.

William entered the room with a nervous smile on his face. Julia had been frustrated with her husband for weeks, but inside her new warmth, she felt affection for him. She *was* love. She beamed at William and thought: *I never needed you. Did you know that? I thought I needed a husband, but I don't actually need anyone. I could have done everything by myself.* William bent his long body to hug her, and Julia wrapped her arms around his neck. She told him how excited she was for him to see the baby girl she'd made.

WHEN JULIA AND BABY Alice were home in the Northwestern apartment with the sunlight streaming through the living room window, they set up in the armchair. The nurse in the hospital had taught Julia how to breastfeed, and Alice had taken to it easily, so they spent their days in that chair with feeding and resting as their only activities. Breastfeeding made both Julia and Alice sleepy. Julia was surprised every time she woke to find that she had slept sitting up, in the middle of the day. Time moved like waves across a waterbed; hours and minutes surged and then settled under her heavier weight. She never knew what day of the week it was, to the extent that each time William told her he was leaving for work, Julia was startled. When he was home, her husband brought her food and glasses of water, and took care of dishes and laundry, and let her sisters in when they rang the doorbell. Julia felt drugged with a kind of dazed happiness with the baby in her arms.

Her newfound power was like a wonderful secret. She smiled to herself at odd moments, thinking of it, but she allowed herself this rest, this recovery, to gather her strength. Sometimes when the baby napped, Julia would lie beside her and daydream about the future. She would become truly independent. When the baby was a little older, she would call Professor Cooper and ask him for work. She would use her gleaming brain, and while William was in graduate school, she would make money. There would be no more financial hiccups, with her in the mix. She could see this new life so clearly. Emeline worked in a daycare, so Julia could leave Alice with her loving aunt when she went to work. With two incomes, she and William could buy a house sooner rather than later. They could afford to send Alice to private school. This vision was less complicated and fraught than any other that Julia had had in her life, because instead of depending on her husband, she was depending on her own capacity, which had been revealed to be limitless.

Hour to hour, though, the baby pulled Julia's attention as if she were a magnet. Julia had thought Alice would be a boy, but regardless of the gender, she'd expected the baby to look like Izzy. Newborn Izzy had been dark-eyed and serious. Alice, though, had sea-blue eyes and a friendly expression. She seemed interested in and somehow optimistic about the landscape around her. Sylvie used Charlie's old camera to take a picture of Julia and Alice in the armchair, to send to Rose. Julia had expected it to be difficult to smile for this particular photo, to express anything other than loss or anger. To her surprise, though, she beamed. The pain of her mother's departure had nearly disappeared; all that remained was the faintest trace of a bruise. The obvious explanation was that Alice's birth had reshuffled Julia's place in her family. *She* was the mother now. Alice was the daughter. Julia wondered if Rose had sensed that she was about to become a supporting character, instead of the main one, and left to avoid that fate.

In the middle of the night, in the armchair, Julia found herself talking out loud, not to her mother but to her father. It was him that she missed in those moments. In the darkness, it was easy to imagine Charlie sitting on the couch, his eyes filled with delight each time Alice waved a tiny hand or pursed her lips. "Daddy, she's exquisite, isn't she? You would adore her. Her middle name is Padavano. Alice Padavano Waters."

Emeline came over most days during the small window of time between her shift at the daycare and her evening classes at the community college. She joked that she was taking the long road to graduation, because she was only able to manage one or two classes at a time toward her early-childhood education degree. She was enthralled with the new baby, though, and couldn't bear to stay away. "I get to snuggle Alice," she said into the newborn's cheek, "and then go home at the end of the night to Izzy. I'm sooo lucky."

Julia smiled at her sister's happiness. "We need to find you someone to make babies with," she said. "You'll be the most amazing mother."

"I know—I wish I could just skip ahead to that point." Emeline was shy, and nervous around men. She stood behind her sisters in social settings, the same way she'd hidden behind them at parties when she was a child. "I'm a homebody," Emeline said, whenever she had to explain herself to someone new. Her propensity to stay home was even greater since Izzy had been born. Emeline wanted to leave Izzy's side only to visit Alice.

Alice was three weeks old when Emeline said, one afternoon when they were alone in the apartment, "I've noticed that William doesn't seem to, well, hold the baby much. Do you think he's scared?"

Alice was asleep, a solid, delicious weight against Julia's chest, so she spoke softly. "You're right. I've noticed that too." William held the baby only when Julia directly asked him to—for instance, when she used the bathroom or took a shower. And he always walked directly to the bassinet or changing table and set Alice down. He never snuggled her or leaned his face down to kiss her soft cheek.

"I don't know if he's scared," Julia said. "I don't know *what* he's feeling, because he won't tell me."

"I wonder if maybe it's because his parents weren't . . . normal," Emeline said. "Maybe he doesn't know how to act with her?"

This hadn't occurred to Julia, but she shook her head. "I don't think that's it. He always says he's fine, everything is fine." She shifted in her chair, careful not to wake the baby. She found she was relieved to have the chance to share her frustration with her sister. "I thought it was so nice that William was doing the dishes and laundry, and I know it is, technically, but he's clearly doing those things because they keep him away from Alice. Emmie, he doesn't even look at her."

"Well, he might just need more time. Men aren't naturals with babies like we are. He'll come around, though. How could he not? Alice is scrumptious," she said, and peppered the baby's foot with kisses.

Sunday was the only day that William had no classes or work, and his presence in the apartment threw off Julia and the baby's normal routine. Julia sent her husband out for any errand she could think of and took a long afternoon nap, but it still felt like every time she looked up, William was in front of her, asking a silly question. Which shirt should he wear? Should he contact the movers about what time they planned to show up on the designated day? Did she want him to ask the super about the elevator button? Did these grapes look okay to eat?

Julia finally said, "I can't give you every single answer in the universe! I'm busy with the baby, and I don't have time to take care of two children."

William looked hurt, and he apologized. This irritated her too. Julia shifted in her chair, beneath the baby, and wished it were Monday morning. She could feel the real questions in their marriage lurking beneath the surface of William's tiny ones. These questions were hers: *Do you really want this life? Me, and Alice? Do you want to be here with us?*

William asked fewer questions after that, but this meant that he spoke less. This irritated Julia too, and the way he avoided the baby made her increasingly sad. Now that one of the main equations of their marriage—William's questions plus Julia's answers equaled a plan—had broken down, they were awkward around each other. "Am I doing something wrong?" he asked her one night, after they'd turned out the lights. "Oh, William, you're fine," she said into the darkness, and then fell asleep.

When Cecelia visited next, Julia tried to explain her revelation while giving birth and how different she was now. She said, "Did you feel like an animal?"

Cecelia considered this. "Well, I don't think I made the kind of noises you made or went quite as feral." She grinned at her sister. "But I know what you mean, I think. If someone tried to hurt Izzy, I'd rip their face off."

"You're more powerful since you had Izzy."

"Am I?" Cecelia said, with doubt in her voice. Izzy was on her lap. The baby could stand on her own now for a few wobbly moments, but she liked to pat Alice with great enthusiasm, so Cecelia stayed close.

"I convinced William to go to graduate school," Julia said. "But I'm the one who should have gone. I could have gotten a PhD in organizational psychology or gone to business school. I could run a business, don't you think?"

Cecelia kissed Izzy's soft cheek. "I think you've got some powerful hormones in your body and you should enjoy them while they last."

That night, in the shadows, Julia said, "I miss you, Daddy. I wish you could have seen me as a mother. It would have made you smile."

JULIA AND WILLIAM MOVED into the bigger apartment in July, when Alice was eleven weeks old. The apartment had two bedrooms and a new kitchen, but the living room windows looked out over other buildings instead of the sky and a peaceful quad. Alice woke up less frequently in the night, so Julia slept in bed with the bassinet beside her. Although Julia had wanted to move before Alice's birth, she'd come to appreciate the timing. This was where she would start her new life. She'd decided, without talking to William, that she'd start working when Alice was six months old. Julia eyed her closet and designated half of it for the business suits she would soon buy. She walked from room to room in the apartment, thinking: *When I'm making money, we'll buy a new sofa to go there and a soft rug for Alice to crawl on.*

William was gone for long hours, studying in the library, attending graduate classes, and teaching a summer course. By teaching and taking classes during the summer, he would earn his degree sooner, but he looked exhausted and glassy-eyed when he was home. Now that the baby was a little older, Julia's sisters visited less often. Cecelia and Emeline had their own apartment—a basement space with a tiny backyard for Izzy—and Sylvie had rented a studio on the top floor of a small building near the Lozano Library. Her sisters were busy, and Julia was no longer their focus.

Once a week, Julia phoned Rose. The call sounded like the long distance it covered: Sometimes there was static, and Rose sat on her condo's balcony, where she could see a sliver of ocean, so there was noise on her end too. Wind, occasional car honks, perhaps the sea.

"The air is different here," Rose said. "Softer. Saltier too."

"Alice can almost roll over," Julia said. "Did you get the last set of photos? The ones I took in the park?"

"Yes," Rose said. "She looks healthy. Did I tell you the ladies and I take turns cooking dinner?"

Julia looked down at Alice, who was lying in her lap. The baby was holding and inspecting one of her feet. *What a marvel,* Alice seemed to be thinking. *Look at this craftsmanship.* Julia smiled.

She heard her mother say, *You have to let me go.*

"What did you say?" Julia said.

"I made enchiladas for the first time. They weren't bad either."

Julia shook her head to clear it. She said, "Mama, did you feel different after having me? After becoming a mother?"

"What a question! I barely remember that time, Julia. By the time you were Alice's age, I was pregnant with Sylvie, wasn't I? I was far too busy to think about how I *felt.*"

Julia nodded. What had happened seemed to have happened only to her. "I have to go now, Mama. This call is expensive."

When she hung up, Julia put Alice down for her nap. The baby was always amenable to the idea of sleeping. Each time she was laid in the bassinet, she seemed to set her mind to the task at hand. Alice closed her eyes, a small smile on her lips, and tried her best to sleep.

Julia pulled the shades and lay down on her own bed. She'd figured out why it was her father she'd yearned for since Alice was born. She wanted to explain to Charlie how she now saw the world, because he was the one who would understand. Her father had seen her power—understood its scope—before she had. When Julia told him that she and William were getting married, Charlie had looked disappointed for a split second. That reaction hadn't made sense to Julia at the time, because she knew her father liked William. But Charlie had stopped calling her his rocket around the same time, and Julia realized now that her father had hoped for more for her. He'd seen her potential and wanted to watch her soar, not marry and make a home. "I can do both, Daddy," she said now into the room softened with the sound of light baby snores. "I'll figure out how to do both."

Sylvie

THERE WAS A THREE-MONTH GAP BETWEEN WHEN SYLVIE
stopped sleeping at Julia and William's apartment and when she got
her own place. She'd told Julia that she had an apartment to stay in
when she moved out. This wasn't true, though. She didn't have anywhere lined up. She'd simply known, the evening she'd forgotten her
keys and spoken to William on the bench, that it was time for her to
live somewhere else. That was the second time Sylvie had cried since
her father's death; the first was after she'd read William's manuscript.

She'd been surprised to hear herself talk about how she missed
Charlie, and surprised to talk about the stars, and surprised to start
crying, and surprised to feel William's sadness beside her too, as if in
answer to her own. It felt like she'd tripped a switch and ended up in
a place where she saw her brother-in-law's true state, and he saw hers.
William had recognized the loss she was carrying inside her and spoken it aloud. No one else in Sylvie's life had identified the specific
swirl of her pain; no one had *understood* her since her father died. That
recognition had felt like drawing in giant mouthfuls of air after holding her breath for a long time.

Later that night, lying on the couch while her sister and William
slept in their room down the hall, Sylvie decided it was too risky for
her to continue to stay there. She felt vulnerable, at risk to her own

elements, in William's company. This didn't feel like his fault or her own; it felt as if the amalgamation of her grief over Charlie, plus reading William's footnotes, plus the handful of minutes when she was too tired to put up boundaries on the bench, had made it impossible for Sylvie to act like a normal person around her brother-in-law. She was also aware that when William had announced they should go inside, she'd almost grabbed his arm and said no. She'd felt *seen* during those minutes on the bench, and she'd wanted to remain with William in that spot. Sylvie knew it wasn't appropriate for her to crave more time alone with her sister's husband; she knew better.

After she moved out, she slept on co-workers' floors and sofas and several times with Emeline in her single bed. When Head Librarian Elaine went on vacation, she put Sylvie in charge of the library, and on those nights Sylvie slept in the library's lunch room. The room had a soft yellow couch that functioned well as a bed, and Sylvie used a washcloth to clean herself in the bathroom sink before opening the library's doors for the day. She often carried her overnight bag to evening classes, because she'd be sleeping in a different location from the night before. The wind off the lake was brutish that spring, and she had to fight for every step.

This transience made Sylvie feel skittish and unfocused—without a home, her movements often felt random. She'd always lived with family, and she hadn't realized how big a role waking up in the morning to the sounds of her parents, or Julia, played in her feeling like herself. Her family was a mirror in which she recognized her reflection. When she woke up on a co-worker's couch, not sure where she was for a few moments, she didn't know who she was either. She was visited by William's questions: *What am I doing? Why am I doing this? Who am I?*

Sylvie had to come up with tricks to create a sense of continuity and keep track of herself. Wherever she was staying, she went into the bathroom first thing in the morning and studied herself in the mirror. She had never done this before. She'd never been particularly vain or interested in her appearance, but now she needed to remind the girl standing in front of the mirror that she was roughly the same person day after day. She looked at the state of her hair, which was never negotiable—she accepted whatever crazy angles or cowlicks appeared after a night's sleep—and noted the green flecks in her brown eyes. She said, "Good morning, Sylvie," and then brushed her teeth.

She started rereading her father's copy of *Leaves of Grass*. Charlie had underlined passages and written in the margin too many times to count: *Wonderful!* It had been several years since she'd read the collection from start to finish, and this time Sylvie was surprised by how much death was in it. In "Song of Myself," Whitman listed numerous definitions of grass, but Sylvie's favorite was *the beautiful uncut hair of graves.* Sylvie thought of this when she visited her father's grave. According to the poet, death wasn't final, because life was tangled into it. Sylvie and her sisters walked the earth because of the man they'd buried. These thoughts, and reading Whitman's words, made more sense to Sylvie than the polite chatter of the lady in the seat next to her on the bus or the fact that there never seemed to be enough money in her purse.

Rose left for Florida in the middle of that period. Kissing her mother's cheek goodbye, and then rushing to the hospital to meet baby Alice a few hours later, felt correct to Sylvie—it matched the level of upheaval inside her. Her father was gone, and now her mother and their family home were gone too. Sylvie had seen a photo of the aftermath of a massive earthquake once, and the image had stayed with her. A road split in half lengthwise, revealing the middle of the earth, and how silly humans were to build houses and schools and cars on top and pretend they were safe. Sylvie felt like she spent her days carrying an overnight bag and a book, leaping over that chasm. The morning that Rose left, Sylvie stood in front of the bathroom mirror and said, "Goodbye, Mama. Good morning, Sylvie."

Head Librarian Elaine made Sylvie's promotion and new salary official a few weeks before she received the requisite credits for her library-sciences degree. Sylvie had enough money saved by now for a deposit, so she rented a tiny studio around the corner from the library that same day. When the realtor put the key in her hand, Sylvie said, "I'm sorry I'm so emotional."

The realtor, who had been working in Pilsen for decades, shrugged. "More people cry than you would think. Having your own apartment is a big deal."

Sylvie owned no furniture, so moving in was simple; Julia and the twins had removed a few items from their childhood home before Rose left, but Sylvie had been homeless and so had taken nothing. She bought a mattress for the floor and paid a neighborhood kid two bucks to help carry a kitchen table she'd found on the street up into the apartment. Because Rose had always spent trash night trawling the neighborhood for treasures other people were throwing away, Sylvie knew where to find what she needed. Bookshelves, a box of dishes, a pot and frying pan. Pretty embroidered pillows and curtains that looked brand-new. She wondered what could make people throw away items in such good condition.

After months of trying to make herself small in other people's homes, Sylvie slept spread-eagled on the mattress. She kept the window open for the breeze. She invited her sisters and nieces over for eggs, which she cooked in her scavenged pan. She listened to the noises of her apartment and the surrounding streets—children laughing at the playground, the city bus hissing to a stop, the man who ran the bodega downstairs talking in Spanish while he drank endless cups of coffee on the store's steps. Sylvie started reading novels again and had the giddy pleasure of tipping into new fictional worlds. She was grateful she was steady enough on her feet to do so.

She called her sisters from her own phone line whenever she desired to hear their voices. She was careful to call Julia only when she knew William was at work, though. She didn't trust herself on the phone with him. She still thought about their half hour on the bench while she lay in bed at night. She'd memorized their short conversation and played the scene over in her mind. She told herself that it had been no big deal. She was simply a mess, and had been since Charlie died, and so what she wanted or even dwelled on no longer made sense. But Sylvie couldn't imagine making small talk on the phone with William; the polite words would get stuck in her mouth. She wanted to ask, *What is it like to be William Waters? What was your experience on the bench that night?*

Sylvie secretly thought it was Julia's fault that she'd ended up in this odd predicament with her brother-in-law; her sister knew about the footnotes, knew the manuscript included William's personal thoughts and questions, and she'd asked Sylvie to read it anyway. If Sylvie hadn't read his manuscript, none of this would have happened. The day after she'd cried on the bench beside William, she lied to her older sister for the first time. She told Julia that her fictional new apartment didn't have a phone and that, no, Julia couldn't visit her there, because it was too small and messy. "I'm fine," Sylvie had insisted to Julia over and over during those three months, even though she knew her sister could tell she was lying. That lie chipped away at both of them every time Sylvie uttered it.

Sylvie's college graduation took place in the stuffy community college auditorium on a Tuesday morning in June. She told her sisters not to come, because the ceremony would be hot and boring. *And anticlimactic,* she thought, when she threw her cardboard mortarboard in a garbage can on her walk home. Sylvie was now a college graduate, which was what her mother had always wanted, but her mother no longer cared. Sylvie didn't even tell Rose that she'd officially graduated. She didn't want to hear her mother sigh at the news; Sylvie knew Rose had lost faith, and perhaps interest, in the finish line she'd set for her daughters when they were young.

Three months after Sylvie moved into her studio, on an August afternoon, Ernie walked into the library and into the row where she was shelving young-adult literature.

Sylvie stared; she hadn't seen him since Charlie's wake. She hadn't seen any of her boys since then. She'd been walking the library rows alone for all this time. She managed to say, "Well, look what the cat dragged in."

"I've been thinking about you," he said. "Been busy. I just graduated—I'm officially an electrician."

"Congratulations. I graduated too."

They smiled at each other, and she took in his wavy hair and the dimple in his chin. They'd known each other since elementary school; she'd watched him grow from a skinny boy into a thickset young man. Sylvie inventoried what was inside her: She'd wanted this boy in her arms once upon a time, but she was no longer sure she did. She wasn't the girl she used to be; that girl had a father and a mother and dreams for her future. Now Sylvie was a librarian struggling to make her own home. Her fantasies had gone on hold when her father died, the third doors had sealed shut, and the only man she thought about was the one married to her sister.

Sylvie shook her head, trying to clear away those thoughts, and said, "Are you going to kiss me or what?"

Ernie's smile deepened and they each took a step forward, till their bodies met. Her hands on the back of his neck, his arms around her waist. Sylvie felt her body issue a silent moan of relief. It felt nice, like it used to. Thank goodness. She wondered over the synchronicity of Ernie showing up now, when her apartment key was sitting in her hip pocket, when she needed to be distracted. Maybe this was a chance for Sylvie to start over. Maybe this version of her *would* date Ernie, like her sisters had wanted her to.

When they stepped apart and glanced around for patrons or Head Librarian Elaine, Sylvie said, "Did you know that I got my own apartment?"

He shook his head. "No way. That's amazing."

It *was* amazing that she had her own place. Most of the kids they'd gone to school with either still lived with their parents or had, like Julia, moved directly from their father's house into their married home. Sylvie appreciated that she was unusual. Cecelia was even more unusual, of course, with her fatherless baby and apartment with Emeline. Julia was the only one toeing the traditional line. Looking at Ernie, with the key in her pocket, Sylvie felt hopeful. She was back in her own life, on her own terms.

She said, "Would you like to see it? My apartment?"

Ernie tilted his head to the side, then said, "Sure."

They made a plan, and when he left the library, she walked to the empty desk in the back corner and picked up the phone. She knew William might be home at this hour, so she dialed her other sisters.

Emeline answered the phone. "Padavano sisters' residence."

Sylvie laughed. "Why are you answering the phone like that?"

"For some reason it amuses Izzy. Are you at the library?"

"I just needed to tell someone that Ernie came back. Today. He found me in the stacks."

"Oh, thank goodness!" All the sisters knew that Sylvie's boys had evaporated when Charlie died. They'd discussed, numerous times, why this might be the case. "Did he say why he'd stayed away?"

"Emmie, I invited him to my apartment tonight."

There was a silence. Then Emeline said, "Wo-o-o-o-w."

Sylvie could hear her sister smiling and Izzy burbling somewhere near the phone line.

"I'm going to be the only one of us who's still a virgin," Emeline said. "You have to call me after and tell me everything."

"Do you want me to ask him if he has a nice friend to set you up with?"

"Heavens, no." Emeline said this cheerfully. "I'm too busy with classes and work. But this is so exciting, Syl! Don't forget to shave your legs. Look at your body and try to see it like a stranger."

"He's not a stranger. I've known him my whole life."

"You know what I mean."

Sylvie looked down at her jeans and tennis shoes. She tried to remember which pair of underwear she had put on that morning.

Emeline said, "You told Julia he came by, right?" When Sylvie didn't respond right away, she said, "You have to call her, Sylvie. She'll be hurt if you don't tell her."

Sylvie sighed. By the complicated math that tied the sisters together, Emeline was correct. There were four of them, but inside the four there were two pairs: Sylvie and Julia, and Emeline and Cecelia.

"You're in your own place now," Emeline said. She meant: *It was excusable for you to be weird with Julia while you were homeless and sleeping next to me at night, but now you're settled, so you need to do better.*

"God damn it, Emeline," Sylvie said. She knew Emeline didn't like it when she swore. "Why do you have to be so wise?"

"I'm the only one without my own personal life, so I have time to watch you all."

"I have to go back to work," Sylvie said, and hung up. She told herself to call Julia whenever there was a lull at the library, but she didn't, and the next thing she knew, it was time to close up.

———

ERNIE ARRIVED AT EIGHT on the dot, and Sylvie suspected he had been walking around the block until the exact time arrived. He wasn't wearing his usual uniform of a white T-shirt and dark pants with pockets designed to hold tools. He had on a button-down shirt, and his hair was combed. He held a bottle of red wine.

"Do you like wine?" he asked.

Sylvie nodded, though she wondered if she would be able to drink. She was so nervous she was finding it hard to swallow. She looked around her tiny apartment and tried to see it through his eyes. Did it look worn and sad in the lamplight?

Ernie touched her cheek and said, "I can go if you want. We don't need to do this, whatever this is."

"Yes, we do," she said. This was her new life, *her life,* whether she was ready for it or not. "Kiss me. That will make me feel better."

Kissing did make her feel better. They had been kissing for years, after all. They never opened the wine. They didn't have to step apart after ninety seconds or think about patrons or Head Librarian Elaine. Sylvie put her fingers in Ernie's hair. When he unbuttoned her shirt and gently moved her bra aside to kiss her breast, Sylvie thought she might die from pleasure.

He rose up to check her face and said, "You like this?"

She said, "Oh yes."

More kisses, and then they were tugging clothes off each other. Sylvie couldn't believe that her body could feel this much. She couldn't believe anything could feel this good. With her eyes closed, she saw warm colors: reds and oranges. They spoke, but Sylvie barely paid attention to her own words. Her body was responding to his body, her mouth to his mouth.

Afterward, though, when they were lying in each other's arms, panic tickled the back of Sylvie's neck. She heard herself say, in a voice that sounded too loud to her own ears, "Just so you know, I'm not looking for a boyfriend."

"Okay." Ernie's stubble rubbed against her shoulder. "What are you looking for?"

Sylvie pictured William sitting on the bench and squeezed her eyes shut to make the image go away. "I'm not sure."

"So we can just have fun together," Ernie said, and rolled her over. *Can we do that?* Sylvie thought. This certainly *was* fun. She'd never been this close to a man's chest. It was so different from her own. Hairy. She ran her finger down the rivulet in the center of his abdomen. He ran his finger down the center of hers. He had to wiggle his finger slightly to fit between her breasts.

Kiss them, Sylvie thought, and somehow he knew, and did.

"I guess I shouldn't have expected anything normal," Ernie said finally, "from the girl who siren-called me to kiss her."

He stopped touching her for a moment, and Sylvie almost yelled at him to resume. Her body arched toward his. "I siren-called you?"

He smiled at her body's eagerness and pressed his cheek to the side of her breast. "A couple years ago," he said, into her skin. "I was in the library. To write a paper for Mrs. Brewster. You came out of a row of books and gave me a look. No one had ever looked at me like that. I looked back. Then I pushed my chair back and followed you."

"And we kissed." Sylvie liked this story; she liked what he was doing to her body; she liked the girl she used to be.

"Mmm-hmm. Even when my life was terrible," Ernie said, "I knew I could go to the library and kiss you." He pulled back a little, looked at her. "Although one time I went there and you were kissing another guy."

Sylvie blushed. "I didn't see you."

Ernie lowered back down with his sturdy body. She held on to his upper arms. "I was angry," he said. "At first. But I had no right to be, you know? We weren't dating. When you asked me to come over here, I thought of that other guy, though. I wondered—I wonder—if he was here first."

"You're the first." Sylvie suddenly felt sad, and her voice sounded sad too—was there some basic human truth that if you were naked, you couldn't control the tone of your voice? Like, her voice was naked too? She said, as evenly as she could, "There's been no one else."

But she was relieved when Ernie said he had to be at work early the next morning and needed to go home. "Maybe we can see each other tomorrow night?" he asked, and she made a noise that even she didn't recognize as a yes or a no.

Sylvie waved to him awkwardly while he let himself out of the studio. Alone in bed, she covered her face with her hands. She felt a jumble of emotions at the same time: embarrassed, pleased with how great sex was, uncomfortable about Ernie. He'd said they could just have fun, and she found herself repeating the word *fun* inside her head. She didn't think there was anything morally wrong with having sex with someone she liked but didn't love, but a new loneliness had arrived deep inside her. She was aware that if her mother heard what Sylvie had done, Rose would drag her to St. Procopius and leave her there on her knees. But Rose lived on a beach in Florida now, and that felt like a punishment too. Sylvie curled into a ball under her covers and pushed herself into sleep.

The phone rang next to Sylvie's mattress early the next morning, and she rolled over to answer it. She squinted at the sky through the window: pale light striped with pink clouds. Dawn.

"I hope it's not too early," Julia said. "Alice was up, and I know you wake up early."

Sylvie yawned. "Are you all right?"

"I think so." Julia paused. "But something strange happened."

Her sister's tone made Sylvie sit up, and she realized she was still naked. She'd never slept naked before. She thought, *In a minute, when it's my turn, I'll tell Julia the strange thing that happened to me.* She said, "What is it?"

"I called the history department to ask William a question yesterday. I don't remember what the question was. And the department secretary, when she found out I was his wife, said he hadn't shown up for over a week and that he'd missed teaching three classes. She said she'd overheard a professor saying that he might be put on probation. I think she told me because she felt bad for me."

Sylvie tugged the covers closer; her sister's words had given her goosebumps.

"I was mad when I hung up, because I thought she must be wrong. I thought she was confused and it was irresponsible to tell someone's wife such nonsense."

"That sounds wrong to me too," Sylvie said.

"Yes," Julia said thoughtfully. "But the woman was correct, and I just didn't know William as well as I thought I did."

Part of Sylvie's brain noted that her sister had used the past tense. She remembered the footnote from William's book: *This is terrible, I'm terrible.* She leaned forward, trying to understand what Julia's words meant.

"Last night I asked William how his day was, and he told me about a class he taught, what one of the students said, and who he ate lunch with in the faculty cafeteria. I told him that I'd called and spoken to the secretary in the department. I told him what she'd said, and he got very pale." Julia hesitated. "And then he left me."

"What do you mean, he left you?"

"He gave me a note and a check and walked out."

Something was terribly wrong. This knowledge broke over Sylvie like a wave. "I'll get dressed and be there as soon as I can," she said. "We'll figure this out, Julia. Don't worry."

"There's nothing to figure out." Her sister's voice was calm. "William has been lying for a week, at least. And he doesn't want to be married to me anymore."

William

AUGUST 1983

WILLIAM MISSED THE FIRST CLASS BY ACCIDENT. IT WAS LATE
summer, and there was a baking heat. He'd just completed the final
batch of player interviews Arash had asked him to conduct, and he'd
stayed in the Northwestern gym a little longer to watch practice. He
knew he was too busy with studying and teaching, not to mention a
baby at home, to spend time there, but he couldn't seem to help himself. It was summer training camp, and he knew only half of the players
on the team now; the juniors and seniors had been William's teammates, but the freshmen and most of the sophomores were strangers.

When the training camp began, Arash had asked William to help
by interviewing the incoming players about their prior injuries.
"You're the man to do it," he'd said. "The youngest kids aren't clear yet
about which staff member is important and which isn't. They look at
me and think I can bench them, so they won't tell me the truth."

"My job is to open them up," William said.

"Share your story, and they will."

And so William had found himself in a small office in the back of
the gymnasium with a clipboard containing the details of every player
on the roster. One by one, the students came in to see him. Over and
over again, William told the story of his knee. The details of the first
injury in high school, and then what had happened to him in the air
under the net in his final season.

When he was done talking, the player almost always said, "How's your knee now?"

The first few interviews, William said, "Fine."

But with repetition, he thought, *That's not true, and the whole point of me being in this stuffy room is to tell the truth, so they'll tell the truth.* After that, he said some variation of: *The knee still hurts, but I didn't rehab it properly. I can still feel the places where it broke.* Invariably, the players leaned away from him at this point, as if the damage might be contagious.

But telling the truth worked. The boys—the freshmen looked young to William—told him what had happened to their bodies, growing up. Only one or two were unscathed and fully intact—that's what they claimed, anyway. *Nope, zero injuries. No accidents. I've been lucky, I guess.* Everyone else had a story. Two of the boys had been in car crashes because of drunk drivers, leading to a broken shoulder in one case and a herniated disc in the other. A freckled kid from a famous basketball high school in Oklahoma had recurrent Sever's Disease: terrible heel pain from growing so tall so fast while playing a lot of basketball. The boys who had also played football had histories of concussions. A cocky freshman who introduced himself as "A-one from day one" had torn a hamstring. A sturdy six-and-a-half-footer with a prominent forehead told William that his shoulder frequently dislocated but he'd never told a coach or trainer, because he knew how to pop it back into place. A player from Los Angeles said, "Does it count if I was stabbed? Because I was stabbed in the lower back a couple years ago."

"That counts, yes," William said, trying to hide his shock. "It certainly does."

At the end of the final afternoon of interviews, William stumbled out of the warm room. He felt the impact of all the injuries he'd heard about. When those young men ran the court, they didn't look like college kids; their preternatural athleticism made them appear superhuman. The isolation scorers set screens for the lumbering bigs, who in their turn made plays from the post, shoveling passes to the open man. The scrimmages were punctuated with shouts of pleasure because of how good it felt to play at this level. Before the interviews, William never would have guessed at the pain inside the talented young players. He remembered seeing Sylvie's sorrow. He remembered some of his own anguish, with the shattering of his knee and the opening of the envelope from his father. Now William could see pain as if it were a dark cloud chasing each of the players across the court. They were outrunning it, for now. William had outrun it for a time too.

"They're telling me about all the bad things that have happened to their bodies," William said to Arash. "Not just what happened on the court."

Arash nodded. "I'm glad."

"You're glad?"

"They need to let that out to someone. We hardly ever ask each other how we've been hurt. You did better than I'd hoped for, William. Excellent work."

William was surprised. Arash rarely gave compliments. But as the words settled inside him, he knew that those boys wouldn't have shared as much, or at all, with someone else. William wasn't sure exactly why this was; his broken knee was part of it, but not the entire reason.

After leaving the gym, William walked the sunbaked paths of the campus, looking at strangers and wondering not *if* but *how* they had been hurt and how well they'd recovered. When he paid close attention, he could almost see their stories in their silence, like the wake that trails a boat. Abusive fathers, distant boyfriends, bad choices, debt, dreams of success of one kind or another that they feared would never be achieved. When William was close to the university library, he spotted the elderly history professor sitting on a bench. There was a droopiness to his posture that sent William over to him.

"Are you okay, Professor? Can I help you?"

The old man looked up at him, and William had a flash of Charlie peering up at him from his armchair. "You're the tall one."

"Yes, sir, William Waters. It's very hot out here."

"Yes, it is, William Waters. Yes, it is."

William positioned himself in front of the old man so that he cast him in shade. "Do you need help?"

"Oh, well, don't we all? Why don't you sit down beside me, William Waters? A little sunshine never did anyone any harm."

William sat down beside the old man. He watched students—

about half the normal number, because this was the summer semester—move groggily across the quad. He could hear the old man's ragged breathing. The professor smelled of lemons, or perhaps lemonade. William closed his eyes for a moment. The baby woke up a few times a night to be fed, and Julia and Alice would fall right back asleep afterward, but William was often unable to. He would listen to Julia breathe, more deeply than she used to, as if she needed more air now. The only way to make sure the baby was breathing was to lean over Alice's bassinet and put his ear to her mouth. Her inhales and exhales were almost silent, so William would get up and listen, to make sure she was breathing, several times each night.

When William opened his eyes again, the air was light purple, and the professor was gone. It was twilight. The trees in his line of sight were darkening to silhouettes. William blinked several times, trying to make sense of what he was seeing. His body was stiff. His knee throbbed. He looked at his watch and took in such a sudden breath that he coughed. His Scientific Revolution class had ended forty-five minutes earlier. He was the teaching assistant. There was no one else in charge; for all intents and purposes, he was the professor. William scanned the landscape, looking for a solution. The outlandishness of this predicament would require an equally strange fix. Perhaps a magical tree that could turn back time to when William had sat down on this bench.

In all of his education, William only had one teacher not show up for class, and it turned out that the man had been locked out of his house during a torrential rainstorm, with no access to keys or a phone. Other than that occasion, every teacher had walked into the classroom right on time, if not early. In cases of illness or a family emergency, enough notice was given for a substitute to be called. A college classroom with a mysteriously absent professor was unthinkable. William pictured his students, first bored, then confused. They would have told the department secretary on their way out of the building that he'd never showed up.

William sat very still on the bench. The baking heat of day was gone. The sunlight was gone. He thought of the players' torn ligaments and concussions and painful heels and dislocated joints, and he felt immovable. He had made a terrible mistake, one he couldn't erase. When darkness cloaked him, when he had to hold his hand in front of his face to see his fingers, he walked home. He was relieved that Julia greeted him normally; this told him that the department hadn't called looking for him. He thought that maybe he should tell her what had happened. Julia was great at solving problems, and this would probably seem like a softball to her. He could hear her saying that he simply had to call the department first thing in the morning and apologize, and all would be fine. But, he thought, his wife was no longer interested in answering his questions. She wouldn't understand why he'd been at the gym either—Julia had no idea he'd embedded himself in the basketball team. He'd be embarrassed to tell her that he'd fallen asleep on a bench in the middle of the afternoon—what kind of a man did that? He wondered what the old professor had thought of him slumbering beside him.

"Are you all right?" Julia asked him, near bedtime.

"Yes," he said. "Of course."

His sleep was even more disrupted than usual that night. Alice cried out, and his heart jackhammered in his chest. *What do I do?* he thought, so many times that he forgot what problem he was swimming away from in the darkness. He was just left with the question and the visceral sensation of panic. When William woke up early the next morning, he opened their front door to pick the two daily newspapers—one local and one national—up off the mat. *It's a new day,* he thought. He decided that he *would* tell Julia about missing the class. He was exhausted and didn't know what else to do. He imagined his wife before he'd disappointed her, before the baby was born. That version of Julia would wrap her arms around his waist and issue clear instructions. His head aching, he thought that maybe the old Julia would come when he summoned her, sensing from the shadows of the past that William had no other hope.

He bent down to pick up the Evanston newspaper and scanned the front page. He was about to go into the kitchen when he saw, in the lower-left corner of the page, a small photograph of the elderly professor. The text below the photo said that the man had died of a massive stroke around dinnertime the night before, in his home. The professor had won a prestigious history prize earlier in his career and was widely known for a best-selling book about World War II. *He's dead?* William thought, and the word *dead* dropped to the bottom of him like an anchor.

With this news, and the weight of that word, the silence inside William expanded until it filled him completely. He'd had to fight for coherence, to make sense of his life, for a while now, but the fight was no longer possible. He knew this, holding the paper in his hand.

William took the newspaper with him when he left the house. For five days, he left the apartment at the usual time, with his packed lunch and his academic books and papers. He ignored the library and only walked in and out of the gym. He watched training camp for a few moments, from the shadows in the back. He didn't let anyone see him. He looped the quad and the bench where he and the professor had sat. He walked past strangers and cataloged their pain. He stayed far away from the history building, but he noted, as if to document his own disappearance, the time as he missed his second class, and then his third. He missed a meeting with his adviser too, and William imagined the deepening confusion in the professor's eyes while he waited at the appointed time. The bow-tied professor loved history so deeply, he could only feel bewildered by William's lack of commitment.

The part of William that knew history—the dates, the statesmen, the critical moments when the future hung in the balance—had become inaccessible to him. The idea that he could stand in front of a full classroom and hold forth for an hour was unthinkable. When he bought a sandwich from a food cart, his voice was so soft that he had to repeat himself three times in order to be heard. William closed his eyes and saw his notes on the players' injuries. The rough drawing of an elbow or a knee. He'd been so surprised when the baby-faced freshman told him about being stabbed that William had drawn a picture of a knife.

He went home each evening at the normal time. Julia looked at him with mild curiosity but didn't ask any questions. William knew, in his bones, that she wouldn't want to hear about his experience these last few days. He was nothing like the husband Julia had planned into existence when they'd married; he had the urge to apologize to her for this fact but knew that the apology would annoy her. He pressed a bag of frozen peas against his knee; walking all day had made the joint ache. He felt faintly relieved that the department hadn't called his wife yet. He knew these were the last days of his marriage—he couldn't continue like this or continue to be married. When Julia offered him her cheek, he kissed it; he tried to memorize the sensation of her weight in the bed beside him. William was pretending to be a husband, but there wasn't much left of him, and the clock would run out. And it did. On the seventh night, with his fork in a chicken breast, after telling flat lies about his day, he learned that Julia knew the truth. Some of the truth, anyway.

"I don't understand." His wife stared at him. "Why would you miss your classes? Where were you?"

William was letting everyone down: his wife, his adviser, his students. William remembered the younger version of himself being drawn to history because it taught cause and effect. If a person does this, then that happens. But the cause-and-effect levers inside William had malfunctioned; he was a defective machine.

"I wish I could have been better for you," he said.

"I literally don't understand," Julia said, and mixed in with her confusion now was anger. She hated surprises, hated to have her feet swept out from under her.

"I know." He couldn't explain; he couldn't build a case. William was a fake, a liar, a pretender. He pushed his chair away from the table, walked into the bedroom, and pulled down an over-the-shoulder bag from the closet shelf. He considered putting his manuscript inside but didn't. He grabbed a sweater, with the thought, *I might be cold.* He opened his dresser drawer and took the old wallet from the back. He removed the check from the wallet and scrawled *For Julia Waters* on the blank side. He wrote a few sentences on a piece of paper from the pad Julia kept bedside. He was careful not to think about what he was writing and careful not to reread the text once it was finished.

He walked into the living room and handed the check to his wife.

"What is this?" she said, her eyes on her husband's face. "What's happening?" When William didn't respond, Julia looked down at the check. "Ten thousand dollars. From your father? Your father gave this to you?"

"You should deposit it," he said. "It's for you." Then he handed her the folded piece of paper and walked out of the apartment. Later, it would occur to him that he didn't look at Alice in her bassinet, didn't think of her before walking out. Julia called after him, but he kept a steady pace down the stairs.

Time worked strangely for him that night. He started walking and eventually found himself on the shore of Lake Michigan. The lake had always been a presence—spotted from between trees or from the windows of some campus buildings—but William never went there deliberately. The lake reminded him of Boston, of the choppy ocean that sat alongside his home city. The fact that this enormous expanse of water was a lake, even though it had no end in sight, felt like a mistake. Surely this flat, seemingly endless basin deserved a different designation than *lake,* the kind of thing that you could jog around in thirty minutes.

The lakeside path suited William tonight, though. He was able to walk in a line, and when he was too tired to go on, there were benches. He could rest his eyes on the black water. He slept sitting up a few times, buffeted by the soft summer wind. Drunk or homeless men were sprawled across some of the benches, and William spotted dark forms curled beneath a few trees. He alternated between walking and sitting in this night world. On his final bench, before the sun began to climb back into the sky, he wondered how far he could walk into the lake before he would be entirely covered by water.

With the arrival of the new day, William's brain restarted, as if fueled by the light. But the engine was made of remnant parts. He didn't know what to do. He would never return to the apartment he'd called home. Julia and Alice deserved the best possible husband and father, and they were better off without him. He couldn't go to Northwestern—he'd been pretending to be a graduate student all along, and surely they had figured that out. He shouldn't have been accepted into the program in the first place; he imagined that they'd already offered his teaching-assistant position to someone else. It felt meaningful too that his own pretend teaching career and his life with Julia had expired with the ancient professor. William had met Julia in the old man's class, before the professor's skin became translucent and his eyes watery. The true teacher had died and, like a wave crashing against the beach, wiped away all of William's measly efforts at a life. The university gym was harder for him to attach his attention to. Thinking about Arash and the sinking of balls through nets felt like putting his hand on a hot stove. Not painful, exactly, but searing, and designed to keep William and his thoughts away.

He had the sensation that he had cut himself out of his own life, the way a child cuts a figure out of a blank piece of paper. The sun glared from a cloudless sky, while William wandered through unfamiliar sections of Chicago. A part of his brain kept working on the same question: What would the cool lake water feel like, rising over his skin? William crossed the river and canals, passed thumping factories, traversed neighborhoods that would have frightened him in the past because everyone was poor and outside in the summer heat. No one said anything to him that day, though, not even about his height. He was either disappearing or he looked too dangerous—too other—to engage. Later, he would think, *No one wants to be near someone who's that close to gone.*

In the dark center of the night, he saw Charlie standing in a doorway. His father-in-law met William's eyes and offered his warmest smile. William was able to see the pain in Charlie, the same way he'd seen it in the college basketball players, the way he'd seen it in Sylvie on the bench. His overtaxed liver, his unsatisfying work, his broken heart: William saw it all and said, "I'm glad to see you," because he was. But by the time the words left his mouth, Charlie had disappeared. William stared at the empty space his father-in-law had occupied, and then continued to walk.

Julia

AUGUST 1983

WILLIAM LEFT THE APARTMENT JUST BEFORE EIGHT AT NIGHT. The dinner dishes were still on the table. Julia looked at the check he'd handed her. She studied her father-in-law's signature. She'd never seen the man's handwriting before; his name looked scratched onto the paper, as if it had been dashed off as quickly as possible. Ten thousand dollars seemed like an impossible amount of money to be lodged behind this handwriting. Her father-in-law had apparently sent the check to her husband sixteen months earlier, and William had never told her.

Julia found it hard to wrap her mind around this fact. The previous fall, when she was pregnant and William had asked to be excused from his teaching position, her financial anxiety would have been lifted entirely if she'd known they had this extra money. Instead, the worry about how much she could afford to give Cecelia and spend on food plus her father's death had braided themselves together inside her, and she'd had a constant headache.

Julia washed the dinner dishes and wiped the kitchen countertops. She cleaned her face and put on her nightgown. Alice was asleep in the bassinet, her face peaceful. Julia watched her perfect features for a few minutes—her tiny nose, her pink cheeks, her long eyelashes—and then sat down on the couch. She'd finished her normal evening routine, even if this wasn't a normal evening. For the first time, Julia considered the sheet of folded paper William had handed her. When he'd walked out, she'd put it down, still folded, on the coffee table. She was aware of a prickly sensation in her chest, aware that she was scared to unfold the sheet. *Don't be silly,* she thought, and with feigned confidence smoothed the page flat on her lap. William's handwriting was different from his father's: His letters were round and easy to read. His handwriting was as familiar to Julia as her own.

> *I'm no good for you and Alice. If I stayed, I'd ruin your life.*
> *You deserve to be free, Julia. Our marriage is over. I'm sorry*
> *for everything.*

She read the sentences on a loop, as if they were a book she restarted as soon as she reached the last page. After a while she stopped and lay down on the couch. She wished Sylvie was beside her on the cushions, to hold her. Julia wasn't ready to talk, but she was alone in a way that felt dangerous. She got up and double-checked the lock on the front door. She dug out the old toolbox from under the kitchen sink and removed the rusty hammer they'd used to hang pictures when they moved. She placed the hammer next to the letter and check on the small coffee table, in case she needed protection, and lay back down. She told herself to sleep but found she couldn't close her eyes. Any small noise and she pushed herself upright, wondering if it was William's key in the lock. Had he ever been out past ten? No. It was now midnight. After midnight, the bars would be closed. The campus buildings were shut. Alice woke up, and Julia fed her back to sleep. She was still on the couch at three in the morning. She thought, *Is this actually happening?*

Julia hadn't lost her clarity from Alice's birth. When she paid attention, she could see everything. But she'd paid as little attention to William as possible since Alice was born. She'd kept her gaze averted, partly because Julia had come to know what, apparently, her husband had also figured out: They didn't work together. Or perhaps they *had* worked, while Julia was intent on fixing the world and people around her. She had pushed William into the career of teaching, pushed him into graduate school, even pushed him to marry her. But Julia had stopped pushing when Alice was born. And when she stopped pushing, something in their marriage sputtered to a stop. She'd continued to play her role as a wife, and he'd continued to play his role as a husband, but they'd done no more than go through the motions for a while now.

"I was going to stay with you, though," she said to the empty room. "I'd made a commitment."

It hurt her that William didn't feel the same way. But still, she thought, it was brave of him to leave. He'd always struggled with decisions, and this had to be the boldest move of his life. Julia thought she'd masked her new sense of independence after Alice's birth, but he saw through her. He saw that she didn't need him. He noticed that she'd taken her hands off his back and that he was no longer being moved forward in a direction she'd chosen.

Julia called Sylvie when the sun rose, then showered and put some care into her appearance. She would set the stage for her new life by making sure the woman in the mirror looked presentable. She'd always believed in dressing for the part she wanted, and she didn't want to appear like a disheveled victim. Julia remembered her childhood self twirling into a room, singing, *Ta-da!* She took her time in front of the mirror and put on some lipstick and a little eyeliner. She wove her hair into a neat updo. When Julia was fully dressed, she left a professional-sounding message on Professor Cooper's machine, explaining that she was available to work and that she was sure she could bring a lot of value to his company. *I can do this,* she thought, when she hung up. *I can do anything.*

But this confidence twanged, like a rubber band, into doubt. Did she have a good sense of what she was capable of? Julia had known that she wouldn't leave William, even when he'd disappointed and irritated her. She had married him for better and for worse. But she'd also known that if their marriage were ever to end, it would be her decision, not his. William had needed her; she hadn't needed him. How was it possible that she was the one being left behind?

Julia rubbed her forehead and forced her thoughts elsewhere. As if answering an essay question for school, she tried to figure out who

William would be without her pushing him. *He'd probably like to be a high school basketball coach,* she thought, and felt pleased with herself for being so mature and generous about the man who had lied to her and walked out on his family. Equally true was the fact that she never would have married a high school basketball coach. Men like that lived in small houses in Pilsen like the one she'd grown up in. They wore sweatshirts on workdays and barely made enough money to pay the rent.

Julia had wanted to be married to a college professor. She'd had secret aspirations for William: that he would be a college president in his later career or perhaps even run for public office. These aspirations had disappeared after she'd read his book, though. She realized then that there was something wrong deep inside him—after all, what kind of man would type the words *I'm terrible* on a page?—which meant he would never be successful. A college professor still seemed possible, though, and even inevitable. Julia had sat in on one of William's classes during the spring, and at the end he'd said, nicely, that the sight of her grinning like a Cheshire cat at the back of the room had made it hard for him to concentrate. But William had been remarkable, breaking up the material with small jokes, fostering an interesting discussion on the ethics of war even though it was a lecture course. For the first time, he'd seemed to utilize his size off the basketball court. His height gave his presence significance. He was meant to stand out, so it made sense for him to be alone in the front of the room. *Look at me,* his body said, and the students complied.

Julia would have stayed married to the man at the front of the classroom. But the man who had just walked out, the one who had hidden ten thousand dollars and who knew what else, was a stranger. She hadn't known, hadn't wanted to know, who William was for a long time. When her husband came home after being out for the day, she never asked him where—or *who*—he'd been.

Julia needed to see Sylvie, because nothing in her life seemed real unless her sister shared it. But Sylvie showed up pale and panicked, as if the building were on fire. Julia was unsettled by her sister's intensity from the moment she opened the door. It felt like her sister had arrived with a problem, instead of showing up to help Julia with hers.

Sylvie studied the evidence on the coffee table: the five sentences, the check. She said, "Before he left, did William explain why he'd missed his classes? What else did he say to you?"

"He didn't say anything."

"Nothing at all?"

"It's in the note, Sylvie. We haven't gotten along since the baby was born. Since I got pregnant, really." The reasons she and William didn't work were like a series of dead-end streets; Julia walked quickly down one and then doubled back to try another. "We're like a clock that doesn't keep time anymore," she said. "He's not ambitious. He never knew what to do, so he wanted me to give him instructions for everything, big and small. I'm a fast walker, and he's slow. I thought I needed a husband, because that's what we were told as little girls, right? Or maybe not told but shown. It didn't occur to me that I might be better on my own. I was carrying him, Sylvie."

Sylvie listened, bent slightly at the waist as if leaning forward helped her understand.

With her sister in front of her, Julia felt less clear than she had when she was alone. She could feel the effects of staying up all night; her eyes felt gravelly, and her hands shook slightly. She put her hands in her lap so Sylvie wouldn't see. She said, "Alice and I will be fine. I don't *need* a husband. William"—she hesitated for a split second—"was right to leave."

"Do you think he's okay?"

Julia blinked at her, confused. "Do I think William's okay?"

"Yes." Sylvie looked at the pieces of paper and the hammer on the coffee table. "I think for him to do this—to miss classes, write that note—something must be really wrong."

Julia rested her eyes on the note too so she and Sylvie were looking at the same thing. "I don't think the end of a marriage is supposed to feel good for anyone," she said. "Why are you worried about William?" She heard the tremor in her voice. "You should be worried about me."

"I am, of course!" Sylvie said. "I feel terribly for you. But, Julia"—she hesitated—"it's just that if there's an emergency, we should do something."

"My husband left me," Julia said. "I don't think that qualifies as an emergency." She felt far away from Sylvie, even though the sisters shared the same couch. A strange thought occurred to Julia. Could it be that Sylvie somehow *knew* the man who had lied to Julia, handed her a check, and then left? Had her sister seen a version of William that was a stranger to his own wife? She shook her head; that didn't make sense. Julia was tired and not thinking clearly.

"We're the only ones who know what happened, though," Sylvie said. "I think maybe we should call Kent, just so he knows too."

Julia considered this. "William's probably with Kent. If you want to, fine. His number is in the book by the phone."

Sylvie nodded, her lips pressed together. "Do you want to make the call?"

"No," Julia said. "This is your idea."

Sylvie stood up and moved to the armchair. The small table beside the chair held the phone and address book. She stared at the phone while she pressed the numbers.

Julia could tell her sister felt uncomfortable, and she thought, *Good. You should feel uncomfortable. You should be sitting here hugging me. Why are you worrying about William?*

"Hi, Kent? This is Sylvie, William's sister-in-law. We have a situation here, and I wanted to let you know." She was quiet for a moment, then said, "William has been gone since last night. He wrote a note to Julia." Sylvie cleared her throat. "Saying he was leaving their marriage. He missed work too. . . . No, no one has heard from him. He didn't say where he was going. You haven't heard from him?" There was a pause. "Yes, of course, thanks." And then Sylvie put the phone down.

"He's going to drive down here," she said to Julia. "He's concerned."

A hot anger flashed through Julia. "He's not coming inside this apartment," she said. "If you want to meet Kent outside and talk to him, fine. Forgive me if I'm not *concerned* about the man who just walked out on me, Sylvie. And you shouldn't be, either. God!" She stood up. "I'm going to take a nap. I was up all night."

Sylvie looked like she was going to speak and then changed her mind. She nodded.

Julia went into her room. She lay on her bed and watched Alice in her bassinet. Julia hated that Kent now knew that William had left her. He would think Julia was a victim, even though she wasn't. He wouldn't know she was wearing a nice dress. He wouldn't know she'd done her hair and put on lipstick and called Professor Cooper. He might think she hadn't been a good-enough wife. She was in the middle of these thoughts when she fell asleep.

When Julia woke, thick yellow light was pushing through the blinds, which meant it was late afternoon. She realized she must have slept for hours. Alice was awake in her bassinet, playing with her feet. Julia scooped her up and kissed her soft cheek. "You are literally the best baby in the world," she said.

The apartment was quiet when she opened the bedroom door. "Sylvie?"

There was no response, so Julia carried the baby into the living room. She noticed a piece of paper on the coffee table and picked it up.

> J—Kent has organized a search party. I have your extra key
> from the spaghetti pot, so I can let myself back in. I'll be
> back soon, I promise.

A search party? The phrase felt needlessly dramatic. Julia shook her head, annoyed and still groggy from sleep. Why had Sylvie gone with Kent? Julia didn't understand what her sister was thinking, and this had never been the case before. Even when Sylvie had skipped high school classes or kissed boys in the library, Julia understood her reasoning, even if she disagreed with it. But this morning Julia had told Sylvie that her husband left her, and her sister had left her too.

"Why would you do that?" she said into the silence.

Julia fed Alice and then laid her on a blanket in the middle of the living room floor. She walked into the kitchen, aware that she was hungry. She made a sandwich from what was in the refrigerator—tuna salad, lettuce, tomato—and put it on a plate. Julia hadn't eaten since the day before, and she devoured every bite of the sandwich, licking her fingers at the end. When the sandwich was finished, Julia was still hungry, so she ate an apple all the way down to the core. She drank one of William's beers that was in the refrigerator. Finally sated, she changed Alice's diaper and then read her *Goodnight Moon*. "You're such a good girl," she cooed at the baby. Alice stared up at Julia. Her expression was mild, optimistic. She was four months old and had begun to shine love at her mother like a sun. When Julia walked into a room, Alice's entire body would shake with excitement. Now she reached up to pat her mother's chin, which was something she did for comfort while she nursed.

There were knocks on the door at six o'clock. Julia looked through the keyhole and then opened the door for Cecelia and Emeline, with Izzy in a stroller. Both women hesitated just inside the apartment, sizing her up. "You poor thing," Emeline said. "You must be so upset."

"It's been a strange day," Julia said.

"Sylvie didn't say much on the phone," Cecelia said. "She was in a hurry. From what I could understand, she seems very worried, far more worried than makes sense to me. I'm sure William is fine. Emmie and I are more concerned about you."

Tears came to Julia's eyes. "I appreciate that," she said.

"I didn't know things were so bad between you two. Was it because of how he was with the baby?" It was as if this news had turned back Emeline's biological clock—with her eyes wide in her face, she looked like a child. "How could William leave you?"

Cecelia was studying William's note, which Julia had handed to her. "I don't understand any of this: him leaving you; Sylvie and Kent searching for him as if he's lost. None of this makes sense."

"I know," Julia said. "This is unexpected, all of it, but it's not . . ." She shook her head. "I can make it work. I'm still young, right? I have a college degree, thanks to Mom, and it's the eighties, not the fifties. Alice and I will make a fresh start."

"Bah," the ten-month-old in the stroller said, and waved at her aunt. Julia crouched down and pressed her nose to Izzy's, which made the baby chortle with pleasure. Across the room, Alice kicked her feet on her blanket, excited to see her cousin.

Julia felt better with the twins there. Sylvie had made her feel like there was a problem in addition to her husband walking out, and that had been disorienting. But Julia had her feet under her now; she knew that William had ended their marriage at the start of the night, and almost twenty-four hours later, Julia had caught up. They were both done. She believed she would be okay on her own, but to convince herself, she tried to imagine a possible day in a possible future. The future Julia was wearing a gorgeous business suit and sitting behind a modern black desk. Her hair was contained in a masterful bun. Her competence was on full display. *I'll be better than okay,* she thought, and felt her face light up. *I'll be amazing.*

She saw that Cecelia and Emeline looked concerned. They didn't trust her optimism in this moment and thought it might be a warning sign of an impending collapse. Julia turned her attention to the baby blanket in the middle of the room. Cecelia had placed her daughter beside Alice, and Izzy was handing the younger baby a toy. Julia remembered the earlier version of herself that had gotten pregnant in order to place her baby beside this one on a sun-soaked blanket. The two babies were meant to be the magnet that drew all the grown-ups together, but in reality they had done the opposite. The babies had arrived, and the adults had scattered. Izzy had started something, the same way Julia had started something with her own birth, but what trajectory had Izzy hurled everyone on? Charlie died, Rose left, and now so had William. Julia didn't blame the baby, of course; she felt a shot of love while gazing at the dark-haired, dark-eyed child.

"Have you called Mama?" Cecelia asked.

Julia looked at her sister, who had a streak of bright-yellow paint on her right hand, and knew that because Rose had abandoned Cecelia, she would always think of their mother first. "Not yet," Julia said. "There's nothing she could do but worry. I wish Sylvie was here, though. She's acting so oddly."

"What can we do to help?" Emeline was standing by the window. She was looking for Sylvie, or perhaps William, the same way, as a tiny child, she'd stared out the front window after school was dismissed, watching for her older sisters. "We could make you dinner? Do you want us to sleep here?"

Julia shook her head. She appreciated that Emeline and Cecelia had shown up for her, the same way she'd shown up for Rose in her garden when their mother's heart was broken. But Julia's sisters couldn't take the next steps with her, even though pulling herself together had always meant pulling her sisters to her side. Now being strong meant standing on her own, with her child in her arms. This was a lonely position, even though it felt like the correct one. She was a grown-up, and a mother.

"If Mama *was* here," Cecelia said, "she'd drag us all to St. Procopius to pray."

This statement rang true. The four girls had gone to church and said rosaries for Rose, not God. There had been no way to know this while they all lived on 18th Place, because the church and their mother were so intertwined. Catholicism succeeded because it kept its parishioners feeling guilty and therefore in the pews every Sunday, but none of the Padavano girls had stepped inside St. Procopius since their mother moved away. The girls' only genuine beliefs, growing up, had been in fictional characters and their games and one another.

When Julia was in middle school, a girl had accused her and her sisters of being a coven of witches. Julia hadn't known what a coven was and had to look the word up. The definition had delighted her, and she'd hoped the girl was correct. The four Padavano sisters dressed up as witches for Halloween that year, and Charlie gleefully quoted *Macbeth* at them. Julia, in the height of her girlhood, with a pointed black hat on her head, knew that they *were* a coven of witches, at least to some extent. She, Sylvie, Cecelia, and Emeline had a shared power, a fierceness.

"You should go," Julia said. "I'm fine, and the little girls need to go to bed."

The twins kissed Julia's cheek in turn when they left. They pressed their bodies to hers, briefly, before walking through the door.

Julia returned to the couch. It had been a strange day, and she felt strange. William's departure had been sudden, but it had struck like lightning in the middle of a storm. Unexpected yet natural. In the bright flash of electricity, Julia had been able to see clearly, for the first time, the similarities between her husband and her father. She'd wanted to marry someone the opposite of Charlie. She'd chosen William because she thought he was that: serious, mature, sober, attentive. Charlie was a dreamer—Rose used to say that he walked among the clouds. He was also regularly demoted at work and spent money that Rose needed to pay bills at the bars in their neighborhood.

William did not walk among the clouds, but, like her father, he lacked ambition and reliability. Charlie had been a loving father but a deadweight as a husband. He'd given Rose nothing she could use. Perhaps Charlie had recognized that facet of himself in William. Julia remembered the disappointment on her father's face when she'd told him about this marriage. Her father had known so much, she thought. She'd never given Charlie enough credit when he was alive, but she knew enough to understand that if her father were here now, he would wink at her and say, *Let's see what my rocket can do.*

Sylvie

SYLVIE WALKED THE CITY WITH KENT AND THE OTHER BASKET-ball players, even though she slowed them down with her normal-length legs and normal-person fitness. They were all over six feet tall, most of them six foot five, at least. They strode ahead of her, a visually intimidating pack that cleared the sidewalk. More than once, Sylvie saw people stop to watch them. It wasn't just their height that was arresting but the purpose with which the men walked. They moved as the team they'd been in college—matching strides, taking directional cues from one another. Several of the guys addressed Kent as *Captain,* which amused Sylvie at first, since Kent hadn't been their captain for two years and they were no longer on a team together. But they referred to William as their teammate too, and Sylvie began to wonder if being on a team was a different kind of commitment than she had previously understood. Neither she nor her sisters had ever played sports—it hadn't been an option for girls in their neighborhood—so she had no way of knowing. She admired the unspoken understanding between these men: Kent made the decisions, and the others followed his orders in the most efficient way possible. When the group crossed roads, one of them would wave a long arm, as if greeting the waiting cars, while they continued to move at a pace only they could keep.

Sylvie kept thinking she would break away, turn a corner, and walk back to Julia. She hadn't meant to leave with Kent. She'd spoken to him in front of the apartment building, the sun beating down on them. She'd planned to hand over the news like a bowl of bad apples and then back away. But she hadn't been able to do it; she'd followed him to meet his and William's friends, driven by a strong feeling that if she didn't help, William wouldn't be found. This made no sense, of course, but from the moment Julia called her, Sylvie had been scared—scared as if her body knew something about this situation that her brain did not.

She remembered feeling William's emotions on the bench that night and how tired he'd been. She remembered how little light he'd contained. She remembered the questions in his manuscript. Sylvie had talked to William about missing her father and only later remembered that he had a father and mother who wanted nothing to do with him. She'd showed Kent the note and the check because she wanted him to make up his own mind. Maybe Sylvie was wrong. If Kent thought the situation was as clear-cut as Julia did—simply a man leaving his wife—Sylvie would force herself to calm down. She would climb into the bed beside Julia and lie there until her sister woke from her nap. Sylvie would make Julia a comforting dinner, and she would stay with her sister until she was back on her feet. For weeks, or months if necessary. Until the ache had disappeared from living in that apartment without her husband.

"William may have wanted out of his marriage," Kent said, after studying what she'd handed him. "I can buy him not telling me that. But I don't like the tone of the note, and William would never skip his classes. Something is wrong. We need to find him."

Sylvie knew that her concern for William had confused Julia. She knew it wasn't right that she had left her sister alone in that apartment. But with Kent's words, Sylvie's fear became so loud that she knew she had to do something to quiet it or she would be no good to anyone. Before leaving with Kent, Sylvie had gone back into the apartment to return the note and check, and she'd called Emeline and Cecelia. She asked them to keep Julia company and then hung up before the twins could ask any questions.

Sylvie had met Kent only once before, at the wedding—where he had been jovial and charming and several girls in the neighborhood had declared him dreamy. Now he looked weary and stressed and like the kind of person who had no time to waste. Sylvie jogged down the now-dark Chicago streets, trying to keep up. The young men glanced over their shoulders and slowed down for her. They had covered Northwestern's vast campus, spoken to the security guard for the history building, checked out the gym. They waited on the sidewalk while the tallest guy stuck his head into every bar and restaurant Northwestern students and faculty frequented and scanned the room for William. They wove through the neighborhoods that bordered the university, sweeping up one street and down the next. This took a long time, a few hours at least, though Sylvie couldn't be sure because she wasn't wearing a watch. Now they were headed to collect a man named Arash, whom all of the players seemed to know.

Sylvie watched Kent become more drawn. He didn't joke with the other guys, who occasionally laughed because, even though this was a grim situation, they were happy to be together. Most of the players assumed they would find William drunk somewhere, unhappy about his failed marriage. *He must be on a bender* was a comment Sylvie heard more than once. This seemed unlikely to Sylvie, since William drank very little, but she hoped they were correct. In the meantime, Kent seemed to be aging as the minutes ticked by, as if he were living out a long life with his missing friend, compressed into a single night. The only person he spoke to regularly was a player named Gus, who seemed to have endless energy. The young man jogged ahead of the group and then circled back and talked into Kent's ear.

A player named Washington said to Sylvie, "You look worn out. You okay?"

Sylvie peered up at him in the shadows. She had been near tears as she ran after the men. She was wearing sneakers that she'd thought were comfortable but had given her a blister on her heel. She was worried about William. She was worried about her sister. She was worried, in a detached way, about herself. Sylvie was also moved by the players' commitment to help her brother-in-law, and in the face of it, she realized that she was committed too. She had to see this search out until the end, whatever the end turned out to be.

"I'm okay," she said, and stopped paying attention to the discomfort in her body. She just kept moving forward, as fast as she could. In the players' wake, Sylvie was aware of how different her physical life was from theirs. The players were powerful, unassailable. In Sylvie's normal life, she avoided quiet streets after dark and crossed the road if she sensed any aggression or worrisome behavior from a man. She ignored catcalls, kept her head down, turned the nearest corner. In the library, even, she knew when to slump her shoulders, minimize her hips when she walked, and cross her arms over her chest. She, and all women, were prey. But in the company of these men, Sylvie dropped her usual worry over her physical safety. Their proximity meant that strangers would leave her alone.

Each block they covered looked like a puzzle, and Sylvie turned her head from side to side, trying to spot the missing piece: William. When they reached a far corner of Northwestern's campus, they met Arash—an average-sized man with heavy eyebrows and an intense stare. He reported that he'd asked all over the university and that it had been several days since anyone had seen William. "Arash is our physio," Washington told Sylvie, and she nodded. She no longer questioned Washington's use of the present tense. These men were still on a basketball team together in their hearts, and they had a physio and probably a coach or two. Her own team was her sisters, and she was apart from them. She knew Julia must be awake now and upset at her. Sylvie felt like part of herself *was* in that apartment, on the couch beside her older sister.

Standing behind Arash were a cluster of young men, who turned out to be seniors on the current Northwestern basketball team. They had been William's teammates too, and Kent had been their captain, and so they'd showed up. Sylvie's eyes smarted, and when she reached up to touch her face, she realized she was crying. Relieved that no one noticed, she stepped deeper into the shadows.

"We should split up," Kent said. "William's been missing for over twenty-four hours. We need to cover more ground." He broke the group in two and sent Arash and the young players in one direction. Everyone else, including Sylvie, would travel deeper into the city with him.

There were now upward of twenty current and former basketball players jogging through Chicago, scouting parks famous for their basketball courts, checking the identity of people sleeping on benches. At some point, the sun began to rise—an orange orb filled the spaces between buildings. Sylvie tried to remember the last time she had seen a new day begin. She tried to remember what day of the week it was and what time she was due at the library. She asked Washington, who was wearing a watch, what time it was, but she was so tired that the numbers he said didn't make sense. She wouldn't show up at work, she knew that. She also knew that Head Librarian Elaine wouldn't be happy; she had a few favorite themes, and one of them was accountability.

At one point, Kent dropped back to walk next to Sylvie. He spoke like a man conserving energy, and she had to lean closer to hear him. "William's gone dark before. He has this in him. He stopped talking and eating for a week once when he thought Julia was mad at him and the coach had benched him. He bounced back pretty quickly, but I think I'm the only one he let see him like that."

Sylvie's entire face ached with something like relief. It was nice to know that she wasn't crazy. She almost told Kent about the footnotes in William's book, but instead she said, "We've been up all night." Sylvie rubbed her eyes, because that was a stupid thing to say. She had a memory of Ernie's hands on her waist and remembered how it had felt to lie naked beside him without any fear or knowledge that her world was about to tip off its axis. It felt like a memory from another life. It occurred to Sylvie that she might have disappointed Ernie, the same way she was about to disappoint Head Librarian Elaine. He had probably waited at her apartment door last night, confused that she never came home. *I'm not anywhere I'm supposed to be,* she thought. *And I have no idea where I am.*

They visited three midtown libraries in a row and went inside to check the carrels. Midmorning, Sylvie, Washington, Gus, and Kent entered a deli to buy everyone sodas. Sylvie noticed that, under the store lighting, the young men's faces looked cracked with fatigue. She could only imagine what she looked like and was careful to avoid any reflective surfaces. It had been hours since anyone had mentioned benders or bars. It felt now like if they found William, it would be terrible, and if they didn't find him, it would be the same.

When they exited the deli, they paused on the sidewalk, the icy sodas sweating in their hands. The rest of the players were halfway down the block, waiting. Sylvie noted the pause; she suspected Kent didn't know where to go next. The air had a new heaviness; the sun was climbing into the sky, bringing with it a dense heat. A loud noise approached them from the side—the keening of a siren. Sylvie turned toward the sound, but it immediately split, or doubled. An ambulance thundered past them as cars pulled over to get out of the way, and two police cars, sirens shrieking, turned a corner and followed the ambulance. The air pounded with noise. Kent, Sylvie, Washington, and Gus looked at one another, a shared fear on their faces. Sylvie knew they were having the same thought: *William?*

"Gus," Kent said, "run!"

Gus was gone, down the block before Sylvie could understand what was happening. He was unbelievably fast. Later, Sylvie would be told that he was their point guard and could run the three-quarter sprint in three seconds flat. The rest of them ran after Gus, while he ran after the ambulance and police cars. Soda cans were dropped on the sidewalk, where they spun away like tops. Kent was fast too, and so were most of the guys; they sprinted across the avenue, hands raised to keep the traffic at bay. They needed to cover enough ground to keep Gus in sight. Washington was apparently the slowest player; he trailed his teammates. He was seven feet tall and ran like a tree that had been uprooted from its forest. Sylvie couldn't keep up with Washington, but she could see his long back weaving through the pedestrian traffic ahead, which allowed her to stay connected to the group.

The lake appeared abruptly, and the shimmering surface made Sylvie squint. She was panting now, her heart thudding in her ears. The water looked like a shining plate, extended to the horizon. Charlie used to take his daughters to the lake on occasional Sunday afternoons when they were little. He would drink beer and chat with strangers on the beach, while the girls built sandcastles and tried to see how many somersaults they could do underwater. Sylvie felt a pang of grief for her father, and then the grief inched further. She had lost the only other man in their family. What if they'd lost William? She tried to feel what her brother-in-law was feeling—stretching out beyond her own boundaries to do so—but she felt nothing.

She was on the lake path now, still running. The ambulance and police cars had stopped up ahead but kept their flashing lights on. Sylvie was dizzy and slightly nauseous. There were gray spots in her vision that she knew weren't part of the landscape. She was sprinting but falling behind, at the tail of this group. *Please don't be William,* she thought, in rhythm with her footsteps. *Please don't be William.* She stopped when she finally reached the parked ambulance. She stood, shaking from exhaustion and nerves, on the edge of the path. Because of the heat, the beach in front of her was already half filled with families and sunbathers. On the sand, kids had paused playing, and men and women in bathing suits were standing on their towels, hands shading their eyes so they could see what was happening in the lake. *What could be happening in the lake?* Sylvie thought. Kent and the other players had jumped down to the beach, where the paramedics and a handful of cops were standing at the very edge of the water. She turned in the direction they were looking and watched a boat approach at a very slow speed. One of the paramedics and a few of the basketball players waded into the lake. The other two paramedics waited at the water's edge with a stretcher. The boat was close enough for Sylvie to see a man lying on the deck. She couldn't see enough to identify him one way or another. Kent and Gus were up to their waists in water. With the paramedic, they raised their arms over their heads, and then they were lifting the man. His face turned to the side. It was him.

"William," Sylvie whispered, as if to call him, as if in his current state he could hear only whispers.

William's eyes were closed, and he was limp in his friends' arms. He was wearing an untucked button-down shirt and pants. He didn't have on any shoes. One of his arms hung down, touching the water, while the other rested on his chest. More friends joined Kent and Gus; more hands supported William as they struggled to carry him out of the lake. Kent staggered once, and Washington was immediately at his side, his arm around Kent's shoulders. They laid William down on the stretcher, the movement gentle.

A teenage boy standing near Sylvie said, to no one in particular, "That guy looks dead."

"Sylvie," Kent yelled, and that was what unfroze her. She ran to them and, not knowing what else to do, how to help, held William's freezing-cold hand as they carried him off the beach and across the path. When they reached the ambulance, a paramedic said, "Only one of you can come in the vehicle." He looked at Sylvie. "You the wife?"

Sylvie stared at the paramedic. She felt like she couldn't let go of William's hand. His fingers were so cold that her skin seemed frozen to his skin, and if she was the wife, she would be the one to ride in the ambulance. So, without looking at Kent or anyone else, Sylvie nodded yes and climbed into the back of the vehicle.

The ambulance was in motion before Sylvie realized that William was breathing—shallowly—and she almost threw up with relief. She was wedged between the wall of the ambulance and the cot he had been strapped onto. The paramedic leaned over William. He pulled up his eyelid. Pressed his fingers to the side of William's neck. Covered his body with a blanket. William's face looked swollen, and his skin was a gray color. He had a bruise near one of his cheekbones. He was very still. *Too still,* Sylvie thought.

The hospital they drove to was the same one where Julia and Cecelia had given birth and Charlie had died. Time kept slowing down and then speeding up. Medical people wearing scrubs lifted William out of the ambulance. Kent was there; he must have taken a cab. He was talking to the paramedic about blood pressure, and she remembered that he was in medical school. "I should call Julia," she said, and walked into the hospital, unsure if anyone had heard her.

While the phone rang—she was in a booth just off the emergency room waiting area—Sylvie blinked and touched her face. Her hair was stiff, probably from dried sweat. It felt good to sit on the booth's tiny seat. Her body was a collection of aches and pinpricks; muscles she didn't know she had were confused and upset by the ordeal of the past hours.

"Hello?" Julia said.

"It's me." Sylvie found it hard to speak. She realized she didn't want to put what had happened into words. When she told the story to her sister, it would be real. It would have happened, and what happened would have consequences. What those consequences would be, she had no idea. She was too tired, and her imagination had been run over by reality.

"Where have you been?" Julia said. "Where are you?"

"I'm at the hospital. You should come here. We found William." Sylvie hesitated. "He was in Lake Michigan. He tried to kill himself."

There was a pause, and Julia said, "No, that can't be right. It's hot out, so he must have gone swimming, and he's not a strong swimmer. He never learned when he was a kid."

"He was unconscious, Julia . . ."

"No, no, he couldn't have done that." But there was hesitation in Julia's voice now.

"You thought the history department was wrong too, about him missing classes. Julia, this is real. This is happening."

Julia was quiet at the other end of the phone. Sylvie felt terrible in every part of her body. Terrible for her sister, terrible for William. "Just please," she said, "find a cab and come here. I'll call Emeline too, and she can meet us here to watch Alice."

"He left me," Julia said, in a slow voice. "He was very clear. He wouldn't want me there."

Sylvie stared at the foggy plastic wall that lined the booth. She was facing the seating area, and nearby there was an older man sitting with his head in his hands. Next to him, a woman wearing sunglasses stood with her arms crossed over her chest. Even if she hadn't known where they were, Sylvie would have known they were waiting for bad news.

She said, "You're not going to come?"

"He has Kent. Kent will take good care of him." Julia cleared her throat and then said, "I need you, Sylvie. Please come back to the apartment."

Sylvie opened her mouth to speak. She felt like a collection of rusty hinges: her jaw, every joint in her body. She said, "Let me wrap things up here first." She returned the receiver to the cradle and then stood in the booth until a man knocked on the glass to indicate that he needed to make a call.

She had no trouble finding Kent in the waiting room. He and his friends occupied seats in the far corner. They looked like what they were: a basketball team that had waded into a lake. Everyone else in the waiting room seemed to have chosen seats as far away from the team as possible.

"The doctor won't speak to us," Kent said. "You need to go to the desk and ask if you can sit with William until Julia gets here. I don't want him to be alone."

"She's not coming."

Kent gave her a sharp look. "At all?"

"Not now. I don't know."

Kent closed his eyes for a second, then said, "Fine. The ambulance driver thought you were his wife—tell the lady at the desk the same thing so they let you in. And when you talk to the doctor, make sure William is not only being looked at physically but has a psychiatric consult."

She thought, *Tell Kent you have to leave. Tell him your sister needs you.* She said, "You're in medical school. Shouldn't you go?"

Kent shook his head. "Only family allowed. I can't pretend to be related to him."

Tears filled Sylvie's eyes, though she couldn't have guessed what she was feeling, because it felt like everything. She nodded at Kent and walked to the desk.

She said, "I'm William Waters's wife," and the nurse led her through a door and then down two hallways, past open doors that showed men, women, and children in various urgent states: crying, bleeding, unconscious. Sylvie felt increasingly unwell herself. Her clothes rubbed against her skin. The blister on her heel stung with each step she took.

The nurse stopped and pointed to a doorway. Sylvie walked through it, alone. William was lying on a bed. His eyes were closed. His feet were covered by a blanket, but they hung off the too-short bed. With William spread out in front of her, Sylvie could see that his skin looked wrong. Extra pale, and somehow stretched. Like he had been inflated and was now returning to his normal size. The nurses had taken away his wet clothes; he was wearing a hospital gown, and his arm was hooked up to an IV. This was the first time Sylvie had been alone with him since the night on the bench, six months earlier.

"I thought you were dead," she whispered.

There was one window in the room, which had a view of a green leafy tree. The childbirth floor was above this one and on the other side of the huge building. That was where Sylvie had been before, where her nieces were born, and where her father died. There was a hard chair next to the bed, so she sat on it.

Sylvie closed her aching eyes. She was aware of a sensation inside herself—a pattering, like light rain—and, slowly, she realized it was relief. She was relieved. She was relieved that William was alive, in front of her. And she was relieved to be the person in this chair, in this room. When she'd spoken to Julia on the phone, Sylvie had been focused on what was *supposed* to happen—a sick man's wife was *supposed* to come to his bedside—but it was better for William to be with her. Sylvie could trace the dots that had led him to this room; she'd known, somehow, that this wasn't impossible. With her eyes closed, Sylvie could imagine William walking into the lake, feeling like a tablespoon of water that could no longer stay on a spoon. There had been no more gravity holding him together, and so he'd tried to dissolve into the giant body of water. Sylvie sat at his bedside, loose inside her own skin, so she could share some of her strength with him while he slept.

William

H E WALKED THE CITY FOR MOST OF THE NIGHT AND THEN returned to the shore of the lake. It was still dark out. No one was around, and even the air was motionless as he waded into the water. No birdsong, no traffic noise behind him, no human voices. It felt like the world had paused. William had to walk for a long time before the water was deep enough to go over his head. He hadn't thought to bring any weighted objects; he'd stopped thinking hours earlier. William contained only a yearning for water, for darkness, for quiet. He wanted to sink, but his giant body kept trying to float. Even after a long time in the water, when he was pretty out of it, his feet would shoot sideways, and he would be on his back, as buoyant as any boat, staring up at the sun. He was no longer a person with a name and a history; at that point, he was a cork bobbing in liquid, and he could only note the soft, pruned feeling of his hands, the sun burning his face, the water making its way into his eyes and ears. He was sleeping, or unconscious, when there was a roaring noise, and voices, and hands tugging at him. He couldn't open his eyes to see what was happening. He listened—heard Kent call his name after a time—but only because he had no choice. When he woke up in the hospital, dry, and saw Sylvie on a chair next to him, his first thought was that he'd failed. The fact that he had failed meant he had to continue to walk forward with his life history—his mistakes—slung over his shoulders like a heavy backpack. This fact exhausted him, but he was too tired to reject it.

WILLIAM WAS IN A different hospital from the one he had first woken up in; after nearly a week of evaluation, he had been moved to an inpatient psychiatric facility in downtown Chicago. The lake was three blocks away, out of sight. William was aware of the body of water, though, despite the distance. While he drifted in and out of sleep, he still felt soaking wet, far from shore, and unable to stay underwater.

During the first few days at the new hospital, either Sylvie or Kent was always in the room when he shifted in and out of sleep. He saw them but wasn't strong enough to speak. Kent spoke to him, told him he was going to get better, told him his doctors were excellent, finally told him he had to return to school but would be back in a few days. Sylvie rarely said anything, just sat in the room's one chair and read her book.

As he became more alert, her presence felt complicated. He suspected that Sylvie was the only person, other than Kent, who hadn't been completely shocked at what he'd tried to do. She'd seen the bleakness inside him that night on the bench and in the footnotes of his manuscript. His wife had read his footnotes too, of course, but he knew Julia's primary response had been dismay that William contained those kinds of thoughts. For Julia, this meant he was the wrong man for her, not that there was something wrong.

William was aware that he was glad Sylvie was there, even though something about her presence didn't sit right—the Padavano family should want nothing to do with him. Every time Sylvie was in the room, he half-expected the door to swing open and Julia to walk in. He tossed and turned under the weight of this possibility and tried to stay unconscious for as many hours of the day as possible. "Sleep is a great healer," Dr. Dembia told him. She was the doctor assigned to him in the psychiatric unit. "You've been working very hard for a long time, William. Give yourself a rest."

One afternoon, when William woke from a restless nap, Sylvie said, "Can I ask you a question?"

He heard distress in her voice. He had to clear his throat to say, "Yes." And then he felt resigned, because no matter what she asked, he had to answer. He couldn't lie anymore. Like a piece of fine porcelain unable to bear any weight, he could no longer take it.

"Do you want Julia to visit? We're not sure what to do."

His body emptied of air under the force of the question. He knew the answer, though. He'd written it into the note before he left the apartment. He understood that this was a necessary postscript, a clarification. "No," he said, his voice winded. "Julia and Alice should stay away from me. Forever."

He didn't know how Sylvie took this announcement, because he didn't look at her. He knew it was a horrible thing to say, but he meant it, more than he had ever meant anything before. "Tell her that I give Alice up," he said, and turned his face to the wall. He stayed that way, his eyes closed, until Sylvie was gone.

His words had been so brutal, and his rejection of Sylvie's sister and niece so final, that William knew Sylvie would never return. The night that followed was long. William remembered being in the lake. He tried to reckon with what was left of his life: Kent, and his other friends from the team; the medications Dr. Dembia had prescribed him. That was all he had, and he knew he was lucky to have anything. His old life sat at the bottom of the lake. He'd just pushed away the last piece, Sylvie, and it was a loss that ached. William had experienced a strange peace beside her on the bench that night—as if he'd been able to set aside his pretending and just *be*—and he'd felt relief each time she walked into his hospital room. But William had revealed himself to be the kind of monster who abandoned his wife and child, and there were consequences to that.

THE DOOR TO WILLIAM'S room had to remain open, even at night, so the nurse patrolling the halls could lay eyes on him at any time. There were no locks inside the unit, not even on the bathrooms. The unit itself was secured with a thick metal door, which was always bolted shut. Visitors had their bags searched, and the main door had to be unlocked to let them in and locked again once they were inside.

Dr. Dembia met with William for a half hour every afternoon. She had short gray hair but a youthful face. William didn't know if she was old or young: Perhaps her hair color meant she was older than her face looked, or perhaps her hair had prematurely grayed. He'd been in her care for a week when she said, "I was finally able to speak to one of your parents. I called your father at his office."

A chord buried deep inside William vibrated. He wished he hadn't taken things so far that his parents had to be involved. He'd given the doctor his mother's and father's names when she'd written down his life history. "I assume he said that he couldn't help," William said.

"He said you were an adult and therefore on your own. He actually hung up on me. William, I want you to know that that isn't a normal parental response. It's unkind and unfair. You deserve, and deserved, better from your parents. You were born to two broken people, and that's part of why you're here."

"You think he's a jerk."

She smiled. "Well, that word doesn't really fall under my technical vocabulary. I would say that I suspect your father also suffers from depression."

William found it hard to picture his parents' faces. He saw them at the train station, waving, but their forms were blurry. The idea of his father being depressed had no traction in William's mind; it just slipped away. These sessions with this doctor, who paid attention to him—sank her eyes into him like fishhooks—were exhausting. The other two doctors who visited him were distracted; William only got a sliver of their focus. He was more comfortable with that arrangement.

"He and my mother haven't been part of my life," he said. "Not for a long time, anyway."

The doctor tilted her head to the side, and William could see her considering the veracity of this statement. It occurred to him, for the first time, that just because you never thought about someone didn't mean they weren't inside you.

WILLIAM WOKE UP ONE morning nauseous and sweaty. He knew this was a reaction to his medication; finding the most effective combination of antidepressants and anti-anxiety medications was a process of trial and error. He kept his eyes closed for a few more minutes, because he knew this would be a difficult day, and he was in no hurry for it to begin. When he did open his eyes, he saw Sylvie sitting next to his bed. William blinked at her. She was sitting very straight in the chair, as if she were being tested on her posture.

"I didn't think you'd come back," he said, uncertain whether she had in fact come back or he was hallucinating.

She nodded. "I had another question," she said. "You said you didn't want Julia or Alice. Is it all right if I visit you? Or do you want me to go away too?"

Go away? William thought. He'd been dreaming about his conversation with Dr. Dembia regarding his parents. In the dream, William was swimming away from his mother and father, while they swam away from him. And he had told his wife and daughter to go away. So many people leaving each other. There had been a claustrophobic atmosphere in the dream, a foreboding, as if they were all about to find out they were swimming in a fishbowl. They were trying to get away from one another, and they were doomed to fail.

William looked at the young woman in the chair. He knew she was real and not a hallucination. He knew he wanted her here. He didn't know why, but that didn't matter right now. William was trying to relearn what it felt like to want anything at all.

"Don't go away." His voice was tired, fuzzy with drugs and sleep. "I'm sorry I hurt your sister."

Sylvie said, "You hurt yourself too."

He shook his head, rejecting this. "Is Julia okay?"

Sylvie sat even taller; she looked stretched, as if she were trying to be in more than one place at once. "Julia is upset," she said. "Obviously. But she'll be all right. She doesn't know I'm here. It's just that I think"— she hesitated—"that you deserve to have visitors. I know Kent visits, but he's too busy to come often. You don't deserve to be alone."

This sentence struck William like he'd been shoved in the chest. He didn't deserve to be alone? He didn't think this was true, but he believed Sylvie meant what she said.

"Thank you," he said.

Sylvie nodded, and then they were both quiet for a few minutes. The quiet was loud, like the ambient rush of a white-noise machine. William wondered if there was something else he should say. Sylvie looked uneasy too. It felt like they'd reached the end of a script, and now one of them needed to either make something up or leave the stage. William thought longingly of sleep. Maybe he could disappear from this moment, into unconsciousness.

Sylvie leaned forward and said, "I was wondering if you could tell me about Bill Walton."

"Bill Walton. The basketball player?"

She nodded.

William was surprised, but he knew the answer, so he gave it. "He's a playmaking big. Played for Portland and was a season and finals MVP. He was plagued with injuries, though. Broke his wrist twice. Sprained his ankle. Dislocated fingers and toes."

"Goodness." Sylvie looked lighter, relieved that they had found something to talk about.

"Walton broke a bone in his foot, and they had to make a kind of sling-slash-cast for the foot to try to reduce the pain. They gave him painkilling shots, which he played on, and that messed the foot up even more." William couldn't believe he was speaking this much, but now that he'd started, he needed to give Sylvie enough information so she truly understood. "Walton's a great player, maybe the best passer in the game, definitely for a center. He loves basketball, but his body is terrible. His knees are . . . impossible, and he has endless foot injuries. He's on the bench for the Clippers this year."

Sylvie said, "It seems impressive that he was able to play at all, much less win MVP, with that body."

"It is," William said. "It is impressive." But talking so much had exhausted him, and he fell asleep. The next time he opened his eyes, Sylvie was gone.

DR. DEMBIA TOLD HIM that she was giving him homework. "I want you to write down every secret, every part of your life that you kept from the people close to you."

He looked down at the plain notebook he'd been handed. William nodded and then put the notebook to the side. For as long as he could remember, he'd tried to push away from anything uncomfortable, to not allow it close. But he had pushed away so much that there was nothing left. He knew that to get well, he needed to consider his wife, his childhood, and his failure to manage what had looked from the outside like a great life. He wasn't ready yet, though. It was enough to simply know that the time was coming and that he could no longer hide. When William slept, he dreamed about water, and while he was awake, he walked the psych unit's halls.

Kent sat in the chair in the corner when he visited, his long legs reaching into the middle of the room. He looked sleepy and sometimes closed his eyes. "Stop feeling guilty," he said. "You would have done the same thing for me."

"I'm not in medical school with two part-time jobs. You shouldn't be here now. How many hours of sleep did you get last night? And now you have to drive back to Milwaukee."

"I'm only coming here once a week. My buddy is covering my shift today. You can't make me stay away."

Kent's affection for William was too clear and too uncomplicated. It shone on William like the sun. No one had ever loved him unconditionally like this, and that love, when he was the most undeserving he'd ever been in his life, made William feel like he was burning up. He paced the room, trying to cool himself down with motion.

"I think you think I'm still in danger. But I'm not. I won't do it again," he said. "I promise."

Kent studied him from beneath lowered eyelids. "I want more than that, you know. I want you to feel better. To love your life."

William laughed, a brief, dry sound. When had he last laughed?

"That's not funny," Kent said.

William felt chastened. "I'm sorry," he said. "I thought it was." He thought for a moment. "Do you love your life?"

"Shit, yes." Kent said this with force.

William looked at his friend. Kent was still at his playing weight and seemed to glisten with youth and health. They were both twenty-three years old. William felt at least forty—which was ancient. He put his hand over his busted knee.

"I'll give you something to live for," Kent said. "I've got my eye on Michael Jordan—you know, the North Carolina kid who made that big shot last year? He looks *good*. Maybe the Bulls can get him when he enters the draft."

William nodded. He thought of the conversation in which he'd told Sylvie about Bill Walton. Michael Jordan was much harder for William to think about. Kent was excited about Jordan because he looked like the future of basketball, but William found it impossible to contemplate the days and weeks in front of him.

"Listen." Kent studied him. "Are you sure about your marriage being over? Because I can talk to Julia, if you want. Help you mend fences or whatever's necessary."

"I'm sure it's over."

"All right." Kent sat up straight in the chair for the first time. "We're going to watch the Bulls together on TV this year. Every game. You'll come to Milwaukee, or I'll come to you."

Come to me, William thought. *Where? Where will I be?*

WILLIAM HAD ENTERED THE hospital in August, and it was now late September. The leaves outside his window were losing color, their dark summer green washed away. William appreciated this small moment in time when the colors faded, a visual deep breath before the new season arrived.

Dr. Dembia said, "Have you finished your homework?"

It had been a while since she'd asked him about the notebook; he knew this was a nudge. He shook his head. "Not yet."

When Sylvie arrived at William's door, he was aware he felt grateful to see her. He was becoming more aware in general. What had been a dull paste of emotions inside him had more texture. Sylvie had recently brought socks that Emeline had knit for him and an art book from Cecelia. It had become clear that the twins were concerned about William too, even though they'd stayed away from the hospital.

In different ways, three of the four Padavano sisters continued to care for him, as if their sheer number, and adjacency to Julia, could paper over the hole he'd created in his own life. *You're not alone,* their attention told him, and he was moved by that kindness.

William knew Julia would hate that Sylvie visited him. His wife would have rightfully considered the note he'd left—along with the addendum he'd given Sylvie—the end of their marriage. The fact that Sylvie had decided to continue, even temporarily, her relationship with William was messy at best and bordered on disloyal. The Padavano sisters had acted with complete unity, he knew, for their entire lives. He had watched Sylvie and Julia sleep in each other's arms on his couch. He found it hard to believe that Sylvie had crossed that line for him.

Sylvie set down her purse on the corner chair. She said, "I'm curious about Kareem Abdul-Jabbar—why did he change his name in the beginning of his career?"

William smiled; his thoughts were still on his estranged wife, and Julia wouldn't have asked him this question in a million years. Julia had no interest in basketball and was always trying to shoo William and his attention away from his favorite game. She'd had her eye on who William would *become,* after the next job offer or once he had a PhD after his name. He didn't blame his wife for this conditional acceptance; he'd grown up with parents who'd never accepted him at all.

"William?" Sylvie said, her head tipped to the side. "You all right? You look far away."

"I'm here," he said.

He knew, with his new awareness, that he should tell Sylvie to return to her sister for good. He should tell her that he would be okay without her visits. The nurse who patrolled the halls and peered into each room had just walked by and would walk by again in four minutes. William felt more grounded in his body. Kent would be here on Saturday. *You should go,* he thought. But he couldn't make himself say the words.

—

SYLVIE WAS SITTING IN the chair, and William was pacing from one side of the room to the other. He'd been in the hospital for over two months. It was almost Halloween, and the nurses had taped posters of jack-o'-lanterns to the walls in the common room. William wasn't able to open his window, but he could see that people outside were now wearing jackets or vests while they walked down the sidewalk.

"How many rings did Bill Russell win in total?" Sylvie said, after several minutes of watching him slowly ricochet from one wall to the other.

"Eleven in twelve years," he said, and stopped walking. The warmth—that discomfort he felt when Kent gazed at him with his wide-open face—flared inside him. Sylvie shone affection at him too, and even though it was hard, he was trying to accept it. He'd smiled once, during Kent's last visit, and his friend had slapped him on the back, delighted. Dr. Dembia had said to him, "Discomfort is just a feeling, William. It's okay to let yourself feel your feelings."

He said, "I know you bring up basketball to make me feel comfortable, Sylvie. It's very nice of you."

Sylvie raised her eyebrows, surprised by this.

"And I know you read my book." Without stopping to think, William reached for the empty journal on his bedside table. "I have homework from the doctor. Maybe you could help me with it? I appreciate your visiting me. I should have said that before."

"I'd like to help you," Sylvie said, in a careful voice.

"Can you write down what I say, as a list? I'm supposed to write down the secrets I kept from . . . well, Julia."

Sylvie reached out for the notebook. Like him, she'd grown up going to confession in church. Entering the dark booth and lowering herself to the kneeler. Confessing her sins to the screen that separated her from the priest. William thought of that sacrament now and felt bad for all the children who were forced to divide their ordinary lives into sins and not-sins so they would have something to say to a cassocked stranger.

"The first one is that I knew you read my book," he said. "I never told Julia that I'd figured that out." His manuscript was still on the top shelf of the closet in his apartment, unless his wife had thrown it out.

Sylvie wrote in the notebook, her head down.

He sat on the side of the bed, ready for his body to be still. "I never wanted to be a professor." He paused to see if there was a reaction, then went on. "I never told Julia that I was eating lunch in the Northwestern gym every day and that I was helping Arash with the basketball players. She had no idea how much time I spent in the gym. I didn't tell her how unhappy it made me that she read what I was writing. That it was more a journal, more for me, than a book." His head dropped lower. "I didn't want to have a child." He closed his eyes, sank into the deepest part of himself. "I didn't tell her I had a sister."

There was a gasp. "You had a sister?" Sylvie whispered this, as if the words were sacred, too important to be uttered at volume.

"She died when I was a newborn. From the flu, or pneumonia, maybe. It destroyed my parents. I think they were never able to look at me without remembering her."

"Oh, William."

He and Sylvie sat in the same stunned silence. They sat in the unthinkable—William never thought of it—loss that preceded all the other losses. He had never told anyone about his sister, and something blossomed out of the confession. When William closed his eyes, the little girl sat beside him. He had given her substance by telling her story. He was confident that his parents never mentioned her because they couldn't bear to. If only three people remembered her short story and never spoke it aloud, she was erased from history. William was in this hospital to try to inhabit his own body, his own history. His sister was part of that, but she was also a person in her own right.

"What was her name?"

"Caroline." He'd never said her name out loud before.

William felt the little girl beaming because she was the subject of so much attention. He could also feel the bright red and yellow color of the leaves outside the window and the heightened emotion of the woman across from him. He'd never had this level of molecular awareness before, never felt so much in a single moment. William had always evaded the pointed spears that emotions threw at him and been quick to smother any uncomfortable sensations. He had a hard time believing that other people were able to stand being alive if it came at them with this intensity.

"I couldn't have told this to anyone else," William said. "I don't know why, but I had to tell you."

Sylvie looked at him, and he knew they were both remembering that night on the bench, under the stars. She said, "Can I ask you a question?"

He nodded.

"In your manuscript, in the footnotes, you said something like *It should have been me, not her.* Was the *her* your sister?"

William stared. "I don't remember writing that." How was he still surprised by the secrets inside him? But it was the truth; he'd always known that his parents would have preferred him to be the one who died. "I imagine I meant my sister, yes."

He looked at Sylvie's open face, and he knew that he could tell her anything and she wouldn't judge him. He had told her every terrible thing inside him, and she was still holding a pen, ready and willing to write down more.

"I think that's all," he said. "Maybe you should tell all of this to Emeline and Cecelia too. These shouldn't be secrets anymore." William paused to take a breath. "I don't think there's anything else to add to the list. I wasn't a good husband to Julia. She deserved much better."

Sylvie shimmered in front of him, and that was how he realized he was crying.

When she was leaving—looking as exhausted as William, as if they had just run a marathon together—Sylvie stopped in the doorway. "You said you didn't want to be a professor. Did you want to be a professional basketball player?"

"Yes, but I wasn't good enough, even before the injury."

"That must have been terribly disappointing," Sylvie said, and he nodded.

———

WILLIAM KNEW HE HAD one more thing to say before Dr. Dembia would allow him to leave the hospital. She kept saying, "Just a few more days," and he understood that he hadn't said everything. He didn't understand why he had to say everything, but there were rules to getting well, and he had to follow the rules. The doctor was pleased with the medication levels, and William no longer felt like he was hanging off the fender of a car that sped across town and then hurtled to a stop. His hands were no longer clammy, he could sleep at night, and there were moments of calm. He was learning the difference between calm and disconnected and was working to make his days more the former than the latter.

Arash visited and gave William a stern look. "Remember how I told you we keep tabs on our players?"

William nodded.

"Not everyone has good news to share when we follow up, and we try to help out when we can. You think you're the first one who got in trouble? The coaching staff had a meeting about you."

"Oh God," William said, horrified.

"You brought value to our program when you interviewed the players this summer. I can't guarantee you a job on staff. Obviously being here"—Arash frowned—"is a hurdle to overcome. But the university always needs resident advisers, and your doctor said you could handle the responsibility, so we're going to get you a room in a dorm. That will cover your living expenses. We'll see what happens from there."

William found himself unable to speak. He'd been worrying about where he would sleep when he left here. He had very little money in the bank and no possibilities. The only option he'd been able to think of was to travel to Milwaukee and sleep on Kent's floor, but that was problematic too, because Kent had a new girlfriend, a fellow medical student. She would understandably not be thrilled to have her boyfriend's depressed former teammate taking up her space in the room.

"You pity me," William said finally, and the words were sour in his mouth.

Arash shook his head, hard. "You're depressed, not crazy. It's not insane to be depressed in this world. It's more sane than being happy. I never trust those upbeat individuals who grin no matter what's going on. Those are the ones with a screw loose, if you ask me. Also, I'm not offering you a job. I'm offering a room."

William's brain clung to a new refrain, after the weeks in the hospital: *No bullshit and no secrets.* He could recognize both now, and when he reviewed what Arash had said, he knew it wasn't bullshit. The coaches did track their players, and he had given value to the team in the past. The hours he'd spent listening to the boys explain how they'd been hurt meant something—to William, perhaps to the boys, and to Arash, in his mission to keep all the players strong and undamaged. The memory of those hours in the stuffy room—when so much else in his brain was water-damaged or frayed—remained intact, and it was a place William didn't mind revisiting. When he considered this further, he realized it might be the only memory he had that didn't cause feelings of regret or dismay. He had been helpful.

"Thank you," William said.

When he walked the halls that day, he realized that he'd stopped feeling lake water against his skin. The cool liquid no longer tickled up his spine. He had a room to sleep in, which allowed him to believe, for the first time, that there would be a next step.

William wasn't surprised that afternoon when Dr. Dembia said, "You never mention Alice."

He was standing; he turned away to look out the window. This was what he needed to speak about. This was what he had to say in order to leave. This was what he had to know in order to start over. This was the last secret, which he could no longer keep.

He said, "I started getting darker—everything was getting darker— before she was born. It wasn't because of her, but she showed up when nothing made sense anymore, and I had to keep turning off lights in my head to make it through the days. The thing was—" He stopped, looking for the right language.

"Yes?" the doctor said.

"Alice is a lamp. A bright lamp, from the moment she was born. She kind of shines. Looking at her hurt my eyes, and I was afraid to touch her."

"You were afraid of her light?"

"No. I was afraid I was going to put her light out. That my darkness would swamp her light."

"So you felt like you had to stay away from her, to keep her safe."

"I have to stay away from her, yes."

Julia

AUGUST 1983–OCTOBER 1983

WHEN THE PHONE RANG ON THAT HOT AUGUST MORNING, William had been gone for a day and a half. Julia was sitting on the couch with Alice in her lap. She was tickling the baby's stomach. Alice gurgled when she laughed, and it was the best sound Julia had ever heard. It made Julia laugh too, every time. Julia carried Alice to the colorful blanket on the floor and laid the baby down. Then she picked up the phone next to the armchair, and everything changed.

Something inside Julia froze while she listened to Sylvie talk. The news that William had tried to kill himself was so enormous, she couldn't take it in. Her hands went cold, and when she hung up the phone, she blew on them as if it were the middle of winter. She carried Alice from room to room, even though the baby hadn't asked to be picked up. She visited each of the four windows in the apartment; she appeared to be looking for something, and yet she wouldn't have been able to relay the weather outside or the time of day.

Cecelia and Emeline came to her apartment, and Julia told them that she needed time alone to think. They nodded, their faces grave. They'd all been shaken by the idea that William had wanted to leave them, to leave everything. His choice made them feel vulnerable; they'd never considered anything other than a natural death, and he'd pointed out another exit. The world felt scarier in the wake of what had almost happened.

The three women stood by Julia's door for several minutes.

"How could he have done that?" Cecelia's voice was hard.

Emeline rubbed her sister's arm. "I don't think it makes sense to be angry at him."

"But," Cecelia said, "I literally don't understand how he could give all of this up. He was going to abandon Alice? There's nothing more wrong in the universe."

Julia listened to the twins talk the same way she'd listened to Sylvie on the phone. Everything was new to her now; it felt like her prior understanding of the world had been wiped away. She considered each sentence as if she were hearing words for the first time.

She said, "How could I not have known William was so unhappy?" Her husband's lack of ambition, his unreliability, had turned out to be small symptoms in an ocean of darkness. Julia remained cold with fear. She had scared herself—how clueless she'd been—and William's darkness terrified her. She had lain in bed, night after night, beside a man who didn't want to live. Now, when she looked back at even the recent past, the memories were covered by shadows. Her own experience was a lie.

"He's sick." Emeline looked miserable. "Sylvie said he'll probably need to be in the hospital for a long time."

"Still," Cecelia said. "No one should give up. It's so selfish to do that. So wrong."

Julia found herself nodding in agreement.

When the twins were gone, Julia became aware of her own anger. She felt like she'd caught it from Cecelia, as if the emotion were a cold. She walked from window to window again, her heart beating out questions:

How could William have done something as embarrassing as trying to drown himself in Lake Michigan?

Was life with me so unbearable that he had to not only leave me but kill himself?

Why didn't he tell me how he felt?

Even though Julia had sworn off solving problems for the people around her, she still had all her skills at her disposal and could have helped. She could have at least stopped him from doing something so dramatic, so hopeless, so humiliating.

When Sylvie appeared later that night, Julia let her sister into the apartment but stayed by the front door again. She couldn't bear long visits. She needed her home to be occupied by just her and her daughter.

Sylvie apologized. "I don't know why I went with Kent," she said. "I'm so sorry. I should have stayed with you."

She wrapped her arms around Julia and Julia did the same, and the two sisters held tight for a long time, each leaning into the other's body like buildings that required support.

"What do I do? Do I have to *do* something?" Julia said into her sister's hair.

Sylvie had suggested, when she'd called from the hospital, that a mental breakdown erased the note William had written and the check he'd signed over to her. Was that true? Did Julia still have to be a wife, in a worst-case scenario, to a man she no longer recognized?

"I don't know," Sylvie said. "But I'll find out."

THE NEXT MORNING, JULIA decided to deep-clean the apartment. She needed movement. She pushed the coffee table to the side and rolled up the thin living room rug. Wearing Alice in a baby carrier, she dragged the rug down to a massive laundry machine in the basement of the building and wrestled it into the drum. When the rug was clean, Julia pulled a small ladder out of the hall closet and used it to take down the curtains from the living room window. They'd used these curtains in the smaller Northwestern apartment too. They were magenta, made of a thick weave Julia had chosen in the early days of their marriage because the fabric felt grown-up to her. *I was an idiot,* she thought. *A young idiot.* She carried Alice and the curtains down to the basement and set the washer to an extra-long soaking time.

She had a hard time sleeping. When she tried to rest, she worried. Anything seemed possible after William had tried to drown himself in the lake she swam in as a child. She thought in *if . . . then* scenarios. If William's hospitalization did somehow nullify the note he'd given her, then Julia would have to go to the hospital eventually and stay married. If she and William divorced—a preferable scenario—then he would still be Alice's father. He would still want a role in their child's life. Julia would have to find a way to protect Alice from whatever had sent William into that lake. If William spent time with Alice, then their daughter might find his depression contagious. Julia kept returning to the idea that it couldn't be good for Alice's happiness to spend time with someone who saw life as disposable. Life was opportunity, a chest of drawers to open, one after the other, and William had tried to hurl the chest out the window.

At three o'clock in the morning, Julia used the ladder to empty the top shelves of the kitchen cupboards. These shelves were filled with wedding gifts, items too impractical for regular use. A crystal bowl that was absurdly heavy. A set of china teacups, much too delicate to use in a house with a child. Miniature wineglasses, which were intended for some kind of old-fashioned after-dinner alcohol. Brandy or sherry—Julia couldn't remember which. She filled the sink with soapy water and carefully cleaned each breakable piece, until the sun began to rise in the sky and Alice woke up.

Julia felt trapped: in her apartment, in the strange limbo of her marriage, in her own skin. She was waiting for William to call her, perhaps, and tell her he wanted her back and needed her now. Or for Sylvie to return with the same answer. She was waiting for some clarity on whether she had to be a wife or not. When Sylvie came to the apartment again, a little over a week after William had tried to kill himself, Julia's younger sister looked so tired she seemed to have aged five years. Her hair was in a ponytail. The skin under her eyes looked bruised.

"Sit down," Julia said, worried. "You look like you might faint."

Sylvie shook her head. "William told me to tell you that he doesn't want you to visit."

Relief soaked through Julia, and she sank down into the armchair.

"He also said"—Sylvie's voice was flat, like a correspondent reporting the news—"that he's giving Alice up."

"Giving her up?" This term didn't make sense to Julia, and she thought she might have misheard. "What does that mean?"

"I think it means he won't be her parent anymore. You'd be her only parent."

Julia turned her head slowly and looked at Alice lying on her baby blanket. She was wearing a pink onesie and kicking her bare feet in the air like she was riding an upside-down bicycle. Her round cheeks were flushed with effort. Julia held the words in her mouth: *give her up.*

"He seemed to mean it," Sylvie said. "He used the word 'forever.'"

Another word, held inside Julia: *forever.* She thought, *Oh, thank God,* though she hadn't prayed since her father died. But still, the relief was so enormous that she thought again, *Thank God.*

Sylvie put her hand against the wall as if to steady herself. She looked like she'd been sleeping as little as Julia had.

"You should lie down on the couch in the nursery." Julia found she didn't mind the idea of her sister staying in her space now. She no longer needed to hole up with Alice. Julia had felt free after William left her, then trapped when he'd tried to die, and now she was free again. This freedom felt like falling backward onto a plush bed; it was decadent, delicious. "Please rest for a little while, at least," she said, glad to have the chance to worry about someone other than herself. "You look like a ghost."

Sylvie offered a thin smile. "I'm okay. I have to work at the library. I just wanted to tell you first."

"Thank you for telling me."

"I wanted everything to be clear for you," Sylvie said. "It was too confusing as it was, too unresolved, and I know you hate that. I wanted to know if he really wanted your marriage to be over."

Julia considered her sister before her, who seemed to have unraveled with Julia's marriage, with the almost-end of William. Sylvie was suffering in front of Julia now, as if she'd been caught in the gravity field of William's depression and was unable to fully break free. It seemed to Julia that Sylvie was suffering on her behalf, in an effort to deliver clarity to her sister as a gift. Julia appreciated this. She loved Sylvie for this. But she wanted to make the suffering stop, before her sister was permanently changed: permanently sad and weary. "I need to help you," she said. "I'll make you eggs the way you like, before you go." She took Sylvie's hand and walked her into the kitchen.

After Sylvie left for the library with slightly more color in her cheeks, Julia put Alice in her stroller and went outside to run two errands. She found herself smiling while she walked, and her face felt oddly stretched, because it had been a long time since she'd smiled this fully. Julia was loose with relief that William wanted nothing to do with her. She hadn't damaged him, and she wasn't required to fix him. And, most important, he wanted nothing to do with their daughter. This was unfathomable to Julia—she could barely stand to be out of the baby's sight—but it eliminated her biggest concern. William had chosen to give Alice up.

Julia decided she would speak to a lawyer as soon as possible, to make everything William had said legal before he could change his mind. She walked to the bank and deposited the check William had given her. Then she bought an answering machine for her apartment so she could manufacture some control over her life. She never again wanted to answer the phone not knowing what terrible news might lie at the other end of the line.

JULIA SPENT HER DAYS packing the contents of the apartment into boxes. This apartment had been intended for a different future, one that would no longer happen, and she needed to move. Julia had imagined a happy family here: a successful professor and a career woman with a perfect daughter. But that future had been doomed, without Julia's knowledge. Now she felt embarrassed by her own foolishness, while she emptied closets. A new home was imperative so that she and Alice could start over.

One early October morning, the phone rang while Julia was pulling a sweatshirt over her head. It had gotten chilly overnight. She felt irrationally pleased by the drop in temperature, because it indicated a new season, and that meant a small step into her future and away from her disastrous past. When the answering machine clicked on, the caller hung up. The phone rang again immediately, though, and after the beep Rose's voice said, "Julia Celeste Padavano, you better pick the phone up this instant. How dare you ask your mother to speak—"

Julia sprinted across the apartment, tripping over a box, righting herself, and climbing over a chair that was trapped between two boxes. Alice watched her from her spot on a blanket. First she was wide-eyed, and then she chortled, apparently thinking her mother was putting on a show for her amusement.

Julia was breathless by the time she picked up the phone. "Yes, Mama, I'm here!"

"Julia?" Rose sounded distrusting, as if perhaps the technology was imitating her daughter's voice.

"It's me."

Julia could almost hear her mother nod and resettle into her chair on the narrow balcony. "Is it really you? I would have thought that *my* daughter would have called me if her husband walked into the lake."

Julia had asked her sisters not to tell Rose what had happened, and they'd agreed. Julia had called her mother once since William had left, but she'd kept the conversation short and busy with questions about Rose's life in Florida. Julia had wanted to buy time until the chaos settled, until she knew how to frame what had happened, until she had the strength to absorb her mother's reaction. But a story this dramatic couldn't be muffled for long, and the gossip Julia had feared must have ignited in Pilsen and spread all the way to Florida. "Well, obviously I've been upset, Mama. And busy—"

"You haven't been busy. Don't lie to me, young lady. Emeline tells Grace Ceccione everything, and Grace told me that you've barely left your apartment and you haven't set foot in the hospital. And that you put *Sylvie*"—Rose said Sylvie's name with the same incredulity with which she might have said *Santa Claus*—"in charge of dealing with William's doctors. I couldn't believe my ears."

"Sylvie's not in charge. You don't under—"

Rose interrupted her. "You refused to go to the hospital. What was she going to do, leave him there alone, almost dead? William's an orphan; you know that. He has no other family."

Julia glanced down at Alice, who was lying on a blanket on the floor. The baby looked drowsy now, which pleased Julia. That meant her child wasn't hooked up to her mother's adrenal system. If she was, Alice would be crying right now. Julia wanted to cry.

"William left me, Mama, before he ended up in the hospital. We're getting divorced. This has been a very hard time."

"Don't use that ugly, ugly word. I heard that William left you a note." Rose said *note* in a dismissive tone. "Your husband is in the hospital because he's sick, Julia. Have you spoken to him?"

"No," Julia said. "He said he didn't want me to visit. And, Mama, you won't believe this, but he doesn't want Alice to be his daughter anymore. He's giving up his rights to her."

She expected her mother to be horrified by this statement, but Rose sighed, a noise that sounded exactly like the sighs of Julia's sisters. The blurring of the sound and the women made Julia rub her forehead. Her mother and sisters were all tied together in her mind and heart, but no one could make Julia trip over the cords that bound them like Rose.

"William's not well," Rose said. "No person in their right mind would say that about their child. It's blasphemy."

Julia wanted to say, *You gave up a child. You gave up Cecelia.* But she didn't want to hurt her mother, and she knew Rose would say that was completely different because Cecelia was already grown. When Julia played this argument out in her head, at the end, she and her mother both lost. She sighed and said, "William meant it."

"He's upset, and you're upset too. Listen to me. Your husband is a nice man. He doesn't drink, and he doesn't play around. Maybe graduate school didn't work out, but he can get a job. You have a baby, for heaven's sake. You have to think clearly. It's a horrible thing to be a divorced woman. Men can recover from a marriage ending, but women don't. Do you really want to throw your life away? You're only twenty-three."

Julia shook her head. "More people get divorced now than they did in your day, Mama. It's not that big a deal."

Rose blew air into the phone. "Not a big deal! It's a big deal in the church, I can tell you that. And we're the talk of the neighborhood," she said. "Everyone loves a disaster. Father Cole baptized and married you—imagine how heartbroken he'll be if you go through with this. Remember how Mrs. Callahan stopped combing her hair after her husband left and no one else wanted her?"

"I would never be like that," Julia said, offended.

"William is going through a rough time, but we all do. Nothing as flashy as trying to drown in Lake Michigan, hopefully, but we all run into a wall at full speed at one point or another. A wife's role is to stand by her husband when that happens. Twenty years from now, you'll look back together on this time and it'll look like a small blip in your marriage. You'll be glad you stuck it out."

Julia surveyed the boxes that surrounded her. She thought of the broken expression on Rose's face in the garden after Cecelia announced she was pregnant. Rose had run into a wall. And William had too, of course. But Julia hadn't. She was healthy, and whole, and full of capacity. She had watched her mother stick out her own marriage, and that path wasn't for Julia. She was her father's rocket. She and Alice would be better on their own. "I'm going to move," she said. "I'm waiting to hear about work from Professor Cooper, and I have to leave this apartment, because William is no longer enrolled at Northwestern."

"Right now you have to move? Those people won't give you an extra month, after what happened?"

"No, they won't." This wasn't true, or at least it wasn't true as far as Julia knew. She didn't know when she had to move out by. She had a stack of mail to go through, and perhaps some of it was from Northwestern, but she'd already put the mail, unopened, into a box labeled *Julia*. Almost all the boxes were labeled *Julia* or *Alice*. Her husband seemed to own only clothes, a few basketballs, and his manuscript, which was still wrapped in its paper bag.

"That's ridiculous," Rose said, and Julia could tell she didn't believe her. "You want me to help you find an apartment in Pilsen? The ladies I'm friends with here have real estate connections everywhere. Let's take care of this. I can make some calls in the neighborhood. We can get you moved, and when your head's clear, you'll reconsider things with William."

"You're too far away to help with moving," Julia said. "Thank you, though."

"Don't be a fool. And don't use me as an excuse for bad behavior, Julia. You were raised better than that. How's my grandbaby?"

Julia looked over and smiled, because Alice had fallen asleep on the blanket. In the middle of stacks of boxes; in front of her mother, who was wearing jeans and an old sweatshirt; despite her grandmother hollering through the phone into Julia's soul.

"She's perfect," Julia said. "I'm going to make sure she stays perfect."

PROFESSOR COOPER HAD TOLD her that he was waiting for a particular project to come together so he would know which positions he might need filled. He called one afternoon and left a brief message on the machine. Julia knew he was too intelligent not to have realized that she wasn't answering her phone at all, since she always called him back directly after he left a message. She didn't mind if he suspected something was going on in her life, though. Suspecting was fine. Julia didn't know anything about Professor Cooper's personal life either. She liked that their relationship was purely professional.

When she phoned him back, Professor Cooper said, "Julia, I'm sorry to say that I won't be able to use your services right now. Probably not until next May, to be honest. I'm sorry, as I know that's not what you hoped to hear."

"But it's"—Julia searched her mind for the date—"October twelfth."

"I know. You see, I've been offered a large six-month project in New York, so I'll be out of town until it's finished. My work here will pick back up in the late spring, and at that point I'd be very pleased to have you work with me."

Julia tried to process this information. What would she do for the entire winter and spring? Besides babysitting and the kinds of jobs you did as a teenager, she'd never worked for anyone other than Professor Cooper. And he paid her enough that she could afford a good daycare for Alice. She'd planned to put the baby in Emeline's daycare when she started working so the baby could be doted on by her aunt and play with Izzy, who was there most days.

Julia considered herself very lucky to have taken a class with Professor Cooper; she'd signed up for the organizational-psychology course out of curiosity, not understanding the nature of the subject.

Cooper was a reserved man; he'd appeared flustered when she approached him as a student and asked if she could help him during the summer break. She'd offered to run errands, fetch coffee, whatever he wanted. And she had done some of that, but the professor seemed to realize that having her with him when he went on location to meet clients made the clients happy. Julia was smart, with insightful ideas. "I value your beginner's mind," Professor Cooper would say, and then tell her the complicated workflow problem he was struggling to solve. Sometimes she didn't understand well enough to help, but several times she had suggestions or ideas that sent him off in a new direction.

"I'll come with you," Julia heard herself say now. "I can help you with the big project."

"Come with me to New York?" The man sounded shocked.

Julia was shocked by the suggestion too.

"Forgive me"—Professor Cooper hesitated—"but don't you have a husband and a child?"

"I'll bring the baby," Julia said. "They must have good daycares in New York. And it's only six months."

A plan formed in Julia's mind. This could solve, or at least delay, several of her problems. She could store all of her furniture and belongings and put off finding a new apartment until she'd returned from New York. She would be far away from William while the divorce and his revocation of parental rights took place, which she thought might help keep the process businesslike. If William changed his mind and Julia lived in Chicago, he could argue with her in person. But if she was in New York, he would have to resort to a phone call or write a letter. The dust and drama would have settled in half a year's time. Perhaps when Julia returned, she would be able to live in Pilsen, near her sisters. Rose's friends would be less likely to chase her down the street asking why her marriage had ended and what she'd done wrong. Six months would offer a very different terrain from the hot coals her family was currently standing on.

"That's an interesting proposal," Professor Cooper said. "Hypothetically, I would pay for your plane ticket, of course, but everything else . . . I was planning to hire someone local."

"I'll cover the move," she said. "I can afford to do that." She almost said, *I've never been to New York, so seeing it would be exciting,* but she feared that would make her sound unserious about the work and also less helpful than a local hire, who would almost certainly know where to eat and how the subway system worked.

"I have a rule about not making decisions on the phone," Professor Cooper said.

"Of course," Julia said. Professor Cooper had many rules, most of them having to do with sound decision-making and efficiency. He bought one suit a year and no more, so that he stayed with the styles but also got good use out of his clothes. He kept trim by eating six large salads a week. It didn't matter when he ate them or what else he ate besides the salads; eating six large salads was the rule.

"But if you think you can handle the move, Julia, I accept your offer. You're the best assistant I've ever had. I'll get back to you with the details shortly."

When Julia hung up, she was flooded with a ticklish energy that made her do a frenzied dance in the middle of the boxes. She knew she should be scared, having made this wild decision, but she wasn't. She was excited. She thought about telling Rose and grinned; it would be fun to shock her mother with this news. Rose had run away, and there were consequences to that. One was that Julia had every right to run away too, if only for a little while. In fact, it occurred to Julia—in the middle of her dance—that her mother might be able to help her find an apartment in New York. Rose had said that her Miami friends had real estate connections everywhere; surely one of them would know of an available apartment in New York City. Perhaps one of the old ladies had a place sitting empty right there that Julia and Alice could simply occupy.

Julia pulled a bound atlas out of one of William's boxes; it was one of his few non-clothing belongings. She found New York State and then a close-up page of New York City. She traced the island of Manhattan with her finger. She had grown up in a city; how different could big cities be from one another? She looked around at the stacks of boxes, at the sleeping baby. She had figured out her next step, and neither her mother nor her sisters could stop her.

—

JULIA PUT OFF TELLING her sisters the news until the details had been confirmed with Professor Cooper and until Julia and Alice had plane tickets to leave for New York in two weeks' time. One or more of her sisters came over most nights for dinner, but Julia didn't want to tell them in person. She was scared that if her sisters became upset in front of her, she might lose her bravery and change her mind about the move. After all, the sisters had never been apart like this, never lived more than twenty minutes from one another, never not seen one another at least once a week and often every day. Julia decided the best plan was to tell one of them over the phone and then let that sister tell everyone else. She hoped she would be on the plane before they were able to hurl their collective emotions at her.

When she contemplated which sister to tell, she thought of Sylvie first, but Sylvie felt like a complicated choice. Sylvie visited Julia as often as the twins did, but she was quieter when she was in the apartment. She and Julia hugged more than they used to, and after dinner they sat side by side on the couch watching television with one sister resting her head on the other sister's shoulder. They held hands occasionally, reaching out to squeeze each other's fingers. Their bodies pulled together as if magnetized, as if their bodies were communicating during a period when the two oldest Padavano sisters both seemed hesitant to speak. Julia had never asked *why,* in the twenty-four hours after William walked out, Sylvie had been more concerned about William than her own sister. She'd never asked to hear the story of the search. She assumed Sylvie had stopped going to the hospital after William told her he wanted nothing to do with Julia and Alice, but something William's doctor said made Julia wonder if that was true.

Dr. Dembia had left a message on the answering machine, asking for ten minutes of Julia's time. The doctor was hoping Julia might provide some insight into what she referred to as William's "crash." But Julia hadn't known he was depressed; she hadn't seen this coming; she had been shocked by everything. When the doctor asked her for information, she realized she didn't even know much about his childhood. William had never talked about it.

Julia said, "I think our marriage would have ended no matter what."

There was a pause and then the doctor said, "I know this must have been very upsetting for you, even if your marriage was already in trouble."

For a moment, Julia couldn't speak. There was a lump in her throat, and she thought she might cry. She'd expected the doctor to chastise her for not knowing her husband. She'd expected the doctor to judge her for never coming to the hospital, even though she'd been told to stay away. She hadn't expected kindness. And the doctor had diagnosed her correctly: What had happened *had* upset Julia. She'd been knocked over like a tower of children's blocks, and even when she'd had a chance to gather herself back up, she felt like she'd lost part of her heart for good.

"I'm sorry I can't be more helpful," Julia said, when she could trust her voice.

"Thank you for your time, Sylvie."

Julia blinked. "Sylvie?"

"Oh, I'm sorry. I misspoke. Julia. I really do appreciate your speaking with me."

After she hung up, Julia wondered why Sylvie's name had been on the doctor's mind. Had Dr. Dembia seen Sylvie recently? Had her sister been standing in front of her during the conversation? The doctor's verbal slip may have meant nothing, but now Julia had questions, and those questions put Sylvie at a distance from her. She decided to call Emeline to tell her about moving to New York. Emeline had a kind voice and was almost always holding a baby, so she never shouted. Cecelia was prone to anger when she was surprised with what she might consider bad news. So on a Wednesday in the last week of October, Julia called Emeline at the daycare.

"It's the busiest time of the day," Emeline said. "The babies are losing their minds. Can I call you back when I get home later?"

"I need to tell you that I took a job with Professor Cooper."

"Oh, congratulations! That's wonderful."

"The first six months will be in New York City, and then I'll be back working here."

There was a silence, and Julia heard Emeline say, away from the phone, "Josie, can you cover for me? I need to take this call in the kitchen." There was a pause, presumably while Josie held the phone until Emeline picked up the line in the kitchen. "Thanks, Josie," Emeline said, and the other extension clicked off.

"New York City?" Emeline said.

"Just for six months. It's a great opportunity, and I need the job."

"You can't do that," Emeline said, and her voice sounded sharp, like Cecelia's. Emeline was a butter knife; Cecelia, a steak knife. "You can't leave now. In the middle of everything. That's a mistake, Julia. You can't run away."

"It's short term. I'm not running away." This frustrated Julia, though, because she knew Emeline meant running away from her marriage, and as far as Julia was concerned, that wasn't even possible. William had been perfectly clear. Their marriage was over. There was nothing to run away from.

"You need us with you," Emeline said. "You might not realize that, but you do. We need each other right now."

"You can come visit me in New York, Emmie. Wouldn't that be fun?"

"I'm disappointed," Emeline said, and Julia realized that she'd had her calculus all wrong. She'd called the wrong sister. Emeline was their conscience. Julia should have called Cecelia and they could have shouted at each other. She could have even called Sylvie and listened to the news bounce off her sister's silence. Emeline was operating from a place of right and wrong. She wasn't trying to win an argument. Cecelia and Sylvie would have been trying to win. Julia would have been better able to find a foothold in those contests.

"Alice is crying," Julia said. "I love you. I have to go."

When she hung up, she knew she'd failed even in ending the conversation. Crying babies were life to Emeline. Five or six were probably crying their way to nap time in her presence right now. Julia could picture her sister making her way back to her responsibilities, picking up babies and perching them on her hips, pushing pacifiers into mouths, cooing love at infants she had no relation to, simply because it was the right thing to do.

Sylvie

Dᴜʀɪɴɢ ᴛʜᴇ ꜰɪʀꜱᴛ ᴛᴇɴ ᴅᴀʏꜱ ᴏꜰ Wɪʟʟɪᴀᴍ'ꜱ ʜᴏꜱᴘɪᴛᴀʟɪᴢᴀᴛɪᴏɴ, the nurses and doctors all believed that Sylvie was William's wife. Sylvie had claimed that she was, after all, the day William tried to kill himself. She never used those words again, but neither she nor Kent corrected the mistake either. As a spouse, Sylvie was privy to information about William's medical care. Doctors and nurses treated her with respect and showed her William's chart, and Sylvie told Kent everything they said.

A few days after William was transferred to the second hospital, though, Sylvie told Dr. Dembia the truth. The aim in this unit was to treat William's diagnosed severe depression, and when Sylvie heard Dr. Dembia tell William, "I need you to be ruthlessly honest," she was immediately swamped with guilt. She felt like she had been caught lying during confession at St. Procopius. Sylvie followed the doctor into the hall and struggled to explain how she'd ended up in this situation. She was grateful that Dr. Dembia was a woman; Sylvie tried, while she talked, to pretend that the intense doctor with short gray hair was one of her sisters.

"William told my sister Julia that their marriage was over right before he tried to kill himself. So Julia didn't want to come to the hospital when it happened, and William's parents . . . I don't know what the issue is there, but they have nothing to do with him. Kent couldn't claim to be William's brother, for obvious reasons, and someone needed to advocate for William while he was unconscious. The ambulance driver assumed I was his wife, and I didn't correct him. So that's how this happened." Sylvie shrugged, feeling slightly dizzy at the contents of the paragraph leaving her mouth.

Dr. Dembia raised her eyebrows. "It sounds like you did the right thing," she said. "I'll change your designation to sister-in-law on the visitors' sheet. Thank you for letting me know."

If Sylvie's sisters had heard any of this, they would have been surprised; Sylvie was surprised too. She felt like a stranger to herself. She had been changed by the night and day she'd spent running through the city streets with William's friends. That time had been different from any other set of hours in Sylvie's life—the exertion, the company, the fear, the sleeplessness. She would never forget it; she felt marked by the experience, as if she'd gotten a tattoo.

Sylvie told herself that she continued to visit William for two reasons: First, because William was still physically unwell and unable to take charge of his own medical care, so it helped to have someone there to speak to the doctor. Kent couldn't do it, because he'd had to return to medical school. And second, because Julia had asked Sylvie to find out if she had to come to the hospital, if she still had to be a wife. "Do I need to *do* something?" Julia had asked when Sylvie visited. Sylvie had already disappointed her sister once, by leaving her to search for William, and she didn't want to disappoint her again. Sylvie waited by William's bedside for him to become alert enough to talk.

The many hours William spent in the lake had temporarily affected his eyesight, his electrolyte levels, and his thyroid. He had a hard time staying awake, and Sylvie read a favorite collection of poems while he slept. Poems suited her fractured attention span, but she also chose them to feel closer to her father. Charlie was almost always on Sylvie's mind while she sat beside the sleeping patient. Her father had understood her, and she knew he would have recognized William's brokenness too. Sylvie knew with all her heart that if Charlie had been alive, he would also be in this hospital room, able, like his middle daughter, to follow the inner journey of the man in the bed.

One afternoon, William blinked awake and pulled himself up to a seated position, and Sylvie put her book down. Her body became fretful beneath her, and she knew it was time. She could almost feel Julia fretful in her own apartment across town. Did William mean what he had written in the note? Did he really not want Julia to be his wife? When William said—in a flat, clear voice—that, no, he didn't want Julia to visit, and he didn't want Alice either, and he was giving both of them up more completely than Sylvie or Julia or the twins would have considered possible, Sylvie looked at his turned-away face, his long body in the bed, the white sky out the window, and felt her body gather and release into silent sobs.

It turned out that she had needed that answer too. Sylvie was composed of question marks and feelings that she didn't know what to do with, as if her hands were full and she was wearing pants with no pockets. Sylvie was going through something herself in this hospital room. She missed her sister, but if Julia showed up at the hospital, there would no longer be a place for Sylvie beside William's bed. And if Julia and her husband reunited, Sylvie knew she would fit nowhere; their apartment and this room would somehow no longer hold space for her. Sylvie felt like she'd checked into this hospital room alongside William, and she needed more time. She wasn't sick, but she wasn't well either.

Sylvie intended to stop visiting after that. She'd met both of her goals: William was well enough to speak to the doctor, and Julia had been given the news she desired. But Sylvie found that she couldn't stay away. She told herself every morning that she wouldn't visit that day and then climbed onto the bus that traveled to the hospital. She felt pulled, as if by magnetic force, between the library, the hospital, and her older sister's apartment. She stamped books, sent out overdue notices, sat by William's bed, and ate takeout with her sisters.

What am I doing? she asked herself repeatedly, and she never had a good answer. In the hospital, Sylvie spent hours sitting next to someone who had wanted to be dead. He certainly didn't seem to be fully alive. Sometimes his eyes were blank when he looked at Sylvie, and she could tell he had to work to remember her name. She sat in silence, a book open in her lap, willing the man in the bed to restitch himself to life's fabric. Dr. Dembia had talked to her about the stickiness of depression, about the art and science of finding the right mixture and levels of medication. "He'll need to be on medication for the rest of his life," Dr. Dembia said. "He won't be able to manage this depression without it. It's remarkable he made it this far."

Sylvie struggled to think of a safe subject to talk to William about as he became more alert. She couldn't attempt small talk; she couldn't bear to talk to him about the weather or the terrible hospital food. The idea of chatting with William about nonsense made her mouth so dry she couldn't say anything at all. Once, out of desperation, she asked him a basketball-related question. This worked and became the solution for conversations that weren't stilted or awkward. Sylvie recalled a specific player or a piece of basketball history from his book and asked him about it. She felt a wave of relief because of the relief on William's face when he answered. A light went on behind his eyes in those moments, which made Sylvie think of the pilot light on a stove. She found a basketball encyclopedia in the library and took notes on possible questions she could ask. She wanted to turn that pilot light on again. She wondered whether, if she asked enough questions, it might turn on for good.

SYLVIE, CECELIA, AND EMELINE left Julia's apartment one night after a dinner. Julia had looked lighter since hearing that William didn't want her or Alice. She smiled, and teased her sisters, and gave opinions on the food they were eating, and talked about Alice and Izzy. Sylvie watched her older sister and envied her lightness. Sylvie felt trapped within herself, as if she were snowed in with secrets. Whenever she opened her mouth to speak during dinner, she felt a bleary confusion about what she was free to say and what she wasn't.

Cecelia had borrowed a car from a sculptor who wanted to date her, so they climbed into his small green sedan. Emeline sat in the back next to a sleepy Izzy, who was buckled into a car seat.

"No speeding," Emeline said, in warning. When Cecelia drove, she drove fast.

"I don't think I like Buffalo wings," Cecelia said. "What chickens have wings that small, anyway? It seems suspicious."

"And she's out," Emeline said, because Izzy had fallen asleep. The little girl's expression was serious, as if her unconscious mind was contemplating difficult problems: how to optimize budget deficits in a modern economy, perhaps, or whether free will is compatible with determinism.

Sylvie's muscles were so tight she had struggled to buckle her seatbelt. When the car accelerated after turning a corner, she knew she had to say something or she would be entirely snowed in and unable to speak at all. She coughed and said in a rush, "I have to tell you both something. I've been visiting William. Sometimes. I've visited him a few times. I don't want to tell Julia, but I can't not tell you too."

Cecelia looked at Sylvie from the driver's seat. Sylvie could see her sister weighing up what she'd said.

"Oh, I'm glad," Emeline said, with obvious relief.

Sylvie turned to look over her shoulder.

"I've been really worried about William," Emeline said. "He has no family. I know we're supposed to side with Julia, and I do, of course"— Emeline's eyes were wide—"but William isn't a jerk. He must have been in such terrible pain to do what he did. It's an awful situation, really. I can't bear it. I'm so glad you're visiting him."

"Oh, Emmie." Sylvie felt her shoulders relax. She felt how stressed she'd been, carrying this secret. "That's how I feel."

Cecelia was bent over the steering wheel. "What?" she said, feeling her sisters' eyes on her.

"Are you mad at me?" Sylvie said.

"I'm glad you told us," Cecelia said, "but I'm not going to visit him."

Sylvie knew Cecelia was angry at William for attempting suicide. "Any of us would have helped him, if he'd asked," she'd said several times in the days after it happened. Sylvie thought that her sister couldn't stand the idea that someone she cared about would try to wreck himself in secret. Cecelia operated with honesty and bluntness. She believed that if you were unhappy, you should say so. If you needed help, you should ask for it. William's silence offended Cecelia as much as his choice to walk into the lake.

"I don't think you *should* visit him," Sylvie said. "Julia would hate that I'm doing it. We shouldn't all have something to hide from her."

Cecelia didn't seem to be listening. She said, "Emmie's been hammering me about how much pain William must have been in. She wants me to understand, even though it makes no sense to me."

Emeline nodded in the back seat.

Sylvie said, "I'm glad you're not mad at me. I couldn't bear that."

"That possibility's not on the table," Cecelia said, and Sylvie smiled, because she knew her sister meant it. Cecelia had certain nonnegotiables, and during this time of familial turbulence, she would bend in any necessary direction to support her sisters.

When Cecelia dropped Sylvie off at home, Ernie was waiting outside her apartment door. She hadn't seen him since the night they'd slept together, and she'd thought of him only rarely, but it made sense that Ernie would appear now. Sylvie had started to tell the truth—at least some of it, to some people—which meant she could no longer avoid her previous self.

Who do I want to be now? Sylvie thought. *Do I have a choice?*

"It's been a while," Ernie said, and she agreed. They were both clearly nervous about how this would go. Ernie said that the front door of her building was broken and that she should tell her super. Sylvie said that the door had been broken for a while now. Ernie was wearing jeans and a bowling shirt, and she noted—as if adding up numbers in a column—that he looked cute. Sylvie smiled, and he smiled back. She allowed him to take her into his arms and allowed him to kiss her neck.

Then she stepped back, her arms by her sides. There was a buzzing sensation in her body, a kind of warning signal. She told Ernie what had happened after she'd last seen him, and it turned out that Ernie had heard about the lake rescue on the radio. He said, "I can't believe that was your brother-in-law."

"Yes," Sylvie said. "I'm busy helping him and my sister now, so I really don't have any free time." She paused. *I don't want you,* she thought. *I wish I did. I wish I was a normal girl who wanted to sleep with the handsome man in front of her.*

"Oh . . . right," he said, understanding on his face. They were still in the hallway.

"Maybe I'll see you at the library?"

"Sure thing," Ernie said, and then he was gone.

Sylvie leaned against the wall. Because she was clear about what she didn't want, she was alone. She was no longer who she used to be, and she wasn't yet whoever she was becoming. She was grateful that her father had prepared her for this type of hard, lonely ground. Because of him, Sylvie knew she could exist outside the boundaries of her past and future selves, for a little while, anyway. Even though it hurt. She understood now, though, why her father had tempered the brutal beauty of this kind of life—this kind of honesty—with alcohol, and why she had always been more comfortable in the library with books than in the world with people.

She was still in the hallway. She wanted to go inside her cozy studio; the scuffed walls and fluorescent lighting of the hall made the scratches of despair inside her deeper, but the discomfort felt necessary. There was a question she needed to ask herself—a question covered with pointy brambles.

What do you want?

Sylvie wouldn't have asked this question before, because she would have been afraid of the answer, but she wanted to be deeply and truly herself and to experience the world in the deepest and truest way. She'd been compartmentalizing herself for a long time, certainly since her father had died. She was one person with Julia, a slightly more honest person with the twins, and she controlled her own thoughts and feelings, trying to battle herself onto paths she felt like she should be walking. There was only one person Sylvie felt fully herself with: William. She was *all* of herself with him and even felt there was room for her to become more. When he rested his eyes on her, it was without judgment or expectation, and in that space, Sylvie felt her potential: for bravery, brilliance, kindness, joy. All of these sails rested on the deck of her ship; they were hers, but she hadn't seen them before. She hadn't been aware of them prior to the many hours she'd spent in William's hospital room. Her father's love had said, *Do everything. Be everything.* She knew, when she was near William, that she had the capacity to raise these giant, beautiful sails and *go.*

She thought, *I want to be with him,* and had to catch her breath at the enormity of this desire. It felt like she'd been holding an umbrella to deny that it was raining, and now the umbrella was gone, and she was standing in a storm. Sylvie was awash in surprise, shame, and sadness because, of course, she *couldn't* be with him. Not once he left the hospital, and not in any way that mattered.

ONE AFTERNOON, DR. DEMBIA stopped Sylvie in the hospital corridor. "I'm trying to piece something together, and you might be able to help. William said you'd been talking to him about basketball."

Sylvie nodded, pleased that the doctor was asking for her assistance. "He likes to talk about it. He's . . . happier when he's talking about basketball."

"Yes," the doctor said. "Why do you think basketball is so important to him?"

"Well, he's played it since he was a kid. He was on his college team." Sylvie thought about this. "Have you asked Kent?"

"He said that basketball was William's first language. That he dribbled a ball more than he spoke when he was a kid."

"His first language," Sylvie repeated. That made sense. She had stumbled into speaking William's first language with him, perhaps the only language he spoke fluently. That was why his pilot light had turned on.

"I do think that's part of it." The doctor nodded at a patient walking by but kept her eyes on Sylvie.

"He told me once that his parents didn't love him," Sylvie said. "I think they barely spoke to him when he was young." Hearing the sentence out loud shocked her a little. Rose and Charlie had never *stopped* speaking to their girls when they were children. Sylvie tried to imagine what it would have been like to grow up in a home with no affection or laughter and envisioned a cold, echoing space. She saw a little boy dribbling a basketball in order to make a comforting, repetitive sound. Sylvie had the sensation she often had when she was reading a good novel and the story came together suddenly inside her, accompanied by a new understanding.

She said, "Basketball was the first thing in William's life that loved him back. The only thing that loved him, for a long time."

"Yes," Dr. Dembia said, her eyes bright. She was a scientist, and Sylvie had just handed her a useful part of an equation. "That's it. Yes."

THE DAY WILLIAM ASKED Sylvie to write down his secrets, she left his room and noticed that her hands were shaking. What had happened in that room was how she'd always thought church should feel. The air seemed to break open, and what passed between them felt sacred.

Sylvie usually caught the bus right in front of the hospital, but that afternoon she walked to the library. She wanted to feel the wind on her skin. She broke into a jog a few times, because her body craved motion, and she liked that mid-stride both of her feet were off the ground for a split second. That night at Julia's apartment, she whispered to Emeline and Cecelia that she needed to talk to them. They understood that she meant without Julia, so when they got into the sculptor's car after a meal of curry and samosas, Cecelia drove a few blocks away and then pulled over. Mrs. Ceccione was watching Izzy; it was just the three sisters in the car. Sylvie and Cecelia turned their bodies so they could both see Emeline in the back seat.

"What is it?" Emeline said. "Is William okay?"

Sylvie told them everything William had told her. The only thing she left out was his comment that he wouldn't have been able to share his secrets with anyone other than her. That sentence warmed Sylvie's insides and belonged to her alone.

"Oh my heavens," Emeline said, when Sylvie was done. She was quiet for a minute. "That was so brave of him."

"I can't believe he had a sister," Cecelia said.

The three women looked at one another with shared wonder. A hidden, lost sister was momentous. Sylvie said, "The doctor, who I really like, told him that to be well, he couldn't keep these things inside him anymore. She gave him a mantra: No bullshit and no secrets."

"I have to tell you something." The words burst out of Emeline as if from a blocked tap. "Part of why I've felt so bad for William," she said, "is that I've been depressed sometimes. Over the last few years. I've even had those kinds of thoughts."

The car windows were closed. It was a gusty October night; the wind rattled branches above their heads, making it sound like the trees were clapping. "No, you haven't." Cecelia's voice was sharp. "Don't say that. It isn't true."

"I wouldn't have done anything," Emeline said. "I promise."

"Why would you hide that from us?" Sylvie said. "Why wouldn't you tell us you felt sad?"

Emeline turned her face toward the car window. "I've been afraid to tell you. But William's doctor is right. We shouldn't have any secrets."

Cecelia studied her twin's profile. She was clearly surprised to hear that there were any secrets between them. "Emmie, you can tell us anything."

"I have a crush on someone. A big crush."

Sylvie and Cecelia both brought their hands to their chests, which was what Rose did when she was told big news. Julia did this too.

Emeline's eyes were closed now. Her head was still turned away, as if she feared a physical blow. "It's not a man, though. It's Josie, the woman who works with me in the daycare."

"Josie?" Cecelia said.

"I was sure I was wrong and that how I felt just meant I really liked her, because I do. We work wonderfully together, and she makes me laugh. The babies follow her around. But my heart beats faster when I'm near her, and I want to kiss her so badly."

Sylvie's body was stiff with surprise. She tried to think of what to say.

"I know," Emeline said, with sorrow.

Sylvie had never known a lesbian personally. There was a lady who rode her bicycle around the neighborhood wearing a baseball cap, and it was rumored that she lived with another woman, but she never came into the library, so Sylvie had never seen her up close. She thought of lesbians as being somehow hard and manly, and Emeline was the opposite of that. She was the sweetest and softest of the sisters.

"Oh, Emmie," Cecelia said. "Are you sure?"

Emeline's eyes filled with tears. Sylvie reached into the back seat to touch her younger sister's knee. "We love you," she said. "This is just . . . unexpected, that's all."

"I have no idea if Josie likes me in that way," Emeline said. "She probably doesn't."

"Mom would be horrified," Cecelia said. This was undoubtedly true; Rose was Catholic all the way to her bones and had said several disparaging or insulting things about gay people in front of the girls over the course of their lives. A terrible new disease that seemed to afflict mostly gay men had been identified recently, and this news story disgusted and fascinated Rose in equal measure.

"I know. It's the first time I've been happy that she moved away."

The relief in Emeline's eyes made the other women laugh.

"I thought if I told you, you would hate me. But William told you awful things, and I only feel sympathy for him." She hesitated. "I won't be able to have babies, though," she whispered. "I won't be able to be a mother."

Sylvie and Cecelia traded the quickest of glances, to share their surprise at what they'd just learned and their grief at the last statement. William didn't want to be a father, and Emeline couldn't have what she most wanted, to be a mother. "You can adopt, maybe?" Sylvie said. She felt another small fissure inside herself; another piece of life was separating the sisters from the dreams they'd once held for themselves and one another.

Emeline shook her head. "I wonder how William feels. I feel better." Her face was brighter; she sat taller. "Now you have to tell me a truth from your lives," she said. "Your turns. In honor of William."

This reminded Sylvie of the future-predicting game they used to play. Even though they'd just left Julia, Sylvie missed her sister, a sensation like a painful stab in her side. She could see that her sisters had also remembered the game, and there was a crease between Emeline's eyebrows that meant she regretted how she'd phrased the request. They had recently learned that Julia was leaving them for six months. The departure had struck each of them as a mistake. "The timing is awful," Cecelia said. "She's running away," Emeline said. But Sylvie suspected her sister was running *toward* something. A new life. Julia wanted to reimagine herself, and it was hard to do that in the presence of people who had known her since she was a small girl. Sylvie worried, though, that Julia had sensed Sylvie was keeping something secret from her, and that secret had opened space for Julia to leave. If Sylvie and Julia had stayed close-knit, and stayed honest, the older sister wouldn't have considered departure a possibility. Deep inside herself, Sylvie believed it was her fault that Julia would soon be gone.

"I'll go first," Cecelia said. "I wish I could have sex. I've only had it once."

Emeline must have known this, but Sylvie was surprised. She had assumed that Cecelia had bedded many lovers on a painter's tarp, before or after a project. She felt like Cecelia had pulled on the fabric of adulthood more easily than the rest of them. She moved with a confidence that Sylvie lacked and seemed unfazed by other people's expectations. When Cecelia was with Izzy, they both laughed a great deal; they visibly delighted each other. Sylvie had assumed that her sister had cherry-picked men to delight her physically too.

"I know I make it look like everything is great," Cecelia said, to answer Sylvie's expression. "And it's really good, but not great. The guy who owns this car would happily have sex with me, but he's a billion years old, and sleazy. I have bills to pay, and the boys anywhere near my age are so immature I can't stand it."

"Sylvie?" Emeline said.

"Oh," Sylvie said, and the syllable came out like a little moan. It was warm in the car now, and the windows were fogged up. Sylvie had *become* a secret. She was changing in ways she couldn't keep track of, much less explain. Would she tell them that she thought about William all the time and missed him as soon as she left his room? That sometimes, when he was sleeping in the hospital bed, Sylvie wanted to lie down next to him in the hope that he might mistake her for his wife and hold her? Instead, she said, "I'm writing something."

Her sisters' faces opened with pleasure. *Of course,* Sylvie saw them think.

"No," she said, "it's not like you're thinking. It's not a book. I'm having trouble sleeping, so when I get home at night, I write something about our childhood. It's only scenes. Last night I wrote about the birthday party where that boy dared Julia to hold her breath for as long as she could, and she held it for so long she passed out."

"Our ninth birthday," Cecelia said. "The one with the terrible cake."

"Bright-yellow icing," Emeline said. "Sylvie! How wonderful. I'm so glad you're doing that."

"It's not good." Sylvie tried to impress this upon them with her eyes. She needed her sisters to understand. "It's not about making it good." She had gotten the idea, the possibility, from reading William's book, of course. And from Whitman too. Sylvie had always thought that when, *if*, she wrote, it would have to be perfect. A beautifully crafted novel, ready to hand to the world. But William had shown her she could write for, and to, herself. And Whitman had rewritten, expanded, cut, and reimagined his poems across his life. He'd created not one beautiful book but different attempts at excellence and beauty as he aged and loved and reconsidered everything.

Sylvie found inhabiting herself in the present difficult; her skin had felt uncomfortably tight ever since William was rescued. She was aware that she was writing about her childhood in an attempt to make a third door; she needed to take a sledgehammer to a wall to find a way out of the here and now. When Sylvie did sleep, she was stricken on the beach, watching men carry a dead William out of the lake. And an ache ran through her, because Julia was leaving Chicago and she had no idea of the pain and longing Sylvie carried inside her. Every night, Sylvie sat at her tiny desk by the window, overlooking Pilsen, remembering and trying to re-create the times when her family was whole. When Charlie was alive, Rose in her garden, the twins giggling in their bedroom, Julia striding around the house doling out plans like gifts. Every moment Sylvie captured on the page couldn't be lost.

SYLVIE FELT EXHAUSTED BY her desire for honesty but also drawn to it, as if the quality were a magnet. She loved that she could see a fuller version of Emeline now, after she'd told Sylvie and Cecelia her truth.

Sylvie had stopped by the daycare one afternoon, because she wanted to meet Josie; she wanted to smile at the young auburn-haired woman who held her sister's heart. Emeline was flushed and shooting off sparks of happiness in her work setting, surrounded by babies, with Josie nearby. Seeing the breadth of Emeline excited Sylvie, even though her sister hadn't yet confessed her feelings to Josie and didn't know if they would be reciprocated.

Sylvie appreciated that William's healing was built on truthfulness. She remembered Dr. Dembia telling William that she wanted him to be relentlessly honest. The problem was that in her new state of heightened awareness, Sylvie had spotted a glaring dishonesty in William's behavior, and it bothered her. She kept her mouth shut, because it was none of her business, and William was under the care of Dr. Dembia, not her. Surely the doctor would see what Sylvie saw and fix it? But nothing seemed to change, and it felt to Sylvie like William was building his new life on a rickety foundation.

One afternoon, William said, "You seem grumpy. Is something wrong?"

"I'm not grumpy," Sylvie said, though she could feel herself scowling.

"If you say so," he said.

"Well," she said. "There is one thing that's bothering me. William, of course you can do whatever you want, and I'm not judging your choice. Really." She hesitated. "But I know your mantra, and I think you're lying to yourself about something important."

He looked at her, and she knew he could see her fear. He could see her concern that she might say something that could set his recovery back. "Don't worry," William said. "I'm all right. Just say it."

"It's about Alice."

He flinched, but almost imperceptibly; this was the first time either of them had mentioned the baby.

Sylvie said, "You gave her up because you think you'd hurt her, but that's wrong. You wouldn't hurt Alice. I know you wouldn't."

William was quiet for a minute. "Dr. Dembia thinks the decision to give up custody is bullshit too." His face looked worn, as if he had been alive for all of time and had seen every possible heartbreak. "I disagree, though, and I can't take that chance. Alice is better off with Julia."

Sylvie felt her shoulders relax. William *had* spoken to Dr. Dembia; he'd given the subject thought and made a careful decision. She still thought he was wrong, but it wasn't her decision to make, and it occurred to Sylvie that perhaps the truth was more complicated for William because of his past. Now that she knew about his lost sister— a baby girl who had died—it made sense to Sylvie that his worry over his daughter might be heightened. Perhaps the two babies shared space inside him, and the right thing for him *was* to step away. She could see this possibility and the way grief and depression tangled inside him; Sylvie found that she could accept his choice even if she didn't fully understand.

William leaned forward and said, "Do you have any concern, any concern at all, that Julia won't take excellent care of Alice?"

Sylvie didn't even have to think about this. "No."

He nodded. "I'm the risk factor," he said. "That's why I removed myself."

JULIA DIDN'T WANT A group goodbye; she said it would be too painful. She asked Sylvie to come over the morning before her flight to New York. Sylvie found her sister and Alice in a small clearing in the middle of stacks of boxes in the living room.

"I can't actually do this," Julia said, without looking at Sylvie. "I can't say goodbye."

"I can't either." Sylvie gave her attention to Alice, who was sitting on the small blanket on the floor. Julia had clipped a pink bow into the baby's scant blond hair, and Alice looked tremendously pleased about this development. Sylvie felt slightly breathless. She'd been missing her sister since William had been hospitalized, and now Julia was leaving. It felt like compounded loss. And this beautiful baby, who was beaming up at her mother and aunt, was going to disappear too. Sylvie loved Alice so much, and six months was such a long time in a baby's life. Alice would be one year old the next time Sylvie saw her. She might be walking. She might have forgotten the sight of her three adoring aunts.

"Bah," Alice said with delight, and Sylvie leaned down to kiss her cheek.

Julia was wearing jeans and an old T-shirt. She seemed over-caffeinated, jittery. "I never thought I would leave Chicago. But I never thought Daddy would die. And I never thought Mama would move away." She paused and then said, "I never thought you would visit my husband in the hospital every day."

Shocked, Sylvie took the words like a punch to the stomach. She had been on her knees, to be close to the baby, but now she rose to her feet. "Not every day," she managed.

Julia nodded. "I wasn't sure you were visiting him at all."

Sylvie looked at her sister directly for the first time. She could feel the distance that had grown between them over the last few months. "You didn't have to trick me," she said. "You could have just asked."

"I wasn't sure you'd tell the truth."

Sylvie took this in. "He has no one else," she said. "I feel bad for him."

Julia left the clearing of boxes and came back holding a folder. "These are the divorce and custody papers," she said. "Please give them to William the next time you see him."

Sylvie felt despair. She felt her sister cutting at the threads that connected them. Was this Sylvie's fault? Or was Julia lashing out because otherwise she couldn't bear to leave? "I love you," Sylvie said.

Julia pushed her hair off her face. She shook her head at the same time, as if annoyed, as if this sentiment were not the point. But she said, "I love you too."

SYLVIE SHOWED UP EARLY on the cold November morning that William was due to be checked out. She knew Kent was coming, as was Arash. Dr. Dembia would probably be on hand. Sylvie could tell that the doctor cared about William as a person and would miss her time with him. Cecelia, whose antagonism toward William had been extinguished with the revelation that Emeline had also been depressed, was going to meet them at his new Northwestern apartment to judge whether the walls would benefit from colorful paint. When Sylvie stepped out of the elevator on the psych-unit floor, she found herself glancing around for Julia. Her sister was gone, eight hundred miles gone, but still Sylvie half-believed she would find Julia here, her jaw set, ready to organize her husband back into her life.

William was standing by the window when Sylvie got to his room. He barely had anything to pack. He hadn't wanted to ask Julia for any of his belongings when he first arrived in the hospital. He had been adamant about this, although he needed clothes, and he was so tall he couldn't wear anything from the hospital's lost-and-found bin. Hearing this, his friends from the basketball team had dropped off clothes from their own closets. William was wearing a pair of khaki pants, worn sneakers, and a Northwestern sweatshirt. He had signed the divorce and custody papers, and Sylvie had mailed them to the lawyer. When she left Chicago, Julia had arranged for his possessions to be put in a storage locker for him. As of the day he was leaving the hospital, William was no longer married and no longer a father.

"Big day," she said.

"Sylvie," he said. He looked down at his hands. "I don't know how to thank you for everything you've done."

"You don't have to."

"I've been selfish. I should have told you to stop coming, but I liked when you were here. I hope you know that when I leave the hospital, you don't have to worry about me anymore. Please know that. I have my medication"—he gave a trace of a smile—"and my mantra. I'll try to help Arash." He paused. "Everyone has been so kind to me. I'm not going to waste their kindness."

These words hit Sylvie strangely. It felt like William had put together sentences that took aim at what was inside her. She could tell, intellectually, that he'd said a nice thing, something she agreed with. William was healthier. He was telling her she could walk away, but she knew—the knowledge sharp, like pain—that she didn't want to, that she might not be able to. This was her real secret, the one no one could know. Sylvie's eyes smarted, and she had a flash of worry that she might cry. She said, "Did you know that I searched for you for that whole night with Kent and the other guys?"

William squinted, as if there was light in the room that hurt his eyes. "Yes," he said. "Kent told me."

Why am I thinking about this? Why am I talking about it? She said, "When they carried you out of the water, I thought you were dead." She couldn't stop herself from picturing it now: the tall, tired young men bearing William's limp body. "I didn't know what to do. I couldn't help move you, but I wanted to do something to help. So I held your hand while Kent and Gus carried you to the ambulance. And in the ambulance too."

William was quiet for a moment, then said, "I didn't know that. I don't remember most of that day. Sylvie, I'm really sorry you had to go through that. It must have been very frightening."

When Sylvie lay in bed at night, she recalled, over and over again, Kent calling her name and her running across the sand. She remembered the shards of panic and grief in her chest because William was gone. She remembered when she reached out and took William's ice-cold hand. She didn't want William to be alone, even if he was no longer alive. And yet, in that moment, she had never felt so alone.

She heard herself say, "Can I hold your hand again, for one second?"

William crossed the room to stand in front of her. He held his hand out, palm facing up. His skin was soft and warm, so different from that day. A wave of feelings ran through Sylvie. A radio dial spun inside her, the volume loud. *I love you,* she thought, and the words—impossible now to deny—brought her both desolation and deep joy. William was her one. He was her heart. He had changed all the molecules inside her. Sylvie had known love would come for her with the force of a tsunami. She'd dreamed of this ever since she was a little girl, and her dream had actually come true. But she hadn't known her love would be impossible, a dead end, unspeakable, because he had been married to her sister.

She thought, *I'm in so much trouble.* The thought made her laugh.

"Are you okay?" William asked.

She didn't want him to worry, so she said, "I'm okay."

She and William held hands for a few more seconds, until there was a noise in the hall, and they stepped apart.

Kent arrived, bouncy with excitement as if he were showing up at a playoff game, ready to celebrate a win. "You're out of here!" he said, and gave William a big hug. Normally, only one visitor was permitted at a time, but because William was checking out, the rule had been waived.

Arash walked in, took one look at Kent's face, and said, "You'll always be a damn fool." But he was grinning too.

William opened his mouth to speak and then closed it. He gave a small shake of his head. Kent, understanding that his friend wanted to say *thank you,* or even *I love you,* but was unable to say the words without starting to cry, slapped William on the back, and the four people in the room just smiled at one another.

SYLVIE WALKED OUT OF the hospital with those three men an hour later, the hand William had held tingling at her side. The November sky was gray, and the forecast predicted the first snowfall of the year that night. They walked beneath a canopy of leafless trees on the way to Kent's car, and Sylvie thought about the memory she'd written down at her small desk the night before. She wasn't writing her family history in any particular order, though the recollections did seem to lap into one another like waves. Last night she'd found herself remembering the time when Mrs. Ceccione's mean, yippy dog had chased Emeline up a tree. Even after the dog was put away, the eight-year-old girl had refused to come down. Julia, Sylvie, and Cecelia stood at the bottom of the tree for an hour, coaxing Emeline with snacks and promises to braid her hair—she loved to have her hair played with—to no avail. *I can't live without you,* Cecelia said at one point, as if in warning. *Don't be ridiculous,* Julia said. *None of us can live without each other.* Rose was alerted, and she yelled at her daughter to get her little bippy down on the ground immediately. *No, thank you,* Emeline said, gripping the tree branch. *I have a nice view. I can't come down.* Kids from the neighborhood gathered around the trunk too, wanting to see how the story would end. Sylvie remembered that her neck had ached from gazing upward for so long. Cecelia started to cry, which made Emeline cry too, but she now seemed rooted in the tree, unable to leave her perch. It was hard for her sisters to imagine her returning to them as the sun set and darkness began to fall. When Charlie got home from work, he joined the crowd at the bottom of the tree, still wearing his white short-sleeved shirt and tie. He didn't speak. He gazed up at his daughter, like a tractor beam sending love. Emeline didn't say a word either, but she climbed down into his arms.

Sylvie had avoided thinking about what her life would look like after William checked out of the hospital. She'd kept her head down and showed up in his room, knowing that that was where she belonged. She'd hoped, at first, that his release from the hospital would return her to her former self. But now she felt like she was seated on the tree branch beside the small Emeline, not wanting to get down. Her previous life was the ground beneath her. She saw Ernie, with his dimpled chin and jovial expression. Her solo commute from her studio to the library. Her co-workers chatting about quirky patrons, the weather, their weekend plans. But there was no tractor-beam gaze from Charlie, because there was no Charlie, and there was no Julia either. She would see William less, or perhaps not at all, because the crisis was over, and it would be dangerous for her to spend time with him. She might reach for his hand or be unable to silence her feelings. Sylvie scooched closer to Emeline's small body and held tight to the branch. There was no way she could go back to that heartbroken, lonely ground, where the sisters, who'd believed they would die if they were separated, had separated.

William

AFTER HE LEFT THE HOSPITAL, WILLIAM LIVED THE WAY HE imagined drunks did after they stopped drinking: carefully, and one day at a time. He felt newly housed in his body, aware that any negligence could cause the entire building to collapse. Each morning, he got out of his single bed, took four of the eight pills he had to swallow every day, and did as many push-ups as he could—five, at first—and then the knee exercises the surgeon had assigned him years earlier, which he'd ignored. William was almost amused at how his knee audibly creaked during the stretches, issuing loud complaints about being asked to function. But he didn't stop, and he never missed a day; he had to take deliberate actions toward stability and health. "When I visit, we're going to go for runs together," Kent said, on one of their phone calls. "You have to get in shape."

William nodded into the empty room. He'd been lucky that the dorm suite was furnished with a couch and bed when he arrived; these walls had seen a revolving door of questionable adults over the years: grown men who had lives small enough to fit into the miniature set of rooms, who were willing to handle middle-of-the-night emergencies and usher college students out of the building if there was a fire. "Another divorced guy, huh," the aged security guard had noted when he gave William his keys, as if he was keeping an inventory of the reasons men ended up here. William could have said, *Mental hospital, actually,* to shock him, but he didn't. The fewer people who knew where he'd come from, the better.

William said to Kent, "I'll go running, but not near the lake." He knew he probably didn't need to say these words, that Kent would naturally steer them away from the shoreline, but William wanted to be clear about what he didn't want, when he knew what that was. Before his hospitalization, he'd done things he didn't want to do all the time, and he'd gotten so good at muffling his own preferences that he was rarely aware of them. Knowing he didn't want to jog along the lake path, and saying so, felt like progress.

He tried this tack again with Cecelia when she brought over a painting of Alice to hang on the wall in his dorm suite. She'd deemed his set of small rooms—a bedroom and a tiny living area with a kitchen along one wall—acceptable. "At least they gave you bookshelves," she said. "They could use a coat of paint, though. I see Sylvie brought you a haul from the library." It was true; all the books on his shelves were covered in plastic and had the Lozano Library seal on the spine. Sylvie had arrived one afternoon with equal amounts of fiction, nonfiction, and poetry; the nonfiction was all basketball-related—biographies of players and histories of the sport.

"Careful, Iz," Cecelia said. The thirteen-month-old was walking slowly around the rooms, her small face fixed with concentration beneath her unruly curls. She appeared to be judging the space: the walls, the furniture. She looked under the bed, then walked into the bathroom to check out the bathtub. When William had gone into the hospital, Izzy was still a baby everyone carried around; he kept doing double takes, startled by the tiny independent human studying his belongings.

"Sylvie said she was going to switch the books out when they're due back at the library," he said. "I mean, I told her she didn't have to, but . . ." He shrugged. He was acutely aware of his relief that Cecelia, and not Sylvie, was here now. He was comfortable with Cecelia. She was who she'd always been with him, and his feelings for her remained unchanged. This wasn't the case with Sylvie. It felt like William had seen Sylvie through a sliver in a doorway, and now the door had been thrown wide open. She commanded his full attention in a way that mystified him, and whenever they were together, goosebumps rose on William's arms. Sylvie showed up at his place every few days, and her presence always jolted him, as if he'd been dealt an electric shock.

He knew, rationally, that this change could be explained by the fact that Sylvie had accompanied him through the most turbulent moment of his life. She'd sat beside his hospital bed, spoken to the psychiatrist. She had received his secrets. He'd been confused when he woke up in the hospital to find Sylvie next to him, but she'd looked confused too, and somehow they'd started over from the same groggy place. She had accepted him unquestioningly, even when he was bloated with lake water. This had surprised William, and still surprised him. No one in his life, except perhaps Kent, had ever accepted him just as he was, and Sylvie had accepted him when he was so broken he was barely a person.

"The kitchen is a bit drab," Cecelia said, frowning at the sink, mini-refrigerator, and hot plate. "Not sure what we can do about that."

"Cecelia?" he said.

She looked at him. Of all the sisters, she reminded him the most of Julia. She shared her older sister's searing focus. Cecelia was more curious than Julia, though, and more interested in getting to the bottom of things. He'd heard Cecelia tell her sisters once, "I don't give a shit what people think of me." William had been startled by this, partly because he believed her, and partly because it hadn't occurred to him that this was an option.

"Thank you for the painting of Alice, but I don't want to hang it up. I"—he hesitated—"I don't want it."

Cecelia didn't look offended; she studied William's face the same way Izzy was currently studying the knob on the bedroom door. "It's too painful to look at her?"

"I'm not her father anymore."

Cecelia's eyes flashed; William was engaging with her, and that pleased her. "You're still her father," she said. "You gave her up because of your depression. And to please Julia. That doesn't mean you don't love Alice. And it doesn't mean you don't deserve to look at her."

William had been raised by unhappy parents, and he'd been unhappy from his own earliest memories. William knew that a father could be present and nonviolent in a child's life and still destroy that child. William's parents' grief had shaped him, like a glacier moving silently through a valley. Alice would be better off if her universe was filled with Julia's light and none of his darkness. He said, "I don't want to."

Cecelia gave him an appraising look. "It's an interesting thing to get to know you now," she said, "after being in your life for so long. You've made a bold decision. I'm not sure it's right, but it's bold. It's the kind of decision Julia would make."

William nearly smiled, because Cecelia was right. His ex-wife was the orchestrator of big plans and life-shifting moves. It felt ironic that he'd made the same kind of decision in her absence. William almost told Cecelia that he would be fine with a portrait of Julia on his wall, that the idea of that didn't bother him. Their marriage was over. William had said goodbye to his parents in a train station and goodbye to his wife in their living room. He was grateful that Julia had left Chicago. He'd departed his old life, and so had she. But William turned away from thoughts of Alice, so he naturally turned away from Cecelia's painting.

"I'll paint you something else," Cecelia said. "You know you're coming to Sylvie's place for Christmas, right? She said you were making noises about being alone, but that's not acceptable. Our family has gotten too small as it is." She picked up the painting of Alice from where she'd leaned it against the wall and slung her purse over her arm. "Come on, bean," she said. Izzy appeared out of the open closet and headed toward them. *Were you counting my sneakers?* William thought. He took a step back, out of her way, but Izzy walked toward him. She walked straight up to his leg, her head level with his hurt knee, and hugged his calf hard.

"Good job, Iz," Cecelia said, and Izzy let go and went to hold her mother's hand. After they left, William stood still in the middle of the room until he could breathe normally again. It was hard for him to be touched, and he hadn't seen that coming.

WILLIAM SAT IN THE bleachers of the gym and watched the practices. He had no official role on the staff; he was there just to be helpful, for now. The program was strong this year, with an excellent roster of athletes. The NBA was in thrall to the rivalry between Magic and Bird, and the college players were inspired to mimic their no-look passes. The practices were loud, full of trash talk and whoops of pleasure when one of the players attempted a flashy move and managed to pull it off.

Arash had given William a binder of information that included the transcripts of his interviews from the summer; William had documented them on a miniature tape recorder, at Arash's request. The player on the team with the highest vertical jump was the one who'd told William he'd been stabbed, and William noticed the worried expression on his face while he played. The young man with the large forehead tapped his shoulder sometimes, and William wondered if it had dislocated recently and if he was in pain. The boys with past concussions sometimes shied away from contact, and he wondered if they were scared of their brains thudding against their skulls a second time. William watched the players, and their histories, sweep up and down the court. He reread the contents of the binder at night in bed, because the better prepared he was, the better chance he had of being helpful. William could feel the information swirling around inside him. He believed—even if that belief was couched in worry—that he *could* provide a service to this team that no one else could. It might be something small, almost unnoticeable, but there was something. He just had to figure out what it was.

In rereading the transcripts of his interviews with the boys—his eyes so tired they landed heavily on each word—William was reminded of his own manuscript, where his questions also appeared in typeface. The manuscript was in an unopened box in his closet, along with other items from the Northwestern apartment; William and Kent had emptied the small storage locker shortly after he'd left the hospital. Written on the outside of the box, in Julia's handwriting, was: WILLIAM'S BELONGINGS. He wasn't ready to look at the manuscript, to consider whether he wanted to write more about the game of basketball. When William tried to recall his questions in the footnotes, all he could remember was self-doubt and anxiety, as if he were standing on thin ice. He could read a note of worry in his questions in the transcripts too. There, he seemed concerned about the state of the ice the boys were standing on. William had asked: *Have you been hurt before? During high school or the summers? How bad was it? Was anyone there to help you?*

HE SHOWED UP AT Sylvie's apartment on Christmas, but only because he thought one or all of the sisters would come and get him if he didn't, and he didn't want them to ruin their holiday waiting in the snow for a bus to Northwestern. He would have spent the holiday with Kent, but Kent was traveling to Des Moines to meet his girlfriend's family for the first time. William understood that the three sisters were trying to continue to be a family to him, and he deeply appreciated their kindness, but he knew he had to stop spending time with them.

He had a clear vision of what his new life should look like. He would be a lone, monkish figure. That was the safest way not to hurt anyone else, after all. He had his hours with the basketball team, his friendship with Kent, and a roof over his head. Most of his new life would take place on the side of a basketball court, where he might be able to help young players avoid the kind of injury he'd suffered. It would be a fine life, full of purpose and friendship. He didn't need family, or sisters-in-law, and he certainly didn't need whatever Sylvie had become to him. He promised himself, on the bus ride to Pilsen, that this would be his last evening with the Padavanos. They would be better off without him.

He arrived with a wrapped fire engine for Izzy and three identical women's sweaters he'd panic-bought in the Northwestern campus store. Sylvie's apartment was small, especially with a Christmas tree taking up one corner, so William leaned against the wall, near the open window. The cold air felt good against his back. Izzy marched in circles around the space, wobbling occasionally because she'd been too excited that afternoon to nap. Sylvie served Charlie's favorite holiday food: turkey sandwiches. The three sisters seemed happy together, but they took turns glancing at the closed apartment door. It occurred to William that they hoped their missing family members might magically appear: Julia and Alice, Rose, even their father. The Padavanos had never spent a holiday apart from one another like this, and the three sisters still here were haunted by ghosts.

William hadn't asked, but he assumed Julia had no idea her sisters were spending Christmas with him. He wanted to apologize for giving them another reason to lie to their older sister, but he knew that would make everyone uncomfortable. He shouldn't have come. Loss and ghosts were his shadow, and his darkness was spreading across the small apartment.

"You all right?" Emeline said, coming to stand next to him. She was wearing the white-and-purple-striped sweater he'd given her; so were Cecelia and Sylvie. They looked like members of some unidentified winter-season team.

He nodded and sipped his wine. "I'm going to head back soon. The city buses end early tonight."

Emeline looked at him, her eyes wide, and then put her hand on his arm. William realized she was tipsy. "Do you know," she said, "that I'm a lesbian? Did they tell you? I only just started calling myself that."

He hadn't known this. He considered it for a moment, then disregarded the subject as none of his business. "You look happy," he said, because she did. Her face was wide open, and he realized he'd never seen Emeline look like this before. She'd carried a hesitation inside her ever since he'd met her at his basketball game when she was fourteen. Emeline had always seemed occupied with watching everyone else and trying to be helpful, but she'd stayed on the sidelines, as if it weren't her turn to live. William had thought the hesitation was part of Emeline—part of her personality—but now it was gone. She seemed fully alive in front of him.

She leaned close to his ear and said, "I'm in love."

Something happened inside William's head; the words made his cheeks flush, and he felt a longing so powerful that for a moment he thought he might cry. That phrase—*I'm in love*—sent an ache like an arrow into his past. He knew that he never would have been able to love Julia in a true, deep way, nor she love him. And now, in his new, safe life, he was landlocked, and love was the sea; William had chosen stability over any more risk or loss. He smiled brusquely at Emeline, grabbed his coat off the couch, and said his goodbyes and Merry Christmases and thank-yous as he walked to and out of the apartment's only door. He felt a great relief, under the snowfall, as he stood at the bus stop beneath the dim lights of the city. This was where he belonged, alone in the semi-darkness.

William had been back in his dorm for just half an hour—most of the building was emptied out, with only a few foreign students and committed athletes remaining over the holidays—when there was a knock at his door. He sighed, knowing it would be a lonely student, or perhaps the elderly security guard hoping William would offer him a drink. He tugged the door open slowly, reluctantly.

Sylvie stood in the hallway, with melting snow on the shoulders of her winter coat. She shrugged the coat off as she walked inside. She was still wearing her striped sweater.

He blinked at her, confused. "What are you doing here? Did you take the bus too?"

She walked past him, into the middle of the small room. "Do you think I don't see what you're doing?"

"Excuse me?"

"You're trying to pull away, to disappear. From me, from us. It's like"—she bit her lip for a second—"Julia left and so you're leaving too."

The wall clock in the corner ticked loudly. It was one of the original furnishings in the apartment, provided perhaps to remind everyone who lived here that time was passing. Sweat broke out on the back of William's neck. He'd worked hard, when he and Julia were first together, to convince the Padavano family to accept him. He'd read a book on plumbing to figure out how to fix a rusty pipe under their kitchen sink. He'd spent afternoons pulling weeds in Rose's garden. He'd taken poetry books out of the library to try to understand the references Charlie made during conversations. Now he felt guilty about those efforts and how effective they'd been. He and his wife had split up, yet he was still somehow part of her family. A week earlier, Cecelia had called him when her bathroom flooded, and William had traveled there with tools. The three Padavano sisters still in Chicago seemed to be willfully oblivious to the truth of the situation: William didn't deserve the family Julia had felt compelled to leave behind.

Please go away, he thought. His body and brain wanted to pull him to the dim, submerged place where he wasn't aware of his emotions, where everything was dulled. But he couldn't do that anymore.

"You're not supposed to be here," he said. "There are rules about having female guests after hours."

"Oh, please," Sylvie said.

He silently agreed with her. That excuse was weak. He was weak. The truth was, William felt awake, and uncomfortable, and he *wanted* things, in Sylvie's presence. Things he didn't deserve and that would create more mess. When he'd decided to separate himself from the Padavanos, he really meant Sylvie. Every time she'd entered his hospital room, his heart beat faster. He knew he needed to walk away from her. He could have done so more easily if Sylvie hadn't asked to hold his hand on his last day in the hospital. For William's entire life, he'd been trying to hold himself together. There was the little boy coughing in his closet, trying not to upset his parents. The unsteady college student, always a second too slow to smile or to return a high five. The basketball player, at home only with a ball in his hands. The young man who was relieved to be chosen by a powerhouse of a woman who'd handed him plans and schedules and even thoughts. He'd followed her every instruction, but eventually the directions had led him so far away from himself that he was no longer a person.

In the hospital, William had allowed himself to feel sympathy for the lonely child he'd once been and for the young man who'd lost hope after injury forced him off the basketball court. William had found his voice in the hospital, and the medication meant that when he opened his eyes in the morning, his first thought wasn't about how he could get to the other end of the day. His ongoing goal—and, he thought, his doctors' too—was that he be healthy *enough,* good *enough,* and happy *enough.* But when Sylvie put her hand in his, William experienced a sensation he hadn't known existed. With her hand in his, he'd felt whole. The shock and pleasure of this had reverberated within him.

Right now he wished Sylvie weren't in this room, forcing him to have this conversation, and yet he wanted to hold her hand. He wanted the feeling that came with her touch. He wanted it badly.

She said, "You barely looked at me or spoke to me tonight, and I think you pretended not to be home when I came by a few days ago."

He nodded. He had left the lights off and kept quiet when she'd knocked on his door. "You should leave me alone," he said. "You should go on dates and have fun. I'm a broken-down man. You have to go live your life."

Sylvie listened while he spoke, and whereas Cecelia had given him a curious face, Sylvie gave him a pensive one. "But that breaks your mantra," she said. "You can't pretend not to be home if you're going to live with no bullshit and no secrets."

William took this in. She wasn't wrong. He was making mistakes, which was why he needed her to go away. He needed to live quietly and carefully, alone.

"I'd rather you answered your door and told me why you wanted me to go away." Sylvie took a jagged breath, and the sound made William think of a window being yanked open. She said, "I don't want you to hide yourself, and I don't want to hide myself either."

You're not hiding yourself, he thought. *I see so much in you, more than in anyone I've ever known.* This had started on the bench that cold night, but he could see the ache inside her now. He could see that she was filled with want too. William was still standing near the door. Sylvie was in the middle of the small living space, in front of the red couch. William wondered for a second what his parents might be doing right now. He imagined them sitting quietly in their living room, a fire in the fireplace, drinks in their hands. Their faces faded with age and unhappiness.

"Aren't you going to say *anything*?" Sylvie said.

He looked at her, tried to express with his face that he was sorry, because he didn't seem to be able to speak; he felt incapable of reaching into the maelstrom of feelings and language inside him and pushing words out of his mouth.

She shook her head, clearly frustrated. "I'm going to tell you something. Something I figured out because of you. When I was a kid, my dream was to find a great love, like the kind you read about in a Brontë novel. Or Tolstoy."

William pictured this, as if flipping through an album: He turned from the image of his worn parents to Sylvie wearing a high-necked gown, standing in a Russian train station.

"When we were teenagers, my sisters wanted me to date boys and not do what I was doing, which was making out with them in the library. But I didn't have any interest in being a girlfriend, and I didn't care about becoming a wife. I knew that if I never found my great love, I would rather be single than settle for a mediocre relationship. I can't bear to pretend happiness." Sylvie waved her hands for a second, as if they were wet and she wanted them dry. "Here's the thing I realized, though: I always thought that I wanted that dream because I was romantic and destined to live a big life, but that wasn't true. I created that dream because real life scared me, and that dream seemed so far-fetched I didn't think it would ever happen. I'd never seen that kind of love in person. My parents loved each other, but badly, and they were miserable. So were all the other couples in my neighborhood. Have you ever actually seen that kind of love?"

William shook his head. He had married out of fear, because he didn't think he was capable of steering himself into adulthood. He'd needed Julia to be his parent more than his partner. He was ashamed of this, but it was true.

"I didn't think I would ever find a man, other than my father, who truly understood me. Who would see the way I look at the world, what reading means to me, how I wonder about everything. Someone who would see the best version of me, and make me believe I could be that person." Sylvie blinked several times, as if trying to hold back tears. Her hands were in fists at her sides. "I thought that type of love was a fairy tale. I thought that kind of man didn't exist. Which meant I got to feel good about the fact that I had a dream and yet I could stay safe with my sisters."

Sylvie gave him a long look, and William knew he was in terrible trouble. He wasn't walking away—he was standing in fire. "I see all of you," he said, but his voice was quiet.

"I know you do. I knew it was possible when I read your book. And when I held your hand." She stopped.

He remembered Emeline saying, *I'm in love.*

"This can't happen, Sylvie." William spoke firmly now, from the center of the fire, to make this clear. *I was married to your sister,* he thought. He wished that when he'd first met Julia Padavano on the college quad, he'd walked away and left her alone. He'd known, even then, that there was something wrong with him; he just hadn't known what it was or what to do. The eighteen-year-old Julia shone at him like a beacon, and he'd used her brightness to light the path in front of him. "I can leave Chicago," he said, knowing even as he said the words that if he left the Padavanos, and the university grounds, and Arash, and the basketball team, he would break apart into pieces too small to be put back together. "Look," William said, desperate now. "There must be other guys. Find another guy. Keep looking."

"There is no other guy," she said. "You're the one."

"I don't deserve this." He meant all of it: this moment, this woman in front of him, her hand in his, because she had crossed the room, and she was holding his hand now. Warmth rushed through him.

"Well, I do," Sylvie said. And she leaned forward and kissed him.

Sylvie

THE FINAL DAY IN THE HOSPITAL, WHEN SYLVIE HELD WILLIAM'S hand and admitted to herself that she loved him, she'd intended to keep the realization to herself. She would limit her contact with him. She would work extra hours at the library, take up new hobbies—what exactly, she wasn't sure—to busy herself, and, starved of oxygen, the feelings inside her would go away. But that plan hadn't worked. Nothing worked. The feelings seemed to only expand. In the library, Sylvie's hands shook while she shelved books. She found she was unable to read, because if she turned her imagination on, she entered not the world of the novel but a room inhabited by William. Her eyes met his, and Sylvie and William silently told each other everything that mattered. She made herself go for long walks after leaving work, to tire herself out for sleep, but each night she climbed into bed and felt her invisible seams strain to the point of bursting.

On Christmas Day, when William surveyed every inch of her apartment except where Sylvie was standing, when his gaze surgically cut around her until she felt, again, like a ghost, she'd chased after him in the snow. She was angry. She planned—to the extent that she planned anything during the bus ride—to show up in his dorm and make him look at her. That's all she intended to do. But in his presence, gazing at his sweet, sad face and the blue eyes that haunted her dreams, she wanted more. She wanted peace and the ability to lie in bed without feeling like she was going to explode. She wanted to speak the words manacled inside her. She wanted everything, because she could feel the walls they had both erected to hold back their desires, and she could sense the enormous beauty that lay on the far side of those walls.

When they finally kissed, in the middle of William's tiny living room with snow falling outside, the pressure within Sylvie disappeared. Her body light, she experienced a new kind of joy and meaning. Sylvie thought, *This is why we live.* She and William held each other and talked: Sylvie into William's chest and he into her hair. In between sentences and sometimes words, they kissed. Sylvie ran her hands across his shoulders, through his hair. She'd been wanting to touch him for so long that the pleasure almost ached through her, and the closeness of their bodies made it hard for her to concentrate on their conversation. She wanted everything at once. She'd been lonely and fractured since Charlie died. She'd been lying to Julia since she moved out of her and William's apartment. The evening on the bench had opened William and Sylvie to each other, and she'd tried to run away from that connection, but her efforts to escape had throttled her. In his arms, she was able to breathe deeply for the first time in almost a year.

Neither of them bothered with punctuation, and neither worried that they might offend the other. They simply shared their feelings, which, on some level, each already knew. Sylvie told William how she had felt seen on the bench and had seen him too, in his footnotes, and he told her that he felt an ease with her, a wholeness, that he'd never felt in his life. "We can't tell anyone," she whispered, and he agreed. Sylvie told herself that they weren't breaking the terms of William's mantra, because there were no secrets between *them.* Their love and honesty would have to stay inside this room, but this room felt enormous after the confines of Sylvie's body.

Sylvie imagined her father smiling in approval as she and William sidestepped labels and held each other in the shadows. She returned to his small set of rooms the night after Christmas, and almost every night after that. With William, Sylvie felt free to unfurl. She showed him the scenes she'd written about her life with her family when she and her sisters were young. She told him about the conversation with Charlie behind the grocer's shop. She delighted in the fact that she could show and tell William anything that came into her head without worrying that he would misunderstand or think her strange. She recited the terrible jokes a library patron—an old man with Coke-bottle glasses—shared with the librarians every afternoon, and some of them were so ridiculous that she and William laughed until they had tears in their eyes. Sylvie was everything with him: silly, sad, inspired, contented in every cell of her body.

"Our relationship doesn't feel like a relationship to me, anyway," she said one evening, while he was watching a Bulls game on his small television. She had been sitting next to him, dipping in and out of a novel. The game was turned low, and the door was double-locked, to give Sylvie time to hide in the bathroom if anyone knocked. She slept in William's room a few nights a week, which involved leaving before dawn and being quiet so William wouldn't get in trouble.

"What does it feel like?" he said, without looking away from the screen.

"Like all the walls have been knocked down. Like we're past needing a roof or doors. They're irrelevant."

"So we're outside." He turned his head and smiled at her. It was his new smile, which had appeared after their first kiss. William used to smile rarely, and when he did, the smile looked obedient, like he knew the moment called for a smile and so his face pulled the correct levers to form one. Sylvie wanted to spend the rest of her life causing this new smile. William's face looked alive, and grateful, and happy. Sylvie knew William was happy with her, knew he was grateful; he whispered his happiness into her skin at night.

He also wanted to keep their relationship secret forever, which to him meant until Sylvie came to her senses and broke up with him. William didn't feel like this contradicted his mantra; *this* secrecy was actually just a delay tactic, a moment of stolen joy before they gathered the strength to walk away from each other. "I don't deserve this," he said almost daily, until Sylvie told him to please not say it anymore. But he said it again now, because he couldn't help himself.

She said, "Do I deserve happiness and wholeness?"

"Of course."

"Then do this for me."

"Love you for you?" William stood to switch off the TV. Hung above the television was the painting Cecelia had recently dropped off. William had told Sylvie about how Cecelia was flustered when she showed it to him. "I always paint portraits," she'd said. "But I like a challenge. I'm not sure what this is, but technically something about it works." Sylvie thought the painting was beautiful. If she hadn't known her sister painted it, she never would have guessed. It was part landscape, part exploration of light, and rain. Sylvie remembered Cecelia telling her sisters that she wanted to paint rain like Van Gogh painted stars. There was pelting water on the canvas, intermixed with faint light. It was the light that drew your eye.

"I'm going to love you no matter what," William said. "But I don't want to hurt anyone else. I couldn't bear to hurt you, Sylvie. I'm supposed to be alone. What is your family going to say? What about Julia?" He grimaced as he said her name. "Those memories you're writing down. Most of them are about you and her."

"Well, of course. They're about the four of us."

William shook his head sadly. She could hear him thinking, *No bullshit, no secrets.* He said, "I can tell how much you miss your sister, when I read your writing."

Sylvie was annoyed, enough to motivate her to close her book, push her nightgown and toothbrush back into her purse, and leave. She walked through the campus toward the bus stop, the cold air chilling her hot cheeks. She was annoyed at herself for overreacting to what William had said. She would phone him when she got back to her apartment. He was right, of course. For her, this was about Julia. William wanted them to stay secret so they could walk away from each other without anyone else being pulled into, or even knowing about, their orbit. Sylvie wanted to keep their love secret because of her older sister. When she tried to imagine what it would be like if

Julia found out that she and William were in love, Sylvie had to shake her head hard to dispel the images of heartbreak. Julia would hate her; Sylvie was betraying her; the only solution was that no one could know.

It was March, and Julia and Alice had been gone for almost five months. Professor Cooper's project had been extended, and Julia, without consulting anyone in the family, had decided to stay in New York. "For how long?" Cecelia had asked her on the phone. "We'll see," Julia said. "I miss you, but Alice and I are doing well here." Sylvie had been relieved to hear about the delay. She and her older sister spoke twice a month after Alice was in bed at night; they traded off on initiating the expensive long-distance call. Neither she nor Julia mentioned the tension embedded in their goodbye; they both pretended that hadn't happened. Julia was always tired from a long day of work, but she was excited too, about the city, about the smart people she worked with, about the clothes the women in New York wore. She sounded shiny, burnished by exhilaration, and more alive than she'd been in a long time. "Tell me about you," Julia would say to Sylvie when she was done sharing her news. "I miss you. Tell me everything." And Sylvie would talk about the fringes of her life—her job, the leaky sink in her studio, the last time she'd babysat Izzy—but leave out what mattered.

"You sound happy," Julia had said at the end of one call.

"So do you."

"I'm happy for us," her sister said.

Beneath the heavy-limbed trees of the campus, Sylvie imagined her older sister shaking her head at her now. *You can't pull this off forever,* the imagined Julia said. *You have to make a choice.* Sylvie's older sister was part of her, in a way her younger sisters were not; the two older Padavano girls had been woven together as children. Perhaps because of this—or perhaps because Sylvie knew there were no boundaries, which meant Julia *was* part of her—she carried her sister with her, even though she'd left Chicago. Julia walked down the street beside Sylvie, sat across the table from her in restaurants, and stood by her side staring into bathroom mirrors. Sylvie was grateful for this version of her sister's company. Recently something had come up in conversation, something about Julia, and Emeline had said, "You must miss her."

And Sylvie said, "Yes, but not too much." And this was true, but in a way no one else could understand except perhaps Julia herself.

KENT FOUND OUT FIRST. He and Nicole—an upbeat young woman with a grin to rival Kent's—came to visit William in early April, and Kent knew immediately that something had happened. William tried to ask about their engagement and admired Nicole's ring, which used to belong to Kent's beloved grandmother, but Kent just stared at him and said, "Tell me what's going on. You look completely different."

"I don't look different," William said. "I'm in slightly less terrible shape, maybe. I can run three miles now."

Kent shook his head.

"Maybe it's a girl," Nicole suggested, studying William like he was a patient who'd come into her clinic.

Kent started to shake his head again, because that was impossible, but something changed in William's face with those words, so he stopped. He stared at his friend. "A girl? Who is it?" Kent knew everyone in William's small life, everyone involved in Northwestern basketball, everyone from the hospital.

William watched his friend comb through the possibilities and then said, in a quiet voice, "Sylvie."

There was a pause while Kent took the pieces that had been handed to him and fit them together. The lakefront scene, the ambulance ride to the hospital, Sylvie seated by William's bedside. "Of course!" he said, and tackled William with a hug, which made Nicole laugh with pleasure.

"Careful—don't hurt him, Kent," she said, because Kent weighed fifty pounds more than William.

Kent phoned Sylvie at the library and told her she needed to come over right away. He hugged her too, tightly, and she could feel his relief in the embrace. "This is wonderful," he said. "I should have seen it coming. I'm a little disappointed in myself." He looked at both of them. "I can see the inherent complications, though."

Sylvie felt awkward in front of Nicole, who was beautiful, and whom she'd just met for the first time. She wondered if this young woman thought she was a terrible person for falling in love with her sister's husband. This was the first time Sylvie had considered what the opinion of strangers might be, and she felt naked, lacking, under Nicole's gaze. She could tell William had been rendered almost unconscious by sharing the news. He sat on the red couch with a stupefied expression on his face. Sylvie squeezed his hand to remind him she was here. To keep him from sinking beneath the water inside himself.

"This isn't going to continue. We're going to break up soon," William said. "For Sylvie."

Kent looked at Sylvie, and she shook her head.

"We need to keep this a secret, though," she said. She'd been running the math and thought it was okay that Kent and Nicole knew. They weren't in contact with the twins or Julia. They lived in Milwaukee. Their knowing simply meant that the tiny dorm room that William and Sylvie's love inhabited had grown a little bigger. Sylvie thought this might be nice; she and William could, perhaps, go out to dinner with Kent and his girlfriend. A double date, like a normal couple. She and William could engineer a small, controlled expansion of their secret life. William would be able to talk to his best friend.

Kent paced in front of them. "You love each other?"

They moved their heads up and down. William reluctant; Sylvie bold.

"Wonderful. This is wonderful. But the secrecy has to stop. Immediately. It's not healthy, and your health is the top priority, William. You know the drill."

Sylvie put her hands over her eyes. She felt like a three-year-old on the verge of a tantrum, flushed with annoyance and embarrassment. Kent was directing his attention at William, to remind Sylvie that he was the fragile leg of the table. To remind her that if William weakened, everything would fall to the floor.

"Have you told your therapist?" Kent studied his friend's face. "No? That's no good. You have to tell everyone. That's crucial." *Crucial for William to survive,* Kent's expression said. "You can't hide love," he said, and Sylvie, her hands still over her face, wondered, *Is that true?*

Where was their love? Could it be hidden? Sylvie saw love coming out of William's face when he looked at her, like light streaming through cracks in a wall. Sylvie's love for him was as much a part of her as her own hands, her face. She never would have *chosen* to love William; she never would have chosen to sweep her sister's husband into her own heart. It wasn't a feeling she and William gave each other, though; they *were* their love. Sylvie felt that if she walked away from him, she would end. She would no longer be Sylvie; she would be a shell of who she had been, moving through days that meant nothing.

Kent said, "To be clear, you have to either break up or tell everyone." He looked at Sylvie. "Those are the only two options."

A fog inside Sylvie cleared. She knew that William's survival required him to live his life on his own terms. Lying to himself, and lying to others, was a departure from solid ground, and Sylvie couldn't be party to that. William had been right, since their first kiss, that this secret needed to be temporary, and Sylvie had known, since their first kiss, that she couldn't go back to living without William. He had become oxygen that she needed to breathe. Sylvie just hadn't been able to merge those truths, until now.

Kent was still walking the floor. "You'll tell your doctor, William. I'll tell Arash. Don't worry, I'll be casual about it. And he'll be thrilled—he loves Sylvie. That will take care of the people you spend your days around. Sylvie." Kent looked at her, to chart her progress. He nodded, seeing that she had caught up. "You have to tell everyone else."

Sylvie nodded and said, "Yes, Captain."

SHE TOLD THE TWINS together. She called them to her apartment on a sunny May afternoon. The window was open, and the air traveling inside smelled of spring.

Cecelia was wearing painting clothes—a pair of olive-colored overalls with many pockets for brushes and rags. She was working on a mural on Loomis Street almost around the clock. She would paint during the day but then leave her house again at two o'clock in the morning—Izzy safe with Emeline—and work on the wall until she wanted to sleep again. This was the first mural commission she'd received, from a local arts council, for which she could paint whatever she wanted. Sylvie stopped by to visit her sister on her way to and from the library each day. She knew Cecelia didn't like to talk about a painting while it was in progress, so she just watched. The outline of a woman's face and shoulders had appeared on the wall first. In the past week, as the woman was filled in, she'd begun to seem familiar to Sylvie. She looked proud and fierce. Sylvie wondered if the woman was Cecelia herself, or perhaps Emeline or Julia. Today she'd felt a shiver of worry that her sister might be painting her. Cecelia might be revealing Sylvie's own true self on the wall. If the woman on the wall *was* Sylvie, then her love and unfurling would be on display for everyone to see. It was this possibility that had made Sylvie stop procrastinating, made her call her sisters and ask them to come over. The idea of being revealed by Cecelia's brush was unacceptable; she needed to reveal herself.

"We knew something was coming," Emeline said, "because you've been acting weird." She'd come from the daycare, which meant she looked slightly sticky with jelly and Play-Doh.

"Are you gay too?" Cecelia said with a smile. She sat down next to her sister at Sylvie's small kitchen table.

Sylvie shook her head. She thought, *I wish that was my news.* "Would you like water? Or"—she tried to think what she had in her cupboards—"crackers?"

"Spill it," Cecelia said. "Em has a class tonight and Mrs. Ceccione is watching Iz, so I need to get home soon."

Sylvie took a deep, gathering breath, as if she were about to dive underwater, and told them the contents of her heart. She started with taking William's hand by the side of the lake and explained that she was alive with him, a whole circle with him, her whole messy self with him. "When we hold hands . . ." she said, but she hadn't been able to finish that sentence with William, and she couldn't now. Sometimes words were like pebbles thrown against a window, and what she was reaching for was the window itself.

Her sisters were quiet when she was done. There was faint traffic noise from outside. The squealing brakes of a bus.

"Oh, Sylvie." Cecelia looked tired from lack of sleep, from holding her world together by herself. Izzy had discovered the word *no*, and the toddler woke up in the morning yelling it from her crib.

Emeline looked away from Sylvie. "Pick any other man on earth, and I'll be happy for you," she said. "Any other man at all."

"I know," Sylvie said. She hadn't expected her sisters to be pleased, but their sadness was palpable, and it pressed against her like a heavy blanket. "If I could, I would."

Emeline's eyes were pleading. Sylvie remembered sitting with Julia and Emeline at Rose's dining room table, begging their mother not to move away. Sylvie was the one with the unwanted news now. She was the one her sisters wanted to hold back.

"Julia's been through so much," Emeline said. "Can't you just be friends with him?"

"Could you just be friends with Josie?"

Emeline tightened her lips. Shook her head. It had occurred to Sylvie that she and Emeline had made choices with similar stakes. Sylvie was sitting here breaking her sisters' hearts because she couldn't imagine life without William, and William couldn't survive inside a secret. Emeline had muzzled her sexuality—not admitting it even to herself—until she'd met Josie. "I had to tell her I loved her," Emeline had said. "Even if it killed me. And I thought it might." This resonated with Sylvie: This moment felt like life *and* death. She was breaking open, but still breaking.

"How do you know he's not with you because he misses Julia?" Cecelia watched her sister while she spoke; she always wanted the truth. "You look like her, you know. It's unhealthy, Sylvie, isn't it? It's like you're getting in bed with her marriage."

Sylvie had nothing to say to this. In the beginning she did wonder, when she took off her clothes, if William was disappointed that her breasts were smaller than Julia's, her hips less curvaceous. Had Julia been a better lover? Sylvie never asked William if he had these thoughts, because she didn't want to hear the answers.

She was surprised to find that she didn't feel defensive in response to her sisters; she wasn't inclined to argue. She thought of the woman Cecelia was painting onto the three-story wall a few blocks away and how the outline was slowly filling with color and detail. Sylvie was filling herself in, discovering and showing her own colors. She could feel the sorrow emanating from her younger sisters like heat off their skin. Sylvie had known this wouldn't go well. She knew Cecelia and Emeline loved William like a brother; they'd known him since they were in ninth grade. But this was hard news, and they weren't thinking about William. They were thinking about their personal versions of the gleaming bridge that existed between the three sisters in Chicago and Julia in New York. Sylvie knew that Emeline mailed Julia newspaper clippings about available apartments in Pilsen. Cecelia continued to paint Alice and Izzy together. She took photographs of the canvases and mailed them to Julia, asking her which one she would like. Julia hadn't chosen one yet.

"But if you do this," Emeline said, and then paused, as if she were about to dive underwater too, "Julia and Alice will never move back home."

The sun sank behind a cloud or a building, and the three sisters were draped in shadows. The gleaming bridge was crumbling to dust at their feet. Sylvie thought of her childhood dream and how Julia had complained to Sylvie that the novels she cited as depictions of great love were all tragedies. Sylvie, in her innocence, had insisted that the tragedy part was avoidable. It wasn't woven into the romance. But she had been wrong.

"I know," she said. "I'm so sorry."

EMELINE AND CECELIA DREW back from Sylvie after the news. She knew they were bruised and tender and needed time away from her. She worried they might need forever but pushed that terrible thought away. She felt bruised and tender too. Sylvie continued to visit the mural Cecelia was painting on Loomis but timed her visits for when her sister wasn't there. The woman on the wall showed more of herself each day. Sylvie finally recognized her when Cecelia had finished painting the woman's eyes. It wasn't one of the Padavano sisters; it was St. Clare of Assisi—the saint Rose had made her daughter carry around as penance. But Cecelia—by painting her over and over again—had made St. Clare into her talisman.

The woman on the wall looked powerful. She didn't look like a warning for how not to live. In fact, she radiated from the wall, like an example of the opposite. Studying her, Sylvie remembered that when the girls were little, Rose had used the saints as inspiring examples of accomplished women. She only started using them as warning systems and punishments when Sylvie and her sisters grew older—when sex and marriage and pregnancy were on the table. St. Clare took up three stories of the side of the building. She had bucked the expectations of her family and society by refusing to be a teenage bride, by refusing to give her life away before it had even started. She embodied bravery, and the woman painting her was certainly brave too. Perhaps, Sylvie considered, testing out the thought, all the Padavano sisters were brave. Cecelia had done the equivalent of running away at seventeen and was a single mother whose art was increasingly in demand. Emeline was in a relationship with Josie now and wasn't hiding that fact. Mrs. Ceccione had almost had a heart attack when Emeline and Josie held hands in front of her, and Emeline had apologized for upsetting her—Cecelia cackling with laughter in the same room—but would not apologize for her love. Julia, when confronted with a husband who needed to be saved, had defied centuries of misogyny that demanded wives prioritize husbands and had chosen to save herself. And Sylvie thought maybe she was brave too, for allowing herself to inhabit a dream so extraordinary, she'd assumed it would pass her by.

Sylvie had believed she would stay single, and safe, with her sisters. Her heart had always belonged to them, after all. The four sisters had beat with one heart for most of their lives. Sylvie wondered, looking at the mural, if bravery was wedded to loss: You did the unthinkable thing and paid a price. Julia didn't know Sylvie's truth yet, but she would soon. Cecelia had said that she and Emeline would break the news; one of the twins would travel to New York to tell Julia in person. Sylvie had been relieved to hear this. The twins would tell Julia gently and try to protect her, while all Sylvie would be able to do was cause pain.

When Sylvie called Julia, she thought, each time, that this might be their last conversation. She didn't know when Cecelia or Emeline would arrive in New York; she wasn't privy to their plans. She listened to Julia describe Alice's daycare and how the baby had said her first word: *Mama.* Julia told Sylvie how Professor Cooper had asked for her opinion after a meeting and how he valued her thoughts. Sylvie asked questions, to make the call last longer. She tried to memorize her sister's voice and the sound of her love. Sylvie wouldn't have believed, as a child, that anything could ever make her cleave her older sister from her life; now, knowing that an ax was about to fall and doing nothing to stop it felt like an exquisite torture. *I love you,* she thought, down the phone line. *I'm sorry.*

Resident advisers were required to sleep in the dorm every night, so Sylvie always traveled to Northwestern instead of William coming to Pilsen. She felt like she spent most of her life in the real world, bearing the silence of the twins, waiting for Julia to be told, while William was able to exist in a bubble at the university. She was glad he was in a bubble; she just wished she had one of her own. To her great relief, William had thawed after his initial terror. For a couple of weeks after Kent had found them out, William kept clearing his throat, as if he couldn't trust his voice to speak. But as the days passed, the sky didn't fall on him the way he'd anticipated. He told his therapist that he loved Sylvie, and the doctor—who had been urging him to make real connections with other people—deemed the news an overall positive. Kent informed Arash, and he—as predicted—was delighted. Arash thumped William on the back for a solid two minutes the first time he saw him after speaking to Kent. Cecelia and Emeline stopped visiting William, but their visits had never been regular, and he was more comfortable with the idea of their absence than their presence.

It was Sylvie who took deep breaths while she walked to the library, who held vigil with St. Clare on the sidewalk a few times a day, and who ate scrambled eggs alone in her studio apartment. She lived in a silence she'd created, and she felt herself deepening into it. She didn't regret her choice; sometimes when she was with William her face ached, and she realized it was because she hadn't stopped smiling for hours. She slept pressed against his warm skin at night, and when she jarred awake at four o'clock in the morning, she wrote down memories from her childhood.

Three months into the silence, Sylvie was in the library one August afternoon, pushing a cart of new releases out of the back room, when Emeline appeared by her side. Emeline didn't speak, she just wrapped her arms around Sylvie. She pressed her head against Sylvie's shoulder so their curls lay on top of each other. Sylvie held the only parts of Emeline she could reach: her hand, the top of her bent head. The two sisters stood like that for several minutes, in the back corner of the library. When they let go of each other, it felt like a new start. From a place where they were heartbroken and besotted and free.

Julia

EMELINE VISITED JULIA WHEN ALICE WAS EIGHTEEN MONTHS old and the mother and daughter had been living in New York for a year. The move had been intense for Julia. From the moment she and Alice boarded the flight to New York—the first of Julia's life, and traveling alone with a baby—each day had felt challenging and brand-new. Not in a bad way, necessarily. New was a relief; Julia had rushed away from her home city because she *needed* new and different. Manhattan delivered, though, at a volume and scale that she couldn't have anticipated. The city pounded with noise, and people rushed everywhere; Julia found herself speed-walking down sidewalks, trying to keep up, even when she wasn't sure she was headed in the right direction.

She started her job with Professor Cooper—where every person and task she encountered was unfamiliar—and tried to make a temporary home with her baby. "Six months," she sang to Alice, when she was trying to put the baby to sleep. "We can do this for six months." She and Alice were staying in an apartment temporarily vacated by one of Rose's Florida friends. In lieu of rent, all Julia had to do was water Mrs. Laven's extensive collection of plants. She traveled the length of the apartment at the end of each day with a watering can in her hand and then collapsed into bed to sleep. Julia had never tried to conduct life, much less one with this many demands, on her own before. She'd always had the help of her sisters, her mother, or William. Now Julia carried a stroller in one arm and a baby in the other while she climbed steps up from the subway. She felt like she was always sweating and endeavoring to look presentable at the same time. She was responsible for everything: the daycare having enough diapers for Alice, paying bills, the presence of baby food and milk in the kitchen, and the laundry. Alice generated so much laundry. Still, Julia felt a deep gratitude to Manhattan, both for demanding all of her attention and for offering no reminders of her old life.

She had a brief respite when Rose bought tickets for Julia and Alice to visit her in Florida for Christmas. Julia was the first of Rose's daughters to travel to Miami, and Rose showed off her daughter and granddaughter to her friends with visible pride. When Julia had declined to fight for her marriage, Rose was vocal with her disappointment, but now Rose seemed swept up in the excitement of Julia's new life. "My daughter works for a very important business consultant in the center of Manhattan. My husband always said that Julia had brains and moxie. And isn't her baby gorgeous?" Julia was struck by how her mother had rewritten the story of her eldest daughter and her own husband: Julia was no longer a failure, and Charlie's opinion was to be respected. Still, it felt good to have her mother's approval, and she was happy to open presents for the eight-month-old Alice beside Rose's Christmas tree. In the afternoon, she and Rose phoned Sylvie's apartment to wish the rest of the family a happy holiday. Izzy got on the phone and babbled importantly for several minutes, while the women listening in Florida and Chicago laughed.

When Professor Cooper's project with the communications company was extended in the spring, he asked Julia if she wanted to return to Chicago. "I love working with you," he said. "And I'm going to start taking on additional clients here, so I'll be staying for a while. But I know you have family in Chicago. I completely understand if you want to go back."

Julia took a deep breath at this news; it wasn't a complete surprise, since she'd known the client was thrilled with Professor Cooper's work and the project wasn't finished, but she'd been living inside a six-month calendar ever since she moved. During difficult days, she missed her sisters terribly, missed being in a city that she could navigate without a second thought. She also wanted Alice to have the chance to play with her cousin and be doted on by her aunts. "Can I think about it overnight?" she asked, and Professor Cooper said of course.

She walked the thirty blocks from the office to Alice's daycare that evening and knew her answer by the end of the commute. In Manhattan, Julia felt like she was on a path to fulfilling her potential; she *was* the clear-eyed, powerful woman who had emerged with her daughter's birth. When Julia pictured herself back in Chicago, that version of herself was weighed down with worry. She had been a wife there; she had misunderstood her husband there; she had made bad decisions there. And it felt complicated to consider being back in the same city as her ex-husband. William had legally given Alice up, and the surname *Waters* had been removed from Julia's and Alice's official documents, but what if William came to a Chicago playground where the baby was, to watch her? What if Julia and Alice happened to walk past him on the street? What if he changed his mind?

Julia hadn't figured out how she would explain any of this to her daughter, once Alice was old enough to understand. She knew she still had time to figure it out, so she avoided thinking about it with any seriousness. After all, what were her options to say to Alice? *You technically have a father, but he gave you up? Your father just doesn't want you in his life? He's so sick he couldn't be a parent?* Part of the complication was that *Julia* didn't understand, even though she was grateful for William's decision. Alice was a bright-eyed, smiling, chubby-cheeked one-year-old. The sight of her turned strangers on the sidewalk into clowns—they made faces, stuck out their tongues, endeavored to make the toddler giggle. She was, Julia believed, the most wonderful child in the world, with Izzy running a close second. How could *anyone* not want Alice in their life? The confusion embedded in this question, and in William's choice, reminded Julia of the swampiness of the end of her marriage. The bottom line, Julia decided, was that she liked herself in New York and wanted to stay longer.

The bittersweet part of that decision, of course, was her sisters. At least once a day, Julia thought she saw Sylvie climbing into a taxi or crossing the street, and there was a woman in Julia's apartment building whose laughter sounded like Cecelia's. During every phone call, Julia asked her sisters to visit. "No. Come home," Cecelia would respond. She was the only one who resisted the idea entirely. Cecelia seemed rooted in Chicago with a stubbornness that was surprising in someone so independent in other ways. Sylvie appeared open to the idea, though she was always vague about timing. And Emeline worried over the details: the cost of visiting, her fear of planes, not having the right shoes. "People will laugh at me there," she said. "Everyone in Manhattan is so stylish."

Having made the decision to stay in the city, though, Julia woke up every morning excited. She and Alice started a nightly dance party in their kitchen; the toddler wiggled her butt with great earnestness, to do her part. Mrs. Laven was returning to Manhattan from Miami, but it turned out that she was the head of the building's co-op board, and she helped Julia rent a cute two-bedroom apartment in the same Upper East Side building. Julia loved having her own place and loved the shape of her days in this new, open-ended calendar. She dropped Alice off at daycare, then commuted on the downtown bus to 42nd Street, where she entered a glass office building that reflected the magnificence of Grand Central Terminal in its windows; on a high floor overlooking the city, she attended meetings with Professor Cooper.

When Emeline announced that she was going to overcome her fears and visit in October, Julia was thrilled. She could barely sleep with excitement, leading up to Emeline's arrival. Julia hadn't had time to make friends in New York, but she also had no idea how to do so. Her sisters had always been her best friends; in Chicago, there had never been a need for anyone else in her life. She and Sylvie and the twins knew every version, every age, every mood of one another; Julia couldn't comprehend how to form an intimate friendship with a stranger. Sometimes she would see a mother at Alice's daycare whose style she admired or who seemed to have a full-time job, like Julia did, and she considered approaching the woman. But the gulf between her and the total stranger was oceanic, and Julia had no idea how to cross it. Was it possible that a friendship could start from asking someone for their name? Surely they would have to move in together to truly know each other, and that made no practical sense.

Julia took the week off from work so she could spend every minute with Emeline. The two sisters went for long walks, with Julia leading Emeline by the hand across streets, because her sister peered upward at skyscrapers instead of at the cars around her. They spent a day at the Metropolitan Museum of Art—a place they knew from movies and books—and pretended, as they walked through the rooms, that they were in a movie themselves. They stayed up late every night, talking. Julia had been starved for this closeness, starved for easy, silly conversation. She'd been lonely. They discussed Rose—as if their mother were still the sun they orbited—and how haughty she was with all of them from her perch in Florida. Emeline was great with small children, of course, and she sat on the floor playing with Alice for hours.

"You're the finest Alice in the world," Emeline said to the little girl. They were playing with blocks on the floor, while Julia sat in the armchair, watching.

"Anemie," Alice said, with careful concentration. She was trying to say *Aunt Emeline.*

"Very good!" Emeline clapped.

Alice grinned, showing all her teeth. The little girl had pudgy cheeks, and her hair was straight and golden. Her blue eyes were unmistakably her father's.

"She does look like William," Emeline said. "But her eyes twinkle like Daddy's. And I bet her hair gets curlier as she gets older. In pictures, my hair was straighter when I was a toddler. And at the daycare, I see lots of little kids transform from looking like one parent to looking like the other."

"I hope she ends up looking at least a tiny bit like me," Julia said. The two sisters regarded Alice with shared adoration. "But really, as long as she doesn't have his *darkness,*" Julia said, speaking her secret fear out loud, "I don't mind what she looks like."

Emeline blinked in surprise, but she said, "Of course. You're right."

Julia pinned back Emeline's hair in the mornings, both of them looking at their similar faces in the mirror. *I need you,* Julia thought, knowing that *you* meant more than just this one sister, but the need was so great that she couldn't be picky. She couldn't let Emeline leave without knowing when and how she would see her again. By the end of Emeline's first day in New York, Julia had launched a campaign to convince her sister and Josie to move to her city. Transplanting her sister here would be a perfect solution. There were Manhattan day-cares that would clamor for women with Emeline and Josie's work experience, and no one cared if a person was gay here. Julia had discovered, after moving to New York, that Professor Cooper had been living with a man for thirty years. His boyfriend, Donny, was lovely; he wore beautifully tailored suits, and he'd helped Julia pick out rugs—the rug market had turned out to be secretly very expensive and confusing—for her apartment.

"I can't imagine living anywhere but Chicago," Emeline said when Julia raised the topic. But she was so admiring of the city, and so happy with Alice in her arms, that Julia felt confident that over the course of a few months she would be able to convince her. She planned to speak to Mrs. Laven about her sister renting an apartment in their building. Julia pictured Alice running back and forth between the two apartments, at home in more than one space. And the prospect of sharing her exciting workdays with Emeline over a glass of wine every evening made Julia shiver with pleasure. It felt like she'd been sipping air through a straw since she left Chicago, and suddenly she was able to take big gulps of oxygen. In Emeline's presence, she laughed for very little reason and was pleased that Alice threw her little head back and laughed too. Julia thought, *I'm better with my sisters.*

"How is Sylvie?" she asked. It was Emeline's last day in the city. Alice was down the hall with Mrs. Laven, so the two sisters could spend a few hours alone together. They were drinking coffee in the kitchen. Emeline had told her all about Cecelia's art and the Italian jazz musician she was dating. She'd heard about how the two-year-old Izzy had recently discovered a tube of strong glue in Cecelia's studio and created a skyscraper by gluing together all the canned vegetables and beans she found in their kitchen. But Emeline had barely mentioned Sylvie.

"You're the only one who didn't seem upset by my loving Josie," Emeline said. "Sylvie and Cecelia tried to hide it, but the truth was that they were shocked at first. I mean, I understand. I was shocked too. And I expected Mama to lose her mind, which she did. But you just seemed happy for me."

"I am happy for you. I wish you'd brought Josie with you so I could meet her."

"I didn't *want* to love Josie," Emeline said. She stared down into her coffee cup. "It was hard for me to accept the fact that we don't choose who we love, because who you love changes everything."

They had talked about Josie a fair amount during Emeline's visit, because the two women had decided to move in together and Rose had thrown a long-distance fit. Julia turned to look at her sister and felt a welling of affection for her.

Emeline said, "Do you agree that we can't choose who we love?"

"I guess. Why?"

"I want you to know that I was upset about this at first, and I guess I still am. But . . ." Emeline closed her eyes. "Sylvie and William are in love."

Julia shook her head, in disbelief and refusal. She lowered herself into the nearest chair, in case Emeline's sentence doubled back on her.

"Cecelia was mad at Sylvie. I was too. It had gotten peaceful after you left. Everyone was okay. You were far away, but you were going to come back. I understand now, though. How could I not? Julia, they didn't have a choice."

The shock of this cleared a space inside Julia, and she remembered how Sylvie had somehow known that William needed to be searched for and saved. She remembered her and Sylvie's strained goodbye. The two sisters' phone calls, since Julia had moved, had been filled with facts and logistics, as if they were sharing their weekly calendars with each other. Sylvie, in particular, had never spoken about her feelings or what she was wondering or thinking, even though that was all the younger versions of Sylvie and Julia had spoken about while they lay side by side in their twin beds at night. Julia should have known something was going on; perhaps she had known but had averted her eyes and not allowed those thoughts to rise to the surface. She'd done the same thing, she knew, with William's depression. Sylvie had been the one to tell Julia that her husband had tried to kill himself and then, later, that her husband didn't want to see her, didn't want to be married or a father anymore. Only now did Julia realize how strange it was that Sylvie had delivered all that news. William should have told her himself, even if it was over the phone. But his voice had gone through Sylvie. Whenever Julia studied her face in the mirror, she thought: *Sylvie has freckles in that spot too, but they're lighter. Sylvie's hair is more obedient than mine.* Julia thought about her sister as naturally as she thought about herself: Sylvie was part of Julia. And William had lain beside Julia in bed at night. He was the only man she'd ever been naked with. The two people Julia had been closest to had chosen each other.

Julia stood and walked to the sink. Her chest contracted, an oversized motion as if it were trying to clear a blocked pipe, and she inhaled too much air. She made a loud gasping sound. Emeline rubbed her back, the way the sisters had always rubbed one another's backs when they were unwell.

"They love each other?" Julia said, when she could speak. The word *love* tugged at her throat on the way out.

Emeline rested her cheek on Julia's shoulder blade. She nodded, and Julia felt the movement on her skin. Julia pictured Sylvie standing behind the desk in the library and thought, *How could you do this? I would never do this to you.*

"I'm sorry, Julia," Emeline whispered.

"I'm so glad I decided to move here," she said. "It's the smartest thing I ever did."

Julia realized, her hands pushed against the kitchen counter, that Emeline had come to New York to tell her this news. Sylvie hadn't been home when Julia called her over the last few weeks, and Julia had assumed her sister was simply out, busy. But Sylvie hadn't answered the phone because she knew Emeline was on her way here. And Emeline would never move to New York; that possibility had been entirely in Julia's imagination. She had been an idiot, and she was barely able to look at her younger sister in the remaining hours before Emeline's flight back to Chicago.

For the next few weeks, every morning when Julia went into Alice's room and lifted her out of her crib, Alice said, "Anemie?" in a hopeful voice, and Julia shook her head. She hated to disappoint her daughter, and she was angry at herself for being foolish, again. She had forgotten that her best self was independent and ambitious. During Emeline's visit, Julia had started to place her happiness in someone else's hands, which was a remnant of her Chicago self. Julia didn't want to be that person anymore. In Chicago, she was part of the paper chain of Padavano sisters; they had never operated independently, and if one of them had a problem, they all had a problem. The fact that Sylvie had done something terrible and dispatched the sweetest sister, Emeline, to deliver the damage to Julia was an example of how Julia could no longer afford to live. She alone would make Alice happy, and she would never disappoint her.

At night, after the toddler fell asleep, Julia lay on her bed and stared at the wall. She felt hollowed out. She remembered Sylvie kissing boys at the library and dismissing the idea of a boyfriend, because she was waiting for her great love. Julia had thought the dream was sweet but impractical and at some point Sylvie would realize that relationships were a matter of compromise. How was it that Sylvie's great love had turned out to be her sister's husband? That didn't feel destined or romantic. It felt like a brutal choice. Sylvie had chosen to betray her sister, and the twins apparently thought that was acceptable. Emeline had bought a plane ticket and traveled to the East Coast to pass on the news as if it were a pedestrian piece of gossip.

Late one night, upset, Julia called Rose. "What do you think of all this?" she said. "How could Sylvie . . ." She found she couldn't finish the sentence.

"It's unbelievable," Rose said. "One of my daughters is a lesbian, one is a divorcée, and I don't even know what to call Sylvie. Oh, and I forgot about the daughter who gave birth as a teenager, out of wedlock." She gave a hard laugh. "Thank God I left Pilsen when I did! The amount of gossip going on in the neighborhood about our family is obscene."

"Are you okay with this, in any way?" Julia asked. She wanted to say, *What Sylvie and William did was cruel. I'm in pain. Help me, Mama.*

"No, I'm not okay with it, but who cares what I think?" Rose sighed.

"I know you feel like the victim, Julia, but the truth is that you shoved your sister in front of William by never going to the hospital and then leaving Chicago. And now Sylvie has shoved you out of Chicago by dating William." She made a harrumphing noise. "Sylvie falling in love with him is ridiculous, obviously. I can't even tell my closest friends here about that—it's the stuff of soap operas! Two of my daughters choosing the same man. And it's not like William's a Kennedy, or . . . or Cary Grant, for goodness' sake."

I am the victim, Julia thought. *My sisters have given me up and given up Alice too. Forever.* Sylvie and William had woven their lives together, and now Julia had to stay away from not only her ex-husband but her closest sister. When she did sleep, Julia had a recurrent nightmare in which an eight- or nine-year-old Alice asked if she could meet her father, and that meeting somehow happened. In the dream, Sylvie stood beside William in the doorway of a nice house, and little Alice ran into Sylvie's open arms. The scene was so vivid it felt like a memory, and it made Julia want to throw up. The image was a perverse version of the life she'd run away from, with Sylvie standing in Julia's place. *Please,* Alice said in the dream, *can I go live with my dad and Aunt Sylvie? They're a normal family, with a mom and a dad. I'd like to be with them.*

Julia heard herself say, "I'm going to tell Alice that William's dead."

"What?" Rose almost choked on the word. "What in the world are you talking about?"

"It's the only thing that makes sense. He wants nothing to do with her, and I don't want to tell her that. She'll think there's something wrong with her, and there obviously isn't. She's perfect. And he is dead, as far as I'm concerned. We're not going back to Chicago, ever. This way everything will be cleaner." This idea had occurred to Julia before, but it had seemed too extreme. Now it no longer did. It made sense. She and Alice would be safe in Manhattan, alone in their tiny family. No one would be able to hurt them again.

"William and Sylvie will probably break up. Sylvie's like your father, which means she lacks follow-through. You should just live your life in New York for a little while, and let's see where the cards fall."

Julia knew her mother was unable to accept that William had revoked his parental privileges. Her brain couldn't make sense of a parent giving up a baby. "I've never heard of such a thing," Rose had said, and that was the end of the idea for her.

"I wouldn't tell Alice now, obviously," Julia said. "She's not even two."

"Good," Rose said, with relief in her voice. "You'll calm down in time. Everything will calm down. I love you, Julia."

This was how Julia knew her mother felt bad for her. She very rarely said those words out loud. "I love you too," she said, and they hung up.

Over the following weeks, Julia changed her approach to her job. She'd been so grateful to Professor Cooper for allowing her to join him in New York that she'd dedicated herself to simply being helpful to him. She processed the data he collected in stakeholder interviews and took notes during large meetings where new business processes were debated. She also made coffee runs and spent a lot of time at the Xerox machine. Julia had done everything possible to make sure that Professor Cooper didn't regret hiring her.

Now, though, Julia recalled the future she'd dreamed about, in which she was behind a boss's desk, wearing stiletto heels and an expensive suit. She didn't know if that dream was achievable, but it might be. Sylvie dating William had been impossible, and yet it happened. Clearly, life was more alterable than Julia had thought.

Julia wanted to be promoted. She wanted to earn more money and make her and Alice's life as stable—and untouchable—as possible. A month after Emeline left, Professor Cooper asked Julia to sit in on a meeting and take notes. She did, but she also interrupted the meeting to offer a few ideas. Julia enjoyed watching the men's heads—it was always all men in these meetings—turn in surprise, because her ideas were smart. Six months later, Julia asked Professor Cooper if she could take the initial meeting with a new, smaller client, and he agreed. She prepared for weeks—learning everything about the electronics company that was looking to merge with a competitor, thus duplicating its own staff—and presented a plan to restructure the combined companies that was so elegant the client asked her to be in charge of the entire process. When this call came in, Professor Cooper toasted

Julia with champagne. "I'm so proud of you," he said, and Julia had to excuse herself to cry in a bathroom stall. They were happy tears, and she felt that Charlie was proud of her too, wherever he was. *My rocket,* he said, with wonder in his voice.

Julia became aware for the first time that men were making signals at her. She simply hadn't noticed before. There was a nice-looking bearded man who always stood next to her in the office elevator in the mornings. She complimented his cuff links. He asked her out for a drink. While getting dressed for the date—putting on perfume and a darker eyeshadow than she would wear to the office, choosing a dress that showed off her curves—Julia laughed out loud, because she felt like she'd just remembered that she had a physical body for the first time since Alice was born. When she smoothed her hands over her hips, her entire body tingled, as if excited for a better future.

She told the bearded man the same thing she would tell every man she dated: that she wasn't looking for a boyfriend or a husband, and she would never bring him home to her apartment. She just wanted to have some fun. She and the bearded man drank martinis at a rooftop bar in a rose-colored twilight and then made out on the street, pressed up against a city mailbox. They went on a second date the following weekend; he took her to a Yankees game and they had sex on the floor of his kitchen because they were unable to make it to the bedroom. It was fun, and Julia felt like she had optimized her life: She had a great job, a perfect daughter, and a sexual life on her own terms. Two years after Emeline's visit, Professor Cooper announced that Julia would be in charge of the New York City branch of his business consultancy. He and Donny would travel back and forth between Chicago and New York, but Julia would run the New York office.

Julia told her mother and the twins the good news on postcards. She'd started to collect postcards featuring various New York City scenes to correspond with her family. She much preferred postcards to phone calls. There was only a small space to write, so she included one or two highlights from her and Alice's life, wrote *xoxoxo,* and sent the card off. Rose hated the postcards and claimed that only a psychopath would communicate with her own mother that way. To appease Rose, Julia mailed her a few photos of Alice every couple of weeks, in addition to the cards. Cecelia and Emeline sent Chicago postcards in return, as if they were entering their city into a postcard competition, and Cecelia and Julia occasionally exchanged photos of Izzy and Alice. Julia and Sylvie never corresponded, in any way.

If Julia was with her daughter when she spotted a colorful postcard in the gray locked mailbox in the foyer of the building, she never let Alice see it. She tucked the postcard in her purse, and after she'd read it, she threw it away in a street garbage can. She threw away the photographs of her niece too. Julia read most of the postcards standing alone on a busy sidewalk, buses and taxis swooshing by. That was how she learned that Emeline, Josie, and Cecelia had moved into a new house together. That was how she found out Sylvie and William had gotten married, in a small ceremony in the back room of the Lozano Library.

William

ONCE EMELINE HAD RETURNED FROM NEW YORK CITY, exhausted and pale, William was careful not only with himself but with Sylvie and the twins too. He had an appreciation for living in the center of a hard truth. Kent had been right: William couldn't do otherwise. During the months of total secrecy, when he and Sylvie had limited their love to his small room, William's mind had grown confused, and he'd had to steer his thoughts to get through the days. It hadn't resembled the final months of his marriage, because Sylvie made him soft with happiness, and in the tiny dorm room they shared everything with each other. But the friction between life inside that room and the outside made him feel like a record needle being dragged across the vinyl surface.

William's psychiatrist—a bald Puerto Rican man who enjoyed telling William why soccer was a better sport than basketball—ended each session by saying, "You gotta get outside and exercise, you gotta take your pills, and you gotta take care of other people." *No bullshit and no secrets* went unspoken. It was a given and the foundation of William's life. He often wondered, on his walk home, if healthy people used mantras to organize their lives. Whenever William felt his insides numb or if he hadn't spoken in several hours, he would return to the psychiatrist's list and do one of the commands.

He ran miles around the Northwestern track, and rehabbed his knee, and took his medications. He was now officially on staff as the most junior of the assistant coaches at Northwestern, and he focused on caring for the injured players. William developed a successful rehab exercise for a kid with recurrent ankle issues, and the student's gratitude—he'd worried his playing career might be over—made William feel full, and of use, in a way he never had before. The impact of helping seemed to be cumulative; the more kids he helped, the more solid he felt in his own chest. He reached out to the twins when Emeline returned from New York. He'd stayed away from them, on the whole, since Sylvie told her younger sisters about her love for him. The twins had needed distance from Sylvie for a while, and he understood that they would want distance from him too. But now he knew that Sylvie wouldn't be able to endure her new life without Julia if he, Emeline, and Cecelia weren't on solid ground.

"We're not angry with you, William," Emeline said, when he asked the twins to meet him for breakfast. He hadn't told Sylvie he was doing this; she would have wanted to come to the breakfast to try to protect everyone's feelings, and he wanted the chance, for once, to take care of her.

He looked at Cecelia, who was cutting up a pancake for Izzy in her high chair. "It's true," Cecelia said. "You didn't do any of this on purpose. I get that now. And"—she paused—"I've never seen Sylvie like this before. I keep painting her, to capture it."

"It's not that she's happy," Emeline said, "because I know she's heartbroken about Julia. But she's beautiful. She's fully Sylvie."

William had expected to weather some level of resentment, spoken or unspoken, from the twins, but they appeared to be letting him completely off the hook. He shook his head, confused, but he remembered the nights when he'd walked out of his bedroom to see Julia and Sylvie sleeping together on the couch. And how Emeline had left home *with* Cecelia, even though she wasn't pregnant or in trouble, and slept on Mrs. Ceccione's floor. Even though William was a major player in this drama, no matter how you looked at it—the end of his marriage, his hospitalization, his relationship with Sylvie—the four sisters managed their hearts among themselves. He was always irrelevant, in a way that used to sadden him but now felt liberating. He was free to live his own life as his true, imperfect self, and Sylvie and the twins accepted him. William felt a pang of guilt toward his ex-wife; he had given Julia and Alice up, and yet he'd ended up surrounded by the women Julia loved most. It didn't seem fair, but he would try not to think about that. He would try to follow his doctor's orders and take care of the people around him.

"If you feel like you need to make something up to us," Cecelia said, "you can be our unpaid handyman. There's a lot of work to do." Cecelia had just bought a broken-down house in Pilsen for very little money, from an art dealer who admired her work. Cecelia, Emeline, Josie, and Izzy would live there together, as soon as the house was livable.

"It would be my honor," he said, trying to sound lighthearted, but he meant it. He felt astonishingly lucky to have emerged from this whirlwind with Sylvie in his bed each night and Emeline and Cecelia willing to keep him in their lives. William remembered seeing Charlie standing in a doorway, smiling at William, the same night he'd walked into the lake. He thought that his father-in-law would have been proud of the twins for keeping their hearts open. He would have liked that Cecelia was making art and that Emeline had allowed herself to love who she loved. William didn't know what Charlie would make of him and Sylvie—since their love impacted his oldest daughter, he probably wouldn't have been thrilled—but Charlie had wanted his daughters to live fully and deeply, and Sylvie was doing that.

For four months, William devoted his weeknights and weekends to replacing the insulation on the second floor of Cecelia's new house, retiling the kitchen, and replacing the tub and toilet. The house was only a stone's throw away from where the Padavano girls had grown up, and it was similar in layout to the house on 18th Place. Sylvie came with him to Cecelia's each time, and she painted walls with her sisters or babysat Izzy while they unpacked boxes. William liked to listen to the patter of the women's voices and murmured laughter while he grouted tiles and unscrewed ancient nuts from rusted pipes. Izzy would occasionally appear in the doorway of whatever room William occupied and hand him random tools. He ended up with a pile of wrenches, screwdrivers, hammers, and bolt cutters around his feet, and when the toddler wandered away, he would place them back in the toolbox.

On the evenings when he wasn't needed at Cecelia's, William met Sylvie at the library and they ate dinner together. There was a Mexican diner they particularly liked, and they would share a margarita and eat tacos. During their secret period, they had been careful when they talked. They'd discussed books, basketball, and the memories Sylvie was writing down. Other permitted topics were what they'd done that day, whom they'd spoken to, and anything funny that was said. They'd avoided talking about the past and anything beyond the current day. In the late fall, though, once they'd been together for eleven months and Julia knew the truth, they allowed themselves to imagine a shared future. They smiled shyly at each other during these conversations. William still believed that he didn't deserve Sylvie, didn't deserve the way she loved all of him, in every mood and every thought, but she beamed at him across the table, and he found that, in her glow, his plans became more concrete, more clear.

He admitted that he wanted to be a physio. He wanted a deeper understanding of the physiology and motivations of the athletes on the Northwestern team. Why were some kids' joints more resilient than those of others? How could injuries be prevented? William had noticed that when players missed shots, they had different reactions. Some got discouraged and were scared to shoot again. Others got angry and went on a scoring run. A few—the rare ones—were the forgetful goldfish the coach urged them all to be: They made a shot and forgot about it, then missed a shot and did the same. They lived in the moment. William wanted to understand all the threads that made up the athletic humans in the Northwestern gym so he could help them not only stay on the court but flourish.

Arash helped William apply for the graduate program in sports physiology at Northwestern. The two-year master's would allow William to keep his job with the team and take classes at night; he was also permitted to include a few graduate psychology classes, and because William worked for the university, the program was virtually free. William repeatedly thanked Arash for his assistance, until the older man became annoyed and told him to stop. But the idea of committing to another graduate program, after having failed so badly the first time, made William so anxious that he knew he wouldn't have been able to do this on his own. One Saturday morning, when they were going over his final application, Arash said, "Stop thinking about who you were when you were living the wrong life, William. You're built for the life you're living now. You have a gift for seeing what's wrong with these boys. And besides, you *can't* fail when you're doing what you love." William was silent, considering this. "Do you not get it?" Arash had said, exasperated. William started to respond, but the older man cut him off: "It doesn't matter if you get it, actually. It's true."

During one of their dinners, Sylvie said, "I want us to live together." She had been sneaking in and out of William's dorm for almost a year, setting an alarm for five o'clock in the morning so none of the students would know she'd been there.

William nodded and allowed himself to imagine that possibility for the first time. The pleasure of coming home to Sylvie every night, of sharing a refrigerator, a closet, and a bed. The peace of being utterly comfortable in his home, with her. He couldn't think of anything more wonderful. William informed the university that he wouldn't be a resident adviser the following semester, and right before Christmas, he moved out of his dorm suite and into Sylvie's studio.

When he was unpacking his shirts into her small closet, he and Sylvie kept smiling at each other, elated. This was the first time William had lived off Northwestern's campus since he'd arrived in Chicago, and he enjoyed making Pilsen his own neighborhood. He chose a favorite coffee shop, a barber, a pharmacy where he picked up his monthly prescription from the psychiatrist. It felt decadent to sleep beside Sylvie all night, with no alarm set, with nothing to hide. William made dinner, teaching himself to cook from books, the same way he'd taught himself plumbing and carpentry. On the evenings when he didn't have class, he studied while Sylvie read beside him. He would turn from his textbook to look at her, not caring if she noticed, not caring if she looked up from the page. Sometimes he would pull her into his arms, or she'd climb onto his lap, and they would entwine their limbs, take off each other's clothes, all their movements soft, gentle, reverent.

When Kent and Nicole visited Chicago, the two couples went out to eat, often at the Mexican diner. Nicole had six brothers and sisters, so she and Sylvie shared stories of growing up in chaotic, loving households. Kent and Nicole enjoyed horrifying the librarian and assistant coach with disturbing things they'd seen during their hospital shifts: a man hopping into the ER, carrying a bucket that contained his severed leg; two college kids who had superglued their bodies together; a toy dinosaur lodged in a part of a man's anatomy where it did not belong. Sylvie recited the titles of the most-checked-out books at the library, because Kent was interested in how that list transformed, or didn't, over time. They discussed Nicole and Kent's ever-changing plans for their wedding. On one visit, the event was to be held on a riverboat; another time, it would be in Detroit in Kent's parents' small backyard, or in a window-lined ballroom in a Chicago skyscraper. "Maybe we'll elope to Paris," Nicole said one night, and Kent kissed her cheek. The couple clearly had fun coming up with plans, but they delayed the actual event while they tried to save money. They were both putting themselves through medical school using a blizzard of loans.

"What about you two?" Kent said. "You'll get married." He uttered this as a statement, not a question.

William and Sylvie hadn't discussed marriage. William waited to see if the subject scared him, but nothing inside him changed. He was sitting next to Sylvie in the booth, the sides of their thighs touching.

"I've never really cared about weddings, and I feel like we're already married," Sylvie said. "Or more than married, if there is such a thing. And"—she hesitated—"it doesn't seem right to do that."

William nodded. He knew Sylvie was thinking of Julia; she often was. She wrote about her sister in the middle of the night; a spotlight shone on Julia in every memory she put on the page. Sylvie cared about her older sister as much as she ever had, and if she could save Julia from more pain, she would.

Kent studied them from across the table. He'd picked William up at the Northwestern gym before dinner, and the two friends had shot baskets for old times' sake. They'd shown Nicole the laundry room in the sub-basement where they worked throughout college. Sareka had already gone home for the day, so Nicole couldn't meet her. When the weather was nice, William sometimes ate lunch with Sareka on a bench in the quad. She told him about her three kids, and he told her everything he'd been through. She listened carefully, her head tilted toward him. Like Cecelia, Sareka clearly appreciated getting to know him after all this time. William felt sorry for his younger self again, because he had missed out on real friendships like hers. He remembered how he used to try to get out of every conversation as quickly as possible so Sareka wouldn't have a chance to realize he was barely holding himself together. Now he told her all the ways in which he had been broken, and she told him about her husband's unemployment and how her middle son had the most beautiful singing voice she'd ever heard.

"Are you trying to hide your love, by not making it official?" Kent addressed Sylvie. He was still the self-appointed watchperson for William's mental health.

She took a sip of her margarita. "I don't think so. We just don't need that label or certificate. And I don't want to do anything more that might hurt anyone."

"Don't take this the wrong way," Nicole said. "But I feel like you forget the fact that William and Julia had already broken up when you got together, so technically you didn't do *anything* wrong. You chose honesty, which was brave. And you chose to be happy, instead of heartbroken and miserable." She paused and gave them her clinical gaze. "You two are adorable, the way you light each other up. I bet you never fight. Kent and I fight all the time." She smiled when she said this. "We're feisty, but you two are always gentle with each other."

This hadn't occurred to William, but it was true that he and Sylvie had never fought, never even come close. Every morning, they ate breakfast together: toast and eggs that Sylvie cooked. Then they both went to work and were grateful to see each other at the end of the day. Sometimes they slow-danced in the kitchen to a song that was on the radio. On garbage nights, Sylvie showed William all the treasures that people left on their curbs. He loved how excited she got when she found a brand-new toaster or a pair of sneakers in Izzy's size. What in the world would they fight about? Who takes out the garbage? Or how much money one of them spent at the grocery store?

"You should get married," Kent said. "Everything you went through to be here . . . deserves to be celebrated."

"We'll do whatever Sylvie wants," William said.

"How about this," Sylvie said, with a smile. "We'll get married after you do."

"Careful," William said. He eyed his friend, who had already cracked a wide grin. "Kent's competitive. He'll go to the justice of the peace tomorrow morning, because he'll see that as winning."

MOST SUNDAYS, SYLVIE READ, and William studied for his classes. Sometimes he studied with Emeline, who still had a year of college classes left. "I do want my degree," she would say, when she was exhausted from working full-time while attending classes at night. "It's important for the daycare, but I know I'm really just doing this for Mama, even though she doesn't talk to me anymore." Her sisters would hug her tightly in response, because they understood completely and knew there were no words that could help. When Emeline did eventually graduate, they would bake a three-layer chocolate cake—her favorite—and shower her with confetti.

Late on Sunday afternoons, William and Sylvie went for a walk. No matter what route they took, they made sure to pass Cecelia's murals. Pilsen had been known for colorful murals since the 1960s, but a local arts commission had set about cleaning the old murals and hiring more artists to create new ones in the past few years. Nearly every corner featured a three-story depiction of Martin Luther King, Jr., or Frida Kahlo, or a painted quote from the Bible. Whenever Cecelia finished a new mural, Sylvie and William attended the unveiling, which usually consisted of a cluster of people standing on the sidewalk and a sheet being dropped from the top of the building to the ground below. There would be photos of the mural in the local paper the next day. When Cecelia was allowed to paint whatever she liked, she painted women's faces. The painted women—some tucked into the corner of a wall, others spanning a full three stories—looked fierce and beautiful. Sylvie laughed at each unveiling, because William always said the same thing: "She looks like you and your sisters." Sylvie would tip her head back to study the woman's face. "They can't all look like us, William. We don't look anything like this fifteenth-century saint." William shrugged, because he disagreed. He saw all four Padavano sisters staring down from numerous walls in the neighborhood and remembered the sisters showing up at his college basketball game, turning their collective gaze on him.

WILLIAM BEGAN TO FIGURE out how he could be more effective at work. His understanding of the physiology of the athletes was better informed now, and he was able to diagnose injuries and vulnerabilities with accuracy. He developed a program in which he interviewed the Northwestern players three times per season—at the beginning, middle, and end. He created a list of questions to find out their injury history and whether they were confident or floundering. He wanted to know where the ice was weakest beneath their feet so he could keep them from falling through. He shared the information he gathered with the coaches, and they all worked to address the needs of each student at this particular moment in his life. They built up the player's physical weak points and tried to build the player up mentally too.

"I knew how to be good to the players after they graduated," Arash said, once they'd finished the first season of the program, "following up and lending a hand if I could. But you built us an infrastructure of kindness." The results had been positive and almost immediate. After several years with a losing record, Northwestern had climbed to the middle of the table in their conference—considered by all to be a big step forward—and William was able to lie down next to Sylvie at night awash in gratitude for his life.

"I want to build more infrastructures of kindness," Arash told William, and a few weeks later he started a free monthly basketball clinic in Throop Park, not far from the Lozano Library. The older man enlisted William and two assistant coaches from Northwestern to help. High school coaches from underserved Chicago districts sent their best players, hardest-working players, and smartest players for advanced coaching. Arash collected proverbs, and he would often make the kids recite back to him phrases like: *Opportunity did not knock until I built the door.* Arash and William looked for bad habits—poor shooting form, unstable landings—that could lead to injuries. They gave the teenagers exercises to strengthen their ankles or told them to do fifteen minutes of yoga before bed.

Sometimes, watching these young kids run the court, hungry for the ball and hungry for praise from Arash, William remembered himself at their age. He would have been in his Catholic school's gym, impossibly skinny and tall, running the court, not expecting praise from anyone. Not expecting his parents to attend the game, not expecting to be passed the ball but deeply relieved when it found its way to his hands. Sylvie had asked him one night, in her gentlest voice, "Do you want to reconsider your decision about Alice?" William had shaken his head. He knew some of the ache he felt in his body watching these boys at this vulnerable age was bearable only because he wasn't a father. He cared about Sylvie with every cell of his body; the idea of watching someone he loved navigate their way from childhood to adulthood was terrifying. He had barely survived his own coming of age.

JULIA HAD BEEN GONE for almost five years when the event space Kent and Nicole had rented for their wedding flooded a few days before the ceremony, and Emeline and Cecelia offered their large backyard. The couple had waited so long to marry that everyone wanted their big day to be special. The Padavanos, Kent and William's old teammates, and Kent's and Nicole's relatives showed up in jeans and T-shirts to make the backyard beautiful in a short amount of time. William, Gus, and Washington built a trellis by following instructions in a library book, and Izzy and Sylvie laced the structure with flowers. Cecelia painted tiny doctor's bags onto the folding chairs and gave the back of the house a new coat of paint. By the time the wedding started, everyone was exhausted, but when Kent cried with happiness under the trellis, everyone present cried as well.

Later that night, in bed, Sylvie said, "I remembered something during the ceremony. Something I never told you."

William was already looking at her; they had just made love and were lying facing each other. It was past midnight, and they were both a little drunk. Sylvie and William were almost never up this late and rarely drank enough to be inebriated. They lived carefully, because sleep was a linchpin of William's health, and excessive alcohol made his medications less potent. Both he and Sylvie felt a little mischievous now, like children who had defied their parents' orders.

"The day we brought you to the emergency room, I told the ambulance driver and a nurse that I was your wife. Everyone in the hospital thought we were married, actually, for the whole time you were unconscious."

"You were my wife for ten days," William said, pleased with the idea.

"What I like about that . . . is that it was the truth," Sylvie said. "I wanted to be your wife. I just couldn't admit it to myself. I said I was your wife for a logistical reason, so the doctors would talk to me, but it was true."

The idea that in some profound, invisible way they had been married before they'd even kissed delighted them both, and William drew her closer to him in the darkness.

They married officially a month later, in the back room of the Lozano Library. Sylvie wanted to hold the ceremony there, and William simply agreed. He knew she felt safe and whole in the library. It was a place that belonged to her alone, apart from her sisters. William bought a silver ring for Sylvie and a new suit for the occasion. Sylvie wore a simple gray cocktail dress and left her hair down, because she knew William liked it best that way. Head Librarian Elaine, ailing and in a wheelchair, attended the wedding, and the other guests were Emeline, Josie, Izzy, Cecelia, Kent, and Nicole. Arash married the couple. William could feel his heart beating during the short ceremony, and he found he couldn't stop smiling.

Afterward, everyone except Head Librarian Elaine went to the Mexican diner for dinner. There was a confusion with the reservation when they first arrived, and for a few minutes there was an extra chair at their table. William knew each of the Padavano sisters pictured

Julia sitting in the empty seat, and a ripple of pain crossed their faces. The chair was taken away by the waiter, though, and Kent told a joke to make everyone laugh. Toward the end of the meal, Cecelia stood and toasted: "To love." Everyone up and down the table said and felt the words—the beauty, and the cost, of love.

Alice

WHEN ALICE WAS FIVE YEARS OLD, JULIA SAID, "I THINK you're old enough to know the truth. Your father died in a car accident last year."

For the rest of her life, Alice would remember this moment, down to the smallest detail. They were sitting at their square kitchen table in their apartment on East 86th Street. Alice's hair was in braids, because her mother said she didn't keep it tidy enough when it was down. She was wearing her favorite mustard-colored corduroy skirt and eating cereal. Julia bought Cheerios because they were healthy, but Alice always added a tablespoon of sugar to her bowl.

Alice put down her spoon and said, "Oh." Her hands felt tingly, so she tucked them underneath her legs. She noticed that her mother didn't look sad.

"Does Grandma Rose know?"

Her mother raised her eyebrows. She was wearing a suit—this one was pale lavender with a small gold chain across the breast pocket— and her Monday-to-Friday makeup. Alice's mother was very beautiful; everyone said so. Mrs. Laven, who was friends with her grandmother and lived down the hall, called Julia *Gorgeous* as if it were her name. Alice also knew that her mother was skeptical about her own beauty. Julia's hair always upset her; whenever she passed a mirror, she tried to reshape it with her hands. "You're so lucky you don't have these curls,

Alice," she would say, at least three times a week. Alice had long, straight, pale hair that was neither quite blond nor brown. She thought her hair was boring compared to her mother's, which moved around as if it had its own plans for the day. Julia wore her hair up at work so it couldn't embarrass her.

"Of course Grandma Rose knows." Julia took a sip of her coffee. She didn't eat breakfast but drank three coffees before lunch. "Don't mention it to her on the phone, though. She won't want to talk about it, and you know what she's like when she's upset."

Alice nodded, even though this confused her. She didn't think of Grandma Rose getting upset, certainly not in a way that was scary or to be avoided. Alice and her mother visited Grandma Rose once a year at her condo in Florida. Her grandmother raised her voice and threw her arms around while telling stories about grown-ups Alice didn't know, but Grandma Rose seemed to enjoy that. Getting worked up was part of Grandma Rose's day, like brushing her teeth or sitting on her tiny balcony. Alice had always found her grandmother's agitation comforting. It made her feel safe, because she knew if someone was ever mean to her, Grandma Rose would let them have it.

Alice became aware that her mother was watching her carefully, so she straightened in her chair.

"I know that you never knew your father," Julia said, "but I didn't want to keep this from you. This doesn't affect us, though, right? It's always been just you and me, baby girl. We don't need anyone else."

Alice nodded again. Every night when her mother tucked her in, the last thing Julia said before switching off the light was: "It's you and me forever, baby."

Alice finished her cereal, then she and her mother walked around the corner to Alice's school, and her mother continued on to work. The news swirled through Alice all day. It felt important, even though she couldn't have said why. In a way, it was like her mother had handed her a father and then taken him away in one sentence. Before this, Alice had been vaguely aware that she had a father, but he was almost never mentioned. Her mother had told Alice once that he hadn't wanted a family, and that was all she'd known until now. Perhaps Alice had been unconsciously waiting for news about her father this whole time. It was like a question inside her had been answered. At the age of five, she didn't carry around many questions, so that made this a big day.

In the schoolyard, she told her best friend, Carrie, "My father died."

Her friend's mouth opened in surprise. Carrie made this face a lot, because she was surprised a lot. Alice would keep track, while she and Carrie grew up, of the life events that *didn't* surprise her friend, because this was a much shorter list.

"I didn't know you had a dad," Carrie said.

"He lived in Chicago."

"Chicago." Carrie said the name like it was its own surprise. "I didn't know that. You never met him?"

"Not since I was a baby."

"Do you need a hug?"

Alice nodded, and she and Carrie hugged until the bell rang and they filed into their kindergarten classroom.

After that, Alice took an interest in fathers. She wondered what distinguished them from mothers and if a child actually needed one. There were mostly mothers and nannies at drop-off and pickup from school, but there would be an occasional dad, and Alice would study him closely. A few dressed like the fathers on television, in neat suits, holding briefcases. Sometimes a dad picked up his child and swung him or her around in a circle, and Alice had never seen a mother do that. Julia certainly never wrestled with her the way Alice watched a dad play-wrestle with his son by the jungle gym one afternoon. Carrie's dad was the only father Alice knew personally, though he rarely remembered Alice's name. He called every child, other than his daughter, kiddo. He wore thick glasses and flannel shirts and generally didn't seem to notice the little girls when they were in the apartment, as if they were too short to enter his field of vision. He was in charge of breakfast—he wore a deadly serious expression while he flipped pancakes—and he was responsible for taking out the garbage, but those were his only specific roles as far as Alice could tell.

Alice felt no need for a father, personally; her life was peaceful and happy. Julia came into Alice's room every morning and woke her up by whispering, "Good morning, baby girl," and in the evenings they made dinner together while watching *Jeopardy!* on the small television in their kitchen. Alice's job was to make the salad, and she did so while standing on a stool by the counter. Julia took off her heels, suit jacket, and earrings before she entered the kitchen, and this softened version of her mother—all the buttons and sharp points gone—made Alice act like the silliest version of herself. The game show questions were usually too difficult for Alice to understand, but she would say a non-sense answer in such a confident voice that Julia would double over with laughter. Fridays were always "girls' nights," and the mother and daughter spent the whole week discussing which movie they would rent from the Blockbuster store on the corner. They watched the film while wearing fuzzy robes and painting their nails. If Julia had a date on Saturday night, Mrs. Laven and Alice would order Chinese food and then play Chutes and Ladders, which was their favorite board game. Most Sundays, Julia and Alice went for a walk in Central Park and bought giant pretzels from their favorite vendor, a Nigerian man named Bou who knew that Julia liked extra mustard on hers. Every day of their week had a regular cadence and routine, and Alice liked them all.

ONE FRIDAY IN THIRD grade, Alice's teacher, an older woman named Mrs. Salisbury—who frowned at the class all day as if it were an integral part of her pedagogy—told Alice to stay in the classroom after the final bell. Mrs. Salisbury left the room, and then returned with Alice's mother. Julia, in her elegant business suit and high heels, looked out of place and uncomfortable amid the sea of tiny desks. She and Mrs. Salisbury seemed like an unlikely pair of adults. Mrs. Salisbury had a headful of giant gray curls that she had set once a week at the hair salon. They looked like waves that would never crash; you could see through the center of them, and they didn't move.

The teacher said, "Mrs. Padavano, I'm sure you're wondering why I called you."

"Ms. Padavano, if you don't mind," Julia said. "Not Mrs."

Alice tilted her head, wondering if her mother would go further. She had heard Julia describe herself as a divorcée recently, but only because a nosy mother had made it impossible to deflect the question. Her mother clearly didn't like saying the word. She normally said she was a single mother. "I say that," she'd told Alice, "because the most important part of my life is being your mom."

"Ms. Padavano, I wonder if you were aware of Alice's report, which she presented to the class today?"

"No . . . I try to give her independence with her work," Julia said. "She asks me when she needs help."

Alice was seated at her small desk. She scuffed her feet against the linoleum floor. "I didn't talk to my mom about the report. I worked on it in the library during after-school."

"I figured," the teacher said in a dry voice. "Ms. Padavano, I've been teaching in this school for thirty-two years, and I have never seen a child come up with a presentation like this one. The students are allowed to choose any subject they like—this helps them feel invested in their work—and then they have to do some very basic research and talk about the subject to the class. Your daughter gave a presentation on automobile accidents. She told us about all the celebrities who've died in car accidents, including details on how Jayne Mansfield was decapitated in a crash—"

"Oh my," Julia murmured.

"Alice gave the class statistics on how many people die in car accidents every year. She made it sound like if a person sets foot in a car, they are risking death. And then she finished by showing us photos of wrecked cars."

Julia looked at her daughter, her eyes wide.

"Several of the children in the class started to cry, Ms. Padavano. I can guarantee you that I will receive many phone calls from upset parents this weekend."

"I'm so sorry," Julia said. "I will speak to Alice."

"I won't be allowing her to speak to the class without running her ideas by me first."

"Of course not. And I'll make sure nothing like this happens again." Julia had Alice by the hand and was walking her out of the classroom. On the sidewalk outside the school, she stopped. "What in the world?" Julia's face was pale. "Why would you do that?"

Alice shrugged, even though her mother had told her that a shrug was an unacceptable response to a question. "I want your words," Julia had said to her since she was small.

"Wait," Julia said, "is this why you've been refusing to take taxis for the past year? Because you're scared of cars?"

"I'm sorry you had to leave work," Alice said. She normally stayed late and either attended an after-school program or read books in the school library. She was picked up by a babysitter or Julia, depending on the day. "I'm sorry I did something wrong." She didn't like to inconvenience her mother; Alice prided herself on not causing Julia difficulties. She got good report cards and often signed her own permission slips for field trips so Julia would have one less thing to do. Alice felt like school was her job, and she was disappointed in herself for screwing up.

Julia's expression changed, as if an idea had just occurred to her. "Is this because of what . . . Is this because of your father?"

Alice shrugged again, but it was a weary one this time. "He would still be alive if he hadn't gotten in that accident."

After a moment, Julia said, "I see."

"I didn't think the kids were going to cry, Mama. I thought they'd find it interesting, and I wanted them to know that cars are very dangerous."

"It sounds like you were successful, baby girl."

That evening, they didn't have their usual girls' night, because Julia had a headache and needed to lie down. Alice ate popcorn with extra butter and used the remote to flip from one channel to the next. She put herself to bed, because her mother's door was closed and she thought Julia might be asleep.

A half hour later, though, Alice's mother opened the door to her room. "Are you awake?" she whispered from the doorway. Julia was wearing her nightgown, and her hair was down.

"Yes," Alice said. "It always takes me at least nineteen minutes to fall asleep." She kept track of this, out of curiosity. She had to think all the thoughts in her head before her body allowed her to sleep.

"I need to know . . . Are you feeling all right?" Julia said. "Are you sad about car accidents? Or"—she paused—"about anything? I need you to tell me if you're sad."

Her mother's voice sounded so anxious that Alice thought, *Am I supposed to be sad?* She considered the question. "No," she said, having made an internal inventory. "I don't feel sad."

"Wonderful," her mother said, in her normal voice. "That's wonderful. You go to sleep now, okay? I love you, baby girl." And the door closed, and Julia was gone.

IN MIDDLE SCHOOL, ALICE hit a relentless growth spurt. It felt like she and her body had been on the same path and then, one random day, her body headed in a different direction at full speed, and Alice was left wondering what was going on. She was always hungry, and Julia had to stock boxes of granola bars to get Alice from one meal to the next. Alice's stomach would grumble so loudly in class that the kids around her would laugh, and she was mortified. She had stabbing aches in her thighs and lower back, which the pediatrician diagnosed as normal growing pains, but Alice, incredulous, thought, *How can this be normal?* The only thing that eased her discomfort was lying on the floor with her legs up against the wall, so that's the position Alice was in most of the time when she was home from school. To her horror, bright-red streaks appeared on her back and upper arms—stretch marks—which the doctor said would fade but never completely disappear.

By the middle of sixth grade, Alice had passed her mother's height: five feet four inches. Alice felt a new kind of sadness when this happened. Her body was galloping her away from childhood and away from her mother. Quickly, Alice was one inch taller than her mother, then three. She found she could reach items on the top shelf in their kitchen. She looked down at the top of her mother's head and understood, for the first time, that her mother was just a woman. Julia wasn't more special or stronger than anyone else, and clearly she would no longer be able to save Alice if she needed saving. If the house was on fire, Alice would have to pick up her mother and run, not the other way around. This reality made Alice feel panicked, and she had trouble sleeping for the first time in her life. She didn't know what to do.

Alice was aware that her growing height discomfited her mother too. Julia often looked startled when Alice stood up out of a chair or entered the room. They shared a look that said, *What is happening?* The balance between them had been disrupted; now Julia had to look up at her middle-schooler when she spoke, and Alice looked down at her mother and thought, *Can I trust you?*

It was at this stage that Alice shifted her investigations from outside their apartment to inside. With this new awareness that her mother was flawed—because all people were flawed—Alice needed to learn Julia's specific issues so that she could compensate for them when the time came. It occurred to her that maybe *this* was why a kid needed two parents and siblings. Brothers and sisters were helpful because they could check in with one another to confirm that a parental bad mood or overreaction wasn't their fault. And in a two-parent home, if one parent's frailties were revealed, the child could lean on the other parent. It was a backup system, and there was no backup system in Alice's home. If something happened to Julia, Alice would be on her own. She made sure her mother went for a checkup with the doctor and suggested that they eat heart-healthy dinners, a comment that made Julia laugh, until she realized her daughter wasn't joking.

When Julia was at the supermarket one day, Alice went through her mother's closet and drawers. She felt no guilt about this activity. In her mind, this was important research, with life-or-death consequences. If Julia had a secret problem, Alice needed to know about it. She shuffled through items she expected to find: clothes, jewelry, makeup, and toiletries. Alice did find one interesting thing, during her search through Julia's bedside table: an envelope with a few photographs inside.

The photographs were all at least fifteen years old, and they were of Julia and her sisters. There was a photo of the four sisters with their arms around one another's shoulders; Julia and Sylvie looked like they were in their late teens. Alice was able to identify the different sisters because, on every visit to Florida, she pored through her grandmother's photo albums, trying to commit the contents to memory. There was no space between the sisters in this picture; they were pressed together as if they were as comfortable with one another's bodies as they were with their own. Sylvie's head rested on Julia's shoulder, and Emeline and Cecelia were pointing identical smiles at the camera. The sisters looked deeply similar, like they were four different versions of the same person. Alice had never seen her mother look that happy.

There was also a photo of an older Sylvie sitting on a couch holding a baby—Alice wondered if the baby was her. But perhaps Sylvie had a baby of her own; Alice didn't know. And the final photo must have been from a party—perhaps thirty people were turned toward the camera. Grandpa Charlie was in the photo, his arms outstretched, his face beaming at his daughters. Rose must have been shaking her head, because her face was slightly blurred. A younger Julia was in the photo, wearing blue jeans, with her hair down. Her sisters were so close she could reach out and touch them. Someone must have just told a joke, because the people in the photo looked both startled and mid-laugh. Alice scanned the photo, looking for a man who resembled her; she'd never seen a photograph of her father, but she knew she had his hair color and blue eyes. Everyone in the photo, though, looked like a Padavano.

After she put the photos back in the envelope and in the drawer, Alice stayed on the floor next to her mother's bed. The discovery of the photographs had somehow confirmed Alice's sense that there was something she needed to find or, in this case, remember. She rarely thought about the fact that she had aunts, living in another city. Grandma Rose told Alice stories about her four daughters when they were young, about Grandpa Charlie, and about their house on 18th Place, but her mother behaved as if her life had started when she and Alice moved to New York City. Why were the only photos from that before-time hidden and not up on their walls? If she had more family in her life, Alice would be safer. This tactile proof that she had family but no connection to them made the fuzz of panic rise inside her, and she had to press down on her legs to stop them aching.

That night, while she and her mother were making dinner, Alice said, "Why don't you speak to your sisters?"

Julia had already taken out all the ingredients for the meatloaf, but she opened the refrigerator door and looked inside anyway. There were a few beats of silence, and Alice knew, for the first time, in her tall body, that her mother was wielding that quiet at her intentionally. It was designed to make Alice stop asking these kinds of questions. Alice could see these pockets of heavy quiet scattered back through her childhood, whenever she brought up topics her mother didn't want to discuss. Alice's father and his death, Julia's childhood, her sisters.

Julia said, "I'm in touch with Emeline and Cecelia sometimes, but we live in different cities. And we have busy lives. When you have siblings, you're close when you're young, because you live in the same house. But when you grow up, you go your separate ways."

In the past, Alice had obeyed her mother's hints and changed the subject. But now she needed to know what was behind the quiet. This was why she had gone through her mother's drawers, in case there was knowledge she might need to take care of herself. "Are the other three—Sylvie, Emeline, and Cecelia—still close?"

Julia looked at her, her face expressionless. "I don't know. They live in the same city, so maybe." She paused, and then said, "I'm a self-sufficient adult, Alice. That's rare for a woman, and I'm proud of that fact. If I raise you right, you won't need anyone either."

Alice pictured her mother on one small deserted island and herself on a different island, within waving distance.

Julia said, "Why are you asking me these questions now?"

Alice wanted to say, *Because I think it's strange that the only family photos we have are in an envelope in a drawer, and I think it's strange that the only family we ever see is Grandma Rose and we spend holidays alone or down the hall with Mrs. Laven and her relatives. And because you have three sisters and I wish I had a sister to share a bedroom with and to talk to in the dark at night.*

"We have a wonderful life," Julia said. "Don't we?"

"Yes," Alice said, because her mother clearly expected an answer, and because it was true. *For now,* she thought. *But what if something goes wrong?*

The next time Julia left the apartment to run errands, Alice phoned Grandma Rose. She said, "Did my mom have a fight with her sisters?"

She knew the question would surprise her grandmother, but she also thought there was a good chance Rose would answer. Traces of her mother's pre–New York life existed all over Grandma Rose's condo. Four framed photos of Rose's daughters hung over the couch, and portraits of female saints from their Chicago home—which her mother always rolled her eyes at—sat on the wall above her kitchen table. And Rose was a talker; there were no pockets of quiet in her company.

"Of course Julia had fights with them. All sisters fight, you know. It's part of being in a family."

"My mom and I never fight," Alice said. "And I've never fought with you."

"Well," Rose said, "that's true. Maybe each generation is better than the one before. But what happened between your mom and her sisters is their business—do you think they told me anything? I'm their mother."

"It just seems odd that I've never even spoken to any of my aunts. I know Emeline visited us, but I was too little to remember. My friend Carrie sees her aunts and uncles all the time. I feel like"—Alice hesitated—"something's missing. My mom never talks about anything she doesn't want to."

"That is the ever-loving truth," Rose said. "And I'm not going to get in trouble by telling you anything without her approval."

"I don't know my father's last name. Can you tell me that?"

"Ask your mother," Rose said, and hung up.

Alice tried to get information about her mother from Mrs. Laven, but the older woman was indignant to be asked. "Your mother is gorgeous and brilliant, and she's worked her derrière off to run her own business," Mrs. Laven said. "You are, bar none, the luckiest little girl in the world." Alice sighed and changed the subject. She knew that her mother had given an internship to Mrs. Laven's troubled nephew one summer and that Julia gave Mrs. Laven an expensive purse from a fancy store every Christmas; it was clear that if this was the last road Alice had access to, it was closed. She considered, as a final resort, writing a letter to one of her aunts, but she didn't know their addresses or what to say. *Hi, I'm your niece. How are you?* She knew it was possible that her mother was right, that sisters grew apart when they hit adulthood and no longer had a home in common. How would Alice know? Perhaps they barely thought of one another anymore.

She stopped asking her mother questions. There seemed to be no point, and the practice agitated Julia, which Alice couldn't risk. Stress could contribute to high blood pressure, which could lead to a heart attack or a stroke, and Julia's health needed to be prioritized. Alice told herself: *If I stop asking questions, I'll stop growing.* She'd been making these kinds of bets with herself since the growth spurt began. *If I stop chewing my nails, I'll stop growing. If I give up candy. If I put my hand up in class when the teacher wants me to.* None of these trade-offs had panned out, though, and this one didn't either. Alice went quiet on the subject of her mother's past, and yet she continued to rise.

Sylvie

CECELIA HAD ADOPTED WILLIAM'S MANTRA FOR PARENTING: No bullshit and no secrets. If Izzy asked a question, no matter what it was, Cecelia answered honestly. Sylvie and Emeline both happened to be in Cecelia's kitchen one evening when the six-year-old Izzy asked where babies came from.

Sylvie ate with her sisters a few days a week, when William was at Northwestern for late practices. She and William had been together for almost six years and had married the year before. They'd recently moved into a two-bedroom apartment not far from where the twins lived, and William was about to start a job for the Chicago Bulls. The franchise had created a new position for him, with responsibilities both in player development and as a physio. The Bulls were flush with optimism and eager to expand their staff. They hadn't yet won a championship, but with Michael Jordan on the roster, the trophy seemed inevitable. William's job description stipulated that he wouldn't travel with the team; he would be based in Chicago, and he would use his specialized program to try to target areas where young players needed assistance. William probably would have chosen to stay at Northwestern out of loyalty to Arash and the university, despite the flattering offer from the Bulls, but Arash was retiring, and the head coach was leaving for another job, so Sylvie convinced William that he should move on too. "We have to keep growing," she said, "or we don't live." He'd smiled at her, because she'd avoided saying the word *die*. He knew Sylvie was invested in keeping him away from even the thought of that word.

"A baby is made by a man and a woman having sex," Cecelia said.

Izzy nodded, and her dark curls bobbed around her intent face. "And what is sex?"

Emeline and Sylvie blushed furiously while Cecelia drew pictures of various sexual positions on a sketch pad. Izzy paid close attention and then said, "How do Aunt Emmie and Aunt Josie do it?"

"Oh my God," Emeline said, and left the kitchen while Cecelia drew pictures to illustrate that too. Sylvie laughed helplessly in the corner. She missed Alice suddenly, a feeling that always came at her as if from around a corner, when she didn't expect it. She had the feeling that Alice belonged in this kitchen right now, in this ridiculous scene. She was meant to be here, seated beside her cousin. Sylvie carried Julia with her, but she ached for the baby girl who had left the family with her mother.

This was one of the unexpected sorrows that trailed in the wake of losing Julia. Sylvie knew in her heart that her sister was flourishing in New York. Julia had sounded excited and alive when Sylvie spoke to her during her first year in the city, when she was building her new self and new life. Julia was the rocket their father had known she could be, with nothing to hold her back. But Sylvie had only known Alice when she was a baby; she was in the unusual position of loving her but not knowing her at all, and Sylvie was unable to shake the feeling that the girl belonged with the rest of them in Pilsen. Sylvie imagined Alice playing chess with Izzy in the library, their blond and brunette heads bent toward each other. And she played, as if on a video loop, a scene in which she walked down the street with Alice's hand in her own. The child was half William, after all, and half Julia, which made her Sylvie's heart.

But Sylvie had broken Julia's heart, which meant she had no right to Alice. And William had not only given his daughter up legally, he'd somehow managed to remove the thought of her from his mind. This removal seemed almost surgical in nature; Sylvie watched him carefully and saw no sign that he ever considered the existence of his daughter. There were paintings of Alice in Cecelia's house, and Sylvie watched William avert his eyes from each one as he walked down the halls, an obstacle course so ingrained that he wasn't even aware he was running it. When he joined Sylvie for dinner at the twins' house, he would talk to Izzy about the history she was learning at school. He seemed to have forgotten his own history, though, and the fact that Alice had entered the world on Izzy's heels. He'd forgotten that there had once been two little girls in his universe, and not one. Sylvie never mentioned Alice within William's hearing. The further they traveled from her husband's suicide attempt, the more grateful she was for his steadiness and his obvious contentment. She had watched him put down roots in this life, watched him fill the breaks inside himself with love and meaningful work. Sylvie accepted William's choice to stay away from his daughter; she accepted all of him, every day, and he did the same for her.

IN 1993, WHEN IZZY was ten years old, Emeline and Josie bought the house next door to the one Cecelia had purchased. Josie, a warm, auburn-haired woman with a business degree, was savvy with money. She'd negotiated the purchase of the daycare where she and Emeline had met; shortly after that, she bought another local daycare. The twins decided to share the two homes; after all, they'd been living together their entire lives. They knocked down the fence separating the houses, and the family spent the summer renovating and cleaning up the new house. Sylvie, after a few years of a regular schedule, enjoyed the disruption and the way her family once again gathered and labored together in all their free time.

Sylvie was now the head librarian at the Lozano Library, so she could set her own hours. She'd been slightly surprised to find that she enjoyed running the library; the decision-making the position entailed was satisfying, and she liked being the person who had the final say on issues big and small. Sylvie now knew not only all the regular patrons but, in the case of many of them, their parents and children too. Frank Ceccione, who had grown up two doors down from the Padavanos, read the newspaper at a table by the front windows each day. He'd struggled with addiction for much of his adult life, and she thought they both took comfort in greeting each other every morning. To Sylvie's delight, Izzy loved the library almost as much as Sylvie did and often walked there after school. Nothing made Sylvie happier than watching her niece play chess or read at one of the tables while she worked behind the desk.

Izzy and Sylvie spent the first few weeks of the summer painting the walls of one of the bedrooms a deep-blue color. "I'm going to sleep in here when my mom has a boyfriend," she told Sylvie.

"Sounds nice," Sylvie said. "I would have liked to have my own room to go to, to read, when I was growing up."

"Tell me stories from then." Izzy had been saying these words since she learned how to talk. She loved hearing about when her mother and her sisters were young.

Izzy already knew most of the stories because of her mother's policy of holding nothing back. But during the hot summer evenings they spent painting the room the color of a midnight sky, Sylvie told the stories in chronological order. She stood at the top of the ladder, painting near the ceiling's edge, and tried to remember all the details that she could. She started with their childhood, which of course included the story that, for some reason, delighted Izzy most, about the time when Rose's garden was being systemically destroyed by a mysterious animal that no one ever laid eyes on. The animal was mauling the food, splitting tomatoes in half, and gnawing at the leaves and stems of everything in the garden. Furious, Rose assigned her family members shifts, during which they had to sit in a lawn chair in the middle of the fruits, vegetables, and herbs and keep guard around the clock. Rose and Charlie split the night shift, though Rose always ended up taking over, because Charlie kept getting distracted. He would chat with a neighbor over the fence or fall asleep in the lawn chair. The girls would come down to breakfast in the morning and see their mother through the back window: her hair wild, a baseball bat in her hand, glaring at the earth around her. "What are you going to do when you catch the animal?" Sylvie had asked, and Rose said calmly, "I'll kill it." The animal wisely never showed itself—the Padavanos never knew if it was a rodent or a bird or a ghost—but the ravaging of the greenery stopped under their vigilance. Eventually, Rose declared herself triumphant and went back to sleeping in her bed.

After a time, Sylvie's narrative reached Cecelia's pregnancy, then Julia's, and then Charlie's death. How Rose had given Izzy and her mother up, how Uncle William had been hospitalized and married two of her aunts, and how Izzy had a cousin her own age whom she would never meet. Emeline wandered in and out of the room while the stories were being told, carrying lamps or books, and she shook her head in what looked like amazement. "Heavens," she said under her breath. A few times she called Josie in to listen. "I know I've told you some of this," she said, "but Sylvie's the best storyteller."

"I wish I'd met Charlie," Josie said once, after listening for a while. "He sounds wonderful."

The stories and the people in them did sound remarkable, Sylvie thought, when spoken aloud. She and the twins had rarely talked about what happened. They'd lived through it, after all, and the loss of Julia had made them quiet. But Josie's wonder at the stories, and Izzy's clear enjoyment of what she saw as a soap opera in which she played a small role, took the sting out of the grief woven through those times. When Sylvie spoke their family history into the air, all she heard was love.

Several times, Izzy shook her head and said, "Adults are idiots. My goal is to grow up and not be an idiot."

"Excellent goal," Sylvie said, thinking that it would be amazing if Izzy made her way through life with no heartbreak. Was that possible? Then something occurred to Sylvie, and she said, "Iz, I've actually been writing these stories down. For years. They're kind of messy, but maybe you'd like to read them?"

Izzy stared at her. She had her own version of the Padavano curls—hers were darker and tighter. Her face was round and serious. For all her questions about her mother's family, she'd shown no interest in learning about her biological father. When asked, Izzy said that she had more than enough grown-ups raising her already, thank you very much, and besides, if her mom didn't want that guy in her life, then she didn't either.

"Are you kidding?" Izzy said. "That would be my dream!"

Sylvie laughed, caught off guard by the child's enthusiasm. She'd written roughly three hundred pages; she had them bound at the copy shop the next afternoon and gave the manuscript to her niece. Izzy read it and then gave the book to Cecelia and Emeline.

"It's really good. You could publish this, you know," Cecelia said, but when Sylvie said she was writing it just for herself and their family, Cecelia nodded. She often painted pieces she had no intention of selling, so this made sense to her. Josie read the manuscript more than once; she was an only child and was now as all in on the Padavano family history as Izzy was.

Working in the disheveled house that summer, with stories filling all the nooks and crannies, the sisters found themselves remembering more of their family history. They shared memories while organizing closets or putting away pots and pans in the kitchen. Sometimes, when Sylvie, Emeline, or Cecelia retold an anecdote over dinner, Izzy or Josie would add details or dialogue, as if they had been there when it happened too.

They were eating pizzas one night on the living room floor when Emeline said, "Hearing all those stories again has made me remember myself, in a way. I know they mostly happened to you two and Julia"— she nodded at her sisters—"but I remember how I felt at every point."

Sylvie and Cecelia smiled, to encourage her to go on. Emeline rarely spoke about herself; she focused her attention on the people around her. She brought toddlers home from daycare most afternoons, and the children would wait on her lap for their parents to pick them up. She remained a homebody, happiest on the couch with Josie in the evenings. The larger spread of the super-duplex—this was what Izzy had named the two houses—made perfect sense for Emeline; home now contained more rooms, more space, and the people she loved.

"What did you feel?" Izzy asked Emeline. She and William were playing chess on the couch, in between bites of pizza. William was the only grown-up in the family who would play her favorite game with her. Izzy was a terrible loser, but she worked to control herself with her uncle, and he liked the challenge of chess. Determining a strategy that involved two teams and a campaign for space reminded him of basketball.

"It made me remember how badly I wanted to be a mother," Emeline said. "How that was all I ever wanted."

William hesitated and started to stand up to leave the room; Sylvie knew he thought the conversation was getting too personal. He was always careful to allow the sisters space and, if they chose, secrets from him.

Emeline shook her head at him, though, so he sat back down. "Josie and I talked about all of this last night." Her face was bright. "And we're going to apply to foster newborns. There's a need for that, and there are babies who need love."

Josie squeezed Emeline's shoulder. "Practically speaking," she said, "we would take care of babies that have been born to drug-addicted mothers or young teens for two or three months, and then the foster agency would return the baby to his or her biological mother or find a permanent placement. The research shows"—now Josie brightened, because she loved research—"that if a newborn is held whenever he or she cries and is smiled at during their first three months of life, their chance for long-term health and happiness shoots up something like fifty percent."

"Amazing," Sylvie said. "Emmie, what a wonderful idea."

Cecelia beamed at her sister and Josie. "Of course you should do that! We'll have to get one of those baby swings that Izzy loved when she was tiny."

"Ahem," Izzy said, with a dark look on her face. "I hear that newborns cry a lot."

"I promise I won't ever ask you to babysit," Emeline said. "And the baby will sleep with us, so you won't hear anything at night."

"Then you have my approval."

The foster application went through quickly. The two women had worried that they might be declined—they sometimes got looks at the supermarket, and a family had pulled a child from their daycare because they were gay—but the foster-care system was so overwhelmed that they seemed thrilled to have applicants with Emeline and Josie's excellent references and background in childcare. By the end of the summer, Emeline was wearing a tiny baby boy in a carrier while she walked through the fully renovated house.

Sylvie would think back on that summer as when her family fully accepted themselves. The super-duplex, with its shared houses and unusual layout, mirrored the unusual layout of the Padavanos, or what was left of them. Sylvie and her sisters and William had built their own lives to suit themselves, to serve the size and shape they occupied. The living space itself shared a backyard and a garden, which was a mixture of food and flowers. Cecelia used the attic in Emeline and Josie's house as a secondary studio, because she liked the light in that space. Emeline built a drying cupboard in Cecelia's house, which both households used to dry herbs and flowers from the garden. Both houses had baby swings and bottles, as well as cribs. William kept his toolbox in Emeline's laundry room, and he and Sylvie had keys to both homes. The twins' kitchen utensils and plates were mixed, from eating together outside and trading off on cleanup duty. Izzy had a bedroom in each house, and she moved back and forth whimsically. If she was in the middle of a good book, she stayed at Emeline's, because her room there had a better bedside light. When her mother was between boyfriends, she slept at Cecelia's.

With William's help, Izzy created a workshop in one of the spare bedrooms and built a speaker system that allowed the two side-by-side houses to communicate without using a phone. Both Cecelia and Emeline thought this was ridiculous at first, but they were soon using the invention daily. *Emmie, where did you put my favorite brush? Josie, are you home? Can you make me a sandwich? Izzy, what are you doing over there that makes so much noise?*

WHEN KENT FINISHED HIS residency, he and Nicole moved to Chicago, and he got a job with the Bulls too, as a sports doctor. The two couples met at the Mexican diner for dinner at least once a month, and sometimes Gus and Washington and their wives would join them. This was the only socializing Sylvie and William did, other than seeing the twins. But when Kent and Nicole found themselves struggling to get pregnant, Nicole stopped wanting to go out, and the dinners became less frequent. William and Sylvie were sad for their friends, but they didn't mind having more nights at home. They were both awkward around strangers. When a new acquaintance asked Sylvie or William how they'd met, they were vague, because the true account was too provocative to tell. Sylvie had read somewhere that the more times a story was told, the less accurate it became. Humans were prone to exaggeration; they leaned away from the parts of the narrative they found boring and leaned into the exciting spots. Details and timelines changed over years of repetition. The story became more myth and less true. Sylvie thought about how she and William rarely told their story and felt pleased; by not being shared, their love story remained intact.

"You and William are so nice to each other," Emeline said one afternoon when they were running errands. "I feel like I'm always throwing a baby at Josie or asking her to pick up her socks."

Sylvie smiled. "Well, we don't have babies, and we don't live in a train station like you do."

"True." Emeline sighed, even though they both knew she loved living in a place rife with crying babies, and toddlers who hadn't been picked up from daycare yet, and half-full paint cans, and a child who was liable to walk into the room with a vibrator and say, *What is this?*

Sylvie also knew that her sister was right—she and William were nicer to each other than most couples. She watched William swallow his pills before breakfast and bed and watched his eyes search out hers in a room when he was beginning to feel overwhelmed. She found herself reaching for his hand at the same moment he reached for hers. William made her lunch every morning to bring to work, and she made sure their life stayed quiet at the edges, because he did best that way. He whispered, "I am so lucky," most nights before they went to sleep, and she knew he was and she was too. Sylvie had almost missed this life with this man, and because of this near miss, she appreciated their moments together, even as they accumulated.

Alice

WHEN NINTH GRADE BEGAN, ALICE WAS SIX FOOT ONE. THIS shocked everyone who came in contact with her. The volleyball and basketball coaches at her private school followed her down the hallways, trying to entice her to join their teams even when she explained that she was too uncoordinated for sports. Her height also pulled her father back into the picture. Everyone from Mrs. Laven to the mailman to the headmaster seemed compelled to say some version of: *Wow, your father must have been a really big guy, huh?*

Julia and Alice now looked almost nothing alike. When Alice was young, there had been something about the shape of her eyes that tied her to her mother, but even that seemed to be gone. Their differing taste in clothes didn't help either. Julia wore skirt suits and silk blouses during the week and skinny black pants and a type of drapey top on the weekends. Alice, on the other hand, had a sneaker collection and wore sweatpants in different colors. It was hard for her to find clothes and shoes that fit her, due to her skinniness and height. Sneakers, though, were unisex, which gave her more options. Her mother had studied her quizzically one morning and said, "You don't look feminine at all." Alice had laughed and said, "It's 1997, Mom. I don't need to look feminine."

Alice took some pleasure in the fact that she apparently resembled her father. It made her feel like she had two parents, even if one of them was gone. Her father walked around with her—or his genes did, anyway—and that made her feel stronger. She needed the strength. When she started high school, she was too tall to make slouching—which she'd mastered in middle school—an effective tactic to look "normal." There was no longer any way to contort her body so that she resembled the petite girls in her school. Carrie had stopped growing at five feet, which shone an even brighter spotlight on Alice's height, since the two girls were always together. When Alice hugged her mother or Carrie, she had to bend at the knees in a way that always felt awkward. She walked faster than everyone else because her stride was so long. Her neck often ached at the end of the day because she had to look down while she spoke to people. She was regularly called *Giraffe* or *the Jolly Green Giant* by the kids she'd grown up with. A female math teacher said to her, clearly meaning to be kind: "You must always wear flats, my dear, to make the boys more comfortable." Men on the street extended themselves to their fullest heights and puffed out their chests when they passed Alice, as if her size somehow challenged their manhood.

Alice decided, when ninth grade began, that she was going to stop wasting time feeling ashamed of her appearance. Whether she felt ashamed or confident, the result was the same: She was very tall, and people were going to talk about it and make fun of her. She was unable to blend in; her height kept her apart from everyone else, quite literally. This meant that Alice felt lonely, but since there was no alternative, she decided to accept her reality. She walked down the school hallways at her full height and made herself smile when some puny boy cracked a joke about how the school was going to need to raise the ceilings. More to prove to herself that she could do it than for any other reason, Alice wore heels to her first high school dance. "You're very brave," Carrie whispered, as they walked into the school gymnasium, but Alice shook her head. "It's not bravery," she said. "Everyone stares at me, no matter what shoes I wear." She was shocked, though, when the captain of the basketball team asked her to dance. He was shy and had a stutter, but he looked her directly in the eyes while they danced, and that was exciting. When he asked her out on a date later that week, she was shocked again. The surprise cleared a space inside

Alice, though, and she heard a small voice—was it hers, or her mother's?—whisper *no*. She had separated herself from the other kids her age, and she would stay separated. She felt safer that way.

"No, thank you," Alice said, in as kind a voice as she could manage, and walked away. She felt a welling of relief inside her. The tall boy had asked her a question she'd never considered before, and the truth had come out of her mouth. She wanted to be like her mother: independent. Alice didn't tell anyone, not even Carrie, but by the end of the day the entire school somehow knew that she had rejected the popular senior.

It was strange, but in the weeks that followed, other kids' faces turned toward her like flowers. Most of them were shy or social misfits in some way. They glanced in Alice's direction from behind their bangs or over a textbook. They timed their locker visits to match hers. They fell in step beside her in the hallways. They thought Alice was brave, and that made them feel brave too. They wanted to feel better about themselves, and they found that they did, in Alice's company. *I'm not brave,* Alice wanted to tell them, because these kids were regularly insulted like she was—called fat, or stupid, or ugly—and she didn't want to mislead them. But she couldn't think of a way to explain herself that wouldn't make them feel bad, so she kept quiet and kept their company.

"What in the world is going on?" Carrie said, wide-eyed. She had spent all of middle school telling boys and girls off for teasing Alice about her height, and she'd started high school poised to do the same. Alice shrugged. She had a sense of what the truth was—she had refused to feel ashamed, and that gave her classmates permission to do the same—but she was unable to put any of this into words. No one else asked her out for a date, though, and that was a relief.

Probably because Alice had more of a life outside her apartment, she now found herself able to accept the silences from her mother about her past and the lack of photographs on their walls. The smallness of their two-person family no longer felt deeply precarious to her. Alice and Julia still made dinner together most nights and watched movies in their fuzzy bathrobes on Fridays, if Alice wasn't sleeping over at Carrie's. She and her mother made each other laugh by putting on silly voices and competing to answer the questions first on *Jeopardy!* But Alice also felt some satisfaction that her very body—with its ridiculous, awkward height and her straight straw-colored hair—was somehow the embodiment of the past that her mother refused to mention. Alice still didn't know the details, or even the broad strokes, of her mother's Chicago life, but she no longer felt like she *needed* the information. She was growing into herself, and she was old enough to be confident that if the time came to save herself, she would have the strength to do so.

By the end of high school, Alice had figured out how to manage her life. She felt less like a zoo animal walking down the school hallways. She slept over at Carrie's most weekends, and in the middle of the night the two friends quoted their favorite movie lines, and sang along to records, and talked about whatever was on their minds. Alice visited her grandmother in Florida once a year, without Julia, because her mother and grandmother no longer got along. Alice was now fully aware that her mother had cut her sisters, her home city, and to a large extent her own mother out of her life, and so Alice was careful to tread inside the lines that her mother had drawn around them. Alice loved her mother, and even though she didn't think she could lose Julia, this data said otherwise. Still, Alice couldn't help but note the look that sometimes passed over Julia's face when her daughter entered the room or stood tall. There was a quiver to her mother in those moments, an opening to another life, and even though Alice wasn't allowed entry, she was glad to be the one who occasionally rattled the door.

JULIA DROVE ALICE TO Boston University at the beginning of her freshman year. Julia talked at her daughter while she drove. Alice thought she knew all of her mother's moods, but today Julia was shooting out sparks that sometimes looked like excitement and sometimes looked like warning signs for an engine that needed repair.

"I want you to have fun at college," she said.

"Sure," Alice said. Her hands were sweating—they did that when she was nervous—and she wiped them on her shorts.

"You didn't have enough fun in high school. I want you to be happy." Julia flashed a look at her daughter, to make it clear that she was taking this conversation seriously.

"I had fun," Alice said. And she had. She'd had fun staying up late listening to music in Carrie's room and watching movies with her mother. She'd started drinking coffee in her junior year, and wrapping her hands around that warm mug every morning had sent a thrill through her—that fell under the heading of *fun*, didn't it? One of her worries about college was that the coffee in the dining hall wouldn't taste as good as what she made at home. She had many worries about college, actually. She didn't like the idea of being crammed inside a dormitory with a lot of kids her age. Kids her age were loud and messy, and Alice would never be alone. Luckily, Carrie was attending Emerson, which was also in Boston; it gave Alice great relief to know that her best friend would be close by.

"Oh, these drivers," Julia said. They were traveling from New York to Boston on Interstate 95, a giant thoroughfare that ran up the East Coast. Motorcyclists, enormous sixteen-wheelers, and cars danced around one another, looking for space. She said, "You should date, go to parties, stay up all night, things like that."

"Is that what you did at college?" Alice asked.

Julia seemed to consider this. "My situation was different. I had to live at home for financial reasons, so I wasn't really part of campus life. But you can do anything you want, baby. Smoke pot, even. Or, what do the kids call it, hook up?"

"Jesus, Mom."

Mrs. Laven had transitioned from calling Alice *my little girl* to— once Alice passed her in height—*my old soul*. Alice hadn't minded; she felt a little proud of the nickname, because it suggested that she was mature. It was a reason that she had no interest in dating boys. She was different, ancient on the inside, and did best on her own. The idea of flirting, kissing, having sex, filled her with horror. Alice's old soul also helped explain the dread in her chest about the next four years.

She sighed. She knew her mother got scared when she thought Alice might be sad, and so Julia was always trying to shove her daughter toward happiness. Alice had taught herself to smile when she walked into rooms her mother was in. She knew that smiling would relax Julia immediately. But this was tiring work, and Alice said, her voice closer to tears than she would have liked, "I'll do my best, okay, Mom?"

The electricity in Julia petered out, and she nodded. They were both quiet for the rest of the ride. When they reached Boston University's campus, her mother helped her carry her things up to the second-floor dorm room. They had arrived before Alice's roommate—a girl named Gloria from Louisiana—so Alice chose the bottom bunk and the desk closest to the window. Alice let her mother hug her goodbye, but she couldn't hug back, because she thought that if she did, something inside her might break and she would cry. Alice never cried—another loss of control she shied away from—and she couldn't afford to start now.

SHE FOUND THE FIRST month of college stressful. She'd worried that the lack of solitude would bother her, and it did. She liked her roommate, who had a wonderful, belting laugh, but Gloria spoke only in terms of gossip—"Did you see the guy with the baseball hat flirting with that blond girl?" or "Those two clearly hate each other's guts." Alice nodded in vague agreement, but it seemed too early for gossip, like going on vacation and buying a house on the first day. She thought, *But we don't know any of these people. I don't know you. We're all strangers.*

Because of her height, she was unable to blend in to the scenery. She crisscrossed the campus on her way to class and felt people staring. Girls looked shocked when they saw her but rarely said anything. Some would adopt a pitying expression, the embodiment of the words *you poor thing.* She knew they were whispering prayers of gratitude for their own smallness, for the fact that they were feminine and could hide themselves when necessary. The boys asked her if she was on the basketball or the volleyball team. When she said neither, they were shocked. "Is your dad Larry Bird?" one guy asked her. She thought he was joking, then realized he wasn't. Certain boys could accept her height only if she was a serious athlete or, apparently, related to one. Otherwise, her size bothered them, like a piece of mail they couldn't find a mailbox for. Still, there were other young men—the slightly older versions of the high school boys who'd walked the halls with her—who grinned at the sight of Alice.

"Hell yeah," a boy named Rhoan said to her when they were introduced at an orientation event. "Right on." His smile was so infectious she couldn't help but return it. He and Alice became friends, and when he was stoned one night, he tried to explain his initial reaction to her. "You were this giantess, and you were owning every inch of it. You're a badass, Alice."

"I'm not, actually," Alice said. "People mistake my height for bravery. It's been happening for a while now."

Rhoan looked like he was considering this. "Okay," he said. "Fair enough. Maybe what I'm seeing in you is the potential for you to *become* a badass."

Alice smiled. "That's not going to happen," she said. "But thank you."

Carrie visited one Saturday afternoon in October, and after walking around Boston University's vast campus, she, Alice, Rhoan, and Gloria hung out in Alice and Gloria's room. Their door was open, so they were able to watch students traffic by. Someone down the hall was playing James Taylor, and his melancholic voice twisted through the air.

"I like you," Gloria said to Carrie at one point. "I'm glad that my girl has a cool friend. Alice is so shy, I was getting worried. I keep trying to set her up with different tall men on campus—she's a beauty, and she's getting looks."

"Oh, please." Alice rolled her eyes.

"I like you too." Carrie was cross-legged on the beanbag in the corner, beaming under her pixie haircut. "Alice is a slow bloomer, that's all. She's going to get there, but she's playing the long game." Carrie gave Alice a warning look: *I'm going to be honest.* "Now that she's away from her mother, I'm hoping she'll start living more."

"Hey," Alice said, surprised.

"So that's the issue?" Gloria said. "I've known my fair share of controlling mothers, that's for sure. You poor chickadee."

"Alice is doing great," Rhoan said. He was encouraging by nature;

he attended college track events just to cheer on the slowest runners. "You and I can look for men together," he said to her. "Or I can look, and you can keep me company. You do you, baby."

Part of Alice warmed at Rhoan's kindness and the attention of these friends, new and old. Another part of her, though, was uncomfortable. This afternoon was exactly what she'd been afraid college would be like. Too much unscheduled time, too many hours at loose ends with your peers, inventing dramas out of perfectly fine lives. "To be clear," she said, "how I live has nothing to do with my mother. I love her."

Carrie met Alice's blue eyes with her own. "I didn't say anything about you not loving her."

Alice frowned, to signal that she was done talking about this. Carrie knew that Alice was touchy when it came to her mother, so Carrie usually kept her thoughts to herself. But Carrie had told her friend once, during high school, not to model herself on Julia. "I like your mom a lot," Carrie had said, "but anyone that dresses and does their hair as carefully as your mom does every single day is unhappy on the inside. She's trying to hide all her messiness, and I want better than that for you."

ONE TUESDAY AFTERNOON IN the middle of February, Alice returned to her room after a class and found her mother there. Julia was standing by Alice's desk. She was wearing a suit, and her hair was in a fancy layered bun.

Alice stopped in the doorway. Her mother hadn't been back to campus since dropping her daughter off at the beginning of the school year—Alice had traveled home for long weekends and holidays—and Julia never showed up anywhere unannounced or unplanned. "Mom?" she said. "What are you doing here?"

Julia didn't look at her daughter. She leaned closer to the wall. "These images," she said, in a tight voice. "Where are they from?"

Alice felt something sink inside her. She walked into the room, shut the door, and slid off her winter coat. The wall above her desk was covered with photographs of Cecelia Padavano's murals. Rhoan was an aspiring art archivist, and he'd helped Alice collect the images from various art magazines. They'd had to send away for a few of them, mailing a check for a couple of dollars to pay for an obscure Chicago art journal that seemed to cover most of Cecelia's work. Rhoan had blown up some of the smaller images with equipment they had in the art department. It was an ongoing project; Alice was currently waiting on the arrival of a magazine that featured a mural Cecelia had painted for a city school.

"They're your sister's," Alice said. She hadn't raised the topic of Julia's family in years. While Alice was in high school, both she and her mother had behaved as if they had no other relatives. Alice visited Rose in Florida but upon her return barely mentioned the trip to her mother. Julia had shut that door between them so many times that Alice had locked it.

It was Rose who'd once mentioned, while her granddaughter was visiting, that her aunt Cecelia was an artist. Alice had tried to find her aunt's paintings during high school, but she'd had no idea where to look. Cecelia's work wasn't in museums or art history books. Alice had also known that, while she was living at home, anything she did find would have to be hidden from her mother. She'd decided that she would renew the search in college, when her belongings and pastimes would be out of her mother's purview. The promise of searching for Cecelia's art and being able to display it was one of the carrots Alice had used to convince herself to look forward to life at college, and it had delivered; the wall above her desk was her favorite view. When Gloria went out to parties, Alice stayed in their room, reading or just gazing at the wall in front of her. The more images she was able to add, the more satisfied she felt.

"She's gotten so good," Julia murmured. She was leaning against the desk now, to get as close to the display as possible.

"Did you notice?" Alice could feel her heart beating in her chest. "You and I are in the murals."

Julia gave her daughter a look that was difficult to read—there was incredulity and fear in it—and returned her attention to the images.

Most of the murals, and therefore most of Alice's wall, were portraits of women. They were close-ups, painted with bright colors on brick walls. There was one particular woman's face that appeared on a few buildings and on the underside of an overpass. In most of the paintings, her eyes were open; on one wall they were closed. There was something ancient about her face—she looked like she was from another time. The murals weren't all individual portraits; there was one image that Rhoan had enlarged of a group of children, perhaps twenty in all. The caption said that the mural was located in a Chicago playground. The children were smiling; they looked like someone had just told them great news. In the back row of the group was a white girl with blond-brown hair that was unmistakably Alice, around the age of ten.

"I sent Cecelia pictures of you when you were little," Julia said, again in a muffled voice, as if she weren't speaking to the people in this room.

"There's you," Alice said, and pointed. The picture showed a wall that had been painted bright blue, overlaid with the outline of a woman's face. Ferocious curls flooded the space around her. Her chin was held high. This portrait was different from the others—more spare. It was Julia, unquestionably, but only those who knew her intimately would ever know.

The room was quiet; Gloria was at a biology lab and would be gone until dinner. Julia looked pale, and Alice knew that if she touched her mother's hand, it would be clammy. "Sit down if you feel faint," she said.

"I'm not going to faint."

"I just like her art," Alice said. "I haven't contacted her or anything. You don't have to worry."

Julia looked from the wall to her daughter. Her lipstick was bright against the pallor of her face. She looked like she was going to speak, but she didn't. She nodded instead.

The mother and daughter walked quietly through the cold to a nearby Italian restaurant. Once they were seated, the restaurant buzzing around them, Julia started to revive. She seemed to remember who she was and why she was there. "I took on a client in Boston," she

said. "I met with them today. Of course"—she smiled at her daughter—
"my decision was helped by the fact that this gives me a reason to
come to Boston and see you. It's lonely for me in New York."

Alice missed her mother too. But she felt lonely right now at the
table with her. She knew her mother was about to ask her if she'd decided on a major—she hadn't—and if she had a boyfriend—she
didn't—and if she was having fun. But she also knew that a part of
herself and a part of Julia were still standing side by side in front of the
wall of images, looking at their own faces, as painted by a woman in
another city, from Julia's other life.

Alice remembered the time in middle school when she had passed
her mother in height and realized that Julia was not a perfect super-
hero, that her mother was a human woman, which meant she had
flaws and a past, which seemed to be at one with her wild hair. Alice
had spent her life watching her mother try to harness both her hair
and her past, wrapping them up, trying to impose her control on them
every single day. Wishing she were back in her room, alone in front of
the wall of pictures, Alice thought: *She's done the same with me.*

Sylvie

SEPTEMBER 2008

SYLVIE LEFT THE LIBRARY EARLY. SHE TOLD THE ASSISTANT librarian that she had a headache. She walked home by her usual route, past Cecelia's murals. Pilsen looked particularly colorful that late-September afternoon, and Sylvie was glad to be surrounded by her sister's art. Whenever she visited the twins' houses, Sylvie traveled the halls to see if any portraits had been added or removed. She was guaranteed to see all the women in her life: her sisters, her nieces, her mother, and herself. Part of Sylvie's desire to go home early today was to visit the piece of Cecelia's art that hung in her own living room: the landscape Cecelia had painted for William shortly after he left the hospital.

Sylvie let herself into the quiet apartment with her key. William wouldn't be home for a few hours. She felt her shoulders relax. The space was peaceful and designed exactly to their liking. She and William rarely entertained here; big communal dinners happened at the super-duplex, and Kent was a foodie, so he always suggested they meet at restaurants he wanted to try. The apartment was where she and William didn't have to mute their love or pay attention to anyone else. They liked to be in the same room, so Sylvie would read next to William while he watched basketball games with the volume off. When Sylvie cooked, she prepared meals she knew delighted her husband: any kind of pasta, any kind of stew. When William cooked, the recipe usually included chickpeas, because they were Sylvie's favorite.

She leaned against the back of the couch and studied the painting of wind, rain, and light. The landscape had always looked like hope to her, and Sylvie needed some. She'd been to see her doctor the week before, because of an odd, recurring headache. Sylvie was able to see the pain when it arrived: It was lavender and emanated from somewhere near her right temple in concentric rings. Sylvie had drawn the headache on a piece of paper for the doctor, and he'd sent her to see a specialist. The specialist had run tests. Sylvie lay in an MRI machine, strangely proud of her ability to lie perfectly still, because it pleased the technician. Sylvie hadn't mentioned her headaches to William or the twins, and she didn't tell them she was going to the doctor. She'd assumed the headaches would turn out to be nothing, or perhaps a symptom of perimenopause. She was forty-seven years old, after all.

The specialist, a man who spoke at a fast clip—presumably because he was in so much demand and therefore had so little time—told her that there was a tumor in her brain. Sylvie nodded in response, to be polite. He talked about the location of the tumor and the size. He used the word *terminal.* Sylvie nodded again, listened some more, and then left his office. The building she exited was near Northwestern, and she decided to walk home. She didn't pay any attention to her direction; she knew that, like a homing pigeon, her body would take itself to Pilsen.

While she walked, Sylvie discovered that she wasn't surprised by the diagnosis. It settled so quickly inside her that she realized she must have known, on some level, that it was coming. When the specialist had used the word *incurable,* she'd thought: *Of course. That sounds right.* Whenever something went wrong in her house while she was growing up—the electricity went out, the washing machine flooded, the refrigerator died—her mother's first words were: "We're being punished." Sylvie was being punished for the choice she'd made twenty-five years earlier. Even though she'd stopped considering herself Catholic after her father's funeral, she recognized the religion's retributive justice in her bones. She *was* surprised, though, to find that she'd unconsciously kept that belief system. She would have thought that she'd evolved past the guilt that was laced through Catholicism and her childhood, past the concept of an eye for an eye. But apparently she had bought into that retaliative framework, perhaps in the pews of St. Procopius as a child. Sylvie had betrayed her sister, so her body had betrayed itself.

It's also possible that you're just in shock, Sylvie thought now. The painting in front of her was becoming less potent; the light, the hope on the canvas, was fading. Sylvie knew this was because she'd been looking at the painting for too long; its meaning was lost, the same way the meaning of a word is lost when repeated fifty times. She knew the hope was still in the painting; she just could no longer see it.

Sylvie hadn't told William yet; she would tell him tonight. She wished her husband could remain ignorant of this; she wished she could simply grow sick and die without him having to watch. Sylvie knew that when William looked at her, he saw the twenty-something girl he'd fallen in love with. It seemed possible, and yet impossible, that she could fade away while staying whole under his gaze. *I wish?* Sylvie thought, but then stopped herself, because *I wish* was a dangerous path to walk down. She needed to stay with *what is.*

Sylvie wasn't worried about herself. She was now in the unusual position of knowing how her own story would end—she would die from an aberrant cluster of cells in her brain—but she was deeply worried about her husband, about how and whether he would live after she was gone. William was so much healthier, so much stronger than he had been as a young man, but she knew they both believed his solid foundation had been built on three planks: his antidepressant medication, daily reckoning with his mental health, and their love. With one third of that equation removed, would he fall apart? If he did, Sylvie would no longer be there to save him. Since leaving the specialist's office, she'd been ruminating on William, wondering if there was a loophole that might allow him to be okay. At the same time, the rest of Sylvie, her mind and body, had turned in a surprising direction: toward Julia. The diagnosis had brought a physical longing for her older sister, a longing so deep that Sylvie felt breathless. Sylvie missed the timbre of Julia's voice when she was coming up with a plan. She missed the specific fit of their hug and her sister's smell. She missed lying in their childhood bedroom in the dark, listening to Julia organize all of their lives. This yearning enveloped Sylvie's entire body now, while she tried to find the light in the painting. She wondered if the tumor was a punishment for hurting her sister and was even created by the separation between them. Perhaps Sylvie's body had been ultimately unable to bear the distance between Chicago and New York.

That night, in the kitchen of their apartment, Sylvie told William what the doctor had said. She wanted to close her eyes so she couldn't see the news fracture his beloved, worn face, but she made herself watch. She needed to catch him if he fell.

"Are you certain?" he said.

"Yes."

After a few minutes, he said, "What do you need? What can I do?"

She didn't say anything, but the longing was still present, and William always saw all of her. Loved all of her.

He said, "You need Julia." Her name sounded strange coming out of his mouth. They never spoke of her anymore.

Sylvie shook her head. "It's impossible. I would never ask her for anything."

William studied his wife, his eyes glassy with shock and sadness. He didn't believe in words like *impossible,* because of what he'd been through. He believed in trying to help; that's what he did at work—helped young athletes stay healthy and whole—and he believed in his marriage to Sylvie. She watched him try to figure out what could be done with the materials at hand, while the sun sank out of the sky behind him.

William

W HEN WILLIAM REACHED THE BULLS PRACTICE FACILITY, HE
nodded at the security officer, then the kid behind the desk. He was
aware that his breath was short in his chest; he was winded from what
Sylvie had told him the night before. He felt the news only in his body;
it moved in and out of his lungs. He'd needed to come here before allowing himself to absorb it fully. William headed onto the courts; the
air thumped with balls hitting the floor. William walked around the
edge of the cavernous space and into the exam room, where he knew
Kent would be. And he was there, taping a rookie's knee.

The rookie spotted William first and got the look that most players adopted around him when they were limping, bruised, or injured
in any way. It wasn't unusual for an injured player to catch sight of
William and try to scuttle away, crab-like.

"This is a small thing, Will," the rookie said. "Kent is confident—
you're confident, right, Doc?—I'll be ready for the first game."

William waved his hand. "I saw you warming up yesterday. You'll
be fine. You've got good wheels."

The rookie collapsed back on the exam table, visibly relieved.

Kent laughed over the tape roll in his hands and the motion made
his dreadlocks shake.

"You see things," the kid said, still lying down. "Everyone knows
that. We've all heard about the injuries you've predicted. You're fa-

mous for being . . ." He paused for a moment, searching for the right words. "Clairvoyant, maybe. Or whatever a guy witch is called."

William leaned against the other exam table, suddenly tired. "A wizard."

"No," the kid said, toward the ceiling. "That's not it. But you can see when we're not okay."

William had no more smiles in him, but if he had, he would have used one now. The rookie was right; William's job was to see when a player wasn't okay.

"Most of the time what William sees can be fixed," Kent said. He pressed the final strip of tape across the knee and studied his work. "You cowards should be begging him to look at you, not hiding from him like little kids. You can go."

"I got good wheels," the rookie said. "I'm happy about that." He hopped off the table onto his healthy leg, grabbed his sneakers, and strolled out of the room.

Kent straightened up. The doctor resembled a football player more than the power forward he used to be. Due to a combination of weight lifting and an enthusiasm for food, he'd widened considerably since college. He and Nicole had divorced a year earlier, and Kent had only recently started to regain his propulsive energy and big laugh. He'd often cut onto the court on his way in and out of the building, trying to steal the ball off a player, even though he was almost fifty and his patients were elite athletes in their prime. The players ran away from William, but they wanted to be around Kent.

Kent's face was serious, though, while he studied his friend from behind his black-framed glasses. He indicated slightly with his head, a signal for William to talk.

"Did Sylvie show you her MRI scan?"

Kent's shoulders dropped. "She told you."

William closed his eyes for a moment. He'd pictured Sylvie handing her medical file to Kent; he was the person they both thought of in case of an emergency. Sylvie might have thought: *Maybe Kent can save me.* "I figured," William said, "that she might have spoken to you first, seen what you thought."

"She saw the best specialist at Northwestern. I made some calls, checked him out. There was a second opinion. The diagnosis is correct."

The air in the room felt dark, but perhaps it was just William turning dark. "She said she turned down most of the treatment. That she has something like six months."

Kent gave a single, effortful nod, as if he had to fight the air to move. "I thought she was going to do that."

"What do you think?"

"I'd do the same thing, in her position. It's the brave choice. The treatment is almost as bad as what she's got."

William noticed Kent's arm twitch, and said, "I don't want a hug."

"I know."

William glanced at his watch, although he didn't care what time it was. He'd gotten what he needed here. Confirmation. Sylvie's news was real, because Kent had said so. He headed out of the room. "I have some things to take care of," he said. "I might come back this afternoon, but I might not."

"I'm gonna get you through this." Kent jogged to catch up with William. "I'm not going to leave you alone. Your meds are solid. It's going to be hard, but you'll be able to bear it."

"I have to think," William said, but by then he had pushed out the front door of the building and was alone on the sidewalk. He could feel his friend behind him, wanting to follow but stopping himself.

William walked toward Pilsen. His skin hurt. His hair hurt. His knee, which rarely bothered him anymore, hurt. He'd hoped Kent would say that Sylvie had misunderstood the doctor or that there was a cure she wasn't aware of yet. He made his way by muscle memory to Throop Park. This was where Arash still held his weekly clinic, so William knew every inch of the outdoor court. He found a beat-up basketball under a bench and began to dribble. The sound of a ball hitting the ground calmed him; it untangled his heartbeats and allowed him to think straighter. William had noticed a change in Sylvie—a slight hesitation in her movements—a few months earlier, but he'd thought it was just due to aging. An infinitesimal slowing of her muscles, joints, and tendons. William had thought, *We're in the middle of our lives, after all.* He never would have reached this point, the middle, without her.

He made the ball pound the cement. His wife had looked at him with her wide-open, beautiful face last night. She was his city, his sky. She had given him a life, two and a half decades earlier. He hadn't deserved it; for the first few years of their relationship, he'd told himself, *You should leave. You should break up with her.* But he couldn't bear to. He'd always known that the rift that had occurred in the Padavano family was his fault. The ensuing silence between Sylvie and Julia was his fault. Julia moving to New York City and staying there was his fault. Sylvie disagreed, but she was too kind, and he knew she had convinced herself that that was the truth because she loved him. William had let the lie continue for this long because he loved his life with Sylvie; he loved her and was as happy as it was possible for him to be. He hadn't wanted anything to change. He'd been a coward.

Not anymore, he thought. William was going to lose everything that mattered to him. But first he could do everything possible to make Sylvie feel beloved and whole.

He had gazed at his wife's face last night and known what he had to do. There was only one answer. When William had dribbled long enough to break a sweat and his entire body was warm, he pulled his phone out of his pocket and called his first wife.

Julia

JULIA WAS AT HER DESK, WAITING TO RECEIVE A PITCH DECK from her assistant and thinking about Alice. She knew intellectually that her daughter was grown up and had her own life—she was twenty-five and no longer lived with Julia, after all—but the patterns in Julia's brain had been set years earlier, and she was programmed to worry about her daughter at least once an hour. Perhaps *worry* wasn't the right word: Julia habitually turned her daughter over in her mind as if she were a Rubik's Cube she couldn't solve. She knew her daughter better than anyone, but there was some part of Alice behind lock and key, and Julia worried that this was her fault. Her daughter's life was too simple, too streamlined, for someone in her mid-twenties. Alice never stayed out too late or got too drunk. She never sobbed over a man, or sobbed at all, as far as Julia could tell. Most concerning, to Julia's mind, was the fact that Alice had never had a boyfriend. Julia was too afraid to ask directly, but she thought there was a strong chance that her daughter was a virgin. This absence in her daughter's life—of love, of touch, of relationship—made Julia panicky. Why would her beautiful daughter have backed away from intimacy? She knew Alice's height must intimidate some men but not all of them; Julia only went to bed with men who agreed to her terms, and although she'd given up on dating a few years earlier, she'd never had any trouble finding agreeable men. This blank space in her daughter's life was presumably deliberate, and Julia wanted to understand why, but Alice was skillful at steering conversations away from her personal life. Once, when Julia had ignored Alice's signposts and pushed too hard, her daughter had said, "Why do I have to live the way you think I should? You never needed a man, and I don't either."

In college, Alice had delayed choosing a major, because she found most subjects equally interesting. This mystified Julia; her daughter was smart but unfocused on any possible career. "How about graduate school?" Julia had suggested. "You're good at science—I'd be happy to pay for medical school." Alice shook her head, a distracted look on her face, and said, "No, thank you." After college, she worked as a free-lance copy editor for a few publishing houses, a job that required her to comb through sentences for ten hours a day and paid barely enough to live on. Alice had never been an avid reader growing up—she'd pre-ferred television—but now she reminded Julia of Sylvie, with her at-tention always adhered to a book. Sylvie had truly loved to read, though; it was unclear what was gluing Alice's eyes to the pages. *What are you really going to do?* Julia wondered. *Who are you really going to be?* Be-cause this controlled, Teflon version of her daughter couldn't be the final product, could it? Julia worried—she had always worried about this—that Alice was depressed, but her daughter seemed too steady, too level, for that to be the case. And when Julia asked her daughter if she was okay, Alice always said yes.

When the light on Julia's phone blinked, she was happy for the distraction from her thoughts. She picked up the receiver and said, in the confident, professional tone she'd mastered long ago: "Julia Pada-vano."

"Hi, Julia." There was a pause. "It's William."

She heard his voice, but it was accompanied by an echoing sound. Julia had closed off her past as if it were a water pipe, and the creak of the valve opening was noisy. She repeated his name, because she couldn't think of anything else to say. "William?"

She never thought about him, because why would she? Her job was to think of Alice, and so she pictured the tall young woman bent over a manuscript, looking for mistakes. At the same moment she had a memory of standing in the Northwestern apartment, her breasts swollen with milk. Julia felt flushed, as if the warm air in that living room had crossed time and distance to find her.

She cleared her throat. "Why would you call me?"

"It's Sylvie," he said.

Sylvie, she thought. Julia looked around, but no one was staring. No one in her office seemed to have realized that Julia's past had just reached through a phone line and grabbed her heart out of her chest.

"Sylvie is dying, Julia. She's all right now, but she has less than a year."

Julia skimmed over what William had said. She couldn't go too close, because the words were hot coals. She had the urge to say, *I love my job, and I'm one of the best in the world in my field. I made three hundred thousand dollars last year.* She wanted him to know that she was successful and therefore too busy, or maybe even too important, for this kind of news. But she couldn't say that. She had the urge to gently set the phone down, like a child who had picked up the extension on someone else's call.

"No," she said.

"The only thing she wants is you, Julia. She needs you."

Julia looked down. She was wearing a gray-blue suit. She had a slight run in her stockings, which she'd stopped with clear nail polish. She tried to understand; it felt like William was asking her to speak in a language that she hadn't used for a long time. "Did Sylvie ask you to call me?"

He paused, and Julia remembered that this was how William spoke: with reluctance and hesitation, never sure if he had the right words. Julia had assumed that William and Sylvie were still married, but only because it seemed like news of their divorce would have made its way to her. Julia never thought about life in Chicago, past or present, at all.

Finally, William said, "No. Sylvie doesn't know I'm doing this."

"I have a full calendar," Julia said. "I run my own business. I don't have time to go anywhere." She lifted her hand in the air and waved it. On the other side of the glass wall, her young assistant popped out of her chair, a notepad and pen in hand, and headed her way. Julia had nothing to say to her, of course. She was going to send her away, just like she was going to send William away. Both were dead ends, blank walls. But she had panicked and set the young woman in motion.

"Julia?" William said.

She waited, and the years pulsed between them, down the phone line.

"I never saw two people love each other like you and Sylvie." He cleared his throat. "I thought maybe it was just because of how I was raised, that I wasn't exposed to that kind of thing, but that wasn't it. I've never seen anything like you and your sister."

Something inside Julia started to crumble, like those awful images of glaciers shedding giant sections to the freezing ocean below. He had said that Sylvie was dying. Her *sister,* who used to be as familiar to Julia as her own body. Her sister, who had not been her sister for over two decades. Julia coughed, and inside the cough was a strange sound, as if her insides had begun to cry, without tears reaching her surface. Her ecosystem was changing beneath her skin.

"Please come home," William said.

Julia knew how to control her voice. She had been manipulating outcomes, with men in boardrooms and on dates, for decades. She was an expert at setting a goal and steering in that direction. When her voice came out confident and clear, she was pleased. She said, "I'm sorry, William, but I can't do that."

When Julia hung up, she noticed that her hands were shaking. *No problem,* she thought. *I can handle this.* She stood up and concentrated on walking gracefully to the bathroom. She chose two different employees at random to smile at on her way across the office. In the bathroom, she splashed cold water on her face and thought: *Stick to your calendar, Padavano. What do you have to do next? Don't think about anything else.* After all, it was none of her business that Sylvie was sick. The phone call changed nothing about her current life. Her sister was no longer part of her world.

When Julia left the bathroom, she started a conversation with one of her smartest employees—an MIT grad who, Julia knew, thought she didn't deserve her position as his boss—about a project they were working on. Julia had a hard time paying attention to the young man's voice, though. Her attention faded in and out—*attention, attention, none*—as if it were her heartbeat. She excused herself, said she had an important call to make, and stepped away. When she got back to her desk, she realized she was barefoot. She stared at her heels, which were sitting neatly under her desk. She must have taken them off while she spoke to William, but she had no memory of doing so. Had the MIT grad noticed she was shoeless in the middle of the office? Julia had a personal rule about not being barefoot at work, even when she worked late, and now that was broken.

She opened and closed her desk drawers, as if she was looking for something, because she needed a few moments of blankness to reset. When her cellphone rang, Julia looked at the screen, saw it was Alice, and felt a hiccup of fear. Had her daughter sensed that she'd just spoken to her father? The fact that William and Alice *could* call her, back-to-back, was supposed to be impossible. William was dead, Chicago was dead. Sylvie was— Julia couldn't finish this thought. "Hi, sweetheart," she said, and poured all her effort and attention into employing her normal voice.

"Are we on for tonight?" Alice said. "I don't mind either way. I have a new project, so I could work."

The mother and daughter watched a movie or television show together once a week. Alice would come to Julia's apartment after work, and they'd order in dinner and sit cross-legged on the couch like they had ever since Alice was tiny. Julia knew they both found the experience comforting, even though Julia also felt uncomfortable, knowing that her daughter should be *out there* living a life, not *in here* with her mother, as if she were still ten years old.

"I'm too busy. Another night would be better," Julia said. She had the sense that today's schedule was tipping away from her, like a plate falling off a table. She was still barefoot; some part of her resisted slipping the heels back on. Then, because the normal Julia—the one she'd been before William called—would continue the conversation, she said, "What's the new project?"

"Oh, I'm copyediting a novel. I told Naveen that I don't like doing novels—I prefer nonfiction—but he said fiction is good for me."

"What's it about?"

"It's a modern take on *Little Women.* Did you read that when you were a kid?"

"*Little Women?*" Julia's body felt like it was filled with wet, prickly sand. She managed to make a noise of assent. She remembered lying in bed next to Sylvie in the dark, in their small room on 18th Place. She'd fallen asleep to the sound of her sister's voice countless times. In their beds, they kept returning to the same argument: which of them was better suited to be Jo March. "I have Jo's spunk and determination," Julia had said. "But I'm going to be a writer," Sylvie said. "I'm the one who could tell our stories."

"Jo runs a feminist publishing company in New York," Alice said. "Meg still marries for love, Amy is a hell-raiser, and Laurie is a woman they're all in love with."

Julia said, "Does Beth still die?"

"Beth dies," Alice said. "It's very sad."

And just like that, the two little girls in their beds on 18th Place were silenced. The child inside Julia lay wide-eyed in the dark, knowing that she *was* Jo, but only because Sylvie was Beth.

Sylvie

SYLVIE PICKED UP A BOOK AND PUT IT DOWN SOMEWHERE ELSE. She rolled three carts of books to the side wall, for the teenagers to shelve the next day. She glanced at the top shelf of one cart—it was filled with new releases. The bright, shiny covers of new books always made Sylvie a little sad. The authors and publishers were hoping their book would take the world by storm, and that was almost never the case. Sylvie had been working in this library since she was thirteen, and she'd seen hundreds of thousands of books move on and off the shelves.

She thought that witnessing this endless merry-go-round of books was what had ultimately put her off trying to publish her own. What she was writing was too precious to her to put into a commercial marketplace. Also, publication demanded an end to a story, and she wasn't done. She had continued to write and revise in the years after she'd printed the book for Izzy, including a few memories the twins had shared with her. Sylvie had become interested in how the different stories and time periods demanded different pacing. Writing about Cecelia's pregnancy, and Julia's too, and Rose's rage, had felt like trying to write her way into a tornado. The childhood memories were separate, though, like puffy clouds in the same blue sky. They didn't touch one another: There was the time Father Cole called Sylvie out in front of the entire church for reading a novel during mass; the time

Cecelia locked their family out of the house for an hour while she finished a painting; the time their rental car broke down on the side of the road, and Rose taught them a song from her own childhood to pass the time. But during the Padavano sisters' early adulthood, events sat on top of each other. Only in writing about them did Sylvie truly comprehend that the same day her beloved Izzy had entered the world, Charlie had left. And the day Alice was born, Rose had departed Chicago.

Sylvie couldn't help but wonder what her own death might bring. What one-two punch would she deliver? No one in her family was pregnant; her sisters were too old, and Izzy was nowhere near motherhood, though she had a nice boyfriend who liked to watch her play chess and who managed the accounts for her tutoring business. Cecelia teased Izzy that he was more like an assistant than a boyfriend. "Works for me," Izzy had said, with a shrug. "The sex is great." *Perhaps Alice is pregnant,* Sylvie thought, then shook her head in self-recrimination. She knew nothing of Alice's life; it was none of her business and couldn't possibly have anything to do with Sylvie's life or death.

Since the diagnosis, Sylvie had returned to *Leaves of Grass.* She wanted to absorb Whitman's optimistic take on death; she wanted to share the poet's open mind about what came next. Whenever Sylvie felt a quiver of fear, she repeated to herself the line: *And to die is different from what any one supposed, and luckier.* She heard these words in Charlie's voice, which placed her in the garden behind the grocer's again. Her father had been close to death that day, and now it was Sylvie's turn. Charlie had told his daughter what he perhaps needed to believe: that everything was beautiful, which meant his life—even though it disappointed Rose, even though it was almost over—had beauty. It was true: It had, everything did. Since her diagnosis, Sylvie saw beauty everywhere: in a perfectly arranged shelf of books, in the smile Emeline offered the baby in her arms, in the familiar lines of William's face. Sylvie would catch herself staring at the stripes of light on the library floor, marveling at their loveliness.

She didn't think about her illness except when she had one of the peculiar headaches that had sent her to the doctor in the first place. She'd continued to draw the headache and its concentric rings, almost as if she were keeping a journal. The headache was so personal, and unique, that Sylvie wanted to document it. If she'd asked, William would have looked at the drawing and listened to her explain how sometimes she even heard dim music inside the pain, but that would have been cruel. Sylvie wanted to help William, not increase his suffering. She wondered every day how she could make sure William lived—more than that, *wanted* to live—after she was gone.

When she'd met Kent at a café, nowhere near Pilsen or the Bulls facility, to show him her chart and MRI scan, she'd said to him, "You might need to save William again, after I'm gone. One way or another. I'm sorry about that."

Kent, heavier in every way since his divorce, said, "Don't worry, Sylvie. I can handle it."

She wished William was still working on his manuscript, because she thought writing might help stitch him to his life. He'd stopped writing about six months into their relationship, though. "I don't need it anymore," he'd told her, and Sylvie had understood. William was working for the Northwestern team by then, and he'd replaced the silence inside him with love and friendship, his medication, and the daily thunder of basketballs hitting the court floor. William's writing had never been a book, after all. It had been a struggle inside himself. Each sentence he wrote about the sport he loved was a match lit against his internal darkness. In his life with Sylvie, he'd no longer required this practice.

A co-worker called her name, and Sylvie turned. Her husband was walking across the library carpet toward her. William smiled at his wife, but it was a manufactured smile, the kind he'd worn when she first met him, many years earlier. He'd gone back to needing levers and pulleys to make his face do what he wanted it to do. She could feel him thinking: *Make Sylvie think you're okay so she won't worry.*

She knew she couldn't afford to worry now. He'd come to pick her up so they could tell Emeline and Cecelia about her diagnosis. Sylvie had told William that he didn't need to come, but he'd insisted. Her husband's face had been set ever since she'd told him she was sick two weeks earlier. Something inside William had turned in a new direction, and he was intent on making sure his words and actions lined up with his new route. Sylvie knew that route had to do with her, but she didn't know what it entailed. She was newly aware of a drain—like in a bathtub—deep inside her, through which her energy was escaping. She could no longer try to understand everything. She had to let this go. She wondered if dying was simply going to be an exercise in letting go of one thing after another.

She and William held hands while they walked the few blocks to the super-duplex. It was the middle of October, and the leaves were changing colors. *What a tree,* Sylvie thought, when they passed an old oak. She nodded at a cardinal sitting on the roof of a car. It was a cloudy day, but there was a triangle of blue in the left corner of the sky. William and Sylvie didn't speak; they didn't need to.

Cecelia and Emeline both met them at the door to Emeline's house, their faces creased with concern. Sylvie had asked them to be home, said she had something to discuss. The four of them stood in the kitchen—Josie was at work, and Izzy wasn't there—while Sylvie said what she had to say. It reminded her of the last time she'd gathered her younger sisters to tell them something they didn't want to hear; the one-two punch of that day had been that they'd all had to let go of Julia, like releasing a balloon. Sylvie was still grateful to Emeline and Cecelia for forgiving her, and she felt terrible that she was about to break their hearts again. It was a relief that Izzy happened not to be there; the young woman had her own studio apartment now, but she still floated from one bedroom to another, the way she had her whole life. It would have felt like too much to have to speak to Izzy too. Sylvie needed to do this slowly, at a pace she could stand. She knew she would have to tell Rose as well, but she couldn't bear her mother's reaction yet. In a few months, when Sylvie was feeling sicker, she would call her mother or ask one of her sisters to.

When Sylvie managed to say the words, the twins responded differently than she would have expected. Cecelia cried, while Emeline got mad.

"Absolutely not," she said, her voice raised. "No way. That's not right!"

William looked at Emeline. "Nothing about this situation is right," he said.

Cecelia said, "You double-checked everything with Kent?"

Sylvie nodded. It was remarkable how deeply they all trusted Kent. He was a sports doctor—not even a general practitioner, and certainly not an oncologist—but they all called him when they had a bad fever or texted him a picture of a cut on the back of a hand to get his opinion on whether stitches were required. *Doctor* was an unshakable identity, and Sylvie and her family, and all of Kent's many friends, showed him their wounds and symptoms with a look that said, *Can you fix me?*

Emeline paced around the kitchen. Cecelia wiped tears off her cheeks, and more came.

"It was supposed to be me," Emeline said, in a hard voice.

Sylvie and Cecelia stared at her. "Why?" Cecelia said.

"I'm supposed to be Beth, out of all of us. Not you. I always knew I would die first." Her voice grew quieter. "Beth and I even have the same personality," she said. "I'm the quiet one, the homebody."

Sylvie stared at her sister with wonder. Emeline had apparently written a narrative for her own life, and Sylvie had just erased the ending. Emeline must have thought this would be the case since they were little girls. She'd always mothered and protected her sisters, and that meant taking the pain for herself. If there was a bullet, Emeline wanted to step in front of it. She had planned to do so and hated that there could be any other result.

"Oh, Emmie," Sylvie said. "I'm sorry."

William said, in a hesitant tone, "Isn't Beth a fictional character?"

"This is awful," Cecelia said.

"We can't bear it," Emeline said.

A great weariness ran through Sylvie, as if her blood had grown heavy. She thought, *We felt that way when Julia moved away. But we got used to her absence, which means you'll get used to mine too.*

LATER THAT NIGHT, SYLVIE sat in bed with a book open in her lap. She was too sleepy to read, but the proximity of the book was comforting. Telling her sisters had required more strength than she'd had, and she was relieved it was over. William was lying next to her; he'd gotten into bed without a book. If he didn't have the attention span or desire to read, he wouldn't pretend to. Sylvie had always admired this about her husband. She carried a book at all times—to read, yes, but also as a handy shield for when she wanted to deflect the attention of other people. She would position a book in front of her face and think, or simply hide. For William, a book was picked up only when he wanted to read the contents.

"You and your sisters have so many reference points, such a dense history," William said. "I never get used to it."

Sylvie studied his face. She saw something new there, a suggestion that he was considering a long-ago piece of his own history. A reference point of his own. She said, "Are you thinking about your sister?"

William gave his smallest smile. "How could you tell? I haven't thought of her in . . ." He paused. "A very long time."

Sylvie thought, *I just knew.* She was aware that she had recently begun to think instead of speaking out loud, as if the two were the same thing. As if both carried the same weight and crossed the same distance.

William seemed to hear her, though; he nodded. "I was remembering when I was in high school and I broke my leg. That's the only time I remember thinking about Caroline when I was a kid. I couldn't play basketball, and I wanted to be gone, like her. But I think . . . I think I wanted to be gone in part because I wanted to be *with* her. I didn't like living in my house without her. It never occurred to me in so many words, but I missed her." He paused. "I somehow miss her even though I never knew her. Isn't that strange?"

Sylvie put her hand over his. They had both seen the raw pain on her sisters' faces today, when Emeline and Cecelia were forced to consider life without Sylvie. It felt true that if one of the four Padavano sisters had died as a baby, the other three would have missed her—and been missing part of themselves—for the rest of their lives.

"It makes sense to me," she said, and tightened her grip on William's hand. She remembered holding his frozen hand in the ambulance, decades earlier. She wanted to hold on now, so tight that nothing could pull them apart.

William

OCTOBER 2008

THREE WEEKS PASSED AFTER WILLIAM HAD CALLED JULIA, AND then four. It was the end of October. Was it possible that she wouldn't come? Julia was the most stubborn and willful person that William had ever known, and his ex-wife certainly wasn't going to appear in Chicago simply because he'd asked her to. Still, William woke up each morning thinking, *Today might be the day.* He hadn't told anyone—not even Kent—about the phone call he'd made. When Sylvie got home from the library each evening, William studied his wife's face to see if something had occurred. Sylvie had made Cecelia and Emeline swear that they wouldn't tell Julia or Rose about her illness, so as far as she was aware, all roads to her older sister were blocked. Each evening, Sylvie looked the same, though: a little tired, and happy to see him. Part of William was relieved, despite his belief that Sylvie needed Julia. The *idea* of his ex-wife, which could also mean his daughter, in his city and life was impossible for him to wrap his mind around. He didn't try, but the possibility—which he had unleashed—remained in his peripheral vision, as if Julia and Alice stood at the far edge of the horizon.

He'd made it this far because he almost never thought of Alice. He'd successfully closed off that part of his history. He had not allowed himself a daughter, so in his mind, he didn't have one. This conviction had not been effortless. There were paintings of Alice that he'd had to avoid in Cecelia's house, and Izzy had gone through a period when she was about ten where she tried to make him talk about his daughter. He'd always liked Izzy; she had no patience for small talk, and he was no good at it. But there had been a time in her childhood when she was painfully direct, and all the adults around her had been stung in one way or another. "You always eat more food than you need," she'd said to Josie once, and the woman had flushed to her hairline, a forkful of chocolate mousse pie in her hand.

"Why don't you drive to New York to see Alice?" Izzy had said. "Aren't you curious what she's like? What if she's not okay because you're not in her life?"

William had forced himself to stay still, to answer. If Izzy had been an adult, he would have left the room. He'd said, "You're fine without your father."

Izzy seemed to consider this. "Yes. But I have you and my whole family. Who does Alice have?"

"She has her mother." This, for William, had always been the bottom line.

Everyone else—Kent, Sylvie, the twins—understood that if they had something to say about Julia or Alice, they said it out of his hearing. This new situation, waiting for a bomb William had lit to explode, or not, was exhausting. William showed up for his days—watched players play, ate lunch with Kent, ate dinner with Sylvie—and waited. He was no longer trying to be comfortable. He was engaged in the long-term project of eradicating the bullshit and secrets from his life and taking care of Sylvie in any way he could think of.

One morning after Sylvie had left for the library, William opened their bedroom closet and took down a medium-sized cardboard box with only one item inside. He pulled the framed photo of Caroline out of the box and looked at it for the first time since it had arrived in the mail after his parents' deaths, two years earlier. The night Sylvie had told her sisters about her diagnosis, William's sister arrived like a surprise guest in his mind. Life seemed littered with small surprises since Sylvie had gotten sick. Emeline yelling about a character from a childhood novel. William calling his first wife. His sister occupying a new place in his heart. And once Caroline had appeared, she'd stayed.

The small redheaded girl, from so far in his past, was accompanying him through his days. He'd wanted to see her face.

William's mother had apparently died first, of liver disease. His father had a massive heart attack at his office desk a few months later. They'd left their assets to their Catholic parish. Their lawyer had called to tell William the news and to ask him to come back to Boston to pack up the house and decide what to do with personal items. "Like what?" William had asked, truly unable to imagine what they might be. "Photo albums," the lawyer said. "China? Jewelry?" William had hired a service to pack up and sell or give away everything in the house, with the exception of the framed photograph of the redheaded little girl that had sat on the end table in his parents' living room. This was shipped to him, and although Sylvie—who was as delighted to see the photo as she might have been to meet William's sister—wanted to hang it on the wall, William had stored it in their bedroom closet.

He ran his thumb lightly across his sister's face now. He remembered telling Sylvie about Caroline when he was in the hospital, but then he'd sealed her back up inside him. He'd always known that his parents would have preferred that he had died instead of his sister. It had been clear, in the house he'd grown up in, that the loss of a little girl was the worst pain imaginable. Losing Caroline had ruined William's parents, and living with those two wrecked people had made William a little frightened of his sister too. He realized now, with the photo in his hands, that he'd turned away from his sister *and* his daughter to protect himself from that specific devastation. He'd made sure that he couldn't lose a little girl. Of course, the irony was that, to ensure that, he'd cut them out of his life.

William's hands grew sweaty, while he felt truths fall into place inside him. His mother and father had shut down under the weight of their immense pain; they'd chosen to go through the motions of living a life, which was very different from *living*. William thought that he might have made the same choice after being released from the hospital if it hadn't been for Sylvie. He would have ticked through days like minutes on a clock, everything locked up inside him, if Sylvie hadn't insisted that he let himself love her. But his parents had no one to save them, and they couldn't look at their son without remembering the loss of their daughter. They'd turned away from William, and he understood now that he'd done the same to Caroline and Alice. He was no better than his mom and dad, really. All three of them had lost time and love with people who deserved both. When William thought of himself as a lonely little boy dribbling a basketball in the park, he believed, perhaps for the first time, that he had deserved his parents' attention. And in that moment, he forgave them.

His sister beamed at him from inside the frame, oblivious to her own power. She looked excited and ready for fun. What would William's life have been like if she had lived? If he'd grown up with a big sister, in a family that wasn't silenced by loss?

With his parents dead, this photo was the only proof of Caroline's existence, and he was the only one who knew she'd lived. William left the apartment with the framed photo. He walked through the zigzag of blocks that took him to the super-duplex. He shook his head, amused, every time he referred to the two houses by the name Izzy had given them years earlier. He'd thought it was ridiculous at the time, but the nickname had stuck. He knocked on the front door of Cecelia's house, knowing she might be next door or up a ladder somewhere in the city, painting. He hadn't seen her or Emeline since Sylvie had told them her news.

He was relieved when Cecelia opened the door. She was wearing jeans, and her hair was pulled back with the yellow bandanna she wore while she was working. She looked pale, but she still looked like Cecelia. William realized that he'd been worried, after watching the usually placid Emeline rage and the usually tough Cecelia weep, that the prospect of losing Sylvie might have rendered them unrecognizable. He had never heard Emeline raise her voice, until that day. Of course, Cecelia might be changed completely under her skin—William was—but her familiar face was still a relief. William loved his wife's younger sisters; this knowledge had crept up on him, with the years. The twins had taken him back after his actions had pulled their family apart. This act of generosity—Cecelia and Emeline had nothing to gain from him, personally—still struck him as extraordinary.

"William," Cecelia said, with surprise in her voice. "What's up? Is Sylvie . . . ?"

"She's fine," he said. "I'm not here about her." He held the framed photo out. "I'd like you to paint her. Caroline." He cleared his throat. His breath was short again; his lungs felt full. "Please," he said.

Cecelia looked down at the photo. "This is your sister," she said in a wondering tone, and studied the image. "William, she was beautiful."

William was afraid that if he stayed still in front of Cecelia, he would cry. He wanted to leave his beautiful sister with her, to be replicated and perhaps painted onto an enormous canvas. That way, she would continue to exist, apart from him. William had done Caroline a disservice for all these years by sequestering her inside himself. He'd somehow feared that if he opened his eyes and heart to her, she would hurt him like she'd hurt their parents. But that had been absurd. The little girl in the picture deserved much better. "Will you do it?" he said.

"Of course." Cecelia held the frame with both hands, as if afraid she might drop it.

William nodded—he couldn't speak—and started to walk away.

"Thank you for asking me," she called after him.

THAT AFTERNOON WAS ARASH'S weekly clinic. William had skipped a few weeks after hearing Sylvie's news, but it was time for him to return. From a block away, he could see Kent, Arash, and several kids on the court. Izzy was there too, chatting with a young female player. She tutored several of the kids through their high schools. Arash was spending his retirement assisting young players, both in this clinic and directly with various public high school teams. "If we help one kid . . ." he'd said when he started the clinic, to convince William and the others to join him. They'd all nodded, understanding that helping a kid could mean many things.

"William!" Arash called out in greeting. Kent waved from midcourt, clearly pleased to see him. Basketballs were being dribbled against the concrete, and William tried to focus on the sound. There were no nets on the park hoops, but William could imagine the swish of the ball with each made basket. Only when he was closer did William realize that more people were there than usual. There were the expected adults, and the kids, of course, already shooting and warming up at the far end of the court. But Washington was there too, and Gus. They both had real-world jobs—that's what he and Kent called any job outside basketball. Washington was a statistician who worked for the city government, and Gus was a high school English teacher. They had never been to the clinic before.

"Hi, everyone," William said, in a wary tone.

"We're so glad you're here," Arash said, and the men around him— Kent, Washington, Gus—nodded at the same time as if to show that they really meant it. Izzy ignored William and continued her conversation with the young player. William felt a note of gratitude toward his niece. She had heard about her aunt, of course, but she wouldn't approach him about it in public.

He went to the bleachers to sit down. He'd known he wouldn't teach a lesson to the teenagers today. He was here simply as one of the columns that supported the effort. He was the least jovial of the involved adults, so his presence kept the kids well behaved.

Washington and Gus sat down on either side of him. "Good to see you, buddy," Washington said. "How are the Bulls looking this year?"

"I'm excited to watch Pooh," Gus said. Pooh was the nickname of the number-one draft pick, Derrick Rose. "He might really be our next Jordan." This was what Chicagoans had been craving ever since MJ left the Bulls nine years earlier. Every new rookie who entered the franchise had an impossible weight on his shoulders.

William glanced at each of the men. "I assume you're here because Kent told you about Sylvie."

Their faces went somber. They didn't look at him now; they watched the kids wash back and forth across the court. Washington said, "Kent's smart. He knows that you'll be nice to us and let us be with you."

If William had had the energy, he would have smiled at his friend's craftiness. The reasoning was correct. Kent was so deeply part of William's life that William didn't need to be considerate of his feelings. But after William's other friends had spent twenty-four hours of their lives searching the city for him and saving him, he had always felt he was in their debt. Once he was out of the hospital, he'd insisted on doing them favors. He'd helped Washington move apartments twice, and he spoke to the basketball team at Gus's high school every season. Two other Northwestern teammates had somehow needed middle-of-the-night appendectomies during a one-year period, and they'd both called William for a ride to the hospital. William was programmed to have nothing but gratitude for the two tall men flanking him.

"You don't have to say anything, William," Gus said. "We're just gonna sit here and watch the kids play. We'll be here next week too. If you want to say something, you can of course go ahead."

"God damn it," William said, and looked around the edges of the park, as if searching for a way out, knowing there wasn't one.

"That's right," Washington said, and patted him on the knee.

Sylvie

TEN DAYS AFTER SHE'D TOLD EMELINE AND CECELIA HER NEWS, Sylvie left the library during her lunch break to buy an ice cream cone. This was her new habit. Before, she'd believed pretty firmly that ice cream and donuts were only for children, but when she removed all rules and guilt from food, she realized, to her surprise, that those were two of her favorite things to eat. Now she went into the expensive, delicious-smelling bakery every morning for a donut and bought an ice cream cone for lunch. It was a three-block walk from the ice cream store back to the library, blocks that were so familiar to her that they operated as memories more than sidewalks, streets, and stores. She was sitting beside Cecelia on that curb when she found out that her little sister was pregnant with Izzy. The laundromat on the corner used to be the butcher shop where Rose had bartered: a Greek varietal of squash that Rose grew in her garden in exchange for meat. Sylvie passed her first apartment and tipped her head back to look at the windows. She'd loved that apartment, had been naked with a man for the first time there. This memory amused her, because right across the street was a bus stop with an ad for Ernie's electrician business. It included a photo of Ernie, heavier now, with a mustache, smiling for the camera. She knew Ernie lived nearby with his wife and four sons. The passage of time, and the details that spun some moments into unforgettable memories and others into thin air, traveled with Sylvie—the swirling atmosphere of her own life—while she walked.

When she walked into the library, she saw Emeline standing with her back to her at the front desk, and she thought, *Oh dear.* Sylvie was tired, and talking to her sister could only be hard work at the moment. Sylvie braced herself and walked toward Emeline. She hadn't seen her younger sister in person since she'd told her the news—they'd only texted and spoken on the phone—and she hoped Emeline had had enough time to regain her normal equilibrium. But as Sylvie moved closer, a strange feeling filled her. Emeline didn't wear silky tops like this, and her hair was slightly wrong too.

The woman turned around, and a static charge filled Sylvie's entire body.

It was Julia.

The sisters stared at each other. Sylvie felt herself wobble slightly on her feet. She had been imagining her sister for so long that it felt like her own reflection had stepped out of a mirror.

"Is it really you?" she said.

Julia, at forty-eight, looked regal. Her mane of hair—similar to Sylvie's, but denser, so it had more height—rose away from her face. She was dressed elegantly; Sylvie was dressed for the library, wearing Converse sneakers and a cardigan. The last time she'd been in the same room as Julia—if she was actually in the same room as her now— her sister had been wearing jeans and an old T-shirt. They'd stood in the middle of moving boxes, a baby at their feet, while Julia told her sister that she knew she was keeping secrets from her. Julia had handed Sylvie her divorce papers, and Sylvie never saw her again.

"I suppose it's me," Julia said, as if she weren't sure.

"I didn't think I'd ever see you again," Sylvie said. "The twins told you?" They had promised they wouldn't, but they must have reconsidered. *It must've been Emeline,* Sylvie thought.

Julia shook her head. "William did."

"William?" Sylvie said in disbelief. But her voice was faint, and she couldn't listen for an answer. The static inside her had grown loud. When Sylvie was a child, she'd watched in amazement when friends, upset about a bad day at school or a slight from a boy they had a crush on, burst into tears at the sight of their mother. Their mother was their safe space, and so, with her, they felt every iota of their feelings. Julia had always been that person for Sylvie. Rose was too volatile, and she seemed to have a bone to pick with Sylvie, even when Sylvie was far too young for that to be likely. Because of this, Sylvie had always run past her mother into her own bedroom, where she threw herself into Julia's arms. She had drenched Julia's school uniform with tears, vented at her, been hugged by her, too many times to count. If she was ever confused about how she was feeling, her older sister's presence provided clarity.

Sylvie had been okay, rational, calm, until now. But now she understood, for the first time, that she was dying. She was losing everything she loved. Everyone she loved. And her sister was here—which was impossible in and of itself—and because of that, Sylvie felt everything.

She closed her eyes and heard a man's voice say, "Are you Julia Padavano?"

"Yes?" Julia said, in a voice that made it clear she had no idea who he was.

"Thought so. I lived down the street from your family. Your sister Cecelia slept in my room when she was pregnant and I was in rehab."

"Oh," Julia said. Sylvie opened her eyes to watch her sister remember the teenage Frank Ceccione, who had walked around their neighborhood on Saturday afternoons in his baseball uniform, looking strong and gorgeous, and how Rose had worn Frank's discarded gear in her garden after he quit the team. Julia said, "What a surprise."

"You always zipped around like you knew what you were doing," Frank said. "Like a bee who knows where the honey is. And you had that tall boyfriend."

Oh Jesus, Sylvie thought. *The tall boyfriend.* She hoped that Julia wouldn't leave because he'd said that, having only just arrived. To Sylvie's surprise, Julia grinned at the old-looking man. Sylvie felt her own face smile in response. She noticed for the first time that her sister looked tired. There were dark circles under Julia's eyes.

"What's the joke?" Frank said, his eyes narrowed.

"Nothing," Sylvie said to him. "Nothing at all." She said in a lower voice, to Julia, "Can we go somewhere to talk?"

"Daddy's favorite bar," Julia said.

The two women didn't speak while they maneuvered down the sidewalks. Neither of them could believe they were together. Sylvie wondered what this terrain was doing to her sister's insides after more than twenty years away. She wondered how William had found the courage to go against her wishes and make a phone call that didn't serve him at all. They passed Mr. Luis's flower shop, where the front glass was so crowded with roses that the old man wouldn't have been able to see, much less recognize, the two sisters. The air was thick with the flowers' scent.

Sylvie had an interior map of Cecelia's murals in the neighborhood and spotted one from the corner of her eye, on a side street. Next to her, Julia looked glassy-eyed and overwhelmed and didn't appear to see it. The painting was of St. Clare of Assisi. Sylvie had seen the mural so often—every day, almost, since Cecelia had painted it—that she felt like the woman was real. More real than the sister next to her, who had appeared out of thin air, who had appeared out of her dreams. The saint felt like an old friend, and Sylvie had the urge to gesture at Julia and whisper to St. Clare: *Look who's here!* But she didn't; she kept walking, wondering if this moment could be true, while the giant woman stared in the sisters' direction, as if from the dining room wall of their childhood.

Julia

JULIA FELT UNSTEADY ON THE SIDEWALK BESIDE HER SISTER; she had the odd sensation of being part of everything she saw. In New York, she walked *on* the sidewalks; here, she was scattered, like pollen, across the concrete. The hardware store; the small, crummy supermarket; Mr. Luis's flower shop. The familiar cut of the buildings against the sky. Old ladies, who looked like her mother, pushing shopping carts down the sidewalk. She remembered the girl and the young woman she'd been when she lived in Pilsen; she'd been in such a hurry to succeed, which she'd believed required an ambitious husband and a house that she owned outright. She'd raced toward adulthood, because she'd always wanted to be in charge. Julia could remember her pleasure, as a young girl, in making her sisters line up in height order and follow her around the house.

Julia noticed one of Cecelia's murals in her peripheral vision. It was a painting of Cecelia's saint; Julia had first seen the image on Alice's dorm room wall. The giant woman stared in Julia's direction, and she sped up her gait. She didn't want anyone peering into her soul. She didn't know what was in there; she felt disrupted in every way. She led Sylvie into the Irish bar, which hadn't changed except for the bartender, who looked impossibly young. The bartenders who had served Charlie had either retired or died. Julia ordered a Scotch and Sylvie ordered a Diet Coke, and they sat in a booth.

"I can't drink alcohol on my medication," Sylvie said in an apologetic tone. She looked older, but she still looked like Sylvie. The scattering of freckles, the slight green tint to her brown eyes. Julia felt boulders shift inside her. Looking at Sylvie was like looking in a mirror, and yet not at herself. This was the other part of her, the part that had been hidden for twenty-five years.

"I wasn't planning to come here," Julia said. "I told William I wasn't going to."

"I thought you hated me," Sylvie said. "I never would have bothered you. I feel like I should apologize for William calling you."

"No," Julia said. "You should apologize for marrying him."

Sylvie froze for a second, then said, "You're right. I'm so sorry. I had no other choice."

Julia took a long sip of the drink, which had been Charlie's favorite. She wasn't much of a drinker; when she drank, she usually chose white wine. The Scotch tasted like colors: red and orange and gold and white. She'd made many choices in her life. She believed in choices, if she believed in anything. Set a goal, and then work your ass off to get it. She hadn't accepted that Sylvie had no other choice when Emeline said so decades earlier, and she didn't accept it now. But she wasn't angry about it either. She didn't know what she was.

After William's phone call, Julia had stopped being able to sleep. She cobbled together only a couple of hours per night. She gave taxi drivers the wrong address twice on her way to work. She also had the strange sense, from the minute she hung up the phone with William, that her shadow had gotten a mind of its own; a few times she caught it pulling away from her, as if it were trying to escape. After a week of sleeplessness, Julia felt like a Picasso painting—her eyes didn't match, and her shoulders were at different heights. She did her best to act like herself, but she got so tired that she forgot what she was like. She forgot how to act and called in sick to work. She texted with Alice but didn't speak to her on the phone, because she had lost faith in her voice.

"I didn't want to go to work this morning," Julia said. "So I got into a cab and went to the airport. I only have my purse. I thought, at three A.M., that maybe if I saw you, like William wanted me to, I could go back to feeling normal."

Sylvie nodded, like this made sense.

"It's only a two-hour flight," Julia said. "And please don't act like what I'm saying is reasonable. I know it's not."

"Oh please," Sylvie said, and for a second Julia saw the Sylvie she used to know, the sister who wasn't afraid to speak to her, who wasn't cloaked in guilt. "What's reasonable? I'm dying, for God's sake."

It occurred to Julia that maybe she felt terrible *because* Sylvie felt terrible. Was it possible that she was falling apart in New York because her sister was dying in Chicago? That there were invisible threads that connected them, which she had been unable to see and therefore unable to sever? Julia felt so confused and fatigued and out of her body right now that when she asked, "How do you feel?" it was like she was asking after herself.

Sylvie spread her hands and looked at them. "I thought I felt pretty good, until I saw you. I have headaches sometimes. I go to sleep at seven some nights." She leaned forward. "Julia. Are you *really* here? Maybe I'm hallucinating because of my medication. I've imagined you with me for years, but this feels much more real."

The bar had a low hum—it was midafternoon on a weekday, and the people in here were professional drinkers. No one was messy or loud. It was mostly older men, some of whom might have known Charlie. Every single person looked tired. The act of living had exhausted them. They didn't know that Sylvie, who was middle-aged but looked younger, wouldn't have the chance to tire of anything.

"I wish you were hallucinating," Julia said. "My being here makes no sense."

Sylvie looked around them, as if assessing what might be real and what might not. "I love this hallucination. Nothing this wonderful has happened to me in a long time."

Julia sighed. "It'll become real when you tell William and the twins that you saw me."

"That's true." Sylvie appeared to consider this. "But I don't usually tell them about my dreams and visions. I'll keep this one to myself, for a little while. Will you tell Alice that you came here?"

"God, no." Sylvie didn't know about the lie Julia had told, and Julia didn't feel inclined to explain. She remembered, with her sister in front of her, that part of the reason she'd killed William off was that she'd been scared that Alice would leave Julia to live in Chicago, because Alice would love Sylvie more than her own mother. That had been a ridiculous concern; Julia knew that now. But the younger Julia had felt like it was possible, because *she* had always loved Sylvie more than she loved everyone else. Julia loved her now, across the wooden table. She had closed a door on Sylvie long ago and triple-locked it, and that had worked until William's phone call. Now, with her sister in the same room, Julia was aware of how badly she'd missed her.

This wasn't a hallucination, Julia thought, but at the same time, no one in her life knew she was in Chicago. This wasn't on her calendar, which meant this moment could exist as a barnacle on the outside of her real life. She was here and yet not here, in a state of quantum uncertainty. "Look," she said, "I'm glad you feel bad about what happened. But you probably did me a favor by visiting William in the hospital. I wondered why his doctor didn't ask for more from me than a single phone call, but that was because you were there. If you'd left him alone like I wanted you to, eventually I would have had to help him. Mama would have made me. Or someone would have needed to sign some paperwork. But you stepped in, and that let me leave. I'm grateful for that."

Sylvie looked at her, and Julia could see the years of their separation on her face. Julia could no longer read Sylvie perfectly. She didn't know what her sister was thinking right now. Julia remembered how frantic she'd felt the last time she saw Sylvie. Her husband had left her, then tried to kill himself, then left her again, and Julia had accepted a job far away from her sisters and home. That collection of weeks had pulled her life out from under her like a rug. Julia had devoted herself to not losing control of her circumstances like that ever again, and she hadn't, until recently.

"Tell me about New York," Sylvie said. "Tell me about Alice."

"Alice," she said, and paused.

Her sister was beaming at her from across the table. Julia remembered Sylvie holding baby Alice in her arms. There was a photograph of the two of them together, in Julia's bedside drawer. Julia could see now, on Sylvie's face, a truth she had overlooked. Sylvie had loved

Alice with all her heart. Somehow it hadn't occurred to Julia that she'd separated the two of them when she left Chicago. She'd worried about the possibility of Alice loving Sylvie, but only as a future risk, not as something that had already happened. But Sylvie was lit up and longing to hear news about the baby girl to whom she'd whispered, *I love you,* every time she saw her.

"She's great," Julia said. "Well, not great, maybe, but good. She graduated cum laude from college, which was fantastic. She has a decent job as a copy editor. Let's see. She's a runner; she runs in Prospect Park every morning." Julia felt Sylvie's quizzical gaze and remembered lying next to her sister in the dark, in the bedroom where they never told each other anything but the truth. They might twist words for other people, but not for each other. Julia said, "I'm afraid I messed her up, though." She told her sister about how careful her daughter's smile was, how deliberately engineered her carefree demeanor was, how uneventful Alice's life was. Julia told her something Rose had said recently: that Alice lived like a cat who refused to leave its cardboard box.

Sylvie smiled at this. "She's still a baby," she said. "Do you remember how young we were when we were twenty-five? If there's something wrong, you have time to fix it."

Fix it, Julia thought. Could she fix it? In her sister's company, she felt brave enough to consider this possibility. She had a sense of what it would take. Julia would have to leap off a cliff, without knowing if she could survive the fall.

"We haven't touched each other," Sylvie said. "You and I. Do you realize that? We haven't hugged. Which makes sense if this isn't real. Ghosts don't hug, because they would pass through each other. Ghosts just enjoy each other's company."

Julia smiled at her sister's whimsy. Sylvie was part of her, and in their separation, Julia had missed these kinds of thoughts. Sylvie was the part of her who walked out of the pages of a novel, who kissed boys for ninety seconds for fun, who talked about third doors and ghosts as easily as she made a grocery list. Maybe she and her sister *were* ghosts, or hallucinations, or maybe it didn't matter. Julia was aware that she felt better—happier, more relaxed—than she had in a long time. She was supposed to be in a different city. She was with Sylvie, whom she'd excised from her life a quarter of a century earlier. Julia felt a shot of joy rise through her like bubbles to the surface of a glass. She was free of her real self, of her real life, for a few hours, and when Julia left for the airport a little while later, she and Sylvie both knew—although neither spoke the words out loud—that Julia would return. They'd found a loophole, which allowed them to be together without anyone's knowledge, which meant this time meant nothing, which meant everything.

Alice

NOVEMBER 2008

ALICE WAITED FOR HER MOTHER AT THE GREEK RESTAURANT that Julia liked. She didn't mind her mother being late. During work hours, Alice lived in her head and in whatever manuscript she was editing—questioning the details of each line—so after hours she initially found conversation, with its awkward pauses, questions, and changes of topic, challenging. She liked her work for the quiet and for the details. She was able to take a book and check, change, and verify that every single fact and timeline was airtight. When she was finished with a manuscript, she knew—and her employer appreciated—that it was as correct as was humanly possible.

The waiter kept refilling Alice's water, and she kept drinking because it felt like the polite thing to do after he'd gone to the effort.

"I don't want to be rude," the waiter said, when he came by with the water pitcher again. "But do you play for the Liberty?"

"No, I work in publishing," Alice said.

The waiter blushed. "I'm sorry. I just thought . . ."

"It's okay." If she was in the right mood, Alice was amused by how her tallness bothered people. Her height immediately exposed men (it was usually men) who had any insecurity. If a guy was a jerk about Alice's size, he was a jerk. She didn't think this waiter was a jerk necessarily, but it didn't reflect well on him that he couldn't come up with more than one career option for a tall woman. Or that he couldn't just keep his mouth shut.

Alice felt her mother's energy enter the room and smelled her perfume. She looked toward the door. "Hi, Mom," she said. A wave of cool air hit the back of Alice's neck; it was the beginning of November, and New York City was toying with the idea of winter. Alice hadn't seen her mother for a few weeks, which was unusual. Julia had been busy with work. "You're wearing too much perfume." Alice wrinkled her nose.

"Am I?" Julia sat across from her and immediately looked down at the menu, even though she always ordered the same thing: a Greek salad with a glass of white wine. "I must have forgotten and reapplied it before I left the office."

Alice studied her mother and noticed she was wearing fresh lipstick too. Julia usually stripped away her office look before she saw her daughter; today she seemed to have doubled down. Julia's hair was in a bun, as usual, but a curl had escaped on one side. Alice was looking at the rogue curl when her mother said, "I have a series of things to tell you."

"A series?" Alice smiled. She assumed this was going to be about a new work client, hiring more employees, and perhaps a piece of art that Julia had bought. Her mother sometimes presented her transactions to Alice because she found them exciting, not noticing that her daughter had never had any interest in her mother's accumulation of wealth or professional prestige. When Alice had taken her first copy-editing assignment, Rose said, "I know you chose that kind of job to drive your mother crazy. And it'll work." Rose meant the kind of job with low wages, no ladder to climb, and no way to *win*. Alice had laughed at this. "You're a little right, Grandma," she'd said. But she also liked her work and the lack of politics involved. The stock market had crashed earlier that fall, and Alice thought the ladders her mother valued so highly were made of rotten wood. Her friends were all struggling financially, despite their college degrees. Carrie was a bartender who had published six poems in literary journals and was working on a collection. Rhoan lived in a one-bedroom apartment with his three brothers and was making minimum wage at an internship for an arts library, even though he'd earned a master's degree.

"My sister Sylvie is dying," Julia said.

Alice's attention snapped back to the present. "Dying?" She remembered the photographs she'd found in her mother's bedside table years earlier. The four sisters with curly hair. "I'm sorry," she said. "Sylvie is the one closest to you in age, right?"

"When I was pregnant with you, I sometimes slept with Sylvie, on a couch. We shared a bedroom when we were children. We used to be very close."

Alice tried to imagine her mother as a little girl, sharing a bedroom with another little girl. Julia had just spoken more about her childhood in ninety seconds than she had in the entirety of Alice's life. Alice felt an uncertainty inside herself, as if furniture were being shoved into an empty room. She said, "Will you go back to Chicago to see her?"

Julia made a strange face, as if she were fighting tears, or maybe a smile. "No," she said. She pushed at her hair lightly and said, "Sylvie is married to your father."

Sylvie is married to your father. Alice ran this sentence through her head, but there were too many errors for a copy editor to fix. The structure buckled under its own weight. She tried a tense change: "Sylvie *was* married to my father?"

Julia shook her head.

The inside of Alice echoed, cavelike. "You're not making sense, Mom."

"Your father was the one who called to tell me Sylvie is sick."

"But my father is dead."

"I told you that because he gave up his parental rights to you while you were still a baby. He had mental-health issues, and I think he didn't feel capable of being a father. But I didn't want you to feel rejected or feel like it had anything to do with you, because it didn't."

"Wait."

Julia waited.

Alice wanted clarity; she wanted to make sure she understood the mechanics of what was being said. "You're saying that my father gave me up, and because of that, you told me that he was dead?"

There was a visible vein in Julia's temple. "It seemed simplest to tell you that. It felt like a kind of truth. His name is William Waters, and he lives in Chicago."

Alice shook her head. She could hear her heart beating in her ears, as if her organs were moving around her body. She wasn't sure what her mother said after that or even if she said anything. Alice smiled reflexively at the waiter, who was passing by, and felt a spear sink through her body. Alice missed *something*. She missed—wildly— everything she had wanted when she was young. She needed a backup to her mother, who was saying crazy things while wearing too much perfume and too much makeup. She needed a sibling to roll her eyes at. She needed someone else to say, *Don't listen to her. She's lost her mind. You're fine. None of this is true.*

"Excuse me," Alice said, not to her mother but to the tablecloth and the waiter, if he was listening. She pushed back her chair and walked with wobbly legs across the restaurant and out the door. She stood in the dim nighttime air. Broadway was in front of her, a steady grumble of taxis and buses. Building windows were lit yellow against the night sky. Alice's heartbeats were still registering in her ears.

Alice pulled her phone out of her backpack, quickly scrolled through her contacts, and pressed the call button.

The phone rang three times, and then Rose said, "Hello?"

"Grandma."

"Alice!" Rose sounded pleased. Alice usually tried to call her grand-mother a few times a month, because she knew Rose was lonely.

"My mother just told me that my father is alive."

There was a shocked silence through the phone. "Gracious," Rose said finally.

"Is it true?" Alice said.

"Well," Rose said, "I mean, I haven't spoken to him lately, but yes, I suppose it's true. I would have heard otherwise." She paused. "Why in the world would she tell you that now?"

"Sylvie's sick," Alice said, as if handing a piece of mail to another person. She wished she were at home in the apartment she shared with Carrie, where one wall was papered with Cecelia's murals. She wished she were standing in front of those images, looking at one strong woman after another, instead of standing on the street while her grandmother made small noises into the phone and her mother was somewhere behind her, a human wrecking ball that had swung into Alice.

Alice had stopped asking about Chicago and her mother's past when she was a child, for her mother's sake. She'd accepted that the place and people her mother had decided to withhold were never going to be part of her life. When the Internet had become easily searchable, in Alice's late teens, she'd considered looking up her mother's sisters, but—apart from tracking down Cecelia's artwork—she'd given the idea up almost immediately. Alice knew her mother wouldn't want her to, and since Alice no longer needed more family to feel safe, she didn't seek out the information.

But Alice had been an idiot. She'd always known her mother was hiding something; that was why she'd gone through Julia's drawers while she was in middle school. She'd thought the secret was Julia's, though, and had nothing to do with her. Alice checked facts for a living. She knew how to look for evidence and confirm sources. Julia had offered the young Alice very few facts, however, and there had been no sources to reach out to for verification. What Julia said went un- verified, and Alice could see that now. She could see the weakness of what she'd been handed, and she could see her own weakness in ac- cepting it as truth.

Perhaps other people might have helped her figure this out—Rose, Carrie, Rhoan—but the young Alice had grown so tall that no one ever thought to help her, and she prided herself on never asking for help. Everyone—men and women—rushed to Carrie's aid, even when she was perfectly fine, because she was cute and five feet tall. But the assumption was that Alice never needed help. She could, after all, reach every high shelf and carry her own luggage with no problem. When someone did try to assist her, she suspected them of ulterior motives.

"Are you still there?" Rose asked.

"Yes." Sound intensified on the street out of nowhere—a tornado of noise. Countless decibels hit at once. Two ambulances passed Alice, driving in opposite directions. Taxi drivers laid on their horns. The air vibrated with sound, and Alice and Rose had to wait to have any chance of speaking or hearing. *The city is talking to us,* Carrie would have said if she were there.

Rose said, "Your mother and aunts have made a real mess of things over the years. There's no point in denying that."

"Why didn't you tell me the truth, Grandma?"

Rose harrumphed, "Do you think I didn't tell your mother she was crazy to lie to you? She didn't speak to me for a couple years because of that. She started sending me those damn postcards."

"No," Alice said. She had taken a home economics class in high school, which mostly involved learning to needlepoint. Alice had been terrible at it, and the teacher would lean over her desk, smelling of cinnamon, and cut away her stitches with tiny scissors. Alice felt like someone—her mother, she supposed—were cutting away tiny stitches inside her now. "That's not what I asked you. If you didn't want to tell me while I was living with Mom, I can understand that, I guess. But I'm twenty-five. You could have told me the real story when I visited you last fall. You could have told me anytime."

Alice could hear her grandmother rustling in her kitchen chair, gathering herself into a storm cloud. "I don't think I'm the one you should be mad at," Rose said. "William could have told you himself, couldn't he? He's your father, and if he'd showed up, it wouldn't have mattered what your mother said to you."

Alice considered this. "That's true," she said. "I need to know the timeline."

"The timeline? What's that?"

Alice shook her head. She heard the restaurant door open and close behind her and sensed her mother's energy nearby again. Alice felt her shoulders hunch up, as if to protect herself. She wasn't going to explain timelines to her grandmother, how if the chronology of a story wasn't clear, nothing made sense. Alice almost cried out, because her mother was standing right beside her now. The tiny scissors were cutting, cutting, inside her.

"What is wrong with this family?" Alice said.

"That's a fair question," Rose said.

Julia was clutching her purse as if it were a life preserver. There was an unsteadiness to her face. Alice looked at her and thought, *I could be mad at you. I could scream at you. But I won't. You raised me to take care of myself, and I will.*

William

NOVEMBER 2008

CECELIA TEXTED WILLIAM AN ADDRESS AND TOLD HIM TO go there. This is just the first one, the text said. There will be more of her. But I want you to see it.

He left work a few minutes early and walked across several neighborhoods. It was a week into November, and he was glad for the cool temperatures and the opportunity to move at full speed. He ended up in North Lawndale, a part of Chicago that the city government had not only neglected but treated badly for a hundred years. William looked around at the sagging housing and remembered walking through this area the night before he'd tried to kill himself. He'd had no idea where he was at the time—he'd known only the terrain close to Northwestern in those years—and he'd seen Charlie. William smiled at the memory of his father-in-law appearing in a doorway. Charlie had been deemed a failure in his lifetime, but almost thirty years after his death, his daughters' love for him ran so deep that he could be considered the most successful person William had ever known. People still came up to Sylvie in the library, after all this time, to tell her about a kind thing her father had done for them. Sylvie, Cecelia, and Emeline had told Izzy so many stories about her grandfather that she could probably win a trivia contest about the paper-factory worker who'd died when he was close to the age William was now. All the memories Sylvie wrote about her family focused on either her father or her older sister, as the two cornerstones of her being.

The address turned out to be a playground. There was a beat-up basketball court, a set of swings, and a climbing structure that was in terrible shape. Several teenage boys were playing three-on-three on the court. One of them spotted William and called out, "Hey, Coach! What are you doing here?"

William waved his arm in greeting—the boy was part of Arash's clinic—and shrugged. The rectangular playground wasn't full, because of the hour and the time of year, but kids wandered in small groups and several girls were perched on top of the jungle gym as if it were their nest. When William reached the center of the space, he turned around in a circle, not sure what he was looking for, until he saw it. A giant mural was painted against the back wall. William walked in that direction and took a seat on a bench that offered a good view. He examined the lower corner and saw the CP flourish, which was how Cecelia signed her work. A handful of young boys ran around William's bench, gulping with laughter, and then sped off in different directions.

The mural showed roughly twenty kids standing together, as if for a school photo. The children were smiling brightly in unison, suggesting the photographer had just told them a joke. William ran his eyes along the top row of kids; this was a habit, because he had always been put in the back row of every picture growing up. At the end of the back row stood a white girl with blond-brown hair, wearing a shy smile. William stopped breathing for a moment. The little girl's face looked exactly like his own as a ten-year-old. She couldn't be anyone other than his daughter. It was Alice. He continued to move his eyes, like a typewriter spitting out words, unable to take in what he'd just seen. William studied the middle row, where one beaming child stood beside another. These kids looked like younger versions of the boys and girls in Arash's clinic, and they might have been, since many of the players lived in this neighborhood. At the end of the bottom row, there was a redheaded girl—brighter than all the other children, probably because she had recently been painted onto the wall. Cecelia had taken care to blend her in and had updated some of the lines in the rest of the mural, so Caroline didn't stick out. But still, with her red hair and excited grin, she looked the most alive, the most keen to leap off the wall and run toward the swings.

William sat on the bench for a long time. He had a flash of anger at Cecelia for tricking him into taking in the visage of his daughter, but the anger was gone as fast as it had come. He made himself look at Alice and Caroline. He made himself look without wincing, without fear that he would extinguish their light and beauty with his gaze. This was the first time he'd ever given his daughter his full attention. Parents shaped their kids; he knew that better than anyone, and he realized now that he must have shaped Alice by his absence, by his silence, even though he'd intended to save her by the same means. This realization was a personal blow, and he said, "I'm sorry," out loud. His premises had been wrong, and he wondered what else he'd been wrong about.

William knew already that he would visit this wall again, many times. He'd assumed that Cecelia would paint his sister alone, because she usually did individual portraits, but he was grateful that she'd placed his lost sister and lost daughter together. The two girls would exist for as long as this wall stood, in the same neighborhood William had wandered through when he was at his lowest point. The fact that he'd also seen Charlie in this neighborhood didn't feel like a coincidence, either. Sylvie had written once about Emeline being stuck in a tree when she was a kid and refusing to come down until her father pointed his tractor beam of love at her. Charlie would have chosen this area of the city to haunt so that he could keep loving his family. He would spend his endless days in this playground, admiring his daughter's art, reading poetry to the two little girls and lighting them up with his affection.

William shook his head, amazed that he could believe in children keeping each other company in a painting and a dead man locomoting through Chicago. As a younger man, he'd believed in very little, and without his noticing, that had changed. William also used to worry about what he did and did not deserve, but no one around him seemed to think in these terms, and it turned out that he no longer did either. He texted his sister-in-law Thank you, and she replied <3. William frowned at his phone, confused, before realizing that Cecelia had sent him back a heart.

Sylvie

NOVEMBER 2008

SYLVIE AND JULIA WALKED DOWN THE SIDEWALK, PAST A RICKETY diner and a taqueria. This was Julia's second visit, which took place only ten days after her first. She sighed and said, "I did something."

Sylvie noticed that her sister still looked tired but also calmer, like a knot had unraveled under her skin. "That's exciting," she said.

"Sure," Julia said in a dry tone. "Very exciting. I did something to try to fix the situation with Alice. I had to mess everything up, though, in order to do it, and now she's angry at me. She might be too angry to ever forgive me."

Sylvie said, "She knows you love her."

"More than anything."

"Then it will probably work out."

Julia made a sour face. "I've always hated the word *probably*." She looked upward, as if checking the street signs, then said, "I had everything under control while Alice was young. I mean it. Everything. It was beautiful. I wasn't prepared for Alice to grow up, though. I don't know why."

Sylvie stopped walking. They were across the street from an old movie theater they'd frequented as children, where they'd seen *Willy Wonka & the Chocolate Factory*, *Star Wars*, and the Buster Keaton films their father had loved. "Hey, let's see a movie," she said.

Julia squinted at the list of titles on the marquee. "I haven't seen a movie in a theater in years," she said. "I never have time."

The movie that was about to start was one neither of them had heard of, but they purchased two tickets anyway. They bought giant tubs of popcorn with extra butter and two massive sodas. Once they were settled in their plush seats, Sylvie looked down and wondered what the popcorn would taste like. Food and drink were beginning to switch up their flavor profiles in her mouth. A donut might taste bitter, even though it was glazed with sugar. Her coffee that morning had tasted like it was doused with maple syrup, even though she hadn't added any sweetener. Sylvie placed one piece of popcorn in her mouth, tentatively, and was relieved to find that it tasted the same as it had her entire life. Salty and crunchy. This was because she was with Julia, she decided, in this time outside both their real lives. Sylvie's headaches had recently become more frequent and intense, but she hadn't had one with Julia by her side; it made sense that with her sister she would also briefly be allowed her normal taste buds.

Sylvie knew she should tell William that she had been reunited with Julia, and she would tell him, soon. These visits with Julia reminded her, though, of the weeks when Sylvie and William's love had been confined to his dorm room, before Kent found them out. At that time, Sylvie and William had assured each other that what they were doing was less a secret than a delay—a few precious stolen moments—before real life, with its inherent complications, intervened. During those private weeks, she and William had breathed air dense with every molecule of their love and their joy at having found each other. Sylvie felt all of these emotions, this magical alchemy, with her sister now. Sylvie had experienced two great loves in her life, after all: her sisters first, and then William. Sylvie could feel something significant happening inside herself now: She was tying together who she'd been in the first half of her life with who she had become. She was stitching her life and heart together, and she wanted to keep it all before her: a beautiful whole.

Next week, Sylvie thought. *I'll tell him next week.* She knew this delay and her reasons were technically both bullshit *and* secrets by the terms of her husband's mantra, but she told herself that the mantra was for the living. She was dying, which meant she could sit next to Julia right now and lie in William's arms tonight.

The movie turned out to be about car racing and was clearly intended for teenagers. Sylvie laughed whenever a car was about to flip over, while the people around her gasped. She had the realization that she could respond to any stimulus however she wanted. If something sad happened, she didn't have to cry. In the midst of a climactic scene involving a ten-car pileup, she reached over and held Julia's hand. They hadn't touched until now. They'd both been careful not to, because it felt like a parameter that kept them in this liminal place where they got to see each other without it counting. It was the bumpers on the strange bowling lane they were playing within. But Sylvie was running out of time, and she was no longer interested in parameters and rules—even the ones she'd made up.

She felt Julia stiffen for a split second, then relax. She didn't pull away, and in the dark of the movie theater, the two sisters were ageless. They were ten, and thirteen, and in their forties. Julia was absolutely confident that she could design her own destiny, and Sylvie opened herself to books and the boys who came into the library. There were so many moments, piled on top of one another, and the long period when they had turned away from each other, for better and for worse.

Sylvie thought, *This is worth dying for.*

A driver with a firm jawline and shocking blue eyes drove in a neat figure eight to avoid an accident. The teenagers in the audience hooted, Sylvie smiled, and Julia held on to her hand. Sylvie thought of the novel she had just started—a classic she'd put off for years, but she no longer had time to put anything off—in which the main character fell asleep while reading, and when he woke, with his brain still foggy, he thought he *was* what he had been reading about: a horse, or the rivalry between two kings, or a chalet. Sylvie liked this idea, and since she'd read the line, she had been reimagining herself. She was Julia's wild hair, she was the lake her husband had once been carried out of, and no matter what happened next, she was love.

———

AFTER HER DIAGNOSIS, SYLVIE had started accompanying Cecelia and Emeline on their biweekly trips to the big box store to buy the enormous amounts of toilet paper, paper towels, ziplock bags, baby formula, and seltzer water needed at the super-duplex. Cecelia owned a car now, a lemon-yellow sedan, so they no longer had to borrow a neighbor's vehicle for their drives. Sylvie didn't need anything from the store, of course; she and William didn't require tremendous amounts of anything for their two-person household. But she liked to ride with her sisters; it reminded her of when they were young and the three of them would drive home from Julia's apartment and talk. She liked looking out the window and watching her city hurry by. She brought a book and read in the car while the twins shopped, and on the return trip she shared the back seat with paper products. She felt no guilt for not telling her younger sisters that she had seen Julia. They would have plenty of time with their older sister after Sylvie was gone. She also didn't think they would be upset at having been left out—not much, anyway. They would understand what Sylvie had needed and be pleased that she'd been lucky enough to reconcile her heart.

On the way home from the store, Cecelia always drove past the playground where the portraits of Alice and Caroline were painted. The sisters stayed in the car; the sedan slowed, and they looked out the windows at the artwork. Sylvie loved the mural, loved that William had asked Cecelia to paint his sister into existence. On their way back to Pilsen late one afternoon, Sylvie almost told Cecelia not to take that route, because she could feel a headache coming on and wanted to get home. But she didn't say anything, and Cecelia drove into North Lawndale, slowing the car in its usual spot. Sylvie turned to look out the window and inhaled deeply, because William was in the playground. Her tall, fair-haired husband was seated on a bench in front of the mural. Only the back of his head and shoulders were visible, but it was unmistakably him.

"Is that . . . ?" Emeline said.

Sylvie nodded; Cecelia had recognized him too, and the car inched to a halt. The three sisters watched William take in Caroline and Alice. He was sitting very still on the bench, and the mild slope of his shoulders told Sylvie that he was calm.

When happiness came at Sylvie these days, it took over her whole body, and she felt flushed with pleasure now to be sitting with her sisters, in front of this view. She didn't want William to see her, and in a minute or two she would tell Cecelia to drive away. But the pinch of worry that had existed in Sylvie's heart ever since she'd found out she was sick started, for the first time, to ease. She was leaving William, but he had this park, this bench, this painting, and his presence here meant that he was no longer looking away from the babies he'd walked away from. He was contemplating the two girls, which meant the doors that had long been closed inside him might be opening, which meant William might be okay without his wife. He was gaining ground, not just losing it.

Alice

DURING HER WORKDAYS, ALICE'S PHONE BUZZED IN HER POCKET every few hours. The texts were from her mother. Julia had sent her at least twenty texts since their dinner in the Greek restaurant. The texts, no matter what they said, made Alice feel tired. But she liked how they were stacking up inside her phone as a kind of documentation of her mother losing her mind. Initially, the texts were incoherent apologies or explanations.

I'm sorry, but I had reasons.

Can we just meet for a few minutes to talk?

I love you I love you I love you. I thought not telling you was the best thing for both of us.

I was afraid that you would want to go to your father if you knew he was alive. I convinced myself that if you went to Chicago to see him, you would choose to live with him and Sylvie. They would have given you a normal family, with a mother and a father. I know this sounds crazy, but I was a little crazy at the time.

You must have questions, which I can try to answer.

I miss your voice.

Alice did have questions, but she wasn't going to ask her mother or grandmother for answers. Her mother had manipulated her with silences for her entire life. Closed-off conversations, deflected questions. She'd left Alice to guess and strategize without any of the necessary facts. They'd both lied to her—Rose perhaps by omission—and weren't trustworthy sources of information.

When Alice had left the Greek restaurant and her mother that night, she'd walked all the way from the Upper West Side to the Brooklyn apartment she shared with Carrie. It was a one-bedroom, with a pullout couch in the living room. The official arrangement was that the two women alternated weeks in the bedroom. There was some flexibility to this if Carrie was sleeping at a date's apartment, or if one of them was too tired to pull out the couch, they would sleep together in the double bed. When Alice walked in, Carrie was already in her pajamas, writing in a journal on the couch bed; it was her week there. She looked like the grown version of the little girl Alice had befriended in kindergarten: petite, with large blue eyes and a brown pixie haircut. Alice, because of how she had stretched and grown over the years, no longer resembled her kindergarten self at all.

Carrie took Alice in from head to toe and said, "Clearly something enormous has happened." She stood and, as if she were preparing to boil water and gather towels, asked, "What do you need?"

Alice stood by the door until she'd told Carrie everything. Then she dropped her backpack and coat on the floor, tugged off her low boots, and curled up on the sofa bed. She hugged her knees to her chest, and Carrie rubbed her back.

"You have a dad," Carrie said, with wonder in her voice.

"Kind of? He isn't my father legally. He didn't want me." Alice's hair was over her face; she spoke into a light-colored curtain.

"Only your mother could keep a secret like this for twenty-five years." Carrie told strangers intimate details of her life minutes after meeting them and had always found Julia's composure baffling. Once, when they were teenagers and Carrie was sleeping over at their apartment, Carrie had asked Julia when she'd lost her virginity. Alice and Carrie had watched something happen inside Julia that made her face turn a light shade of purple, and then she'd said she needed to make a work call—at nine o'clock on a Friday evening—and left the room.

"She could have kept this secret forever." Alice looked at Carrie. "I think she was trying to hurt me with it. She looked . . . I don't know, a little excited."

"About what it might do to you?" Carrie said.

Alice nodded. She felt tears pressing the backs of her eyes. "I don't see why how I choose to live my life, which doesn't hurt anyone, bothers her so much."

"Oh, Alice," Carrie said.

"I like having a simple life." Alice could feel all the stray threads inside her; the tiny scissors had cut through every one. "I don't like to . . . feel so much."

"I know." Carrie was quiet for a minute, then said, "I've been keeping my mouth shut about you and your mom, as much as I could, forever. You know that."

Alice nodded, already resigned to whatever was coming. "Go ahead," she said. "Say whatever you want."

Carrie set her face; she took this permission, this opportunity, seriously. "Okay, here's what I think happened. From my vantage point, you sealed yourself up, probably right after your mom told you that your dad died. The only people you loved before that news—that lie, as it turns out—are still the only people you love with all your heart. The only people you let yourself love. Me, your mom, and your grandmother. I feel like when we were kids, sometimes you almost opened yourself up. Remember you had a crush on that boy with the spiky hair when we were in middle school? But then you closed down completely. You have the best heart, and you don't use it. Your mom is responsible for that. It's like she raised you to be a Navy SEAL or something, with a completely unusual skill set. Julia's even more responsible than I thought, since she freaking *lied* to you for your whole life. She's obviously realizing that now and wants to try to undo her mistakes."

"I don't need to be undone." Alice felt her own stubbornness, like a bump in the carpet, but didn't care. "I wish she hadn't told me."

Carrie leaned over and kissed Alice's cheek. She looked brighter, like a cleaned lantern, after being allowed to deliver the speech she'd been suppressing for years. "Julia did tell you, though, and this is exciting too, you know? Your dad is alive. You can go meet him and ask him why he did what he did. You have all his genes, after all. You can go meet this tall man."

"I have to figure out the timeline before I can consider that," Alice said. "I have to find out what happened in Chicago. I don't know anything, Carrie."

Carrie eyed her. She knew how Alice worked. The two friends were opposites in many ways, but they both were deliberate about how they lived, wouldn't tolerate assholes, and always had each other's back. "How can I help?" she said.

"You can sit with me while I Google him," Alice said. "And give me time to process everything. There's no rush."

The two young women stayed up until four o'clock in the morning on the sofa bed. It was difficult work, because there was a ringing noise in Alice's ears, she had a hard time reading the sentences on the computer screen, and the images were overwhelming. Her father was the head physio for the Chicago Bulls, so there were numerous photos of him online. There were a few pictures of him in conversation with basketball players, presumably about injuries. He was in staff photos too, with thirty other men wearing identical polo shirts. There was only one photo from earlier in his life, from Northwestern University. It was a shot of the college basketball team, and he was standing at the end of a row wearing a jersey but normal pants, and he was on crutches.

"He's super cute in this photo," Carrie said. In the more-recent photos, he looked not only older but worn, like a rock on the beach. She peered closer. "It's from 1982. So, the year before you were born."

Alice nodded. She felt slightly drunk, even though she'd had nothing to drink except a few gallons of water at the restaurant. She and Carrie both fell asleep at some point, and since the next day was a Saturday, no alarms went off, and they didn't wake until late morning. Alice had a headache, but she also felt relieved, as if a burden had been lifted from her. It wasn't until she was eating breakfast that it occurred to her that she'd muffled her questions and avoided looking for answers her entire life, in deference to her mother. She no longer had to do that. She could ask anyone anything she wanted. This made her smile so widely she felt it in her cheeks, and Carrie looked up from her bowl of cereal and smiled in return.

Alice wondered what this might mean. What were her questions? What did she want to know? What did she want to say? She'd never considered these possibilities before; it felt like she'd been wearing blinders and they'd been removed. The horizon was endless, in every direction. There was a knock at their door; it was Rhoan.

"Carrie filled me in." He sat down at the kitchen table, as if joining a meeting already in progress. "Alice—this makes so much sense. I always felt like you were waiting for something, like you had your ear to the ground and didn't want to move in case you missed it. I thought you were waiting for some dude, but this is much cooler."

"Exactly," Carrie said.

"I'm going to put my almost-PhD to use. I'm a world-class researcher, you know. We're going to help you find every scrap of information there is about these people."

Alice started to object, but Rhoan waved a large hand. "Do you know how happy we are to have the chance to help you? You *never* let us help you. You always say you're fine. You have no drama queen in you, Alice Padavano, but this is a goddamn *drama*."

"I don't like drama," Alice said, to her plate.

"We know. But having the chance to help you makes me so happy I could cry."

"I am crying," Carrie said, and she was.

"I know this is hard," Rhoan said. "But let us take care of you, okay?"

Alice put her hands to her face and laughed. With all the threads cut inside her, there was no way for her to resist. She could feel her friends' love pushing past her skin, into her body, and she cried too.

"This table," she said, as something occurred to her. "This was our kitchen table when I was growing up. When I was five, we were sitting at this table when my mom told me that my father was dead."

"Whoa," Carrie said.

"There's history everywhere," Rhoan said. "I fucking love that."

He worked in a research library, and a week later he handed her a folder of photos and biographical data on William Waters and the three other Padavano sisters. He'd found better, less-blurred photos of her father, and Alice's resemblance to him was remarkable. Thin, tall, same colorless hair, same eyes. There was a newspaper notice about William and Julia's wedding. Julia was described as a future homemaker in the piece, and William was in graduate school to become a history professor. The photo was a close-up from their wedding day: Julia was beautiful, in a shimmering white gown. William wore a fancy suit, and his smile looked obedient beside Julia's radiant one. Alice studied the photograph, amazed at how happy her mother looked; there was no evidence of whatever misery would drive her out of the marriage and then out of Chicago sixteen months later.

There was information on William's college degree, his single year of a graduate program in history, a completed master's degree in sports physiology, and his job history. The notes detailed two hospitalizations, once for knee surgery during college, and then again in 1983—when Alice would have been a baby—in a psychiatric hospital. His mental illness was presumably why her parents had divorced and why her father had given her up. She and her mother had arrived in New York City right around when William Waters was in the hospital.

While she was leafing through the folder, her mother texted her: Can you tell me what it means in literature when a person loses their shadow? I feel like I remember Peter Pan stealing Wendy's shadow?

She showed the text to Carrie. Carrie said, "Things are definitely getting interesting in your mother's head. Are you going to answer?"

"No. Check this out: I have a cousin who's less than a year older than me. Isabella. Cecelia had a daughter. She looks like all the Padavanos except me."

They were at the kitchen table. They'd just eaten spaghetti, one of the only meals Alice was able to prepare that tasted good. This was her go-to meal to cook; Carrie's was a salad into which she put everything she could find, with mixed results.

"Did you finish copyediting that sad novel?"

"The *Little Women* one? Yes."

"Then it's time to go to Chicago," Carrie said. "You can take some days off work. And you have all the information there is in that folder."

"There might be more," Alice said. Her body felt heavy, as though it were rooted to the chair. She searched the room for a distraction, but none appeared. All she could see was hand-me-down furniture and a sink full of dishes that needed to be cleaned. She said, "Carrie, he doesn't want to meet me. He never wanted anything to do with me."

Carrie looked at her with her wide eyes.

"Don't cry," Alice said, in warning.

"I won't. Listen. He made that decision a long time ago, when he was in a terrible emotional place. He might feel entirely differently now. He might have spent the last twenty-five years regretting giving you up. Or Julia might be lying to you about some part of this story. Hell, Julia might have paid your dad to stay away. Rhoan can't find those kinds of answers in old newspapers. You have to go there and ask him."

Go there, Alice thought. She had done very little traveling in her life. She was familiar with the four-hour drive to Boston. And she'd visited Rose in Florida. But she'd turned down the option to study abroad and had never understood why people left New York City. This was her home, and surely nowhere else could compete.

"You're a grown-up," Carrie said. "You're twenty-five years old. You don't *need* a dad. You just have to meet him and ask him what's what, so you can move on with your own life."

Alice listened to her friend talk and tried to take the words in, but the ideas of going to Chicago to meet her father and moving on with her life were at odds. She was in her life now; simply boarding that plane would detonate the safe, careful, calm young woman she'd been constructing since she was a child.

William

THERE WERE A FEW THINGS THAT WILLIAM KNEW WITHOUT being told. He knew that Kent had called his psychiatrist, to make sure William's medications were airtight, and that his psychiatrist scrutinized him during their sessions with a new level of concern. William could feel Kent's worry too, a presence that had existed at different levels since the two men had met. When Nicole had moved out of her and Kent's townhouse during the divorce, William slept in the guest room for a few nights so Kent wouldn't go from married to completely alone. He'd been grateful for the chance to help his friend during that period. When Kent had apologized for his sadness, William told him that it was a relief to direct some worry at him after so many years of feeling it pointed at himself. On the other side of the divorce, even though Kent had regained his enthusiasm and love of life, the giant doctor was still a bit weary, and William felt that too. He hated that his friend had to resume the duty of standing guard over his depression.

William also knew that he was the reason Julia was staying away from Chicago. With him in Sylvie's life, Julia wouldn't budge, even though Sylvie deserved her older sister's devotion. And finally, he knew that Sylvie had lost weight over the previous weeks. She hadn't said anything, but she was smaller, and she was always cold.

He made dinner every night now, trying to cater to Sylvie's diminishing appetite. He roasted chickpeas with extra salt to accompany their meals, because he knew she would eat those. He stocked mint chocolate chip ice cream in the freezer and went out first thing every morning to buy fresh donuts. Sylvie smiled when he offered her a granola bar or nudged the bowl of chickpeas in her direction. She saw what he was doing; she always had, after all.

During dinner one night, she said, "I'm sorry. I know I'm not talking much lately."

"That's okay," he said. "You're tired."

"It's more that . . ." She paused, as if searching for words. "Everything is so rich inside me now . . . that it holds my attention. You know the Mark Twain quote about how the only reason for time is so everything doesn't happen at once? I feel like everything that's ever happened in my life is happening inside me. I'm never bored anymore. I think about everyone and everything. I'm with you now, and you're with me in here too." She pointed at her head. "My dad is here too. He and I are in the back of the grocer's."

William nodded, to show that he was listening more than that he understood. He knew he probably couldn't understand. "Is that nice?"

She considered this and nodded. "It's nice."

They went straight to bed after William put the dinner dishes in the dishwasher. Sylvie needed lots of sleep, so they no longer spent an hour or two of their evenings on the couch, reading and watching basketball. After they made love that night, they slept naked, for the first time since they were young. They were dismantling their habits and routines, and it was like pulling up floorboards and finding joy underneath.

Before they fell asleep, Sylvie said, "Oh, I did want to tell you something." She propped herself up on an elbow. "I'm proud of myself."

The surprise in her voice, and the unexpectedness of the comment, made William laugh.

She smiled. "It's just, I didn't expect to be. When you and I got together, I thought I was going to hate myself, a little bit, forever. Because if I was a good person, I would have stayed away from you. Stayed miserable. But when I made this choice . . ." Sylvie paused, and

William realized that she was doing that more and more. Words seemed to be harder for her to reach, like fruit in the highest branches of a tree.

"It's hard to explain, but our love was so deep and wide that it made me love everyone and everything in sight. Which included me." She smiled wider. "I know it sounds silly, but I'm proud of myself. I guess for living a brave life."

William nodded, unable to speak for a second. "You should be proud," he said.

She closed her eyes, the smile still on her face. She fell asleep quickly, and William lay awake for a long time in the dark bedroom. He listened to his wife breathe. Was he proud of himself? William had never considered this before. Maybe he'd felt that way a handful of times, for fleeting moments. When he truly helped a struggling player; when he spotted a problem no one else had seen and found a solution. He searched inside himself and realized, with surprise, that he was proud of himself for calling Julia.

He remembered kissing Sylvie for the first time in his dorm room and how their love had stayed in that room during the first few months they were together. In a way, William never stopped containing their love, cupping it in his hands. He'd felt safer that way. He'd known he couldn't lose Sylvie's love if he knew where it was. His wife *had* been brave—she'd been the one to lose Julia and hurt the twins—but William had never risked anything. He'd been an eternal coward, scared of what he might lose.

But when Sylvie became sick, the worst thing that could have happened was already happening. He'd had to open himself in order to protect her. William reached out to his first wife for help, and just making that request—across the quarter century that separated them—had made him vulnerable not only to Julia but to a reckoning with the broken man he'd been during their time together. He'd always assumed openness was synonymous with danger and that if he wasn't holding on tight to the new life he'd built, it would blow away. But with the barriers down, he'd discovered that life became bigger. A hidden photograph transformed into a mural. Alice and Caroline stood within arm's reach of each other. His father-in-law had found a way to shine his affection across distance and time. And Sylvie's love, once William let it out of his hands, had shown itself to be exponential in its power. It had expanded to fill all the space around him, which was his entire life.

Alice

THE CHEAPEST FLIGHT TO CHICAGO LEFT AT SIX A.M., SO RHOAN borrowed his brother's car early that morning, and he and Carrie drove Alice to the airport. She knew that if they hadn't, she wouldn't have made her way there on her own. She felt strange and heavy-limbed, after two weeks without speaking to her mother, knowing that she had a father. She needed her friends' hands on her back. Carrie had offered to travel to Chicago with her, but Alice knew she had to do this by herself.

She wouldn't let them hug her goodbye. "I'll be back tomorrow," she said.

"You can always change your ticket and stay longer," Carrie said.

"I want you to go there and show those people what they've been missing," Rhoan said. "They're your family. Don't be afraid to tell them off if necessary. But don't be afraid to smile either."

Alice walked through the airport, wearing her gray backpack. She followed the instructions of the flight attendants while boarding the plane and closed her eyes for the duration of the flight. She couldn't bear for anyone to speak to her, even to offer a beverage. Alice squeezed the armrests and was aware of every bounce of the plane, every small disruption of the air and space she occupied.

At O'Hare, a giant, labyrinthine airport with cathedral-like glass ceilings, Alice waited in the taxi queue and then gave the driver the address for the Bulls practice facility in downtown Chicago. She tried to pay attention to the city as the car crossed the river and entered a thicket of tall buildings. Elevated trains rattled above the car. There didn't seem to be as many people on the sidewalks as in New York. She'd hoped to see murals, maybe even Cecelia's, but in this part of the city, the walls were blank.

Alice thought, *This is where my mother grew up. This is where I'll meet my father.* She felt alone almost as a physical sensation: Her skin tingled as if she hadn't been touched in days. She found that she could barely remember the sound of her mother's voice, and this panicked her. Being here made Alice feel like she'd left Julia behind in some way that was important and permanent. She texted her mother for the first time since the night in the Greek restaurant: A shadow represents either the blocking out of light or the other half of a person. When a character loses their shadow, they've lost a part of themselves and have to search to get it back.

The taxi came to a stop. Alice paid and climbed out of the car. She knew she couldn't stand still or allow herself to think. She pulled open the glass door in front of her and walked into a large foyer. She could hear the thumping of basketballs in the distance, and there were a few extremely tall men sitting on couches in the corner, their knees raised high. An older man with a whistle around his neck walked past her, and he was close to seven feet tall. Alice had a strange realization that she was in a place where people wouldn't find her height of any interest; this building was populated with giants.

She walked up to the desk. A young man looked up from his computer. He blinked at her and then said, "How can I . . ." He paused. "Ma'am, you look just like one of our physios."

"William Waters?" Alice said.

He nodded. "It's uncanny."

"Can I see him, please?"

"I don't think he's come in yet. He should be here any minute, though. Do you want to take a seat and wait?"

She nodded and walked across the foyer to where the couches were. She realized, as she sat down, that the furniture was unusually high off the ground, built for oversized humans. Alice tried her best to appear calm and relaxed and not to look startled every time the front door opened, which was often. After fifteen minutes, she texted Carrie: How long do I wait?

The reply came: A long time.

After thirty minutes, the young man from the front desk walked over and said, "I'm sorry this is taking so long. William's usually right on time. I left a message on his cellphone, letting him know you were here. I'm sure he'll arrive soon."

Alice nodded her thanks and wondered, while he walked away, how he'd described her in the voicemail. Had he said, *A tall woman who looks like you is here?* Or, *The daughter you never wanted has shown up?*

An hour passed, and her stomach grumbled. It was almost lunchtime, and she'd woken up well before dawn, too nervous to eat. She saw the pitying looks the people who worked there were giving her. She thought, *I'm an idiot. He clearly knows I'm here and isn't coming for that reason. They all feel bad for me.*

She texted Carrie: In ten minutes, I'm leaving.

Her friend wrote right back. You can leave that building, but you're not leaving Chicago. You committed to twenty-four hours there. Your ticket is for tomorrow. Call one of your aunts. See someone.

Alice considered this. She wanted, more than anything, to go back to the airport. Back to her safe, comfortable life. She had done the brave thing by coming here, and it hadn't worked out. But what Carrie had said about Alice sealing herself off after losing her father at the age of five had rung true. She had been wrapped up in her mother's hair; she'd imbibed her mother's control with her morning glass of orange juice as a child. She was twenty-five years old, and she had never been in love, never had sex. She'd been kissed once, by a drunken boy at a college party, but she had never kissed. She liked her safe life, but she could see how she might need to open some windows, if only to show herself that she could.

"I'm sorry, miss." The young man was in front of her again. "I tried to contact his colleague Kent too, because William is often with him, but his phone also went to voicemail. I hate to see you wait here. How about you give me your cell number and then go about your day? I can contact you when William turns up."

Alice wrote her cellphone number on the pad of paper the man handed her and thanked him. She walked out of the building with her head high, as if she weren't embarrassed, as if she knew what she was going to do next. It turned out that she did, once she was in the clear air of the sidewalk. She would call her aunt Cecelia, whose artwork wallpapered her bedroom and her dreams. Alice had her number—all the phone numbers, actually—from Rhoan's research.

While she listened to the phone ring, she thought, *If no one answers, I get to go back to the airport.* When a female voice said, "Hello?" Alice's heart sank.

"Is this Cecelia Padavano?" she said.

"No—this is Izzy. Are you calling from the hospital? Can I take a message? I'm her daughter."

"What?" Alice said. "No, I'm not calling from a hospital. I . . . uh . . . my name is Alice. Padavano. I think you're my cousin?"

A silence took over then, on both ends of the phone line. Alice sank into the quiet as if into the deep end of a pool, having no idea when or if she would reach the bottom. "Sweet Jesus," Izzy said finally. "Alice! Where are you? Are you in Chicago?"

Alice nodded, and then realized she had to speak. "Yes."

"Come here right now," Izzy said. "We need you. Come home."

Julia

J ULIA WAS IN HER OFFICE WHEN SHE GOT THE CALL. IT WAS after six and most of her employees were gone for the day; they'd become aware over the last few months that Julia's total attention to her work had wavered. They took advantage of her lapses with longer lunch hours and shorter work days. *I've noticed,* Julia wanted to tell them, but she didn't know what to say next, so she stayed quiet. She'd continued to play hooky herself, usually to spend the day alone in her apartment. She no longer expected her actions or thoughts to make complete sense. She glanced over her shoulder every day, wondering if the real Julia would catch up with her, her face dark with disappointment. *That* Julia had worked so hard for this particular kind of success, and *this* Julia was wondering if it had been worth it.

When her phone rang, she saw on the caller ID that it was a Chicago number. It wasn't Sylvie's cellphone, but it was possible her sister was calling her from the library or even from her home. She'd never done this before; Julia had texted Sylvie when she was on the way to the airport for their second visit, and that had been the extent of their communication when they weren't together. But Julia picked up the phone with a feeling of lightness, a sensation that she was about to be the only version of herself that she could stand these days—the Julia she was with Sylvie—and hear her sister's voice.

"Hello?" she said.

"It's Cecelia," the voice said, and Julia was confused for a moment, because Cecelia sounded like Sylvie and of course *was* her sister, but she hadn't spoken to either of the twins for a long time.

"Oh," Julia said, unable to keep the surprise out of her voice. "Hi. How are—"

Cecelia interrupted her. "I need to tell you something," she said. "Sylvie was sick. She had a brain tumor."

"I know." Julia's throat tightened around the words.

"How do you know? Did she tell you?"

"Why did you say it like that?" Julia didn't want to say, *In the past tense.* She listened while Cecelia told her that Sylvie had died suddenly that morning. William had gone out for twenty minutes, and she'd walked into the kitchen and collapsed. When he returned, he found her on the floor.

"I asked him what her expression was," Cecelia said. "I needed to know if she looked scared. He said she was lying on her side, and she looked like she'd gone to sleep."

Julia was aware of holding the phone to her ear. She had to concentrate to keep her grip on the receiver. Her earlier conversation, at this same desk, with William, seemed to sit on top of this one in a way that felt claustrophobic. *Sylvie is sick. Sylvie is dead.*

"It was too fast," Cecelia said, as if she'd heard her sister's thoughts. "We were supposed to have more time. I was going to call you when she got really sick and make you come home. I was going to do the same thing with Mom." She paused. "I called Mom to tell her, right before I called you."

"Mom," Julia said, as if she were naming an approaching storm. Rose would return to Chicago now. Sylvie's death would dislodge her from Florida; they would all be dislodged from everything they'd known before.

Cecelia sighed. "Emmie says I need to keep asking questions to deal with this at all, and she's probably right, but I spoke to the doctor at the hospital too, and he said the tumor had pressed against something in her brain—he said the name, I can't remember what he called it—which meant she would have died in a matter of seconds. She wouldn't have known what was happening."

Julia made herself say, "That's good."

She thought of the last time she had seen Sylvie, a week ago. They'd held hands while watching a movie. It was the first time they'd touched each other, and the energy that came with that contact, with all the years and selves that lay between them, all the love, had brought tears to Julia's eyes. It had almost felt like too much, to be holding her sister's hand while not speaking to her daughter, during an afternoon when she was not where she was supposed to be and yet somehow exactly where she belonged. Had Sylvie known she had only a few days left? Was that why she'd held Julia's hand and then hugged her when it was time for her to return to the airport? Julia could still feel the hug, the pressure of her sister's body against her own.

"Thank God Alice is here," Cecelia said. "I can't believe the timing, but it's such a gift to have her with us."

"Alice?" Julia wondered if she'd misheard. "Alice is in Chicago?"

"She got here this afternoon. Julia, she and Izzy loved each other right away. It was kind of incredible, as if they remembered being babies together." Cecelia stopped, and then said, "Are you listening to me?"

"I'm listening to you."

"You have to come home right now and stay with us."

Julia took a taxi to her apartment and packed a few items of clothing into a small bag. The last thing she added was the wrapped package Sylvie had handed her at the end of their visit. Julia had intended to head straight back to O'Hare after the movie, but Sylvie asked her to come to the library first so she could give her something. "Give it to me next time," Julia had said. Sylvie seemed to consider this, but she shook her head and said, "I should give it to you now." Julia buried the package at the bottom of her bag and returned to the airport. The trip to LaGuardia was familiar and had felt like freedom the two times she'd traveled there during the last month. Julia had unshackled herself from her history and identity and flown to her sister's side. She'd felt, each time, like she was heading toward herself. In the air between New York and Chicago now, Julia knew that all three of her sisters were parts of her. They had grown up together, and for a long time they beat with one heart. Reunited with Sylvie, Julia had felt more alive, more whole.

She'd thought during her life in New York that she'd become her father's rocket, but that identity had felt more true when she was sitting across from Sylvie in a Chicago bar, considering how she could help her daughter. Under her sister's gaze, Julia felt like she had when she'd first arrived in New York City: fizzing with possibility, the panels that held her together shaking with excitement and fear. Now it seemed clear that she'd built a rocket in New York, had burnished and shined the vehicle but kept it on the ground. To be the rocket, she had to be with her sisters, and she had to set her daughter free.

Julia accepted a drink from the flight attendant and tried to imagine Alice in her home city. The idea was perplexing, as if a finished puzzle had been presented with another piece and there was nowhere to fit it in. The image of Alice hovered above the Chicago map in Julia's mind, not because her daughter was in the wrong place, but because Julia had removed her baby from that scene a long time ago and sealed all the entrances and exits. She felt a sharp relief, though, that Alice knew the truth about her father. Sylvie would have approved of Julia's honesty, even though it had arrived late. The thought of her sister's approval fish-hooked Julia's heart, and she had to close her eyes because of the pain. All of her choices, from now on, would be unknown by Sylvie.

When the plane landed at O'Hare, it was after eleven, and Julia decided to sleep in the airport hotel. She knew the twins were expecting her, but she felt an almost physical need to stay outside the city, and her past, and Sylvie's death, for just a few more hours. She texted Cecelia that she would be at their place in the morning and fell asleep with her arms wrapped around herself. In her dreams, she tried to catch up with Sylvie, who was a few steps ahead of her on the streets of Pilsen. In the morning, she drank an enormous coffee during the taxi ride into Chicago. Sylvie had told her about the twins' double house. It felt now like Sylvie had tried to prepare Julia for the time when coming home wouldn't be secret. She had re-familiarized Julia with Pilsen—shown her Cecelia's murals, told her about Izzy, and explained how Sylvie, the twins, and her niece all trafficked through one another's days to an extent that required knocking down fences and sharing homes. Sylvie had prepared Julia for when she wouldn't be there but everyone else would.

The twins, Julia knew, had complicated feelings toward her. They'd struggled over the many years with the limits Julia had imposed on their communication. Cecelia and Emeline had started off deeply sympathetic to her when Sylvie and William first fell in love. But they'd clearly expected and wanted Julia to soften her stance over time, and she never had. *Emeline and I didn't do a damn thing wrong,* Cecelia had written on a postcard once. *Let us see Alice. Let us see you. We could go on vacation somewhere, take a trip together, do something that has nothing to do with Chicago or New York.* Julia had read that postcard standing on a street corner, the avenue beside her strangely quiet in a city that was always loud. She remembered beginning to consider this idea, this opening, and then shaking her head no. She felt unable to bear any compromise. She had closed the valve to her past—to her heart, really—and a half-open valve was a broken one.

Julia would see William today too, for the first time since he'd handed her a note and a check and walked out of their apartment. That had taken place in what felt like another lifetime, and Julia had been a different person. When she thought of William now, she found that she didn't remember his phone call from a few months earlier or the end of their marriage. She remembered him coming out of the gym after basketball practice, young and healthy and handsome. She remembered tugging his coat lapels in the cold, asking him to kiss her. She remembered their youth and their ignorance of who they were and what they really wanted.

When she knocked on the door of Emeline's house, her hands were shaking, because she knew Sylvie wouldn't be on the other side of this door. At their father's wake, a young paper-factory worker had said, *It's impossible he's gone.* And that man had been right—that had been an impossible loss. Sylvie was an impossible loss too. But perhaps what felt impossible was leaving that person behind. When your love for a person is so profound that it's part of who you are, then the absence of the person becomes part of your DNA, your bones, and your skin.

Charlie's and Sylvie's deaths were now part of Julia's topography; the losses ran like a river inside her. She had been an idiot to stay away for so long, to give up time with her sister. Julia had experienced the beginning and the very end of Sylvie's life, and that wasn't enough.

The door opened to reveal Emeline and Cecelia. Her little sisters, who were now in their mid-forties, with fine lines next to their eyes. Julia became breathless at the sight of them. She had tried to do her best, but for the last twenty-five years she'd done it alone, and of course—she realized now—that could never have worked. When she'd told Emeline that she was leaving Chicago, her sister had said: *You need us with you. You might not realize that, but you do. We need each other.*

She heard herself say, as if it were a greeting, "I'm sorry."

"Oh, baby girl," Emeline said.

Julia hugged both women at the same time, her face buried in their hair. The sisters held one another, breathing into this three-person structure, trying to find a new kind of stability, even if just for one moment.

William

WILLIAM DIDN'T ARGUE WHEN KENT CAME HOME WITH HIM from the hospital. There was nothing William could have said to make his friend leave him alone. In the hospital, while William sat in a chair in the waiting room, waiting to hear from the doctor not if Sylvie could be saved, because she couldn't, but what had happened, Emeline had held his hand. No one but his wife had held his hand for a long time, and this gesture from his sister-in-law was one of the ways he knew Sylvie really was gone. Cecelia was on her feet most of the day, trying to get information from any nurse or doctor who made the mistake of glancing in her direction. Kent paced the room too. Beside William, Emeline cried in an undramatic, unembarrassed way. Her cheeks shone with tears under the fluorescent lights. She said, "I want to make you eat, but I know you don't want to."

"I don't want to."

That night, turning the key in the apartment door hurt. It yawned open and revealed the landscape of his happiness. William had walked through this door eleven hours earlier with a box of donuts in his hand, and he'd smiled to himself because even though he'd been gone less than half an hour, he was looking forward to seeing Sylvie. Now Kent stood by his arm, and William didn't go near the kitchen. He wouldn't go into the bedroom either. He told Kent he would sleep in his clothes on the couch, and his friend nodded. Kent got him a glass of water and handed him a pill. "This will let you sleep," he said, and William swallowed it.

The next morning he woke, groggy, and slid his feet to the floor. He sat up, a movement that required all the energy he had. He looked in the direction of the landscape Cecelia had painted but couldn't take it in. He inhaled and exhaled air that tasted like dread. He didn't want to inhabit a day without Sylvie, and yet here he was.

Kent said, "Where are your pills?" and William told him. He took the daily medication Kent put in his hand.

"Things have to be decided," Kent said. "About the funeral. We're going to go to the twins' houses." He hesitated. "I had some messages on my phone last night from work. Are you listening to me?" Kent's tone was gentle.

William looked at him.

"Apparently, Alice showed up at the facility yesterday. To see you."

"Alice?" William said.

"She got here while we were at the hospital. She slept at Cecelia's last night. William, I don't know if this is good or bad."

William nodded, because Kent was being honest. The doctor rarely voiced uncertainty. "I don't know her at all," William said, and pictured the image of his daughter from the mural wall. A ten-year-old girl with a shy smile. "I don't know one thing about her." He felt like he was explaining that Alice was a test he hadn't studied for and that he'd never had access to the necessary papers or books to begin to prepare.

But he also thought: *Sylvie wanted Alice.* William knew that Sylvie had loved Alice as a baby. She'd spent her adulthood longing for Julia *and* her niece. Alice had now arrived, and the person who'd wanted her wasn't here. William shuddered. "It doesn't matter," he said, and stood up.

"I think it does matter," Kent said. He looked down at his phone and said, with a tinge of amusement, "Emeline says Alice is six foot one. She's not a baby you can drop or harm anymore, William. She's a grown woman."

William pictured a giant gleaming lamp and had to squint his eyes against the light. He was standing in a foggy darkness. Something in him didn't turn away from the light, though. He was done running away.

They stopped at a coffee shop on the way to the super-duplex, and Gus and Washington met them there. They patted William on the back but didn't say anything except hello. When they were closer to the twins' houses, Arash climbed out of a nearby cab. It was a mild November day; the men all wore coats but left them unzipped. William was unaware of the temperature or the bright sky overhead. He took in his friends' presence with a nod. Kent had clearly summoned these men so William could be part of a team on a day when he was no longer part of a marriage. Sylvie would have loved that Kent had done that, William thought, while the men took long strides together down the sidewalk.

Kent opened the door to Cecelia's house, and they walked inside. Only Cecelia was there, and because William's senses were heightened to all the machinations that were being performed on his behalf, he realized this was intentional too. This was a briefing stop and a moment for him to catch his breath. Cecelia told them that Rose was on a flight headed to Chicago and would arrive that afternoon. Alice and Julia were next door, with Emeline, Josie, and Izzy.

William nodded, because he couldn't say, *No, thank you,* and leave. Sylvie wouldn't want him to. He followed his friends and Cecelia out the back door, across the yard, and through the back door of Emeline's house. The air inside smelled of coffee and baby powder. They were in the hallway, surrounded by Cecelia's portraits, when the doorbell rang, and so all the women were in motion when the men entered the open living room and kitchen. A baby was crying, and a teenage boy was in the doorway, holding a giant paper bag with the word *Bagels* written on the side, and Emeline was searching in her purse for cash. At one edge of his view, William registered a very tall, blond young woman, and on the other side of the room, his ex-wife. He found himself walking toward Julia, perhaps because he knew what to say to her and because she played a small role in his distress. He said, "Could we talk?"

She seemed startled but nodded, and they moved to the kitchen area. It was strange to stand so close to Julia. He hadn't seen her for twenty-five years, and although she looked familiar, Julia no longer resembled his memory of the woman he'd married. Was it possible that her face had changed? Not hardened but solidified. He'd known her in the softness of her youth. Her curls were still the most ferocious of any of the sisters, but there was no wildness in them, even with her hair down. William was aware that he was looking at her partly because he wasn't yet ready to look at his daughter. Sylvie had left every room in his life, and Alice was here; the shuffle of bodies was almost unbearable.

He said, "Why didn't you come? I told you that she needed you."

"I did," Julia said. "I saw her twice."

He tried to register this. Sylvie had seen Julia? He felt a pressure on his chest, as if he were being tackled by relief. He sat down in the nearest kitchen chair. The pressure was behind his eyes too. He hadn't seen this coming, but he hadn't seen any of this coming. He'd known his wife was dying, but he hadn't expected her to die.

"Do you need some water?" Julia said.

He found a glass of water in his hand. He was aware that everyone was watching him now. This wasn't a private conversation. Everyone in this room, except perhaps Alice, was wrecked and breathless with grief. They were unable to pretend to chat with one another. They could only listen and hope that he would be okay, because if that was possible, anything was.

"She wanted to keep our visits a secret," Julia said. "I'm sure she would have told you eventually, but it seemed to tickle her that we could see each other without anyone knowing. We went to a movie together not that long ago. I flew in and out of the city for a few hours each time. Emeline and Cecelia didn't know either, until this morning."

Long ago, William had written into his manuscript: *It should have been me, not her.* He'd been thinking of his sister at the time, but he would have willingly died yesterday, or this minute, if it could have saved Sylvie. A strangled longing filled him. If he *had* died, perhaps Sylvie would still be here. Or, perhaps, he could be with her wherever she was. William wanted to cup his hands again, to hold close his love for his wife, to hold close her love for him.

That wasn't possible, though. It was too late. He'd opened his hands weeks ago and let everything out. All three of his wife's sisters were near him now, their foreheads furrowed with concern, their curls untamed. William knew that Sylvie had spent time with Julia. The two sisters had reconciled; they'd loved each other not only in the past but in Sylvie's final days. They'd fixed what had been broken between them, which meant his wife had found wholeness. Sylvie had gotten what she needed, and this made it possible for him to take another breath.

Alice

ALICE FELT LIKE AN ASTRONAUT IN HER AUNTS' HOUSE, AS IF she had to wear a clunky suit and helmet because she couldn't breathe the native atmosphere and had to pay attention while she walked to make sure she didn't fall over. Her normal, safe life had been stripped away, and she had no idea how to act, think, or feel. Her aunts kept pulling her close for hugs. Emeline and Cecelia looked both similar and dissimilar to her mother. Emeline kissed Alice's cheek the same way Julia did, and Cecelia's voice sounded almost exactly like her mother's. Izzy was so excited about Alice's arrival, it was clear that she'd been waiting for her cousin her entire life. Izzy talked a lot, and Alice wondered if, in her distress about her aunt, Izzy was talking more than usual to try to quell her sadness. She told Alice stories about their family and chatted about the future as if Alice was going to be part of it. Alice's aunts, too, spoke as if her presence was inevitable, as if she'd gone out on an errand and been terrifically delayed but had finally returned home.

Alice had spent the night in the same bedroom as Izzy, each of them in a single bed. "We shouldn't be alone," Izzy had said to her, "after what's happened." *What has happened?* Alice wanted to say, because she would have liked to hear it as a list, in a form she could try to comprehend. She had arrived in Chicago to meet her father, and on the same day, his wife had died. Now Alice's mother and Rose were on their way here, and she was surrounded by devastated people she'd only just met. Alice had slept with her cousin in side-by-side beds, in a world where two side-by-side houses were shared by all of the inhabitants, most of whom Alice was related to. There was a tiny baby living in Emeline's house—another mysterious development, because apparently the baby was staying there only temporarily. The infant erupted into cries sometimes, and Alice wished it were appropriate for her to do the same. She was alone only when she was in the bathroom. Every time she entered a room, the people there were obviously delighted to see her, even if they'd just seen her a few moments earlier.

Alice had woken up very early that morning, before anyone else, and walked the hallways. She wanted to look at Cecelia's paintings, which were everywhere. No matter where she turned, six-inch-high portraits of women's faces filled the spaces between the floorboards and the ceiling. There was a painting of Julia as a teenager that Alice had stood in front of for a few minutes. The idea of her mother being as young and open as she appeared on that canvas was hard for Alice to believe. There was the ancient, fierce-looking woman whom Alice had seen in prints of Cecelia's art and who also existed on sides of Chicago buildings. Izzy had told Alice that she was a saint, St. Clare of Assisi, who was important to the Padavano sisters. "She looks like a real badass, doesn't she?" Izzy had said.

Cecelia had painted Rose when she was young and beautiful, with her black hair pulled away from her face. A stern great-grandmother, whom apparently no one other than Rose had met, appeared on the wall too; Cecelia had painted her from the one photo Rose had of her parents. The walls were decorated with the matriarchal line of the Padavano family, plus the female saint who somehow marked both their strength and their follies. There was a painting of a red-haired little girl; Izzy told Alice that this was William's sister, who'd died when she was young. *Another aunt,* Alice thought, because having a three-year-old dead aunt made as much sense as anything else. Only one man appeared on the wall: Charlie, the grandfather who was clearly beloved by everyone, and the only family member both Rose and Julia had told Alice stories about while she was growing up. In the portrait, Charlie was sitting in an armchair, his face lit up by his smile.

There were portraits of Alice and Izzy as babies and individual paintings of the two girls as they grew older. Alice was moved to find herself, at different ages, on nearly every wall. She had been inside these houses before she knew they existed. Perhaps this explained the familiarity with which her cousin and aunts had greeted her. They seemed to *know* her, if only because she was one of them, in a way Alice wasn't sure she knew herself.

When Julia arrived, Alice hugged her mother hello, but the two women kept their distance after that. Alice wasn't ready, and she was grateful that Julia knew better than to force her to talk. In any case, there were so many other people who wanted their attention that neither woman had a minute when she wasn't squinting in the direction of an emotional sister, aunt, niece, or cousin, trying to come up with the right words in a disorienting situation. *Also*, Alice thought at her mother, *I came here for him, not you. You gave me questions, and I need answers.*

Alice kept glancing at the front door, knowing that her father would be here soon. She wanted to be prepared, to compose herself as much as possible. She hoped she could give an impression of independence or even nonchalance, her body saying, *I never needed you, and I certainly don't need you now.* But her father entered through the back door, at the same time that the doorbell rang and the baby Josie was holding started to wail. The air seemed to evaporate from the room, and Alice couldn't breathe. There was a rushing noise in her head. *Don't look at me,* she thought, and thankfully he didn't, so she had a chance to take him in. William Waters was accompanied by a few giant men, all of them with grave expressions. Her father didn't look overtly mean or as if he was someone who disliked children and thus had easily abandoned his own. His expression was one of unarmed sadness. He had Alice's face and her eyes. It was true, as Alice had long suspected, that when she'd looked in the mirror, her father had been looking back.

She watched her father walk toward her mother. William was now speaking to Julia, fifteen feet away. The man who had given her up, and the woman who had been Alice's entire family until twenty-four hours earlier.

Late the night before, from her adjacent bed, Alice had asked, "Do you know why William didn't want to be my father?" Izzy had been quiet for a minute, then said, "I think he was afraid he would mess you up, because of his depression."

Izzy appeared at Alice's side now. "You all right?" she whispered.

Alice made a face of some kind at her cousin, because she didn't want to lie. She didn't know if she was all right. She didn't know anything. Alice had locked herself down years ago. She'd never told a boy she liked him, or driven too fast in a car, or gotten so drunk she lost track of the words leaving her mouth, but now she appeared on a mural somewhere in Chicago and in portraits on the walls of this house, and she saw herself in the man across the room. She existed outside her own body—she was scattered across this ground—but somehow this made her feel less vulnerable. She was painted into this family, mirrored in her father's face. She was more abundant than she'd believed possible.

William sat down, and the other men and women in the room immediately stepped forward, as if they were an external structure designed to keep Alice's father from collapse. Towering men leaned toward him, willing him their own great strength. Alice, in the same moment, stepped backward. *Everyone here loves him,* she thought in amazement. *They love him so much.* She realized she'd expected her father to have a smaller life than hers. After all, he'd given her up. That seemed like a retreat, a refusal to live. But someone who turned away from people didn't inspire this kind of response. She had never been in a room with this much love and grief, this much emotion.

Alice backed up until she reached a wall, and she looked away, out the window onto the Pilsen street. Her father's distress was personal, and she didn't know him like these other people did. She didn't want to appear to be gawking, as if at an accident on a highway. She also had the odd sense that she was a counterweight to this man who looked so much like her. They were both washed of color, tall and thin, somber in some elemental way. Alice felt like if she moved forward and pinned her eyes on him, then William Waters wouldn't be able to rise from his chair. She would swamp him there, their energies mixing until he was too heavy to move. She had to stay at a distance, on her end of the seesaw that connected them, to give him any chance. In time, William stood and left the room. Still wearing his coat, he headed toward the back door of the house.

Alice felt like she'd exerted herself simply by standing against the wall. She was aware of her heart beating in her chest, as if she'd just sprinted up a hill. *What is happening to me?* she thought.

A man with dreadlocks and glasses walked over to her. He said, "I'm your father's best friend. My name is Kent. It's an honor to meet you, Alice."

She shook his hand. Every piece of information was new. Her father had a best friend, his own version of Carrie.

"I held you in my arms when you were a baby," he said, and then shook his head as if to clear it. "You must feel like you've walked into a whirlwind."

Alice pictured a baby in this huge man's arms. She'd come to understand that she'd had a life here as an infant, that for a short while before she had a memory, she was part of this world. These people remembered her, even though she had no recollection of them. "Sylvie loved you so much," Emeline had told Alice. "She would have been so happy you're home."

"When an old person dies," Kent said, "even if that person is wonderful, he or she is still somewhat ready, and so are the people who loved them. They're like old trees, whose roots have loosened in the ground. They fall gently. But when someone like your aunt Sylvie dies—before her time—her roots get pulled out and the ground is ripped up. Everyone nearby is in danger of being knocked over."

Alice considered this. Her world had always been so small, made up of many fewer people than currently filled this room. It had been Alice and her mother, their braided roots driven deep into the earth. When she looked around at her aunts, though, and at her mother, who was keeping her distance, and at her dark-haired cousin, whom Alice had somehow loved immediately when she'd thrown open the door in greeting, she knew something was happening to her own roots. Something was happening beneath the ground she was standing on.

"Your father needs a little more time," Kent said. "Please don't leave him."

The last sentence surprised her. William had left *her,* after all. Was it even possible for her to leave a person she'd never met, who had legally declared, while she was still a baby, that he wanted nothing to do with her? But the big man in front of Alice looked like *his* ground had been pulled apart. He looked weary and kind, and so she said, "I won't leave," without knowing what time frame she was agreeing to or what not leaving meant.

THE LONG DAY FELT unbounded by the regular movements of a clock. The hours swelled into bubbles that floated across the crowded rooms. First, bagels were put out, then, later, pizzas and cookies. Occasionally a discussion would arise about funeral plans, but William was still outside and no one wanted to bother him, so no final decisions could be made. "Sylvie wouldn't want a Catholic wake and funeral," Cecelia said, and both her sisters nodded in agreement.

Rose arrived midafternoon, wearing a black dress, dramatic in her sadness. The night before, Izzy had listed for Alice the battles their grandmother had chosen a quarter century earlier. "She stopped talking to my mom when she got pregnant with me, she's never acknowledged that I exist, and she's mad at Aunt Emeline for being gay." Izzy ticked these off on her fingers. "She was mad at Sylvie for marrying your dad. And I think she was angry at your mom for a little while for getting divorced, but she got over that."

Just before Rose arrived, Cecelia said, "Mama's going to pretend like we've been a happy family this whole time, and I think we should go along with it."

Cecelia was right. Rose swept into the house and hugged each of her daughters as if she'd seen them the week before. When Izzy stepped forward, the grandmother and granddaughter stared each other down, a moment that evoked centuries of fierce women from their line. Then Izzy said, "You had a long trip. Are you hungry?" and Rose smiled with obvious relief. She accepted a cookie from Izzy and said it was one of the most delicious cookies she'd had in years. Rose complimented Josie on her hair color and told Emeline that the baby she was fostering had handsome features. She put her coat back on to go outside and talk to William for a few minutes and then took a seat at the kitchen table, as if claiming her throne. Rose wondered aloud how she could have survived her own child.

William's friends took turns walking loops around the backyard with him; sometimes Alice would glimpse his shoulder, his fair hair, when they passed a window. When the sky began to flicker toward twilight, a giant sub sandwich arrived, with bags of potato chips. Izzy and Alice were sent to a corner store to buy more paper plates. There was coffee bubbling in the kitchen and a table with alcohol for anyone who wanted to drink.

"Your mom isn't mad at Rose anymore?" Alice asked Izzy, while they walked to the corner store.

"She said she forgave her right after Rose threw her out of the house, when she was seventeen," Izzy said. "My mom said she forgave her because she wanted to keep loving her. Aunt Emmie says it's the most impressive thing my mom's ever done. Will you forgive your dad?"

Alice was startled again. Forgiving William Waters hadn't occurred to her; she'd wondered only if she could forgive her mom. She'd felt emotionally paused in reaction to her father, as if she were watching a movie and waiting for more information before she decided which character was the bad guy. She shrugged at Izzy, even though that wasn't an answer.

When the young women were reentering the house, they heard Rose talking to Julia from somewhere behind the door, out of sight. They both stopped to listen.

"I wonder if it didn't do you girls good," Rose said, "for me to take my foot off the pedal for a few years. I went off to Florida, and you grew up well. You built your own lives. Josie's a nice lady. I don't see the sense in that baby they borrowed, but it's a harmless hobby, I suppose. And Izzy reminds me of myself—she's terrific." Rose hardly paused for breath, as if relieved to speak after years of quiet. "Did you notice Emeline and Cecelia's garden? It's not half bad, though they clearly don't know a thing about winter vegetables. They're wasting space, and those potatoes looked a little iffy, but I'll have to get another look tomorrow morning to be sure."

Alice couldn't see her mother's reaction, but she imagined Julia rolling her eyes. Still, her mother didn't say anything critical or unkind. Cecelia had set the tone, and on this day, everyone who had been lost—including Julia and Alice, of course—would be accepted as they were.

"Rose is amazing," Izzy whispered, and grinned. "All of this is amazing."

"Is it?" Alice said, with doubt in her voice, and her cousin laughed.

"You made a joke," Izzy said with delight. "You're warming up! You've looked petrified ever since you got here." The young women stepped all the way inside and closed the door behind them. Julia was headed toward them, and she did something Alice had seen her do a few times since she'd arrived. Julia pulled Izzy in for a hug and pressed a kiss into her niece's cheek. Julia had missed *this* baby, while everyone else had missed baby Alice. It seemed to Alice that her mother was able to hold herself back from her daughter in part because she had another girl to shower love upon.

All three sisters were near them—Emeline cradling the baby; Cecelia with circles under her eyes and a stack of paper napkins in her hand; Julia looking uncomfortable, her now-empty hands at her sides.

"Is it true," Rose said, "that there won't be a funeral at St. Procopius?"

Emeline spoke in a soft voice. "It wasn't what Sylvie wanted, Mama."

Rose watched her daughter sway gently on her feet to soothe the infant. They could all see the old woman working to hide her disapproval, working to keep her mouth shut. Alice felt like an astronaut again, with all these women so close by. Aunts, grandmother, mother, cousin. She was filled with static, finding it hard to breathe.

Rose said, "At least Sylvie's with Charlie now."

Her three remaining daughters looked toward her, toward this possible truth. For a moment they looked like young girls, and Alice could see the hope on their faces. They were picturing their sister with their father. It occurred to Alice that she had left home to see *her* father, and Sylvie had left her home—her life—which opened the possibility of a reunion with her own. This parallel was too much for

Alice to consider further, but she felt, like a physical sensation, William's presence in the backyard.

"You know what Daddy would say when he saw Sylvie," Julia said in a quiet voice.

Emeline and Izzy nodded, and Cecelia said, "Hello beautiful."

AFTER A DINNER OF the sliced-up sub sandwich, potato chips, and wine, Julia put her hand on Alice's arm. Alice was no longer angry at her mother. She no longer had space inside her for anger. Besides, if she'd felt like an astronaut in her aunts' houses, she'd recognized that her mother did too. Each of them had been laboring through the rooms of these two homes, because whatever Julia had taken away from Alice for all these years, she'd taken away from herself as well. The mother and daughter had arrived here from the same place, and they were bound by a tight cord of love. For Alice, part of the strangeness of this new Chicago family was that they conducted a kind of love that seemed voluminous; it required talking over one another and living on top of one another, and it was a force that appeared to include people both present and absent, alive and dead. It was remarkable to Alice that the walls of her aunts' houses were covered with portraits of the same women who walked its halls.

"The last time I saw Sylvie," Julia said, "she asked me to give you something after she was gone. I thought she had time left, so I tried not to take it, but . . ." She shook her head slightly. "Let's go over here, out of the way."

The two women wove through the kitchen. It was hard to get out of the way. More people had arrived over the course of the afternoon. Izzy's boyfriend—a stout, freckled young man—buzzed around the house, fulfilling tasks for the aunts. A grizzled man named Frank, who said he'd grown up on the same street as the Padavano sisters, sat in the armchair in the corner. Librarians who'd worked with Sylvie for years gathered by the coffee station in the kitchen, and more giant men had arrived, in such great numbers that it looked like the forty-eight-year-old William must be a member of several basketball teams. Some of the men were young and muscle-bound; others were middle-aged players with a stoop in their shoulders. Kent seemed to know them all, and he moved through the room embracing each man who arrived. It was an eclectic group, and when new platters of food were set out, Izzy shouted the news from the center of the room to get everyone's attention.

Julia saw her daughter taking in the crowd and said, "It's so silly, but I thought life here would have frozen when I left. That if I did come back, it would all be the same. But it's not. It's much bigger."

"It's loud too," Alice said, because it was. She'd noticed, as the hours passed, that there was a hint of relief in the collective sadness over Sylvie. The people who loved her were glad she hadn't suffered more; they were grateful she'd died without pain and that they'd been spared her final, ruining decline. The men and women present laughed occasionally, happy to have loved Sylvie and happy simply to have come together. The only person whose pain seemed too great for relief was William. He came inside once or twice, but he always stayed far away from his daughter and returned to the backyard within a few moments. Maybe he needed the open air, Alice thought. His friends continued to spend time outside with him, next to the vegetable garden or by the back fence. There was a bench near a small stone fountain, and occasionally William rested there with his head in his hands.

Julia held out a wrapped package tied with string. It was rectangular and solid-looking. "This is a book that Sylvie wrote about our family. I haven't read it, but she said it's about our childhood, and your grandfather, and everything that's happened since he died. She said she'd been working on it for years and that it's a mess." Julia looked down at what she held. "Sylvie wanted me to tell you that it's yours now and that you can do anything you want with it. Edit what's here, publish it, or throw it away. She said she didn't mind, but she wanted it to be yours."

Alice took the package. The familiar weight of a manuscript in her hands was pleasing; she felt slightly dizzy at the prospect of this gift. "Did Sylvie know I'm a copy editor?"

"I told her. I told her all about you. She wanted to hear everything."

Alice nodded. She couldn't imagine a more perfect gift; these pages would give her all the stories and people she'd missed. Her own history was in this document. And, as a bonus, Sylvie had given her niece an excuse to hide from the noisy, affectionate world she'd entered into, or to take breaks from it, anyway. Alice had decided—she wasn't sure when she'd made this decision exactly, somewhere in the commotion of the last twenty-four hours—that she would stay in Chicago for a little while. For how long, she wasn't sure. Emeline and Cecelia had told her they hoped she would stay forever and that she could choose a bedroom in either of their houses. Alice had never taken a vacation from work, but she would give herself one now. She would find a quiet room and read.

Izzy had started telling Alice about the Padavano sisters' childhood, and there was something mythic and epic in the tales she was now holding in her hands. The idea that this was a narrative Alice would find herself in by the end felt strangely exciting. The coming together and falling apart of her parents; her own birth. And what would Alice do in the pages that hadn't yet been written? Where would she live? Whom and what would she love?

Julia looked toward the crowded room and then back at her daughter. "I can't believe I'm going to say this"—she paused—"but I think you should go talk to your father."

Alice had been startled repeatedly since she'd arrived, but this didn't surprise her at all. It felt like what she'd been expecting to hear. Alice had always liked to keep things small so she could, if necessary, grab what mattered and run to higher ground. But there was no way for her to gather everything she'd found in Chicago—since that meal in the Greek restaurant, really—in her arms. The Padavanos had shown her a bigger kind of love. It was vast; it felt like everything. And now she sensed, through the same mysterious connection that had told her earlier that he needed distance, that the quiet man in the backyard would be able to bear her. William Waters was ready, and, unexpectedly, so was she.

She put the manuscript down on the table next to her and wrapped her arms around her mother. Julia squeezed Alice tight, the same way she'd squeezed her when Alice was a small girl and Julia wanted to show how much she loved her. Alice smiled and pressed her head on top of Julia's, so her straight hair mixed with her mother's curls. Izzy had talked about forgiveness, and in that moment Alice felt drenched with it. She forgave herself for locking herself away, and she forgave her parents for the bold choices they'd made to protect her. She forgave every mistake she would read about in the manuscript she'd just received. Earlier that afternoon, when Emeline had noticed Alice watching Rose's dramatic tears, she'd whispered into her niece's ear, "Grief is love." Now Alice thought: *Forgiveness is too.* The mother and daughter held each other in the quiet hallway in a house thundering with life.

When they pulled apart, Alice said, "I'm scared."

"I am too," Julia said, but she picked up a coat from the nearest chair and handed it to her daughter. Alice pulled it on, and walked slowly outside.

William

WILLIAM LOOPED THE YARD. HE WAS FEVERISH WITH SORROW, and pacing the grass felt like the best way to expel it, like sweat, from his pores. The onset of grief bore no resemblance to his experience with depression. Depression meant disconnection, shutting down, a dangerous quiet. Now William's feelings whipped around inside him like a flailing water hose. He needed to control this hose as quickly as possible, though, because Alice was here. She had been brave enough to seek him out, and he had to gather himself enough to make her feel like she hadn't made a mistake. Any mistakes, all the mistakes, were his.

His heart beat with words: *Alice is here.*

On the tailwind of Sylvie's departure, Alice had arrived in Chicago. Of course she had. Sylvie had talked about one-two punches, about how Charlie had died on the day Izzy was born, and Sylvie had clearly used her magic to somehow bring William his daughter on the day his heart broke. His wife was trying to save him, yet again.

The sun had just left the sky when William felt calm enough, ready enough. He headed toward the house and then stopped abruptly, because Alice had appeared in the open doorway.

"I was coming to find you," he said.

"Oh," she said. Her face was questioning, pale, anxious. "You were?"

William nodded. He could feel the cool air against the palms of his hands and the nape of his neck. When he'd first met the Padavano sisters, he'd noticed their similarities: their hair, their brown eyes, their shared gestures. The four sisters looked like different versions of the same person: They were parts of a whole. The young woman standing before William didn't look like them at all; she looked like him. A slightly different version of his own eyes looked back at him. William had never recognized himself in someone else's face before. It felt like finding an answer to a question he hadn't known he had.

"What were you going to say?" Alice asked.

William almost smiled, because the answer was so simple. "Hello?" he said. "I was going to say hello."

Her face relaxed; the air between them relaxed too. Neither of them sensed an attack—not right now, anyway. Alice's appearance was more reserved than Julia's; she was contained, behind her face and eyes. William remembered her as an infant, how she had looked friendly, even optimistic, as she took in the world around her. William could see how much time he'd missed, the gap between then and now. Was life constructed of arrivals and departures? He'd married into the Padavano family and then left his first marriage and fatherhood behind; Sylvie had walked into William's hospital room and his heart, and now she was gone. On the same day, the adult version of Alice had arrived in his life.

She said, "I thought you were dead, until a few weeks ago."

"Your mom told you that?" William nodded, though, because this sounded right. He *had* been dead, or deadened, as far as this young woman was concerned. He was alive now, and it hurt. "I need to say a lot of things," he said. "I should explain the choice I made a long time ago."

"You don't have to. Not right now," Alice said. "I'm sorry about your wife. We don't have to talk about everything today."

They looked at each other, and William said, "We have time." He wanted her to know that he wasn't going to run away. He'd accepted his daughter while sitting on the playground bench, though really this meant that he'd finally accepted himself. Alice was the person he'd most wanted to save from himself. She had been a child, and he was hurt as a child, and that anguish seemed to have tentacles that were out of his control. William would have done anything to protect his daughter: When she was a newborn he'd spent his nights leaning over her bassinet, listening to make sure she was breathing; he'd signed away his parental rights; he'd walked into a lake. It was because Alice was so precious that he'd believed he needed to stay away. Now, as they stood facing each other, all that remained was that she was precious.

He may have said, "Let's go sit on the bench," or he might not have said it out loud. He was feeling unsteady on his feet. He led the way, and they lowered themselves to the stone seat, with their long backs to the house. William's whole life drummed inside him, and he knew Sylvie would say it was all related to love—it had been withheld, he'd believed he didn't deserve it, then he had allowed it in. He realized, startled, that he loved the young woman sitting next to him. He'd loved her since the day she was born. William felt a warmth travel through him.

"Don't look now," he said, "but how many people do you think are spying on us?"

Alice laughed, and the sound rang out into the night air. She didn't laugh like him, or Julia, or anyone else. She had a lovely laugh. "Definitely my mother," she said. "She probably has her face pushed up against a window."

"Emeline and Cecelia are looking at us. And Izzy. Kent, for sure." William pictured them, portraits of the people who loved them, framed by windows across the back of the house. He could feel their care and concern. He could feel their hope too. Life had surprised them all—as if the sea had risen dramatically, lifting their boats precipitously high—in the midst of a moment of sadness. If this could happen, if William and Alice could sit side by side and talk under the evening sky, then truly anything could happen. Julia could share her life with her sisters again; Rose could lay down her grudges and walk forward with lightness; Kent could find a new love.

"When I got to college," Alice said, "it took me a long time to feel like I wasn't living with strangers."

She paused, and William waited. He found that he was just fine waiting, sitting on the cold stone bench, with the stars beginning to shine above, with what Whitman called *the beautiful uncut hair of graves* curling beneath their feet. He could feel his wife's pleasure, from whatever window Sylvie was peering through, and Charlie's too. *I'll make you proud,* he thought. *I promise.*

Alice shook her head, and her fair hair waved around her face. "When I arrived yesterday, everyone acted like they knew me." She looked at him. "I know I don't know you, but I feel like I do. It's weird, though . . . because I also feel like I don't really know who *I* am."

Sounds of laughter swept out of Emeline's house. People inside were getting drunk now, making toasts, telling one another how wonderful Sylvie had been. One Padavano sister after another would peel herself away from the windows to share a story from their childhood; they wouldn't be able to help themselves. They would tell everyone that Sylvie had nearly flunked several high school subjects because she'd read in the park instead of attending classes that were boring to her. Guests would laugh when they heard that the head librarian at the Lozano Library used to make out with random boys in the stacks when she was a teenager. One of the sisters would describe how, as a child, Sylvie walked around their house muttering to herself—casting spells, her sisters had claimed—while she memorized pages of poetry in order to delight their father.

William looked forward to hearing these stories repeated in the days ahead. He knew his wife would not be forgotten or set aside. The Padavanos talked about Charlie as if he were still part of their lives, still part of themselves, and because of that: He was. There was a mural of Sylvie on the side of a building not far from the library and framed paintings of her all over the twins' houses. From a distance, because of her height and posture, Cecelia looked like Sylvie; Emeline shared her older sister's thoughtful eyes; and Julia somehow *contained* Sylvie—like vines of roses, the two eldest Padavano girls had woven around and into each other when they were young.

William said, "For a long time, Sylvie knew me better than I knew myself. I think sometimes"—now it was his turn to pause—"we need another pair of eyes. We need the people around us."

Alice turned her face upward, as if to study the night sky, as if she required a different vantage point to sort through what was inside her. William had written a series of questions in the footnotes of his manuscript, a long time ago. *What am I doing? Why am I doing this? Who am I?* He could sense those questions deep inside his daughter now. She was not broken, like he had been. Julia had seen to that. But Alice was taking tentative steps onto a new terrain, wondering if the ice could bear her weight.

"I know you can do this on your own," he said. "But, if you'll allow me, I'd like to help."

Acknowledgments

HELEN ELLIS, HANNAH TINTI, AND I HAPPENED TO SIT NEXT to each other in Dani Shapiro's New York University workshop in 1995. Despite our striking differences, we recognized something in one another, and when the class ended, Helen suggested we continue to meet. These two women are still my first readers, and I hear their voices in my head when I write. I am the writer I am, and this book is the book it is, because of them.

I am both proud and delighted to be represented by Julie Barer and The Book Group and to be published by Whitney Frick and The Dial Press. Susan Kamil was in the room for *Dear Edward,* and I feel like she remains in the room with us now. Many thanks to Rose Fox, Clio Seraphim, and Nicole Cunningham for reading early drafts of this novel and offering insightful notes. Loren Noveck and Kathy Lord were incisive, thoughtful copy editors, and they have my gratitude. Thank you to the team at The Dial Press / Random House, especially Andy Ward, Avideh Bashirrad, Maria Braeckel, Carrie Neill, Debbie Aroff, Madison Dettlinger, and Donna Cheng. I'm very fortunate to have Caspian Dennis, Jenny Meyer, and Michelle Weiner as advocates for my work, and I'm grateful to be published in the UK by Isabel Wall and Viking Penguin.

Growing up, I slept at my friend Leah's house as often as I slept at my own, and her parents, Louis and Cecilia, were like second parents to me. There were many reasons I loved being there, but one of them was the constant parade of Ceil's many sisters (Toni, Celeste, Rosemary, Caroline, and Christine), who walked in and out of the house as if it were their own. The sisters were all short, most of them had curly hair, and their faces resembled one another's to the extent that they looked like different versions of a whole. They inspired my Padavano sisters, and I thank them for always being nice to the shy girl who was usually by Leah's side.

My uncle Ed mailed postcards to me from his home in Chicago when I was a kid, and the greeting was always the same: "Hello Beautiful." I knew that my uncle didn't really know what I looked like—I saw him very rarely—but that's why I loved the greeting. It felt like he believed I was beautiful on the *inside,* and since (as an introverted, bookish child) my insides were the most significant part of me, I appreciated this. The title of this novel, and the fact that it's set in the neighborhood of Pilsen in Chicago, are because of my uncle. In childhood, magical lands rise up inside us, and my uncle's mural-covered neighborhood was one of mine.

Librarians and booksellers are the best people. The librarians Kolter Campbell and Catie Huggins at the McCormick Special Collections and Archives at the Northwestern University Library answered several of my questions about classes and programs at Northwestern University in the 1980s, and I am grateful for their assistance. Katharine Solheim from Pilsen Community Books helped me determine which street the Padavano family might have lived on, and her expertise on Pilsen was invaluable. The wonderful Lozano Library sits in the middle of Pilsen, as it does in my novel. The actual library opened its doors in 1989; I have taken fictional liberties, and my version exists a few years before that date. I hope, in any case, that I have honored the library, and the profound importance of all public libraries to our society.

I'm grateful to my friend JJ Lonsinger Rutherford for answering questions about what it's like to grow up as a very tall girl. JJ is fierce and funny and a great advertisement for growing as tall as you possibly can. I also want to thank Dominic Vendell for generously answering my logistical questions about how one earns a PhD in history. Kevin

Book Club Questions

1. *Hello Beautiful* is a homage to Louisa May Alcott's *Little Women*. What are your thoughts about homage storytelling? Were you a fan of *Little Women* prior to reading this novel? How much of *Little Women* do you see in *Hello Beautiful*?

2. While the novel is very much focused on the four sisters — especially Julia and Sylvie — the story starts off with William's tragic past. Why was it important to focus on William in the beginning?

3. The four sisters are all so different. Do you feel you're similar to any of them? And, if you come from a family of sisters, how is your family dynamic compared to the ones displayed in the novel?

4. What drew Julia and William to one another?

5. Sylvie imagined her life to be full of 'third doors' or unexpected ways of living that allow her to choose her own path. What third doors can you see in your own life?

6. In what ways did William's traumatic upbringing impact him and his relationships?

7. William has been working on a book and when Julia reads it, she's horrified. Instead of something that fits with her polished, studious hopes, it showcases William's insecurities.

How did reading this book change Julia's opinion about William?

8. On the same note, why did Sylvie feel a connection with William after she read his book?

9. Why did William give up custody to his daughter?

10. Julia is completely done with William and even tells Alice that her father died. Do you understand why Julia lied about William or do you think she should have told the truth?

11. The sisters have a fierce bond. But once Sylvie falls for William, everything changes. What were your thoughts about Sylvie and William? Do you think their love was wrong, or a passion that could not be denied?

12. Over the course of the novel, several of the characters experience tragedy and loss. What do you think the novel says about resilience and hope in the face of difficult times? And how, if at all, does this messaging speak to you?

13. Will Sylvie's passing change the family for good?

14. It's eventually revealed that William's cold shoulder to Alice was from deep-rooted insecurity—he truly thought she was better off without him. What are your thoughts about this? Do you think William is ready to finally move forward and leave the past behind?

15. What happens next for the characters?

**A TRANSCENDENT COMING-OF-AGE STORY ABOUT
A BROKEN HEART LEARNING TO LOVE AGAIN**

Dear Edward

One summer morning, a flight takes off from New York
to Los Angeles: there are 192 people aboard. When the
plane suddenly crashes, twelve-year-old Edward Adler
is the sole survivor.

In the aftermath, Edward struggles to make sense of
his grief, sudden fame and find his place in a world without
his family. But then Edward and his neighbour Shay make a
startling discovery; hidden in his uncle's garage are letters
from the relatives of other passengers – all addressed him.

Following the passengers' final hours and Edward's unique
coming-of-age, *Dear Edward* asks one of
life's most profound questions:

What does it mean not just to survive, but to truly live?

'Ann Napolitano's writing is astonishing. I'm in awe'
Marian Keyes

'A very moving and emotional read'
Anne Tyler

ORDER YOUR COPY NOW!